the

secret

of you

and me

the secret of you and me

MELISSA LENHARDT

GRAYDON
HOUSE

GRAYDON
HOUSE®

ISBN-13: 978-1-525-83220-8

The Secret of You and Me

Graydon House
22 Adelaide St. West, 40th Floor
Toronto, Ontario M5H 4E3, Canada
www.GraydonHouseBooks.com
www.BookClubbish.com

Printed in U.S.A.

To my brother, Stephen,
whose courage inspires me every day.

the
secret
of you
and me

"You pierce my soul. I am half agony, half hope...
I have loved none but you."

—JANE AUSTEN,
Persuasion

The legend is dead.

Raymond Arnold Noakes—Ray to his friends, goddamn Noakes to his enemies—died as he lived: too arrogant to admit an error of judgment even as a hundred fifty-seven head of cattle took issue with his presence in their drought-scorched pasture. The meth heads who riled the herd to stampede a man who treated cows with respect sometimes lacking toward his fellow man remain at large.

Personally, I'd like to buy them a beer.

one
nora

I never intended to stay away for eighteen years. What started as a bone-deep sense of betrayal, and shame, morphed over time into anger and eventually habit and distraction. When I finally craved my family, *needed* them, a latent stubbornness I didn't realize resided in me reared its head. To return to Lynchfield, Texas, would be to admit defeat, to see my father's Roman nose lifted in the knowledge I'd been the one to give in. Not him. The idea planted me firmly in Virginia, and I waited. Stubbornness and patience. The twin pillars of the Lynchfield Noakeses.

I won in the end.

"Well, it's about damn time." My sister took me in from head to toe, her expression of disdain not diffused through the screen door. The bobby pin stuck through a small hole in the screen to hold notes from missed visitors pointed to her curling mouth like an arrow.

"Hello, Mary."

She opened the screen door and I stepped into my father's house and saw my sister for the first time in three years. I'd hoped she would be glad to see me, that she would greet me with her big, toothy grin, but I hadn't seen that joyous, and sometimes mischievous, smile since her wedding day, and I wasn't greeted with it now.

Mary's gaze landed on my duffel bag. "I see you're not staying long."

"I have enough clothes to stay indefinitely."

"In that?"

"In this. I assume Clark's still sells toothpaste."

"Clark's Pharmacy has been out of business for nine years."

"Has it? I'm sure a lot has changed, though this room might as well be encased in amber."

We glanced around the den. Brown paneled walls, a '70s-era golden-brown shag carpet which had long since been flattened into submission, a couch upholstered in a waxed cotton of large orange flowers—the last purchase my mother made before she died—a dark walnut side table and matching coffee table stacked with back issues of *The Cattleman, Texas Monthly, Texas Highways*, and *Field and Stream*. A black recliner sat at one end of the couch, angled slightly toward the center of the room to imply a conversation area, but in reality was pointed toward the television sitting on a rickety metal stand across the room. The black leather slashed through the earth-toned room like a deep canyon.

"I've been trying to get him to replace this horrid carpet for more than ten years," Mary said. "Said it worked perfectly fine and was a waste of money."

"I suppose he's not wrong."

"There's hardwood under here, you know."

"Nora!" Jeremy English emerged from the kitchen, a broad smile on his face and his eyes sparkling with good humor. I put down my bag and hugged my brother-in-law.

"Jeremy. Nice to see you."

"You, too." He held me at arm's length. "You haven't changed a bit."

"You just saw me last year," I laughed.

"It's been two years."

"That long? You've gotten fat, I see."

Jeremy was built like a fireplug: short, stocky and all muscle, which he confessed to me at dinner two years earlier he worked harder and harder at as time wore on. We'd always gotten along like a house on fire. He was fascinated by the military, and I reveled in his pure, nonjudgmental interest in my chosen profession. He'd understood when I'd left the service after ten years, but hadn't shown nearly as much interest in my career as a technical writing translator. Still, when he was in DC, we always found time for dinner or a cup of coffee.

"Where are the kids?" Mary snapped.

Jeremy's smile barely slipped, but his eyes dimmed, and his sigh was almost inaudible. "Outside with Dormer. Feeding the chickens. How was your trip, sis?"

"Flight was good, but Austin traffic was atrocious."

"Welcome to the fastest growing city in the country." He picked up my bag and turned away, boxing out Mary. "Your room?"

I shrugged and nodded, sending signals as mixed as my emotions.

"There she is!" A fat woman wearing a leopard-print caftan waddled into the room, arms outstretched.

My face split into a grin. "Emmadean."

My aunt enveloped me in her wonderfully comforting embrace. I closed my eyes and inhaled Shower to Shower talcum powder and White Diamonds perfume, the scent of childhood comfort for scraped knees and barbed wire fence scratches, a broken arm from being pitched from an ornery horse named Tinker. It reminded me of her laughter at my horrified reaction to the birds and the bees, her quiet understanding when I was heartbroken and, finally, her holding my hand as I lay in a hospital bed, sobbing about everything and nothing. Her temple against my cheek was sticky with sweat, but I didn't care.

"Lookitchoo," Emmadean said. "My God, you haven't aged a bit. Doesn't she look good, Mary?"

"Great," my sister said, pushing past us and into the kitchen.

Emmadean ignored her, gripping my elbows while she searched my face, for what? Grief? Fear? Relief? My eyes watered at the love and concern I saw in Emmadean's expression. "I'm all right," I said, voice thick.

She squeezed my elbows and released. "You will be. Come on, let's get some food in you. I've seen fence posts with more curves than you."

I chuckled and shook my head. Emmadean had been pushing food on me, and everyone else in Lynchfield, for as long as anyone could remember. She lived to take care of others, and what better way to show love than to feed them with the best cooking in the Hill Country? If there was a recipe for it, Emmadean would glance at it, and proceed to make it her own. For all her prowess in the kitchen, she couldn't bake to save her life. Baking didn't lend itself well to improvisation; it required attention to detail and precision, which Emmadean lacked in all areas of her life. It had fallen to me to save our weekly family Sunday after-church meals from Emmadean's box brownies and slice-and-bake cookies, because going without dessert was not an option. Looking at the spread of food in the kitchen, including cakes, pies, cookies, and kolaches, I knew the church ladies had rallied the troops as soon as news of Ray Noakes's unfortunate accident had spread.

Mary shoved a red velvet whoopie pie in her mouth when I entered the kitchen. She ate it almost defiantly, as if she wanted me to judge her and find her lacking. I picked out my own and took a bite. "Not bad, but I could do better."

"Course you could."

"Did you make these?"

"No. Since you weren't here, Emmadean and I made all the

arrangements for Pop. I'm sure you'll find something to bitch about, but do us all a favor, and keep it to yourself."

"Oh, Mary, take the stick out of your ass," Emmadean said. "Nora couldn't care less how we plant Ray in the ground, long as we do."

"Wow." Mary made a production of sweeping the crumbs off her hands. "I thought it would at least take ten minutes. But, she's barely walked in the door, and you're taking her side. I've been at Pop's beck and call for the last fifteen years while Nora's been off doing God knows what…"

"Servin' her country," Emmadean interjected.

"…but does anyone ever appreciate what I do? The sacrifices I've made? No. I'm just told to take a stick out of my ass as if *I'm* the selfish one. Fucking priceless." My niece and nephew, Madison and Hunter, stormed into the kitchen in a swirl of preteen energy. They immediately threw themselves at me, and almost knocked me down.

"Aunt Nora!"

"Gosh, you two have gotten big!" I said, hugging the little heathens. "Next time I think a firm handshake is all I'll be able to stand."

They bombarded me with questions, and I listened and watched Mary smolder with jealousy.

"Did I bring you anything?" I said in mock shock. "Noooo." I put my hand up to block my face from Mary and mouthed, "Yes. Go check my bag."

Madison, the oldest, playfully pushed Hunter out of the way so she could be first down the hall.

"When Nora's done spoiling them, I'll meet y'all in the car," Mary said.

The screen door slapped shut behind her. Jeremy sighed. "That didn't take long."

"She'll get over it," I said. I had zero patience with Mary's jealousy. I saw the kids every couple of years, at most, though I tried to Skype with them somewhat regularly. Why she couldn't just let me enjoy being their aunt was beyond me. "I hope Hunter still likes Legos."

"He does," Emmadean said. "Those things get lost in our shag carpet. Dormer and I have been stepping on them for years."

I opened the cabinet door under the sink and tossed my barely eaten whoopie pie into the trash. "When's the visitation?"

"Six," Emmadean said. The clock above the door said sixteen thirty-five.

"Why don't you drive Mary out to Comanche Springs, Jeremy?"

"You want me to go parking with my wife? Now?"

"I'm giving y'all a break from the kids. If she wants to bitch about me, so much the better."

"Why don't you take her? Let her bitch at you directly."

"Don't worry; I'll let Mary yell and scream at me before I go back home. Let her test out her arguments with you first. Refine them a little bit. I want only her best temper tantrum. And, frankly, I'd rather hang out with your kids."

"You are so weird sometimes, Nora," Jeremy said. "Don't take them to Dairy Queen. They've already had three cookies each."

I mock saluted and said, "Yes sir."

Jeremy left, leaving me to study the casserole offerings. I leaned over and inhaled the tangy aroma of an especially delicious-looking green chile chicken enchilada casserole. "What should I avoid, Emmadean?" When she didn't answer, I glanced up.

"You *are* home."

I straightened, confused. "Hmm?"

"You said Mary could yell at you before you go home. *Lynch-field* is your home."

I picked up a paper plate, found a serving spoon in the drawer next to the sink, and dished up a helping of enchiladas while Emmadean watched.

"Ray's dead, Nora. No reason you can't stay."

"My life is in DC. My career. My friends."

"Your family is here."

"I've gotten along without my family for years."

"That was your choice, not ours."

I took a bite of enchiladas, savoring the contrast of the spicy tang of the sauce and the smooth creaminess of the cheese, and wondering what had compelled me to return to my hometown for my father's funeral. I'd managed to sever myself cleanly from him, and, for that matter, from Lynchfield, Texas. I told myself I could come, pay my respects, and leave, unscathed and untouched by memories, and long-buried emotions. I knew it for a lie as soon as Emmadean took me into her arms. By her body language and expression, so did she. The enchiladas turned sour in my mouth, but I continued to eat to avoid answering.

Emmadean shook her head and said as she walked out the back door, "Can't run from your problems forever, war hero."

I dumped the paper plate into the trash.

"Come on, you heathens! Quick trip to DQ before the visitation!" I called.

They let out a cheer. The sound of feet pounding down the hallway made me smile.

two
nora

I'm not a war hero, nor have I ever claimed to be. I'm a war hero like anyone who wears the uniform is deemed a hero, by merely doing the job we signed up for, volunteered for, or were, sometimes, persuaded into doing.

I stared down a never-ending line of people who knew me, but whom I couldn't remember to save my life. I smiled and shook hands and listened to them shower me with platitudes, and thank me for my service, though I'd been out of the army for eight years. Seemed like yesterday. Seemed like forever ago.

"Your father was proud of you."

"Proudest day of his life when you deployed over to kick some Saddam Hussein ass. Thank you for your service."

"To hear old Noakes talk you'da thought you toppled that statue yourself. You didn't, did you?"

"Talked about you all the time."

"Loved you so much."

"So proud. Thank you for your service."

"He missed you but understood how important your job is."

"Kept everyone up-to-date on your career."

I caught Emmadean's eye with a clear *What the hell are these people talking about?* expression.

She shrugged a shoulder and took the man in front of me off my hands. "Earl, thanks for coming."

Mary, on my opposite side, leaned near me and whispered, "Rest assured, Pop hated you. Emmadean's who talks you up." She leaned away and smiled at the woman in front of her. "Hello, Mrs. Wyatt. Thanks for the enchiladas."

"They weren't too spicy, were they?"

"No, they were perfect."

My stomach twisted. *This* woman I knew. Joyce Wyatt's hair had gone from a dark brown *Steel Magnolias* football helmet to a blond *Steel Magnolias* football helmet. Her solution to going gray, I supposed. It wasn't a bad look on her, but hair dye couldn't mask the fine wrinkles mapping her still-lovely face. She held her purse tightly in front of her and looked at me with a hesitant expression as if she wasn't sure how she would be received. I held out my hands. "I should have known those enchiladas were from you. They were delicious."

Mrs. Wyatt sagged with relief. Holding hands wasn't enough for her. She pulled me into her arms. "Nora. I've missed you so," she whispered in my ear.

"I've missed you, too," I said.

She pulled back. "When you left so suddenly, then didn't call…?"

She waited for the explanation that never came, and one I would never give. "Mrs. Wyatt, that was all a long time ago."

She nodded and sniffed as if struggling to hold back her emotions. "I suppose so." She turned her head and stared into the distance behind me, at my father's coffin. "I can't believe it's been nearly twenty years." She shook her head, returned her attention to me and said, "You didn't break only Charlie's heart, leaving like that."

"I would have been a terrible daughter-in-law and an even worse wife."

"Couldn't have been any worse th—" Good manners took over, and Joyce Wyatt didn't finish.

I forced a smile and remained silent. Mrs. Wyatt sighed, understanding that was as close to an apology as I was going to give.

"I'm sorry about your father."

"Thank you."

"Are you staying in town long?"

In my peripheral vision, I saw Mary turn her head slightly in my direction, though she continued to talk to Mr. Wyatt. "I'm not sure. It depends on what needs to be done."

Mr. Wyatt stepped towards me. "Nora. We hope to see you again before you go. Stop by so we can catch up."

The Wyatts nodded and moved on to console Emmadean and Dormer. As sweet as the Wyatts were, and as much as I had loved them when Charlie and I dated, I had no intention of going over for a visit. I didn't want to have to lie to them and try to avoid their questions.

In the brief break between the Wyatts and the next mourner, I looked down the never-ending line. "Christ, is that Jamie Luke?"

Mary leaned over. "It is. And Tiffany Williams and Kim Stopper." Kim saw us, grinned and waved vigorously from her hip as if trying to hide her excitement at seeing me. The other two waved more demurely, in keeping with a Texas funeral visitation where the deceased lay in repose in the open casket not ten feet away. It had taken longer to wrangle the kids than I thought— those DQ dip cones had probably been a mistake—but there had been a silver lining: I hadn't had to pay my respects to my father's body before mourners started lining up to tell us how sad they were to see old Ray Noakes go before his time.

A stout man wearing a polyester Western sports coat and buff-colored cowboy hat, and smelling strongly of Stetson cologne, stepped forward and greeted Mary and me together. When he held out his hand to shake Mary's, I saw the gun holstered on his right hip, next to his Ranger star.

"Rick Michaels," he said, shaking our hands in turn, and wheezing as if he'd just climbed ten flights of stairs. "Worked with Ray for fifteen years or so. Started just after you enlisted. Thank you for your service."

I gritted my teeth and nodded my thanks.

"Pop spoke of you often, Mr. Michaels," Mary said.

"He was a good man. Solid. Trust him with my life. And my wife."

Though he and Pop were sworn peace officers—Texas Rangers—they worked the cases involving farm and ranch crimes through the Texas and Southwestern Cattleman's Association, a surprisingly busy beat since meth heads had taken to stealing and selling cows and farm equipment for drug money.

"Is your life in danger often, chasing cattle rustlers and tractor thieves?" I said.

Michaels lifted his chin, offended, but willing to let it pass because I was grieving. Condescension oozed from him. "We caught the tweakers who killed your dad."

"Thank the Lord," Emmadean said.

"Just took them into custody this morning after they tried to sell the tractor they stole the night Ray died. They were so high that night they didn't even remember Ray was there. Doubt we'll ever know what happened exactly."

"At least you caught them," Dormer said.

"Oh, they'll be put away for a long time, rest assured. Sorry for your loss. Ray's gonna be sorely missed."

The Ranger had barely moved away when Jamie, Tiffany, and Kim were on me, hugging me like I was their long-lost friend. The truth was, there had been a long-running competition between all of us. I'd assumed it had fizzled with time, but if the way Jamie and Tiffany were sizing me up was any indication, the game was still on for them. Nor had the dynamic between the three seem to have changed; Jamie and Tiffany controlled the conversation, while Kim hung on, desperately trying to get a word in edgewise, and be noticed.

"My God, Nora Noakes, you look *exactly* like you did in high school," Tiffany said.

Jamie looked me up and down. "It's good to see being in the military didn't turn you butch."

"Depends on your definition of butch. One definition, my personal favorite, is being able to kill a man with your bare hands. In that regard yes, the military turned me butch."

Mary barked out a laugh. Jamie was stunned into silence (mission accomplished) so Tiffany jumped in.

"You're just as pretty as the day you were crowned homecoming queen. Same haircut, I see," Tiffany said.

"I was football sweetheart," I clarified.

"That's right," Tiffany said. "Sophie was homecoming queen. You two won everything, didn't you?"

"We tried," I said.

"Have you seen Sophie?" Jamie asked, her eyebrows arching.

Of the three, Jamie had always been the cattiest, the one with the instinctive ability to know someone's soft spot and poke at it until it was inflamed. I smiled at her, feeling nothing but pity. She was trying to psychologically torture the wrong person.

"Not yet."

"I'm sorry about your dad," Kim said, grasping my forearm. "I lost my father a few years ago, so I understand how difficult..." She swallowed. "If you want to talk—"

"It's hardly the same thing," Tiffany said. "You adored your father. You lived next door to him, for Christsakes. Nora hasn't been back to Lynchfield in, what? Twenty years?"

"Eighteen. The anniversary is next Saturday. I celebrate it every year. Maybe we can celebrate it together this year?"

Jamie, Tiffany and Kim stared at me, their smiles fixed somewhere between amusement and anger. Kim finally said, "That's Charlie's fund raiser. He's running for State Senate, you know."

"I did not."

"I'm sure Sophie and Charlie would love to have you there."

My smile froze, and there was a spark of triumph in Jamie's eyes. I forced my smile to relax, leaned forward and whispered, "Every fund raiser I've been to in DC has free-flowing alcohol. Think Charlie will too, or are the Baptists around here still pretending not to drink?"

"Oh, I don't think—" Kim started.

"Are you implying we're hypocrites?" a cold female voice said from behind the trio. Jamie, Tiffany and Kim parted, eyes wide, to make way for Brenda Russell: tall, elegant, dripping with gold jewelry and stinking of Chanel No. 5. I struggled to swallow the bile that rose in my throat, an automatic reaction the scent had triggered in me since I was eighteen years old.

"Brenda."

Brenda Russell's nostrils flared at my use of her Christian name. Check that, her first name. Though professing to be devout, there was nothing Christ-like in the woman. I looked for her husband. "Where's Doug?"

"He died of cancer three years ago."

"Did he?" Everyone waited for me to offer my condolences, but I merely stared at the woman. I'd rather be waterboarded than offer her an ounce of sympathy.

"How are you doing, Mrs. Russell?" my sister said.

"As well as can be expected. I'm sorry for your loss," Brenda said to Mary. "Your father was a fine, Christian man. Moral and always willing to do what was right, regardless of the consequences."

I clasped my hands in front of me and kept my expression placid. I might have envisioned her face a time or two during my sparring sessions, but the woman who stood before me bore only a passing resemblance to the woman from twenty years earlier. Her hair was the same style, but entirely gray. Her face, once perpetually tanned and smooth, was lined with wrinkles and freckled with sunspots her foundation couldn't mask. The deepest wrinkles were around her pursed mouth and looked strikingly like spokes on a wheel.

"How's Sophie?" I didn't care or want to know the answer. But, I wanted to see the expression on Brenda's face when I said her daughter's name. Brenda Russell didn't disappoint. I smirked, and she knew I was baiting her. From the corner of my eye, I saw Jamie look on with an admiring expression. Approval from that corner made me feel petty and small, but not enough to apologize to Brenda Russell.

The line was backing up, so Brenda moved on to Emmadean, as did the other three, though reluctantly. I placed a hand on Kim's arm. "Thank you for the offer. I appreciate it, and I'm sorry to hear about your father."

Kim grasped my hand and smiled. She swallowed thickly. "Thank you, Nora. It's so good to see you, I wish it wasn't under these circumstances..."

"It's good to see you, too, Kim."

"I've always liked your hair," she said. "It's classic. Don't let Jamie give you shit. You should see some of the hairstyles she's gone through in the last twenty years." She winked at me and went to pay her respects to my father. I smiled at the sight of Jamie and Tiffany scurrying after Kim for a change to find out what we talked about.

I ran my hand down my hair. It wasn't the same haircut, though it was a variation on the same theme. A *lob*. Long enough for a ponytail but not so long that it took forever to dry. Simple and professional. I'd gotten bangs after getting out of the army. Big mistake. Now I settled for tucking my hair behind my ears and, if I was trying to be fancy, letting it drape across one eye. I was rarely fancy.

"Your hair is fine," Mary said.

Fucking Jamie Luke.

"Why do you hate Brenda Russell?" Mary asked. "She didn't cheat on you; Charlie and Sophie did."

"It's complicated."

"To not offer condolences is incredibly rude, especially for you. Brenda Russell loved you."

It was true. There was a time when Brenda Russell treated me like a daughter. I practically lived at their house each summer from the time I was ten years old. Brenda and Sophie got along better when I was around, and I'd acted many, many times as a buffer when we were young, and a go-between when Sophie and I were teens. I'd admired Brenda, with her beauty and poise and her generous heart. Doug had been a quiet man who worked all the time. He gave me distracted smiles and pats on the head, and always cheered the loudest at my tennis matches, seemingly as happy for my successes as he was for Sophie's. I think he was making up for the fact that my father rarely came. It had been a shock when the Russells turned on me so thoroughly, and cut me out of their lives.

My stomach clenched at the memory, at the lingering—or was it imagined?—scent of Chanel No. 5. "Not at the end, she didn't."

"Hey, look down the line. Charlie's here. No Sophie, though."

I followed Mary's gaze and still only saw a bunch of vaguely familiar strangers. "Where?"

"Last in line."

"The bald guy?"

"Yep. Charlie's still got those eyes, though."

I felt those eyes on me as we went through the remainder of the mourners, willing it to be over, but dreading the final greeting. Charlie Wyatt shook Mary's hand. "I saw Jeremy outside with the kids. They were pretty wired for a visitation."

I tried to look as innocent as possible.

"I better go check on him," Mary said. She looked as exhausted as I felt. My cheeks were sore from holding an appropriately sad smile, one that said it's nice to see you but the *circumstances*. Putting people at ease was a strength of mine, but today's performance had been taxing in unexpected ways.

"Emmadean, Dormer. Sorry for your loss," Charlie said. He leaned in and hugged Emmadean.

"Charlie, thanks for coming," Emmadean said.

Everyone moved away to give us privacy, and I was left alone with my first boyfriend, my first lover, the person I'd thought I'd spend the rest of my life with. He was familiar and foreign all at once. When he looked at me with those eyes and that smile, he still managed to make my stomach flutter, after all this time.

He inhaled, his gaze roaming over my face. "NoNo."

I gritted my teeth at the nickname, but smiled and said, "Hi, Charlie." My gaze landed on his shiny bald head. "What the hell happened to your hair?"

He laughed, the corners of his pale blue eyes crinkled and that damn dimple appeared on his left cheek. The Deadly Dimple, Sophie and I had called it. It still was. "How many times have you heard 'You haven't changed a bit' tonight?" Charlie asked.

"With you, over a thousand."

"Well, you haven't."

"I live a pure life."

"Ha. I doubt that." He put his hands in his suit pants pockets. The top button of his shirt was unbuttoned and his blue tie, which set off his eyes in a mesmerizing way, was loosened. I wondered if Sophie had picked it out. "How have you been?" he asked.

"Good. Fantastic. How about you?"

He shrugged and looked around. "I'm still in Lynchfield."

"Wasn't that the plan?"

A sheepish smile. "Yes."

"I hear you're right on track. Law practice, now running for State Senate?"

"Yep." He nodded. "It wasn't always easy." He caught my eye and looked away.

"Anything worth having is never easy, is it?"

"I suppose not."

The funeral director walked into the room on soft feet and

with a polite, grieving smile. He met Emmadean and Dormer at my father's casket and spoke in a low voice about whatever was next on the list of tasks for a grieving family.

I steeled myself to ask about Sophie when a young woman walked down the aisle, her head buried in her phone. Her dark hair hung down past her shoulders, save a small braided portion near her hairline. She was tall and thin, with coltish legs jutting from beneath her thigh-length black sundress. The sleeves of a pale pink summer sweater were pushed halfway up her forearms. When she finally looked up from her phone, I inhaled sharply, and loudly enough for Charlie to notice.

"I know, right?" he said.

Sophie's daughter stopped by her father and appraised me with aquamarine eyes that she'd obviously inherited from Charlie. But, the Bette Davis eyes, the thick lashes that curved almost to her dark eyebrows, the full lips, those were pure Sophie.

"Nora, this is my daughter, Logan."

"I've heard a lot about you."

I shuddered to think of what she'd heard. "Nice to meet you."

"Logan's a junior," Charlie said.

"Rising senior," Logan corrected him. "School just ended. I'm sorry about your dad. That's gotta suck."

"Logan," Charlie chided.

"What? It does. I don't know what I'd do if you died."

Charlie pulled his daughter into a one-armed hug. "You won't have to worry about that for years."

"You don't know that. I'm sure Mr. Noakes didn't expect to be run over by a bunch of cows, either." She snapped her fingers. "It can happen just like that."

"Well, my pop *was* sixty-five years old," I said.

"True," Logan said. Her mouth twisted into a crooked smile, and I almost burst into tears at the sight of the familiar mannerism. "Still, what a way to go." She appraised me again. "So. Why haven't you been back to Lynchfield?"

"Logan," Charlie said, pulling his daughter into a playful headlock.

"No, it's okay." She was direct and bold, and utterly guile-less, just like her mother had been. I liked Logan immensely. "My father kicked me out of the house. Told me never to re-turn. So I didn't."

"Harsh," Logan said, at the same time Charlie said, "What?"

I ignored Charlie. "Is Sophie hiding in the car?"

"No." Logan became interested in her phone again and said, dismissively, "She doesn't feel well. A migraine." She was lying. Unsurprising, under the circumstances, but Logan's embarrass-ment at her mother's absence was interesting.

"She'll be at the funeral tomorrow," Charlie promised.

"Excuse me. Nora?" The funeral director had impeccable timing. "We're getting ready to close the casket, would you like a few moments before we do?"

"Yes," I lied. "Thank you."

"We should go," Charlie said. "See you tomorrow."

I smiled and offered a half-hearted wave.

Emmadean and Dormer came up beside me. Emmadean rubbed my back. "You okay, honey?"

"Yes. Where'd Mary go?"

"The kids."

I rolled my eyes. The kids were Mary's built-in excuse for everything.

"Come on, Emmadean," Dormer said in his soft drawl. "Let's give Nora some time alone with Ray."

He nodded, his gentle eyes full of understanding. Dormer was a soft-spoken, solitary man of few words. He rarely offered his opinion, so when he spoke, everyone took his word as law and obeyed almost without question. When Dormer closed the door behind them, I sank down into the nearest chair, exhausted. My head hurt, and my face ached from smiling. I rubbed my stomach, trying to massage away the squirming bundle of emotions that woke at the sight of Charlie and Logan Wyatt.

I inhaled and forced myself to look at my father's polished cherrywood casket. Rather showy for a salt-of-the-earth man like Raymond Noakes. Mary's doing, no doubt. It would have been more appropriate for the bastard to be propped up against the wall in a pine box like the bandits of the Old West. I chuckled. "You would have loved that, wouldn't you?"

From my vantage point, I could only see Ray in profile, his broad forehead beneath a thick mane of hair, his nose arching up and dipping down to point to his handlebar mustache, which had gone completely gray in the last two decades. Emmadean told me Ray had been found facedown, his arms covering his head, which explained why his face was unmarred by hoof prints. The back of his head, set deep into a soft pillow, hadn't been so fortunate, but Dormer said you couldn't tell at all. Ray looked like he was taking a power nap, something he'd done in his recliner at lunchtime for forty years. The Mardell Funeral Home always had done nice work.

The crown of Ray's straw Stetson poked up from his stomach, covering his hands, most likely, or possibly his hands were clutching the brim. I had no intention of finding out. I was here to bury my father, not to grieve for him, to make up with him or, God forbid, cry over his cold body.

I sighed and rose. I buttoned my blazer and pulled down the cuffs of my crisp white shirt. I tucked my hair behind my ears, turned around and walked away, praying with every step that Sophie would feign another headache tomorrow, so I could escape Lynchfield without seeing her.

three
nora

God ignored my prayers.

Sophie's was the first face I saw when we walked into the First United Methodist Church, Lynchfield. She stood at the end of her pew, half in, half out, as if making sure I would see her for my entire trek down the red-carpeted aisle. Sophie Russell was still the most beautiful woman in the room, damn her. She, Charlie and Logan sat in the pew directly behind the family and, by some freak of coincidence, or spectacular planning on Sophie's part, she was directly behind me when I sat down.

I heard nothing of the service. There was music, I suppose. "Amazing Grace," most likely. A eulogy where someone stood up and talked about what a great man my father was. The twenty-third Psalm. "In the Garden." I'd buried enough friends to know without having to pay attention. I stared at my pop's closed casket, but my mind's eye was on Sophie Russell, sitting right behind me. I felt her eyes boring into the back of my head. I even heard her breathing. I smelled her perfume. Remembering Sophie as I'd last seen her eighteen years ago, eyes downcast, cheeks wet from crying, apologizing over and over. *I'm sorry, I'm sorry, I'm sorry.*

I tried to square the Sophie of my past with the woman sitting behind me. Try as we might, none of us could stop the march of time and, though everyone in Lynchfield assured me of the contrary, I knew I was no different. Sophie was still striking but, the closer I got to her when walking down the aisle, I saw that the years showed on her more than I expected. Her face had the hollow look of someone who'd lost a lot of weight in a short amount of time. Was she sick at the idea of seeing me, or was her illness genuine? Maybe the headache excuse hadn't been a ruse, after all.

Someone behind me sniffed. I turned my head to the side and listened. Sophie sniffed again, louder this time. Either Sophie was mourning my father more than any other person in the church or seeing me had been too much for her. I smiled and faced the front. *Good.*

Bored, I automatically reached for the Bible in the holder on the back of the pew and opened it up to the Book of Ruth, the closest story to a romance you will get in the Bible. The only book that seemed to have a happy ending. I'd read this book dozens of times during boring sermons. Sophie was partial to Esther, because she was a queen.

One particularly boring Sunday she wrote a note on the back of the service's program: *It doesn't mention God at all.*

?

Esther. The book. It doesn't mention God at all.

I'd shrugged.

What does it say that my favorite book doesn't mention God?

You're definitely going to hell.

She rolled her eyes and scrubbed the line out with the little pencil. Then she thought better of it and wrote: *I want to go to hell for something a lot more fun that reading Esther.*

We'd both started giggling, which had earned us a stern look from the minister. How he could pinpoint us as the culprits when we sat so far back, I never knew. But, he always did. Maybe because we were the only two in the whole sanctuary who were having fun.

With twenty years of hindsight, my choice of Ruth, and Sophie's choice of Esther, fit our personalities, and our relationship, pretty well: I, the motherless child, wanted to love and be loved; Sophie, the only child, wanted to be worshiped and revered. That sounds crueler to Sophie than I mean it to. Whatever her faults, and I'd chronicled many over the years, Sophie had always been kind and never made fun of anyone, especially not the kids who didn't necessarily fit in Lynchfield. It was one of the reasons she'd been my best friend.

The service ended, and the family was paraded back up the aisle after the casket like show ponies. I pointedly kept my eyes on old man Mardell, who held the door open for us. His assistant ushered us into idling cars where we waited for the casket to be rolled into the hearse, and for those mourners who were attending the graveside service to scurry to their cars for the procession to the cemetery.

The Suburban windows were too dark to see in, but offered me the opportunity to watch the crowd. A fair few were laughing and backslapping, and no one looked terribly torn up. Sophie, Charlie and Logan were some of the last to emerge. Logan and Charlie, so close they were almost a single unit, with a gap between them and Sophie. After what appeared to be a terse exchange, Charlie and Logan walked off. Sophie watched them go before her eyes settled on my car window. She paused for a long moment and turned in the opposite direction of her family. The Suburban inched forward behind the hearse, and we kept pace with Sophie walking on the sidewalk until she stopped at the corner, and we drove on.

The good residents of Lynchfield and the surrounding area might not mourn my father's passing, but that wouldn't stop them from a good feed, and funeral receptions were nothing if not a chance to tie on the feedbag.

The food that had looked so good the day before held little

appeal to me today. I made a round of the mourners, always angled away from the group to discourage deep conversations, until I found Dormer on the front porch with five other men who I should have known the names of but didn't. I was more concerned with what was inside their red Solo cups than in the niceties of mourning the dead in a small town.

"Beer?" I asked, disappointed.

"Dormer's just going easy because he's the host, or so Emma-dean says," one of the men said. "All this gawpin' gettin' to ya, Nora?"

"A little. I was hoping this would be just family and close friends."

"Well, I'll be honest, you're the prime attraction to ol' Ray's funeral. Nobody's seen hide nor hair of you for so long, and everyone wants to know why."

"Digger," Dormer warned.

How did I not recognize Digger Stokes? I thought. His family had owned the Stokes Feed and Seed for a hundred and twenty years. It was the Saturday morning gathering place for the local farmers, and Digger had been one of Pop's best sources of information on what was going on in the farm and ranch community for a hundred miles.

"Go getcha a beer," Dormer said. "It's in the green cooler in the laundry room."

"Put it in a cup so as you don't offend no one," Digger said.

"I thought you were a deacon?" I asked.

"Precisely," he said, toasting me with his red cup.

"Be right back."

I was only stopped by three people on the way to the kitchen, a win any way you looked at it. I found the cooler, and as I bent down to lift the lid, I caught sight of the barn out the laundry room window. It hadn't changed much, just a few rusty sheets of metal on the roof mixed with shiny new ones. Ray must not have had the scratch to fix it all in one go. A few chickens pecked at the ground, and one strutted into the dark barn. The chickens were new, but I bet nothing else had changed. I snatched a red Solo cup from the cooler, filled it halfway with ice, thumped the lid closed and snuck out the back door.

Cars pulled in and out of the driveway as if by appointment. I wondered if the town had gotten together and scheduled when they would visit, knowing old Ray's house wasn't big enough for everyone all at once, and it was too damn hot to stand outside. *Now Irma, you go at three forty-five and I'll come at four fifteen.*

Chickens squawked and flapped away as I walked to the barn. The familiar scent of hay and motor oil leveled me like a freight train.

Ray's old John Deere was parked on one side of the barn, next to the shredder and a few old tires. A jumble of farm equipment that didn't work, but Ray refused to get rid of, blocked access to the hayloft ladder. Three empty stalls and the tack room lined the opposite wall. I went to the tack room door and stopped. I stared at the latch, jagged wood, worn smooth with age and use. I hadn't thought of it in years, and all this time it had been here, waiting for me to return, twist it, and steal my father's stash one more time.

There it was, half empty, dusty and covered with cobwebs, tucked behind the sawhorse holding Ray's saddle. The label was dry and brittle with age. I paused before opening it. Surely this wasn't the same bottle I drank from in high school. I shook the thought away and poured a healthy shot into my cup. The ice cracked and popped when the warm Old Crow hit it. I shook the glass, cooling the whiskey and melting the ice into small shards before taking a long drink. I closed my eyes and put the cold cup to my forehead. Sweat trickled down my back and temple. It was mid-June, and the heat in the tack room was oppressive. It was nothing like the heat at Mortaritaville, but I'd been at a desk for too long and had lost my acclimation to heat.

"Nora?"

I opened my eyes and saw her outlined in the doorway, the bright light behind throwing her in shadow. For a moment, I believed it was 1995, and she was waiting for me to nick the bottle, climb into the hayloft and get loaded together. My throat constricted. Or was it my heart?

"I saw you come out here when I drove up."

I lifted the bottle. "Ray was nothing if not a creature of habit."

"As are you, apparently."

I chuckled. "I can't believe it took me a whole day to remember it."

"That bottle looks pretty old. Hope it doesn't give you ptomaine poisoning."

I laughed. Ptomaine poisoning had been Ray's go-to threat, next to getting lockjaw from kissing my horse's muzzle. With Ray's cooking, the risk of food poisoning had been real. It was why we ate most meals at Emmadean's house.

Sophie stepped out of the doorway, and I left the tack room, closing the door slowly as if it would crack into a million pieces unless I was careful.

I wish I could say it was as if no time had passed, that I felt the same affection for her as before. But, I was a different person. She was a different person. How could we not be? The Sophie I'd been imagining was a seventeen-year-old beauty, the life of the party, full of impossible dreams, by Lynchfield standards, not the nervous woman on the downhill slide to forty in front of me.

We'd had it all planned out: attend Texas Tech together, Sophie would get a degree in public relations, me in journalism, and we would set out for New York City, maybe Chicago. Anywhere that wasn't small-town Texas. I would have been happy with Dallas or Houston, but not Sophie. She wanted out of Texas, as far away as possible. I didn't care as long as we did it together. We'd done everything together since we were ten years old. I couldn't imagine life any other way. I'd never wanted to imagine life any other way.

Then, my life went sideways all at once, and it took years for me to straighten it out. The army, language school, night school to get my degree, officer training school, assigned to Army Intelligence right before September 11. I survived nine months at Balad Air Force Base, affectionately known as Mortaritaville for the daily bombings, only to have my convoy run over an IED two days before my tour was over.

After being released from the hospital, I'd asked for and received a discharge, but the government didn't write off their investments that easily, especially a former officer who spoke multiple languages. I'd lived a good life, an exciting life. I was living a version of the life Sophie and I envisioned, and I was happy.

For the first time, I realized maybe Sophie did me a favor by betraying me.

"How are you, NoNo?" she said.

Charlie had used the nickname the day before, but hearing Sophie use it... "Don't call me that." I shook my head. "Not that."

"I'm sorry."

"Yes, I know." I waved it away with the hand holding the cup. I drank and offered her the bottle.

Sophie licked her lips and said, "No, thanks."

I poured more into my cup, melting the ice completely, and drank again. I watched Sophie over the rim. "Did you come to gawp at me like everyone else? Digger says I'm the main attraction, which is why I'm hiding in the barn with a musty bottle of Old Crow."

"That's not why I'm here." She stepped forward. "Logan wasn't lying. You look fantastic."

"I don't have a husband and child to age me."

She grimaced, knowing me well enough all these years later to recognize the veiled insult. She'd been the brash one; I'd been circumspect. I'd never been cruel, though.

"I'm sorry," I said.

"No, it's true. You look happy."

"Yes, well, my father's dead. I hear yours is, as well."

She nodded. "Mother told me she saw you."

"I'm sure she did. How are you feeling?"

"What?"

"Logan said you had a headache yesterday?"

"Oh, right. I wasn't sick. I couldn't face you."

I wasn't sure if the admission gratified me or saddened me. "What changed?"

"I had to see you." Sophie twisted her wedding ring around and around her finger, pulled it off partway, shoved it back on and continued turning it. I went still at the sight of a thin silver band on her right ring finger. When I found my voice, it was brusquer than I intended.

"Why? To ask my forgiveness?"

She glanced away and shook her head. "I lost hope of that years ago."

I stared into my empty cup. A pleasant warmth had spread throughout my body, but it was not enough. I wanted another drink but didn't want to look weak.

"I like Logan." I glanced up at Sophie, who couldn't hide her pride in her daughter. "She reminds me of you."

Her smile slipped a little before she laughed and said, "Oh, don't let her hear you say that. I'm pretty much the most embarrassing mom ever."

I shook my cup as if there was ice in it. Sophie worried her ring some more. "How long will you be in town?" she asked.

"Not long."

She met my eyes then. "Emmadean will be disappointed. She thinks you're staying for a while."

"I have a life in DC. A career. Friends and—"

Mary marched into the barn. "There you are. Everyone's asking."

I held out the whiskey. Mary took the bottle and drank a swig. She coughed and handed it back. "Behind the sawhorse?"

"Yeah. You knew?"

Mary rolled her eyes. "He let us steal it. There was always a fresh bottle, wasn't there?"

Sophie and I glanced at each other. "Yes," we said.

"If he cared, he would have tanned our hide. You don't have to hide in the barn to drink anymore. No one cares."

"Maybe I wanted to be alone."

"God, you're a shit."

"How do you figure?"

"You're here for what? Two days, after nearly twenty years, and you can't handle talking to a bunch of old people for a couple of hours? I've been doing—"

"Don't blame me, blame Ray. He didn't want me here, did he? He's dead now, so you're free. You'll have to find something else to complain about, but I'm sure you're up to the task."

My sister's eyes narrowed. Mary stood between Sophie and me, looking back and forth. "Did I interrupt a big emotional makeup scene?"

"No," I said.

"Yes," Sophie said.

"Do you want to be left alone?"

"No."

"Yes."

"Goodness. You two used to be so in sync. You finished each other's sentences, if I remember correctly."

"Stop being a nosy bitch and leave us alone, would you?" Sophie said.

Mary's mouth pursed, and her cheeks went red. "I heard you're a mean drunk, Sophie, but never believed it."

"I'm not drunk; I just don't like you."

"Feeling's mutual. Ranger Rick is here, said he found something cleaning out Pop's desk. Charlie's here to read Pop's will. Let's get this over with. Jeremy and I need to leave in an hour."

Sophie waited until Mary was out of earshot before speaking. She took a deep breath and said, "I need to tell you something."

"No." The reply was automatic, and I realized I didn't want her to ask for my forgiveness, nor did I want to give it.

"No?"

"There's nothing you can say to change what happened, and I'm not in the mood to be burdened by your guilt. If you even feel guilty."

"Of course I do."

"I'm over it, Sophie. I moved on years ago. I'm here to bury Ray and go home."

Sophie stepped forward, towering over me by a good five inches, two of those from the wedge heels she wore. Her nerves had evaporated, and her brown eyes met mine, bright and challenging. I saw a glimmer of the girl I once knew, the girl who could see through me and into my soul.

"Bullshit," she whispered. "Why did you come back?"

"Maybe I wanted to see how your choice worked out for you."

She scoffed. "*My* choice."

"Wasn't it?"

She inhaled and crossed her arms over her chest. "You came back to gloat, didn't you?"

I mimicked her stance. "Maybe."

She pursed her lips and nodded as her eyes searched my face. Did she see the girl she once knew or an entirely different person? I held her gaze as the silence lengthened, and the tension between us was palpable until finally, I wasn't seeing her at all, but our history: becoming best friends the summer before fifth grade when Coach Cress had given me a tennis scholarship at the country club; riding our bikes all around town, always ending up at the bakery sharing a piece of buttermilk pie; making grunge mix tapes at Sophie's; clinging to each other and crying when we learned that Kurt Cobain killed himself; going through a very regrettable matching flannel shirt stage to honor his memory; celebrating when Sophie made the cheer team; celebrating when I made the basketball, tennis and track teams; Sophie showing up to cold early-morning track meets with a thermos of hot chocolate for me (and even bringing a can of Reddi Wip); reading our required English lit books to Sophie, my head in her lap, Sophie playing with my hair until it was greasy and needed a wash; our senior year.

Feelings I thought I'd long since buried flared in the pit of my stomach as I remembered the best year of my life. I hadn't been sure of my place in the world—what teenager was?—but I was sure of my place in my best friend's life. Until the day it all fell apart.

Sophie remembered that day, too. She blushed and opened her mouth to speak, but nothing came. My throat thickened with emotion—hope—and kept me from saying what I'd longed to say since that June day in 1995. Sophie found her voice first.

"Congratulations. You won."

She walked out of the barn, letting me down again.

four
nora

I decided ice was overrated and finished off the whiskey before I returned to the house.

I stopped inside the kitchen door at the sight of Sophie and Charlie standing close together, talking low. Sophie's arms were crossed over her chest, and she was staring at the floor, her eyes red. Charlie held a briefcase in one hand and had an exasperated expression on his face. They broke apart when they saw me. Sophie turned away, wiping her cheeks. I clenched my jaw, went into the laundry room and shut the door. I reached out with one hand to steady myself against the refrigerator and inhaled a few times. I had barely eaten, and the whiskey was doing its job nicely. But, not well enough. I reached into the green cooler, popped a beer and drank half of it. I stared at the Shiner label and came to terms with the knowledge that coming home wasn't going to give me the closure I sought. Every emotion, good and bad, had been dredged back up. I would listen to Ranger Rick, and to the will, and leave as soon as possible. Tomorrow. The next day at the latest.

There was a knock. "Nora?" Charlie said.

I opened the door. Before Charlie could say anything, I skirted around him. Sophie stood in front of the kitchen sink, her back to me, staring out the window. I set my half-empty beer on the table with a thunk and went into the den. Rick Michaels sat forward in the recliner, talking to Emmadean and Mary on the couch. Dormer and Jeremy stood off to the side. I heard the children in the distance, with an older girl's voice I recognized at once as Sophie's daughter. Charlie came in and edged over by Dormer.

"That's Ray's chair," I said to Rick Michaels.

Everyone stared up at me. Ranger Rick didn't move, or look abashed, but sat back into Ray's chair.

"Get up," I said.

"Nora," Emmadean said.

"What?" I snapped. Everyone went quiet. I walked to Rick Michaels and stood over him. "Get out of Ray's chair, or I'll do it for you."

"No need to be testy, little lady." He pushed himself forward and struggled to heft himself out of the chair.

"I'm not your little lady."

"Nora, good God, settle down," Mary said.

Michaels reached into his coat pocket and held out an envelope to Charlie. I snatched it away. "We found it in Ray's desk drawer," Michaels said.

Ray's distinctive block lettering covered a single sheet of lined yellow paper with a jagged tear at the top. The date in the top right corner was one week previous. The title: Last Will and Testament of Raymond Arnold Noakes.

I looked at Rick Michaels in astonishment. "Ray wrote a new will, and he just happened to be in a freak accident the next week?"

Dormer leaned close to look at the paper in my hand. Jeremy did the same.

Rick Michaels shrugged his shoulders. "I admit it looks mighty strange. But, there's no doubt about those meth heads being responsible."

"Nora," Dormer said. He nodded to the paper I held. I followed his gaze and read one sentence that changed everything.

I, Raymond Arnold Noakes, being of sound mind, leave all my worldly possessions to my youngest daughter, Nora Jane Noakes, and name her executor of my estate.

Ray had scrawled his signature above the notary stamp.

"What the fuck?" I murmured. Charlie took the paper and inspected it.

"What does it say?" Mary asked.

Charlie opened his briefcase and pulled out a legal document.

Rick Michaels put on his Stetson. "Sorry for your loss," he said to Mary and Emmadean. He turned to me and said, "Congratulations," with a smirk, and left.

"Congratulations?" Mary said. Jeremy stepped back with an expression of long-suffering resignation. "Jeremy?"

Emmadean and Dormer exchanged a look that told me they'd known of this bombshell or at least suspected it.

Charlie finally spoke. "It's Ray's signature."

Mary stood and snatched the yellow paper from Charlie. She read it and looked up at me. Here it came, the temper tantrum I'd been waiting for. I steeled myself, though I was swaying on my feet slightly. My mouth was as dry as a desert. I wanted the rest of my Shiner. A whole six-pack, truth be told. And I wasn't even much of a drinker.

Mary burst out laughing. She covered her mouth with her free hand. "Oh my God. What did you do to make him hate you so?"

"Mary," Emmadean snapped.

Mary's laughter didn't stop. Sophie stood in the doorway of the kitchen, watching. Hunter, Madison and Logan came down the hall.

"What's so funny, Mom?" Madison asked. She held the book I'd given her, one finger saving her place.

Logan went to her mother. Sophie lifted one shoulder at her daughter's silent question before her gaze settled on me again.

"Karma, Madison. Karma is what's so funny." Mary handed the will to me. "Ray's your problem now. Finally. Come on, Jeremy," she said.

"But, Aunt Nora and I are going to build the Empire State Building," Hunter said.

"You can do it another time; she's not going anywhere." Mary let the screen door slap closed behind her.

I hugged Madison and Hunter, telling the latter that I wouldn't start building without him. Jeremy squeezed my upper arm. "Sorry, sis."

When the screen door closed behind them, Logan said, "You're staying? That's cool." When everyone remained silent, she said, with less assurance. "Right?"

For a long moment, no one answered. Finally, Emmadean said, "You bet it is."

I pushed the will into Charlie's chest on my way to the kitchen. Logan watched wide-eyed as I stopped in the doorway, which Sophie blocked. Sophie opened her mouth as if to say something, but instead moved aside. I walked to the table, picked up my abandoned beer and placed it to my lips. I felt sticky remnants on the bottle's mouth at the same time I realized it was empty. I saw bright red lipstick against the amber colored bottle. I turned to Sophie and thunked the bottle back down on the table. "You drank my beer?"

Sophie stepped into the kitchen and said, quickly, "If you need help cleaning out the house, I can get you some names."

Logan was on her mother's heels, her eyes riveted on the beer bottle. "Seriously, Mom?"

"Logan, not now," Sophie started.

"Ugh," Logan said, turned on her heel and ran into her dad. "I'll be in the car."

Charlie looked from his retreating daughter to his wife, who shook her head slightly. "Nora," Charlie said, finally tearing his puzzled gaze from Sophie, "why don't you come by the office tomorrow afternoon. We can go over everything."

"Can't wait."

"I'll give the names to Charlie," Sophie said.

"Sure."

There was an awkward pause while Charlie looked between us—me, his first love, and my best friend, whom he'd married—as if unsure where his loyalties lay. He handed me a business card. "In case you need to get in touch with me."

I put the card in my pocket.

He motioned with his arm for Sophie to precede him out of the kitchen, but she said, "I'll be right there."

Charlie nodded and left the room.

"If there's anything at all you need…"

"I'm sure Emmadean and Dormer can help."

"Right." She nodded and unfolded her arms. "Goodbye, Nora."

I didn't watch her leave. I was taking a long pull of a new beer when a business card stuck halfway under the empty Shiner bottle caught my eye. It was thick, bright white card stock with the Lynchfield city logo in the corner and Sophie's name and title in the center—President, Convention & Visitors' Bureau—and her contact information in the bottom corners. I turned the card over and stared at her cell phone number scribbled on the back above three words.

I miss you.

Emmadean and I cleaned the kitchen in silence, while Dormer went to the barn to take care of the chickens. We put most of the food in the freezer for reheating later and divvied up the rest between me and Emmadean and Dormer. Every inch of freezer space in the house was taken up.

"Why're we doing this?" I asked. "I'll just have to throw it out when I leave. If I stayed here a *month*, I wouldn't put a dent in it."

"You're slurring your words," Emmadean said.

"Am not."

Emmadean was at the sink, washing dishes to return to the friends who'd brought food. "Why didn't they use disposable stuff?" I asked. "I suppose I'm going to have to deliver all of these, along with everything else I have to do."

"You sound a lot like Mary."

"Now, that's cruel."

"If the shoe fits."

I dropped down into a kitchen chair, my head spinning and a headache starting behind my eyes. "She sure didn't let the door hit her on the way out. I bet they made it to Austin in record time."

Emmadean washed and rinsed a deviled egg plate and put it in the drainer. She wiped her hands, folded the dish towel and joined me at the table. She lowered herself gingerly into a chair, and I realized how old Emmadean was. I assumed she was stout as an ox, but her grimace of pain said otherwise.

I reached out and grasped her hand. "You okay?"

She gave my hand a consoling pat. "Old bones. Don't try to tell me you wouldn't have hightailed it as soon as you could if the roles were reversed."

"Why did he do it?"

"Well, to make amends, I imagine."

"By giving me this dump? More like getting back at me."

"No, Nora."

"He had nearly two decades to make amends, Emmadean."

"So did you."

"I didn't do anything wrong."

"Ray had his reasons."

I stayed silent. There was no point in arguing with Emmadean. She'd defended her brother for all these years, and it wasn't going to change now he was planted in the ground. I'd long since stopped feeling betrayed by it.

After Ray had kicked me out, I'd been able to get my reporting day moved up, so I only had to live with Emmadean and Dormer for a couple of weeks, which I'd spent locked in their guest room, avoiding the world. I kept expecting Ray to come over and apologize, but he never did. When it became apparent neither Ray nor I would talk, Emmadean'd given up asking what exactly happened between us and settled into her role as mediator, and eventually communicator. Emmadean kept me up on the town gossip, but I'd started tuning her out years earlier, and had finally asked her to stop giving me updates, especially on Sophie and Charlie.

Now their business cards were burning holes in my two front pockets. I knew Charlie was a lawyer, had taken over his father's practice, and was running for State Senate, apparently, but I didn't know anything about Sophie from the last ten years. Why did she say, *You won* when she looked like she had a pretty good life? If you were stuck in small-town Texas, President of the Convention & Visitors' Bureau for a historic town like Lynchfield was about as good as it could get.

"How long has Sophie been at the CVB?"

"If you were on Facebook, you'd know."

"Oh my God," I said, slouching down and leaning my head against the back of the chair. She'd been on me for years to join up, but I had zero desire. I wasn't interested in what my high school friends' kids were doing.

Emmadean studied me for a while before answering. "Five years? I bet she hasn't had a full night's sleep since Logan was born. After Charlie graduated law school she went to school full-time but never missed one of Logan's games, or recitals, practices. She volunteered with every organization she could. She's a firecracker."

"Superwoman."

"Don't you dare mock her," Emmadean said.

"I'm not, it's just…nothing like the life she said she wanted."

"Who lives the life they wanted at eighteen? Are you?"

"No, Emmadean. It never occurred to me I'd be working for—" Luckily my drunk mind caught up to my tongue and stopped me from finishing. Emmadean lifted her eyebrows and waited. She'd casually asked me if I knew Valerie Plame once, a few years after I left the military. I changed the subject. "Charlie and Logan seem close."

"Oh, they are. Charlie is a great dad and husband. Charlie and Sophie are a well-oiled machine. Never seen a couple so supportive of each other."

Jealousy knotted in my stomach and started festering there.

"They're Lynchfield's golden couple. We're competitive with Fredericksburg and Wimberly for weekend tourism thanks to Sophie, and the Republicans have long-term aspirations for Charlie. Maybe the Governor's Mansion, one day."

"No kidding?"

Emmadean nodded. "I'm not sure that's common knowledge."

"How did you find out?"

"Sophie. We meet regularly for lunch."

"Why?"

Emmadean stared at me. "Some people enjoy my company."

I closed my eyes and nodded, ashamed. "Who wouldn't?"

"I used to sit with Logan for her when Brenda couldn't, and we've become friends, after a fashion. At first, I think she just wanted to hear about you, what you were doing. I gave her your address once. Did she ever write?"

"No."

Emmadean nodded her head slowly as if mulling over the information. Finally, she said, "I suppose I'm not surprised. She stopped asking about you after a while, and I stopped sharing. She and Charlie both needed to move on. Like you did."

"I'm glad they've been happy."

"It hasn't been easy."

Dormer came into the kitchen. "Chickens are fed and cooped up," Dormer said. "The pasture needs shredding. I'll come over and do it this weekend."

"I'll do it," I said. "I want to see if shredding a pasture is as hot and miserable as I remember."

Dormer chuckled. "Oh, it is. Have at it. Call me if you can't get the John Deere running."

Emmadean heaved herself up from the chair and motioned for me to hug her. "Come 'ere." She might be old, but Emmadean still gave the best hugs. I settled into her embrace, wanting to never leave. She must have sensed my need because she held me silently for a long time. "Would you do me a favor?" she whispered in my ear.

I pulled back to see her face. "If I can."

"You can. I want you to make peace with Sophie and Charlie."

"Emmadean—"

"They're good people, and deserve to be happy. They won't ever be until you three clear the air for good."

"Why would you think I have the power to make them happy if they haven't been able to do it themselves?"

"Because neither one of them has gotten over loving, and losing, you."

Emmadean's makeup was running in the heat, and she looked tired. If she hadn't seemed so wiped out, I would have argued. As it was, I didn't have the heart. "I'll try."

"Good." She patted my cheek. "It'll do you a world of good, too." Dormer took her arm and escorted her to the front door.

"I'm happy," I called.

"Talk to you tomorrow," Emmadean said.

The front door closed, and I was left alone in my father's empty house.

five
nora

I woke at 7:00 a.m. with a raging headache. Bars of sunlight streamed through the gaps in the Venetian blinds, throwing stripes of golden light onto the Martha Washington bedspread that had covered my double bed for thirty years. It was the only thing from my childhood room which had survived, it turned out. Every personal item I'd left—the Steffi Graff and Pearl Jam posters, all my photos, the yearbooks, the cheap jewelry—all gone. The few clothes I'd brought for the funeral hung from the center of the long, empty dowel rod beneath a shelf that held back copies dating to 1996 of the magazines on the coffee table in the den. The closet floor was barren save for a small box of toys and a Pack 'n Play which Mary's kids had grown out of. I wondered if Ray had burned all of my things, or if I'd find them in the attic when I started to go through his stuff.

I threw my arm across my eyes. Any small notion I'd nurtured that Ray's making me executor, and leaving everything to me, would be an olive branch from the grave was snuffed out the night before when, while drinking my fourth Shiner, I'd opened every closet and cabinet in the house to discover they were crammed full of junk, some of which I remembered seeing in the same spot years ago. I'd stared at the door of his bedroom for the span of Shiners number five and six, before stumbling to the single bathroom, brushing my teeth, stripping down to my panties and crawling into my childhood bed.

How do you even go about reconciling the dead with the world they left behind? How do you do it with a man you hated?

I sat on the edge of the bed, holding my head in my hands. I knew what I had to do, but dreaded it. It was why I rarely drank.

Thirty minutes later I stood in the parking lot of Lynchfield High School, finishing a coconut cream kolache and coffee from Giesmann's bakery, and staring at the faded red-and-gold lion painted on the side of the detached gym. Like Ray's house, nothing much had changed at the high school. It had seen better days when I was there. Today it fit squarely in the trendy midcentury modern style: a building Brooklyn hipsters would fight to save and gentrify. Lynchfield wasn't having it; I'd driven past the construction site for the new high school on the way into town.

With resignation, I started the fitness app on my phone, ran out of the parking lot and turned toward downtown. I hated running. Hated it. Ten-mile runs at the crack of dawn in boot camp will turn you off of a thing damn quick. But, it was a solid fallback workout when I didn't have a gym or sparring partner available. I'd learned long ago I could survive anything for an hour.

Not wanting to draw attention to myself, I ran through the neighborhoods around the edge of town, letting the rhythm of my footfalls focus my mind on what I needed to do to get out of Lynchfield as soon as possible. Meeting with Charlie was the first step, finding Ray's papers and diving into his financials was the second. Ray had never been wealthy, but he'd made ends meet well enough for the three of us. He hadn't given me a dime since I left, and Mary had been married almost the entire time. Ray was single, and apparently didn't put any money back into the house or barn, or only put the bare minimum. There was a better chance he was the millionaire next door than loaded down with debt. Or at least I hoped.

I didn't want his money, though. If there was anything left over, I'd give it to Hunter and Madison. Start a college account for them. Maybe that would put me back on Mary's good side, though I doubted it.

I checked my fitness tracker. Five miles in thirty-five minutes. One mile per beer, but I still hadn't accounted for the whiskey. I looked at the sign at the end of the road in front of me. Lynch-field Country Club. Half mile to the club, a half mile back and a half mile to the high school. That would be enough penance for one day.

Large brick houses with expansive, perfectly manicured lawns lined the road. I cataloged the occupants as I ran, or at least the residents the last time I was here: Lawsons, Hoovers, Richard-sons, Jenkinses and Wyatts on the left. The Tollesons, McGuires, Stoppers, Lynches and Russells on the right. I sprinted past the Wyatts and Russells, the last houses on the street before the country club, and the two reasons I'd spent every summer of my childhood at Lynchfield Country Club.

I stopped in the parking lot, put my hands on my hips to catch my breath, and heard the familiar sounds of summer. Birds chirping from the limbs of the majestic oak trees surrounding the clubhouse. The choo-choo-choo of sprinklers watering the driving range. A lawn mower in the distance. The thwack of a driver hitting a golf ball off the first tee. The thump of a ten-nis ball being volleyed. I walked toward the tennis clubhouse, wondering if Coach Cress would remember me, or if he was even still around.

Goose bumps popped up on my arms as air-conditioning hit my sweaty body. The teenage girl behind the counter glanced up from her phone, did a double take when she realized she didn't know me and set the phone down. "Can I help you?"

"Is Coach Cress here?"

"He died last year."

"Oh."

"Had a stroke, right on the court."

I resisted the urge to say, *At least he died doing what he loved,* but barely.

The tennis clubhouse hadn't changed much. The main room held a few racks of tennis clothes, shelves of balls next to rackets hanging on hooks on one wall, a half wall of shoes next to two doors leading to the locker rooms. But, the centerpiece of the clubhouse was the Wall of Fame opposite the main entrance. Plaques and photos covered either side of the trophy case anchored in the middle. And there it was. To the left of the case, near the end of the bottom row of photos. Sweat trickled down to the corner of my eye, making it sting. I wiped it away.

Sophie and I stood arm in arm. Sophie held a silver plate; I held a gold cup. We'd just won the club doubles tournament for the third year in a row. I'd won the singles tournament, beating Jamie Luke in straight sets without dropping a game. I was grinning into the camera, flushed with victory and sweaty from my match. Sophie, my biggest cheerleader on the sideline, smiled down at me. After the camera had clicked, she kissed me on the cheek and whispered *You're a badass* in my ear.

You're goddamn right I am.

"That's you, isn't it?"

I jumped at the girl's voice. "Sorry," she said.

"It's okay."

"That's you and Mrs. Wyatt. You're Nora Noakes."

"Yeah."

"Coach Cress talked about you all the time. You and Mrs. Wyatt. Said you were the best doubles team he ever coached."

"Huh," I said, staring at the photo, wishing I could go back to that summer knowing now it was the beginning of the end. Would I do anything differently?

"Mrs. Wyatt says you were the best. She's always teasing

Logan and me about it. Says you two would have kicked our butts. I'm Lexa, by the way. Lexa Rodriguez."

"Nice to meet you. You and Logan are doubles partners?"

"Yeah. Club champs two years running."

"Good for you." I jerked my head toward the tennis courts on the other side of the wall. "Why aren't you out there practicing?"

"I'm done for today. I just started my shift. Logan's out there, hitting with my brother."

"Think anyone would mind…?"

She rolled her eyes in a mannerism I remembered from my youth. "Please."

My body relaxed as soon as I walked outside to the four courts grouped in a rectangle to the west of the clubhouse. A green windscreen covered the chain link fence around the court on three sides, with the fourth side open to the restaurant patio. Logan and a teenage boy were in the middle of a long, grunt-filled volley. I found a chair at a table near the court and watched.

Logan moved like her mother. Long legs and arms made her side-to-side movements seem effortless and gave her the ability to reach the ball even when her opponent thought he'd dropped it in the perfect spot. Her ball placement was impeccable, and she kept delivering shot after shot to his forehand. He would try to reposition himself to the center line, thinking Logan was about to go cross-court, but another volley delivered right at his forehand pulled him back every time. He knew Logan was setting him up as well as I did, so he delivered a shot to Logan's backhand. She reached out and, with a two-handed grip, crushed the return. The guy watched Logan's shot whiz by, just catching the in line.

Logan caught sight of me, grinned and waved. I waved back.

I sat back in my chair and let the familiarity of the sights and sounds wash over me. I'd spent half of my childhood on these courts, and in the swimming pool beyond. Summers full of sticky popsicles, nut-brown bodies cannonballing into the deep end, the tang of sweat and suntan lotion on our upper lips when we laid out, chicken fights with Joe and Charlie and whatever other boys were available, choking on chlorinated water when we were dunked. The squeak of tennis shoes on the court, the thwack of the racquet on a ball. Sitting on a lifeguard chair, twirling a whistle around our fingers, noses white with sun-screen.

A glass of water, sweat beading on the sides, was placed on the table next to me by a perfectly manicured hand. "I saw you from inside. Thought you might be thirsty."

My stomach tumbled at the sound of her voice, and then I looked at her.

With her expensive tailored clothes, red lips and Jackie O. sunglasses, she looked like a movie star. A cool breeze brushed my skin, as if she'd brought the air-conditioning outside with her.

"Thank you."

She nodded but was looking in her daughter's direction. I gulped the water, unaware until it coursed down my throat how thirsty I was. The ice clinked in the glass when I set it down.

The breeze shifted Sophie's dark hair across her olive skin. She swept it back behind her ear, and I caught a whiff of her perfume, spicy and sharp. A perfect scent for Sophie. I couldn't help but smile.

"She's better than I was," Sophie said.

"Oh, I don't know. You were a great player."

"Not as good as you."

"Nobody's perfect."

Sophie shifted her face slightly, and I knew she was side-eyeing me.

"Are you here to pick Logan up?"

"No. Breakfast meeting."

"Don't let me keep you."

"It's over."

She looked back toward the clubhouse but didn't move to leave.

"Do you want to sit down?"

"I can't stay long."

I pressed the button on my phone. Zero eight thirty. "Just for a minute."

She studied me a long moment and sat down.

"Do you still play?" I asked.

"A little in the last year. You?"

"Haven't picked up a racket since I left."

"How far did you run?"

"About six miles."

"Impressive."

"Do you run?"

"Only when someone is chasing me."

I laughed, and she smiled. "Same laugh. It's nice to hear."

Her eyes were hidden behind her glasses, but her smile faded into something else, and we looked away from each other. We watched in silence for a while, though I barely saw what was in front of me. I noticed Logan glance our way, and turn without acknowledging her mother. Sophie's mouth tightened, and she uncrossed and crossed her legs.

"Sophie." I sat forward in my chair and held my empty water glass between my hands. I saw my reflection in her bug-eyed glasses and grimaced.

"Are you going to berate me again? Because you'll have to stand in line," she said.

"Berate you? No." I looked down. "Will you take your glasses off?"

She pushed the glasses back on her head, pulling her hair away from her face.

"Thank you." I sighed and rubbed my forehead, the hangover headache sneaking back up on me. "I'm sorry for yesterday. For how I acted. I…"

I resent you. I miss you. I hate you. I love you.

She stared at me with those deep brown eyes, and I wondered if she could see into me like she used to, if she knew I was repulsed by her as much as I was drawn to her? Her expression was inscrutable. I cleared my throat. "I don't know how long I'll be in town, and I don't want it to be awkward."

"Awkward. Is that what you think this is?"

"It's one word for it. Let's not fight, okay?"

"You never did like confrontation."

"And you thrived on it. Seems like that hasn't changed."

"Apparently not."

I lifted my hands in supplication. "Okay, at least I can tell Emmadean I tried." I put a hand on the table to stand, but Sophie grasped it.

"Wait." She held my hand until I settled back into my chair, paused for a beat, and released it.

The tightness in my chest loosened. I reached out for Sophie's right hand and lifted the ring finger encircled by a thin silver band I'd noticed the day before. We'd bought the rings at a local craft fair our senior year and exchanged them in a giggly ceremony where we vowed to be friends for life. Best friend necklaces with two sides of one heart were too trite for us. I'd worn my ring on my right middle finger; we didn't want to give people the wrong idea. I met Sophie's eyes again, and she smiled. "I never gave up hope."

I smiled and released her hand. "I think Ray burned mine."

"That's over the top even for Ray."

"There's nothing left of me in my old room. Maybe Ray put it in the attic, but that would have been a lot of effort for his disgraceful daughter."

"Bastard."

"Yeah. I'm thinking of torching the house."

"I'll bring the marshmallows."

My phone rang. Alima's photo popped up. My finger instinctively moved to answer but hovered over the screen uncertainly. I glanced at Sophie, who seemed intent on the action on the court, said excuse me, walked off and answered.

"Did you survive?" I could hear the teasing in Alima Koshkam's voice, and see her sitting in her office, leaned back in her chair, relaxed and confident. We'd had hundreds of conversations in her office, about work, history, politics, religion. The personal chats came years later, over a bottle of red wine, and through many tears. Alima was the first person I'd opened up to since I left Lynchfield, and Sophie, behind.

"Barely."

"Are you on your way home?" Alima asked.

"No. The bastard left everything to me. Made me executor."

"Why? Is that his effort at penance?"

"Emmadean says so. Mary seems to think he was getting back at me, one last time."

"That sounds more like it. How long will you be there?"

"Not sure. I have an appointment with Charlie to talk about the will this afternoon."

"*The* Charlie?"

"Yes. He's gone bald, but he's still pretty good-looking."

"Hmm. And Sophie? Have you seen her?"

I glanced at Sophie, who shifted her head in a way that told me she'd been watching me.

"Yes."

"And?"

"About what you would expect."

"What I expected and you expected are two different things."

"I can't talk right now."

"She's there, isn't she?"

"Yes."

"And, how does that make you feel?"

She didn't want to know. "I'm giving you a dramatic eye roll right now."

"No doubt."

Alima was silent for a while, waiting for me to continue, to answer the question. I didn't—couldn't—and was surprised when she broke first. "Let me know if you need me to come down, help clean out his house, or whatever."

"I wouldn't wish that on my enemy, let alone my best friend."

The thought of Alima seeing where I came from mortified me. She lived in an exquisitely decorated house in Chevy Chase with her husband. She'd never set foot in Texas, let alone small-town America. No, I preferred Alima to know the DC version of me, the real version, instead of the small-town me I'd out-grown years ago.

"Hmm. Hurry back. It's boring here without you. Davoud is out of town, remember?"

I grimaced. I'd forgotten. "Montreal."

"Oh, you *do* remember."

It was one of Alima's favorite cities, and she was excited to show me all of her favorite spots. With her husband away in Asia on a ten-day business trip, it seemed like the perfect weekend. And I'd completely forgotten about it.

"You aren't coming," she said.

"I didn't say that. You know I want to come. I'll know more this afternoon."

"We've been planning this for months."

"I know, and I'm sorry, but I can't help it that my father died."

"Nora, that's not the point, and you know it. I'll cancel the reservation because you obviously have other priorities right now."

"Alima…"

"I'll let you get back to your friend." She hung up.

I tapped the phone against my forehead. Damn it. I should have called her last night, but I was too busy wallowing in a six-pack of Shiner.

I sat back down at the table and laid my phone down on its face.

"Everything okay?" Sophie asked, keeping her eyes on the court.

"Work stuff."

Sophie nodded slowly, and called out to her daughter, "Nice shot, Lo." Logan ignored her. "One more year, one more year," Sophie chanted.

"That bad?"

She nodded toward Logan and the boy. "They're having sex."

I watched the teens, glad to have something to think about besides my fight with Alima, though teenage sex wasn't high on my list of interesting subjects. They were on the side of the court now, talking and laughing as if they'd known each other forever. "How do you know?"

Sophie side eyed me. "I was the master at sneaking around, remember?"

"Good point. Is Logan on birth control?"

"She will be soon."

I meant the question to rattle Sophie, to put her on the defensive, to see if she'd turned into an ultraconservative protégé of her mother. It would have been understandable, living in Lynchfield where churches outnumbered gas stations by a four-to-one margin. In my youth, there had been two types of people: those who went to church and the heathens. Was there a middle ground in Lynchfield, finally? Or was Sophie playing the small-town game of pious in public, godless in private?

"What will Brenda think?"

"Mother won't know. And neither will Charlie. I'd like to keep it that way."

"Why would I tell him?"

"I imagine you'll be spending lots of time together while dealing with Ray's estate."

"You make it sound impressive when all it is is a bunch of

back issues of *The Cattleman* and *Guns and Ammo* stacked in every closet in the house. Oh, and chickens. Which I guess I need to check to see if they have eggs. Like I need any more food."

Logan and the boy walked across the court. The boy was tall, dark and not very handsome, with a nose too large for his face. But, he had an open smile and kind eyes. "Hello, Mrs. Wyatt," he said.

"Joaquin."

The boy's gaze moved to me, and Sophie took the hint. "Joaquin, this is Nora Noakes. Nora, Joaquin Rodriguez."

I held out my hand. "Nice to meet you."

"You, too. I've heard a lot about you."

"I'm never sure how to respond to that."

Joaquin laughed. "All good things, I promise. I wondered if I could talk to you about the military."

"Oh," I said. "Sure."

He smiled widely, but Logan's brows furrowed.

"I scored well on the aptitude test, and the recruiter won't stop calling me," Joaquin said.

"Same thing happened to me. I'd be happy to talk to you. I'm not sure how long I'll be in town, so don't wait too long."

"How about tomorrow?"

"Sure. Say, twelve hundred? Logan can bring you out to Ray's house. Y'all can help me eat up the food in my fridge."

Joaquin frowned. "I have to work tomorrow. Why don't you come by after lunch, when I take my break? Char-Grill."

I laughed. "I worked there."

"I know. Mel told me you would be in town because of your dad's funeral. Sorry to hear about Mr. Noakes. He was a nice man."

"You knew him?"

"Sure. Came in all the time, and my dad would work for him occasionally."

I nodded, out of conversation. "Well," I said to Joaquin, "see you tomorrow about fourteen hundred?"

"Fourteen hundred. Yes, ma'am."

"Nice backhand, Logan," I said.

"Thanks. I learned it from my mom."

"Yours is better," I said.

"Hey." Sophie laughed and playfully pushed my shoulder.

"I knew it," Logan said, walking backward, grinning. "I told Mom that Lexa and I would take on you two anytime you want."

"We could take you," I said.

"Name your time." She waved, and she and Joaquin continued on, laughing.

"We're going to have to play them now, you know," Sophie said.

"Yeah, I don't know why I said that."

Sophie nodded and stood. "Logan likes you."

"Wait until she gets to know me."

"Then she'll love you. Did you run here from Ray's?"

"No, the high school."

"Want a ride to your car?"

I glanced down at my dirty, sweaty self. "I'm disgusting."

"You're fine. Come on."

"You're still a bossy little thing."

She turned to grin at me, and her hair flowed up and behind her back like a damn supermodel in front of a wind machine.

I laughed.

"What?" Sophie chuckled. "I am bossy. Everyone knows that."

Sophie pushed her sunglasses back on her head again, and I met her eyes, the corners creased with laugh lines. Five years had vanished from her face.

"It really is good to see you," I said.

Her smile wavered a little, before breaking out again. "Come on." She led me to a steel-gray midsized SUV. I laughed again.

"At least it's not a minivan."

"No," I said. "I drive the same car."

Sophie shook her head. "Get in, Gigglesnort."

When we pulled out of the parking lot, I saw Sophie's mom, Brenda, in her front yard, watering a pot of flowers. I rolled down the window and called out, "Good morning, Brenda," with a big grin and a wave. Her expression of horror made it worth it.

I rolled the window back up and looked at Sophie. She was shaking her head, and the smile hadn't left her face. "That'll be a fun phone call to take."

"Sorry. I couldn't resist," I said.

The ride to the high school was too short. Sophie put the car in Park and turned toward me. "I want my best friend back. Can we do that, do you think? After everything?"

My heart clenched, and I wasn't sure if it was pity or happiness. There was such hope, and fear, in Sophie's expression. How could I tell her that I'd finally found someone to fill the hole she'd left in my life? What was the point? As much as I'd daydreamed about hurting her, getting back at her for all the pain she caused me, I couldn't do it. There was still too much emotion, too many good memories. Last night it had been the good memories that had led to me swimming in Shiner. They'd apparently led to my weakening, to wanting to smooth things over. To forgive and truly move on.

"Yes," I said, with more confidence than I felt. "I was a bitch yesterday, and I'm sorry. Chalk it up to years of pent-up resentment."

"You were drunk."

I shrugged, letting her believe it was the cause.

"You're meeting with Charlie this afternoon?"

"I am."

"Don't be surprised if he tries to seduce you."

"You're joking, right?"

"No. It's Charlie's specialty. In his defense, I've never particularly cared before."

"You know I would never..." The implication hung in the air between us, our camaraderie vanished.

Sophie's mouth shrunk and puckered. "I know. You always were the better friend."

"Sophie, I didn't mean..."

"Just watch yourself. Charlie's still in love with you. At least the idea of you."

"But, he has you."

"Oh, Nora, don't you know by now? I'm the villain in this story."

"There's plenty of blame to go around."

"Yes, well, there was only one acceptable narrative, wasn't there?" She put the car in Drive. "Hopefully Ray's papers won't be a mess. Let me know if you need any help. You have my number." She put her glasses back on, effectively ending the conversation. I got out of her car, and she drove away.

six
nora

The offices of Wyatt & Wyatt Counselors at Law were on New Braunfels Avenue in a former midcentury ranch rezoned for business like almost every other house along Lynchfield's main thoroughfare. Holdouts were marked by the early-model Buicks and Oldsmobiles in the detached garages of houses that were struggling to retain respectability as age and infirmary caught up to the occupants.

My nemesis sat at the reception desk.

"Jamie Luke."

"It's Jamie McGuire now."

"McGuire?"

"I married Trent McGuire."

"Oh, right," I said, barely stopping myself from saying *I forgot*. It was one of those local bits of news Emmadean had been feeding me for years. I couldn't be expected to remember everything.

Jamie marrying Trent McGuire was still a shock. Trent had been one of the most annoying guys in our grade. Not athletic enough to play sports, not talented enough to be in theater and no interest in band, he'd been stuck in between groups. Friends with everyone but not fitting in with anyone, he tried to be the class clown but suffered from having a terrible sense of humor and an even worse delivery. Sophie and I had always liked him well enough (probably because he worshiped the ground we walked on) but Jamie and Tiffany had been relentless in their teasing. I couldn't imagine what in the world would have made Jamie marry him. Hell, I couldn't fathom why she would go out with him in the first place unless all her teasing had been a mask for a secret attraction.

"How's Trent doing?"

"Good. You may have heard about our microbrewery?"

"No, I haven't."

"Mockingbird Brewery. We started it a few years ago. He just signed a contract with HEB for his best-selling flavor. Toasted Pecan Porter?"

"Mmm. I'll have to try it."

"We're hoping HEB will put him on the map."

"The next Shiner, huh?"

"That's the plan," she said, with a small long-suffering sigh. "I'll tell Trent to bring you a case."

"Thanks, but I won't be here long enough to drink a case of beer."

"I'm sure you and Sophie can kill a case of beer while catching up. Or, are you two still not speaking?"

"We're speaking."

"Glad to hear it. You know, there were lots of rumors when you left."

"Were there?"

She laughed, but I saw the calculation in her eyes. "Some of them were *outrageous*."

"Are you going to let Charlie know I'm here?"

She glanced at the phone. "Charlie's on a call. No one believed them. The rumors. When everyone found out about Sophie and Charlie, it all made sense."

I turned away from Jamie, sat in the furthest chair possible.

I placed the white plastic grocery bag I carried in my lap and took more interest in the office than I normally would have. When they'd converted the house, the decorator had decided to embrace the honey-colored oak paneling and fill the space with midcentury modern furniture with clean lines and muted colors. The photos on the wall were black-and-white shots of Hill Country landmarks—Enchanted Rock, Gruene Hall, LBJ's homestead, the Guadalupe River (though it could have been any one of half a dozen in the area), Comanche Springs. Not one cowboy, I noticed. I smiled. "Did Sophie decorate the office?"

"She did," Jamie said stiffly. "What's in the bag?"

"Eggs. Do you want some chickens? They could be the brewery's mascots."

"It's a mockingbird, not a chicken."

For some reason I couldn't figure, I was irritating Jamie, which only made me want to keep at it. "Chickens are very trendy, and the eggs are very colorful."

"Maybe on the East Coast, but here they're just chickens."

"I won't tell Patton you said that."

"Who?"

"Patton. The chicken. She's very sensitive."

"You've named Ray's chickens?"

"Well, yeah. Doesn't everyone? MacArthur isn't sensitive, of course. She's a cocky little thing. She does lay the prettiest eggs, so I guess a little arrogance is expected. Ike watches it all from afar, above it all."

"God, you're so weird."

"From you, Jamie, I'll take it as a compliment."

I'd had enough small-talk with Jamie McGuire, and my headache was returning. I closed my eyes and focused on my breathing, chanting *peace, calm*, silently to myself.

"What are you doing?"

I sighed and opened my eyes. "Trying to forget I'm in the same room as you."

Jamie's lip curled. "You know, the most outrageous rumor was the one no one dared say aloud."

"Then it must not have been much of a rumor."

"The unspoken ones are always the juiciest."

"Should I come back another time, preferably when you're at lunch or picking up Charlie's cleaning?"

"When he gets off the—"

The office door behind her opened abruptly, and I flinched. "Have you heard from—?" He stopped when he saw me. "There you are. Why didn't you tell me?"

Irritation flickered across Jamie's expression. "You were on the phone."

Charlie glared at Jamie but spoke to me. "Nora, come in."

In the doorway, I held up the plastic grocery bag. "I brought you eggs."

Charlie hesitated. "Thanks?"

"You're welcome, and there's plenty more. Ray's chickens are shooting eggs out of their asses like AK-47s. I tried to give them to Jamie, but she wouldn't take them."

"The chickens or the eggs?"

"Ah, the age-old question."

Charlie laughed, took the bag and glanced at the eggs. "Can you taste the difference between fresh and store-bought?"

"You can." I didn't want to say how delicious my morning omelet had been. I refused to give Ray credit for anything, even with his chickens as proxies.

Jamie appeared next to us. Charlie handed her the bag. "Hold my calls."

"Do you want me to take notes?" Eggs clicked against each other as she took the bag.

"No." He shut the door in her face.

Charlie's office was like the reception area, right down to the midcentury modern desk. My gaze settled on the credenza and an array of family photos: Sophie, face puffy, holding a new-

born baby, who wore a pink-and-blue-pinstriped beanie on
her tiny head; Logan at four or five in ballet attire; Sophie in
tennis whites, holding a trophy; Charlie with three vaguely familiar men with a long line of dead geese or ducks laid in front
of them; Charlie, Sophie and a six-year-old Logan at his law
school graduation; Charlie, Sophie and a ten-year-old Logan at
Sophie's college graduation; and on, and on.

Charlie looked embarrassed that these photos showed the
events of their life, their life without me. Or was he embarrassed
that these pictures only told part of the story? The happy parts?
What filled the gaps between the moments of smiles, laughter
and achievement?

"I'm sorry. I should have put those away."

"Bygones, Charlie. We were all young and stupid. I'm glad
y'all have been happy."

A shadow flickered across his face and was gone. He held out
his hand for me to sit down, and sat in the chair next to me. He
crossed his legs and smiled. Charlie Wyatt was good-looking in
high school, but he'd grown into the type of man who turned
women's heads. His light blue dress shirt had a faint texture to
it, enough to make the shirt interesting but not enough to dis-
tract from the feature that had defined Charlie since he was a
child: his ice-blue eyes framed by long eyelashes and dark eyebrows. His bottom lip was slightly plump, and his upper lip was
a perfect bow shape. Unlike so many men who were giving in
to age, or possibly found it freeing, Charlie was still trim and
moved like an athlete. He wore his clothes well.

I thought of seeing Sophie at the club, how the classy and professional version of my friend would look on Charlie's arm and
understood all at once how they had slid easily into the role of
the Lynchfield power couple. I suddenly felt very out of place,
with most of my fashion tending toward my military days—
blues, blacks, whites and grays. I'd always enjoyed the simplicity

of a capsule wardrobe, but confronted with the stylishness of my friends, it was my turn to be embarrassed.

If the way Charlie was looking at me was any indication, my feelings were misplaced. His smile was in full effect, the Deadly Dimple sunk deep into his left cheek, halfway between his cheekbones and his square jaw, and his gaze roamed over my face as if mapping out which features he would kiss on his lips' path to my mouth. I had no doubt if I asked him to take me on top of his desk, he would oblige. Despite myself, my stomach fluttered.

"It's so good to see you, NoNo," Charlie said.

"Don't call me that."

His smile wavered and his brows furrowed. "Outgrew it?"

"Something like that."

"Nora." His gaze lingered on my lips, and I shifted in my seat and crossed my legs. I couldn't remember the last time a man had looked at me with such intensity. Alima said I turned more heads than I thought, that I was merely clueless. I didn't believe her, and I didn't trust Charlie's attention, either. Sophie's warning rang in my ears.

"Tell me about this will."

"Right down to business, huh?"

"Let's get it out of the way."

He nodded and smoothed his pants leg. "It's pretty simple. It's authentic. The notary was a woman at the Ranger office, and she said Ray was the same as ever."

"An ornery son of a bitch?"

"Might have been the implication. It's all yours, and you are the executor."

"Is that normal?"

"Yes, and it simplifies things. Unless you think Mary will challenge it?"

"I haven't heard from Mary since she sauntered out the door, laughing her ass off. Which has me worried."

"You think she knows something you don't?"

"Mary is long-suffering and selfish. I suppose she has a right to be."

"I don't think she was that big a help to Ray. Emmadean and Dormer are who deserve something."

"I'll give it all to them. I don't want anything of Ray's. Do you know about my father's business these last few years?"

"No."

"He sold his cattle."

"I heard."

"He loved cows."

"Maybe he was tired of being around cows all day and coming home to take care of more at night."

"But, he kept the chickens?"

Charlie laughed and shrugged dramatically. "What can I tell you, Nora? You father and I didn't exactly socialize, and when he saw me, he barely gave me the time of day."

"My father could hold a grudge."

"What did I do to deserve a grudge? You ran out on me, not the other way around."

"And you got my best friend pregnant in retaliation."

"After you wouldn't answer my letters." Charlie stood and went to the credenza. "You broke my heart, Nora. Can't you even appreciate that? Apologize for it? When I went on vacation, everything was fine. Surely you remember that last night."

I didn't answer, but I did. After four years together, our relationship, our sex life had gotten stale, and Charlie had been on a mission to fix it. I don't know what he read or watched but that night was the first time we ever came together. He held me after and apologized for being a selfish partner, and promised it would never happen again. Most guys when their high school relationship goes south break up, knowing there would be a bigger pond to fish in at college. But, not Charlie. He didn't like to fail, at anything.

"I'm sorry, Charlie. I truly am. You were my first love, and you deserved better."

He nodded slowly, watching me. "What was that yesterday, when you said Ray kicked you out of the house. Is that true?"

"Yes."

"Are you going to tell me why?"

"Like I said, it was all a long time ago."

"Were you pregnant?"

"No. Why would you think that?"

"Nothing else made sense. Nothing. It still doesn't."

"Me leaving had nothing to do with you. You weren't at fault at all."

"That's it? That's all the explanation I'm going to get?"

"There's nothing else to tell."

With his body half-turned away from me, Charlie flipped through some papers on his desk. I couldn't give Charlie the answers he wanted. Little did Charlie know, it wasn't only my secrets he sought. I stood to leave.

Charlie looked up suddenly. "I hear you and Sophie have made up."

My shoulders straightened in my defensive posture. "Did Sophie tell you?"

"Logan said you two were talking and laughing at the club. Did it feel like old times?"

I thought about Sophie sitting there, sunglasses on, head lifted just enough so she didn't look arrogant, but sure of herself. Very much like the girl I remembered. "Yeah, it did."

"So, you did make up."

"We did."

His voice was gruff. "I think having you around will be good for Sophie."

"She looks like she's doing fine. Great job, beautiful family." I paused. "A husband who adores her."

Charlie pursed his lips, as if debating what to say, or if to say anything at all. He opened his mouth, but I continued, suddenly sure he was about to divulge more than I wanted to know. "Tell me about the campaign."

"Yes," he said, sounding relieved. "We're setting the groundwork for the midterms next year. We're having a fund raiser a week from Saturday. If you're still here, you should come."

A year from now the credenza would have a photo of the two of them standing on a stage with Logan, arms raised as Charlie celebrated his win. My heart clenched. Was it jealousy, or lost possibilities?

"Don't tell Sophie, but we're going to get her a cake for her birthday the next week. Double celebration."

I mimed locking my mouth and tossing the key. "It's a busy time at work. I might need to get back. Can I do most of this remotely?"

"If you want to put all this to bed quickly, then you should probably stick around. Probate moves at its own pace, but the house and all Ray's stuff won't sell itself. Unless you want an excuse to keep coming back to Lynchfield, now that you're home."

I laughed. "In that case, maybe I will be here next week. I need to get back to the chickens."

Charlie came around the desk. "Thanks for the eggs."

We stood at the door, staring at each other, neither making a move. I let my mind wander as I hadn't ever before onto what my life might have been like if Charlie and I had stayed together, and gotten married like we'd talked about in high school. It was a dream he had up until the day I left, and one I'd abandoned months earlier, but hadn't dared to tell him. Charlie Wyatt had always gotten what he wanted, and it never crossed his mind he wouldn't have me in the end. He would let me go to Texas Tech with Sophie, graduate, and get a degree, as long as I came back to Lynchfield to marry him and raise a family. Me leaving town without a word or explanation, ignoring all his calls and letters, never returning, was probably the most significant failure of his life. I suppose it had been easy for him to fall into Sophie's arms, the best friend whom I'd abandoned too, though she knew why.

"Why don't you come to dinner," Charlie said. "At the house?"

"Your house? No."

"Why not?"

"Do you need to ask that question?"

He leaned in close and said in a hoarse whisper, "Fuck this town. Let them talk. It was eighteen years ago, and we're adults."

His eyes moved to my lips, and it would have been so easy to let him kiss me. Instead, I said, "If Sophie invites me to dinner, I'll come."

Charlie pulled back as Sophie and the last twenty years descended between us like a brick wall.

"She'll invite you, if for no other reason than to impress you with her cooking."

I nodded, said, "We'll see," and left, determined to think of an ironclad reason to turn the invitation down.

seven
nora

Mel's Char-Grill was in a tan metal building with a tan brick facade partially hidden by the Super Clean Self-Serve Car Wash which was also, you guessed it, tan. A shiny new McDonald's, the bright lights and red-and-yellow signs garish amid all the earth tones, sat on the sliver of land between the car wash and the lumber yard at an angle whose purpose seemed to be to completely block the view of Mel's from the road. I pulled through an open bay of the car wash and parked in front of the diner, slightly reassured and a little surprised nothing had changed: the cursive neon sign on the top of the building, a direct rip off from Mel's Diner from *Alice*. HAMBURGERS TACOS FRIED CATFISH CHILI SHAKES/MALTS painted in white block letters along the bottom of the front windows; a Lynchfield Lion painted on the rest of the window; the green newspaper dispenser for the *Lynchfield Leader* to the left of the front door, a Reddy Ice cooler to the right.

The smell of grilled onions blasted me when I walked inside, and after the initial revulsion, I couldn't help but smile. "It's a proven fact," Mel had told me once, "that the smell of grilled onions makes people buy more food." I didn't believe it then, and I didn't believe it now, but I'd sold a lot of hamburgers from behind the counter in front of me and had left work stinking of onions hundreds of times. I had chopped my long hair into a shoulder-length bob because it took so long to wash and dry after each shift. My hairstyle hadn't changed, nor had my aversion to grilled onions.

"There she is!"

Mel Thompson peeked through the square window between the ordering counter and the kitchen, a huge grin on his round face.

"Hi, Mel."

Joaquin stood at the register wearing a red Mel's Char-Grill trucker hat which, by dint of not changing for forty years, was now stylishly retro. Mel, never one to miss a marketing opportunity, had a handwritten sign on the wall next to the counter advertising Hats–$12, Tees–$15. I wondered if my Mel's hat had survived my father's purge.

"Hi, Mrs. Noakes."

I laughed. "I'm not a Mrs., Joaquin. Call me Nora."

"Oh, right." Joaquin blushed. "Can I call you Colonel instead?"

"I was discharged as a captain."

"Like Captain America," Mel said. He wore all white and a white beanie and had a towel thrown over his shoulder. He'd also told me he was the inspiration for the eponymous Mel of Mel's Diner fame. Another specious claim, but he'd always looked the part.

I rolled my eyes and shook my head. "Hardly."

"They said you hadn't changed a bit and by golly, if they weren't right!"

"Who's 'they'?"

"Oh, you know. You're pretty much all anyone's talking about. Everyone wants to sit in your booth."

"My booth?"

"In the back corner."

I peeked around the wall separating the counter and kitchen from the dining room. Photos of Lynchfield High School sports teams and black-and-whites of the town throughout history lined the walls. Though I assumed some of the photos had changed over the years, at this distance the booth where I'd taken my breaks, and where I, Charlie, Sophie and whatever boy she was dating had hung out in for most of high school, looked unchanged. Then my eyes registered who was sitting in the booth. Sophie raised a tentative hand in greeting. It was thirteen forty-five, and the lunch rush was over. The dining room was empty save a booth of cowboys at the front of the room. I made my way over to Sophie, who stood up to meet me.

"I hope you don't mind," she said. "I knew you were coming to talk to Joaquin and since I don't have your number..."

"Charlie does."

"Oh."

"If you wanted to see me, just say it."

Sophie's mouth twitched into an embarrassed smile, and she met my gaze steadily. "I wanted to see you."

I smiled. "That wasn't so hard, was it?"

Sophie brushed a strand of hair behind her ear. "No." Her smile gained confidence, and I saw a glimpse of the girl I'd known: self-assured with a healthy dose of generosity mixed in so she never came across as cocky or above anyone else. Parents loved Sophie, all the boys wanted her, and the girls? They wanted to hate her, and a few succeeded, but Sophie was so genuine and kind, she was admired more than hated.

Joaquin walked over carrying two red baskets of burgers and fries. "Here you go, Mrs. Wyatt."

He startled us, and I wondered how long we'd been standing there, grinning stupidly at each other.

"Thanks, Joaquin."

"Hungry?" I asked.

"I hope you don't mind. I ordered for you."

"How do you know I eat my burger the same way?"

Sophie lifted a shoulder. "Nothing else about you has changed."

I laughed. She had no idea.

"I'll be on my break in fifteen minutes," Joaquin said.

"Sounds good," I said and slid into the booth. When Sophie sat down across from me, I couldn't help but notice the photo above her head. "Jesus Christ."

My first official photo as a member of the US Armed Forces hung above her head on the wood-paneled wall. My expression was solemn from the memory of basic training I'd just endured, and for the knowledge that the real challenges lay ahead. Basic training had melted my baby fat, and my cheekbones and jawline were pronounced to a degree unimaginable three months earlier when I'd been smiling from ear to ear in graduation photos.

I leaned to the left and moved slowly back to the right, then repeated the action.

"What are you doing?" Sophie asked, before popping a fry in her mouth.

"Her eyes are following me."

Sophie did a cursory glance over her shoulder. "Don't you mean your eyes are following you?"

"Why would he hang that?"

"Mel's very proud of you."

"Hmm." I lifted the top of my burger. Bacon, American cheese, no onions, mustard, and mayo. Sophie slid a knife over to me. I cut my burger in half. When I looked up, all I could see was that damn photo.

"Here, trade places with me," Sophie said. She switched our burger baskets around and changed sides. "Charlie didn't believe it was you when he first saw it. I did." Her eyes met mine again, teasing. "I'd recognize those freckles anywhere."

"Always with the freckles."

"I love your freckles. All forty-two, if I remember correctly."

"There may be a few more. The desert sun is brutal."

Sophie's smile flickered. "I'm so glad you came back in one piece."

I stared at the burger half in my hands, the thin patty, fried on a flattop grill until the edges were crisp. Yes, I'd returned from my tours in one piece, but I came home with a nice little souvenir: PTSD. It had taken years of trial and error, but I'd finally discovered mental peace through meditation and yoga and emotional peace with a healthy relationship. I was luckier than most; I only occasionally jumped at sudden sounds and, in the last few years, the nightmares had almost stopped completely.

I smiled weakly at Sophie and bit into my burger so I wouldn't have to answer. Sophie didn't press me for details, for which I was thankful, but took up her knife and fork and proceeded to eat her burger with them, a habit she'd apparently never broken after having braces in middle school. I chewed and watched her, eyebrows raised. She saw my expression and said, "Shut up."

"I didn't say a word."

Sophie's gaze flickered between the photo behind me and my face. "Will you stop it?" I said.

"I'm sorry. It's just... I can't believe you're back. I'm so glad you're back."

"You know I'm not staying, right?"

Sophie stilled and put her knife and fork over her burger as if she was finished and nodded her head quickly. "How did your meeting with Charlie go?" she said with false brightness.

"Fine. It'll take a couple of weeks to get through probate, I suppose. I'd hoped to leave by this weekend, but Charlie convinced me it would be easier to deal with it all now instead of traveling back and forth."

It wasn't a total lie. After leaving Charlie's office, I texted Alima that I would meet her in Montreal, as planned, and fly back to Texas afterward to deal with the house and probate. Her reply had been almost immediate, telling me not to worry, she'd changed the dates, and for me to take care of what I needed to, and to let her know if there was anything she could do to help. She didn't sound angry, but I wasn't entirely sure.

"Do you want Joe's number? For the estate sale?"

I laughed. "Estate sale? I'm renting a Dumpster and putting everything I can into it. I would have a bonfire in the pasture, but there's a burn ban, isn't there?"

"This is South Texas. There's always a burn ban. What does Mary say about your plan?"

"I haven't told her yet. If she wants anything, she's got to come get it. If not, it's going to the landfill."

"That seems cold."

"Cold? Cold is telling your eighteen-year-old daughter *get out of my house and never come back.* Cold is knowing I'm laid up in an army hospital bed and not bothering to come see me, to even fucking call. Cold is sending your sister to hold your daughter's hand because you're too goddamn stubborn to swallow your pride and apologize." I inhaled and exhaled slowly. "Sorry."

"No need to apologize to me. You're right about all of it. How can I help?"

I smiled. Just like the Sophie I remembered. Willing to do anything, go to any lengths, to help her friends. I nodded toward her burger. "First thing you can do is finish that. You're skin and bones."

"Okay, Emmadean." I rolled my eyes and she laughed. She picked up her utensils but didn't eat. Instead, she opened her mouth a couple of times as if wanting to say something but not knowing how. I had an obscene amount of burger in my mouth and had to swallow before asking, "What is it?"

She put her knife and fork down on the table. "We're getting along so well, I hate to ask this question."

"Maybe you shouldn't."

She studied me. "I have to. It's The Question, the one I could never answer. Not adequately, anyway."

Sophie cleared her throat to forge ahead, though I wished she wouldn't. I wanted to talk and banter and laugh for a little while longer.

"Why didn't you answer my letters?"

I took my time replacing my burger, wiping my hands on a paper napkin and gulping my tea. "You know, you can get sweet tea in DC, and in Virginia, but it just isn't the same as Texas sweet tea," I said. "Must be the water."

Sophie waited.

I set the glass down and wiped the condensation off my fingers with a napkin. Boot camp had been lonely and brutal. I'd been desperate for letters, for a connection to a life that seemed so distant from my reality. I'd drunk in Emmadean's letters as if they were life-giving nectar, my tears dropping onto the pages as I read each sentence, carefully written with a cheerful voice, and without any mention of the events that drove me from home. When Sophie's letter arrived, I tossed it in the trash before I could be tempted to open it. I swallowed, as the emotion of holding her letters came rushing back. Anger mostly, a fair amount of indignation, and a heaping amount of betrayal. Love had lingered beneath it all, which had pissed me off more than anything. "I knew your letters would bring it all back. So I threw them away."

"You *what?*"

I clenched my jaw against the onslaught of guilt Sophie's expression, and the hurt in her voice, woke in me. I would not apologize—*ever*—for what I'd done to protect myself all those years ago. "I threw them away."

She sat back in the booth. "Without reading them?"

"Hi, Captain." Joaquin stood at the end of the booth, a big grin on his face.

"On second thought, Joaquin, call me Nora."

The young man's face fell, but he nodded in agreement. "I'm, um, on my break early?"

Sophie stared at me with an expression I couldn't read. Astonishment? Relief? Anger?

"I'll come back later," Joaquin said, "if this is a bad time."

"No," I said. "Have a seat."

"Joaquin, could you grab me a to-go box?" Sophie asked with a charming smile.

"Sure, Mrs. Wyatt."

"And take your time."

Sophie crossed her arms. "You didn't read my letters."

"I didn't read Charlie's either. It was over. Done. There was nothing you could say to fix it."

Sophie turned her face away. "All this time," she said under her breath. She shouldered her purse and scooted out of the booth. "You were wrong, Nora."

I reached out and grabbed her hand to stop her from standing and felt the first real crack in the hard shell that had grown around my heart. "How? How was I wrong?"

She brushed her thumb across my fingers, and I froze. I stared at our hands, her red nails, as tiny goose bumps broke out on my arm. My eyes met Sophie's, and what I saw there... She pulled her hand away. "I suppose you'll never know, will you?"

She stood to leave, but I was suddenly desperate for her to stay. "You haven't finished your burger."

"I've lost my appetite."

"Please sit back down. Joaquin is staring."

She sat, but she looked ready to bolt.

"Aren't you going to invite me to dinner?"

Sophie held her purse in front of her like a shield and said, "I can't stomach watching my husband flirt with you for three hours."

"Don't you want to show off your cooking?"

Sophie inhaled sharply. "Is that what Charlie said?" I nodded. "That sounds just like him. He can't say I'm a good cook. He has to imply I'm arrogant about it."

"He was probably making a joke."

"You think so?" Sophie narrowed her eyes. "Friday night. Seven o'clock."

"I don't know where you live," I said, grasping for something—anything—I could say to prolong the conversation, to get her to stay.

Her mouth curled into a slow, mischievous smile, one I'd seen many times. My entire body thrummed in anticipation.

"If you want me to stay, just say it."

"I want you to stay."

"Now, see, that wasn't so hard."

I laughed, and looked away, embarrassed to have shown so much of myself. With one smile, Sophie destroyed the shell around my heart, and I mourned its loss.

Joaquin walked up with a Styrofoam box. "Want me to box your burger up, Mrs. Wyatt?"

Sophie's smile and shoulders dipped at Joaquin's arrival. "That would be lovely, thank you." Sophie watched me with raised eyebrows and a small, private smile. "Call me later, and I'll give you my address."

"I can write it down for you, Nora," Joaquin said, ever helpful.

Sophie laughed and waved her hand. "There you go. Enjoy your chat," she said and left.

The memory of her mischievous smile stayed, played in my mind like a GIF, her voice in my ears repeating, *I wanted to see you. I wanted to see you.*

That's when I knew I was still in love with Sophia Elizabeth Russell.

eight
sophie

Logan knocked on the hood of my MDX, startling me out of my trance.

"What are you doing?"

I stepped out of the car. "I just got home," I said.

"The garage door went up fifteen minutes ago."

"Oh. I was listening to 'Fresh Air,'" I lied. The garage door whined and creaked as it lowered. Logan's expression said she wasn't buying it. "How was tennis?" I asked.

"Good. Lexa's still a little slow from her sprain, but she'll get there."

I placed my computer bag and purse on the kitchen island. "Good," I said. The oven clock said five. Had it only been three hours since I left Nora at Mel's?

"What's for dinner?" Logan asked.

"Um, I don't know." I stared at the keys in my hand. Why was I holding my keys? I tossed them on the counter next to my phone. Would Nora call me? Did she even still have my number? It wouldn't surprise me if she'd thrown my card away. Just like she'd thrown away my letters.

"What's wrong with you?"

"What?"

Logan was in front of me, arms crossed, wearing a stormy expression. "Where have you been?"

"I went for a drive."

After leaving Nora with Joaquin, I couldn't bear the idea of being around anyone. I needed to be alone and think and the only way I had ever been able to clear my head was with a drive. I'd headed west with little idea of where I was going, my mind replaying my recent conversations with Nora and trying to process what it meant that she hadn't read my letters. All this time, I thought her silence had been a rejection of me. It had, but not in the way I thought. My pleas for her forgiveness, the plans I suggested so we could be together, the explanation for my seduction of Charlie—she knew none of it. I drove and drove, mourning the missed chances, and daring to dream of a future which would only be possible if I destroyed the life I knew.

"You've been driving for over three hours?"

"What?"

"Joaquin said you left the Char-Grill about two."

I opened a kitchen drawer. "Would you like to test me?"

"No, Mom," Logan said, reddening.

I closed the door with a snap. "I haven't been drinking and driving." I walked back to my car, pulled the forgotten bags out of the back seat and returned to the kitchen. "Dinner. Cooper's Barbecue. Llano, Texas. Two-hour round trip."

Logan looked slightly chagrined. "I was worried about you. You didn't return my texts. 'Find My iPhone' didn't work."

I grasped Logan by the shoulders and pulled her into a fierce hug, my frustration, and anger at my daughter's real, and valid, concerns, leaking out of me. "I'm sorry. I turned my phone off. I should have let you or Dad know what I was doing."

"You always want me to be on call, and you don't even do it."

"I know, and I'm sorry. I'm sorry you have to worry about

me. About all of it." I held her at arm's length. "I'm not drinking again, I promise. The beer at Nora's...it was a blip."

"You've had blips before."

"Logan, I swear to God I'm not drinking again. I made a
promise to you and Dad, and I intend to keep it."

"Have you been to a meeting lately?"

"No, but I will. I promise."

She inhaled and nodded. I pulled her close again and hugged
her, felt her thin arms encircle my waist. I wanted to absorb her
into my being, to protect her from everything—love and hate,
life and death, the truth and lies of my past.

"You're squeezing me to death, Mom."

"Sorry." I released her and turned away before she could see
my tears.

"What's wrong?"

"Nothing, Lo. I'm fine."

"You're definitely not fine. Half the time you're on the verge
of tears and the other half you're glowing like a candle and the
other half your snapping our heads off." She looked up. "Okay,
those are thirds."

I pulled the grease-stained brown paper packages from the
plastic bags. "You've pretty much summed up every working
mother I know."

"This is different."

One by one, I announced the contents of the bag. "Ribs for
me, burnt ends for Dad and smoked turkey for you."

"Pecan cobbler?"

I tilted my head. "What's Cooper's without pecan cobbler
for dessert?"

"I knew there was something I liked about you," Logan said
with a grin.

I opened the pint containers of beans and potato salad while
Logan pulled two plates from the cabinet. "Oh, thanks, honey,
but I'll eat later. I ate a burger at Mel's."

I turned my phone back on and waited—wondered, hoped, feared.

"You never turn your phone off," Logan said.

Missed messages from Logan, work and Charlie popped up one after the other. Disappointment the size of Enchanted Rock settled into my stomach.

"Mom."

I looked up. "Hmm?"

"Is it Nora?"

I swallowed. "What?"

"Stop saying what."

"Stop asking me questions."

"Why don't you listen to me for a change?"

I put my phone face down on the counter. "I'm listening."

"Are you acting so weird because Nora's back in town?"

"Yes."

Logan's head jerked back a little, and her eyes widened. The microwave beeped. "I didn't think you'd admit it."

I chuckled. "Neither did I." I stared at my red fingernails and drummed them on the granite countertop. "I didn't realize how much I missed her until I saw her again."

"Joaquin said y'all fought today?"

"It wasn't a fight."

"He said it was pretty tense."

"Not really. Not as much as it should have been with years of baggage between us."

"What happened? Why did she leave?"

I exhaled. When we heard Nora was coming for Ray's funeral, Charlie and I guessed Logan would ask this question. Neither of us was eager to tell Logan the story of her conception. Honestly, it was astonishing Logan hadn't heard murmurs of the story. Lynchfield was insular and small, and everyone loved to gossip. But, somehow the consensus had been there was no need for Logan to know she was the product of a betrayal and the town had kept the secret. If Nora had come and gone quickly, and if seeing Nora hadn't brought my long-suppressed emotions to the surface, there would be no need to tell Logan at all. I was tired of lying. But, not tired enough yet. I took the cowardly way out.

"She had a falling out with her father," I said.

"About what?"

It was the part of the story only three living souls knew, and I wasn't ready to tell Logan. Or Charlie.

"I don't know."

"She didn't tell you? Her best friend?"

"She left for boot camp and couldn't call or write."

"But, after…?"

Charlie came in through the back door and called out a greeting. He stopped twirling his keys around his index finger when he saw us. "Hey." His brow furrowed at the sight of the food containers. "Cooper's?"

"I went for a drive," I said.

"Mom's telling me why Nora left town."

Charlie stilled, his eyes shifting to me. "She is?"

"I said she had a falling out with Ray."

Charlie nodded. "That's right."

"But, you were surprised when she said that at the visitation," Logan said to Charlie. "Like you thought there was a different reason. What was it?"

Charlie laughed. "I was surprised because I'd forgotten the reason. It was all a long time ago." He came forward and kissed me on the cheek. "How was your day? You okay?" He looked genuinely concerned. He must have just finished fucking his flavor of the month. He was always extra solicitous after his hookups.

"My day was good. Yours?"

"Not bad. Committee meeting about the fund raiser." He unwrapped the brisket, picked up a burnt end, and ate it. A small groan escaped his throat. "God, that's delicious."

"I still think it's a mistake to have it in summer, in a dance hall with no AC."

"There'll be plenty of cold Lone Star."

"Charlie, that's not an enticement to anyone except hipsters who think drinking Lone Star is retro cool."

"So, that's it?" Logan said.

"That's what?" Charlie said.

"The whole story? You don't talk to your best friend, and your high school girlfriend since before the internet, and you aren't even going to say why?"

"We had the internet," I said, a little defensively, before realizing she wasn't entirely wrong.

"There's nothing to tell," Charlie said. "Nora left town and made a life in DC. We made a life here. People lose touch all the time, Squirt."

Logan jerked the microwave door open and removed her plate. "God, y'all think I'm a moron." She pierced us with her blue eyes. "I've done the math, you know," she said and left the kitchen. She called over her shoulder. "And don't call me Squirt."

Charlie made a plate.

"We need to tell her," I said.

"No."

"She already knows, Charlie."

"She thinks she knows."

"Aren't you tired of lying?"

"Nope."

"You *are* exceptionally good at it."

"As are you, Soph. You went for a drive?"

"How else do you explain this?" I said, waving my hand at the barbecue.

"That's not all you did."

"You're right. I listened to NPR and thought."

Charlie laughed.

The thing was, I couldn't blame Charlie or Logan for suspecting me of drinking. Going for a drive was *the* fucking euphemism for my drinking. I pulled the breathalyzer out of the drawer and blew into it. Charlie glanced at the readout—0.0—shrugged and continued making his plate. I was ashamed at having to do it and angry at his dismissiveness.

"It's only a matter of time before she hears the story from someone. She might as well hear it from us."

"No, and that's final." He put his plate in the microwave.

I gritted my teeth. "Don't want to jeopardize your role as the perfect parent?"

"No," he said, patiently. "I know you two are going through a tough time and I don't want Logan to have another reason to resent you." He put his hands on my hips and pulled me toward him. "What's wrong, Soph? Did something happen at work?"

"Work is fine," I said. "I saw Nora today."

"Ah. Did you invite her to dinner?"

"Yes, which is why we need to tell Logan. She'll put Nora on the spot; you know she will. We need to have our stories straight."

"Stories? There's only one story, and Logan doesn't need to know it. Nora's over it. We're over it. Let's let bygones be bygones." He cupped my face with his hands. "I know Nora being back has thrown you for a loop, but she'll leave in a couple of weeks, and our life will go back to normal."

I thought of our normal. We'd been normal, for a while, in the beginning. In love, bonded together by our love for Logan, determined to succeed when so many people expected, and wanted, us to crash and burn. I was the first one to realize the skeptics had been right, so I went to college to take my mind off of it. I faked it for years, was the model wife and mother, reliable civic volunteer. I threw myself into the church in the hopes that God would take the burden of my secret from me. When God couldn't make me happy, I drank. I drank when I heard news of Nora. I drank when I didn't. I drank when the thought of making love to Charlie made my stomach turn. I drank when he came home the first time smelling of another woman's perfume. I drank when I didn't care. I somehow kept it from Logan, and Charlie ignored it for as long as he could, always wanting to put a good face on for the town. Then, normal turned to Charlie covering for my drinking from the town and Logan. A year ago, I'd hit bottom, crawled my way out of the bottle with high hopes we could return to the promise of the early years. Charlie had tried, and so had I. I knew we were doomed, but Charlie still clung to the perfect-couple lie.

For years, I planned my escape from Charlie and this town. But, it never got further than a thought experiment. I felt obligated to stay. I'd seduced Charlie all those years ago, and he'd done the right thing when I got pregnant. I'd repeatedly tried to push him away, to get him to leave, but he'd stuck by me, supported me, encouraged me. Now, with Logan set to leave for college in a year, my thoughts kept wandering to what happened after. What kind of marriage would Charlie and I have when Logan wasn't around to hold us together? What would our normal be then? Did I feel guilty enough to give Charlie the next forty or fifty years of my life?

Charlie continued, "Sophie, we've been through so much, worked hard to get where we are. We're so close to achieving our goals, why risk ruining it by dredging up something that happened so long ago?"

"Achieving your goal, you mean."

His brows furrowed. "Our goal. I can't do it without you. You know that. You're my secret weapon, the brains and the charm of the outfit."

"Maybe I should run for State Senate."

He nuzzled my neck. "You'd beat me in a landslide." He kissed my ear, pulled on the lobe gently with his teeth. I shivered. "Nora's great, but seeing her, talking to her, made me realize I made the right choice. You're who I want next to me when I'm elected governor one day, my tough, strong, intelligent, beautiful wife," he whispered. "You're fucking glowing like you did the summer we fell in love. You remember?"

I nodded.

"I've missed you." His hands slid under my shirt and caressed my back.

I closed my eyes, imagining someone else. "I've missed you, too."

The scrape of Charlie's stubble against my chin shattered the mental image I'd been holding in my mind, but it was too late to turn back. And, I wanted—needed—to make sure, one more time. Maybe this time I would feel what I was supposed to feel for him.

"Dinner can wait," he said and led me down the hall to our bedroom.

That summer, seducing Charlie had been ridiculously easy. I take no credit for it. He was a horny eighteen-year-old boy angry at his girlfriend for leaving without a word and throwing his plans into disarray. So, I let him vent and cry and rage on my shoulder. Soon enough he wanted me and, at the time, I thought I wanted him.

Charlie didn't have the corner on being angry with Nora. Our mutual rage fueled a summer of almost daily hookups, so energetic and passionate I believed for a brief time that it had been Nora specifically whom I loved, that I could marry a man and have a normal life. Not with Charlie, he was a means to an end, but with someone.

Seducing Charlie killed three birds with one stone: it silenced questions about Nora leaving town and the cause of our rift, it gave me hope I could have a normal life, and it proved to my mother that she didn't need to ship me off to conversion camp like she threatened when she caught Nora and me the second time, after we'd sworn it was a one-time thing, an experiment, we'd been drinking—it was graduation, after all—we knew it was wrong and would repent, do anything, even not see each other, as long as Brenda Russell kept what she saw from my father, and Nora's.

Every word out of our mouths had been a lie. Nora and I were in love, had known it for almost a year. The best year of my life.

My mother wasn't stupid, though like all teenagers, I thought she was. She saw through our lies and, like the master manipulator she was, proceeded to separate Nora and me with surgical precision. I finished the job for her, though. You've never seen an evangelical so happy at her daughter's fall from grace as the expression on my mother's face when I told her I was pregnant with Charlie's baby. Forgiveness for that sin was easier than the crime of being in love with another girl.

To his credit, Charlie didn't hesitate in doing the right thing when I told him. He'd convinced himself he was in love with me—energetic, daily sex will do that. But, all that energy and passion was born of anger, fear and lies, not desire. Is it a surprise a relationship would rely on the same to keep it alive?

The only way I could enjoy sex with Charlie was if I was angry. I'd become a master at blowing up small slights and perceived wrongs into mountains of injustice. Today my old anger at Nora resurfaced. By the time I finished rage-fucking Charlie, we were both hot and sweaty and he had come, but I hadn't. I never did, though Charlie had no idea I'd been faking orgasms since the first time we'd had sex.

"Geez, Soph. We need to do this more often."

I smiled at the ceiling and hummed noncommittally. "Do you need my help planning the fund raiser?"

"Nope. Avery's got a handle on it. You just have to show up and look beautiful."

"Hmm."

Avery Rhodes, up-and-coming political phenom, started her career in the Election Industrial Complex as an intern for Bush '04, worked on McCain's technology team in '08, trying and failing to convince her baby boomer bosses social media was the future, worked at the RNC during the Tea Party wave, and finally moved on to Romney's campaign as Anne Romney's media liaison. It had been something of a coup for Charlie to land her as a campaign manager for a piddly State Senate seat, even if it was Texas. Her name was mentioned in reverent tones among a particular subset of political operatives—i.e., Millennials who were determined to take over the world—and I suspected she noted Charlie's discipline, his resume, his made-for-television charisma, and saw a potential to grow her political capital and influence as she grew his career. I had to admit, Avery was impressive in person. She had a girl-next-door attractiveness with a fierce intelligence and a no-bullshit demeanor. She was the best parts of me and Nora rolled into a ruthless package. No wonder Charlie was fucking her.

"Let her know I'm happy to help," I said, more to watch Charlie squirm than out of any real desire to get involved. Showing up and looking pretty was about all I cared to do.

Charlie rose from the bed, turning his back to me. "Will do."

I watched Charlie walk into the bathroom and turn on the shower. With his broad shoulders, trim waist, and muscular legs, I knew I was a lucky woman. Most of the other husbands our age were thickening around the middle, athletes in high school turning to flab. Charlie was disciplined in all areas, but I think his fitness obsession was rooted in his need to balance out his hair loss. He'd seen the writing on the wall and decided to take matters into his own hands before nature did it for him, coming home one night with a shaved head. Thinking he was an intruder, I threatened him with a knife before he smiled, and I saw that fucking dimple.

I found many men attractive, including Charlie. But, I didn't want to fuck any of them, including Charlie. No matter how hard I tried, Charlie had never made me burn with desire like Nora had, or like the woman I met a year earlier in a hotel bar and had given a fake name, knowing on some deep level where we would end up. I'd admitted the truth to myself the next morning. Declaring to the world I was gay was something else altogether.

Charlie walked out of the bathroom, naked. *Nothing.* "I saw your mom today."

"Lucky you."

"She was fishing about why you aren't going to church anymore."

"I go every Sunday."

The dresser drawer slid open noiselessly, and he pulled out a pair of boxer briefs. "You know what she means."

"Charlie, I went to church three times a week for thirty-five years. Over five thousand times. I could skip church for the next one hundred years and still average out to a day a week, which is more than most people can say."

Charlie stopped adjusting his package for maximum effect. He could have been a fence post for all it did for me. "You've done the math?"

I rolled off the bed, felt his semen trickle down my leg. "I'm done with church three times a week. I talked to Jesus about it. He said it was okay." I closed the bathroom door behind me and turned on the shower.

My mother's reaction to discovering me and Nora, extreme as it was, had made me fear the wider world, and how they would see me, and how I saw myself. Seducing Charlie might have saved me from conversion camp, but it didn't save me from sitting between my parents in the pew of Lynchfield Baptist Church every Sunday (fifth pew from the front, far right side), and hearing about the sins of homosexuality, almost weekly. It became such a familiar theme with Brother Smithfield I wondered if my parents had talked to him, prayed for my mortal soul with him. But, no. My parents would rather die than admit my sin to anyone in Lynchfield, even a pastor who was known for kindness and discretion. One Sunday, the August after Nora left, I was distracted by the recent discovery I was pregnant and barely listening to Brother Smithfield. He slammed his Bible down on the pulpit, stomped his cowboy-booted foot and raised his voice. Theatrics weren't unusual; Brother Smithfield screamed, stomped and banged the pulpit on the regular. When I looked up at him, he stared right at me and said, *And Moses cried unto the Eternal One, saying, Heal her now, O God, I beseech thee.*

He held my gaze for a moment more and I understood. It explained why he returned to the same themes of God's forgiveness and understanding, why he dwelt on the sins of the flesh, that the emotions he showed on the pulpit had less to do with his love of God than with his struggle with his belief he was worthy of His love.

When I showed up on Brother Smithfield's doorstep the following morning, he let me in without a word. Before I confessed to him, he placed his hand on my head and prayed for me, and I felt the love of God wash over me, and I thought *yes, this is right. This will fix me. God will fix me.*

I remember Brother Smithfield's dry, papery hand holding mine while I told him everything—about Nora, my mother, Charlie, the baby growing inside me—the thrum of energy I felt coursing between us. He nodded sympathetically and listened until my mind couldn't form another word, and we sat in silence for so long I began to hope it wasn't forgiveness that Brother Smithfield would offer, but what I wanted to hear: *God doesn't make mistakes. Be yourself, Sophie. Grasp happiness. God's love is unconditional.*

"You are an abomination, Sophia, and will surely burn in hell unless you spend an hour a day on your knees in prayer. Pray God will relieve you of these vile urges, pray Charlie will never know how you've manipulated him into a marriage, pray God will work on you, change your personality into one of subservience to him, and your husband. And pray your child will never know how he was brought into the world."

I'd done it. Everything Brother Smithfield said. For years I prayed fervently to change, for forgiveness, for my secret to stay hidden. It worked, for the most part, or I told myself it did. But, I walked around in a world I didn't fit into, that wasn't made for me, that didn't reflect me at all. When I drank, the world shifted, blurred, softened, so I almost felt like I belonged.

Almost.

"You're setting a bad example for Logan."

Charlie leaned against the bathroom doorway, dressed in his grubby lawn mowing shorts.

I turned the water off and stepped out of the shower. Charlie handed me a towel. "Going to church every week isn't a bad example."

"When you used to go more, it is. When you've stopped being involved in the church, it is."

"Charlie, I'm not having this conversation again."

"Logan has to have a good faith foundation before she goes off to college. Who knows what kind of crazy ideas she'll pick up in Austin."

"Logan will be all right."

"She's already pushing back, and you know it. I'm starting to think your mother has a point."

I stopped drying myself. "About what?"

"We should take her to look at Baylor. Abilene Christian. Oral Roberts."

"Absolutely not." I rubbed my body with increased vigor.

"Why?"

"Because she's wanted to go to UT her entire life." I brushed by Charlie and into the bedroom to dress. "You went there and turned out okay."

"But, she's a girl."

"What does that mean?"

"She's more susceptible to being swayed by other people's opinions."

The comment hit a little too close to home. I'd made sure Logan had learned to think for herself, to be independent, strong-willed and strong-minded. When she hit the teen years I regretted it, but I didn't want my daughter to be as easily persuaded as I had been all those years ago.

"Have you *met* our daughter?"

"You remember Laurie Craven?"

"Oh my God."

Laurie Craven was a year older than us and had made quite a stir during her first visit home from her freshman year at UT. She'd walked down the bleachers during a Friday night football game, silencing the crowd as she passed. She was dressed in all black with half of her head shaved and the remaining hair apparently dyed to match her outfit. Laurie plopped herself down in the middle of the student section, endured the jeers with a superior expression, knowing curiosity would eventually take over. It had. She was all anyone could talk about for a week after. All these years later, Laurie Craven was brought up as a warning against going away from home and losing all of your values. Or Lynchfield's values.

"She read *The Handmaid's Tale* in freshman sociology and turned into a lesbian."

"From reading a book? I don't think it works like that."

"How would you know?"

I pulled a T-shirt over my head. "So, if I'm following your logic here, all that stands between Logan reading a classic dystopian novel and turning into a lesbian as a result is me going to church three times a week."

Charlie knew how ridiculous it sounded, so he changed tacks.

"It's important for the campaign, too. Our faith has to be un-assailable."

"Is this what our life is going to be now? Gauging everything we do on how it's going to affect your political career?"

Charlie waited for a beat and said, "Yes."

"Good to know," I replied, and walked out of the bedroom.

nine
sophie

I waited until Charlie started the lawn mower before going to Logan's room. I leaned my head against the closed door, took a few deep, calming breaths and said a short prayer, asking God to give me the right words to say along with a *please, God, don't let her hate me*, before knocking on her bedroom door. When she didn't answer, I knocked again, louder this time. I never entered Logan's room unannounced. I'm not sure she appreciated the gesture, the independence and privacy my small act gave her, but I'd worked hard to be nothing like my mother. I'd always thought allowing Logan to be her own person, with her own secrets, thoughts and opinions, would make our relationship stronger, that she would see it as a sign of respect for her as an individual. Instead, she favored her father, who was strict and unbending, dismissive of opinions that differed from his own. By the time I realized she had read my hands-off approach as disinterest, the damage was done. Turned out the old canard about children wanting discipline wasn't total bullshit after all.

"Logan!" I knocked louder, shaking the doorknob.

"What?"

"Can I come in?"

She opened the door with a jerk. "You don't have to yell."

I touched the noise-canceling headphones hanging around her neck. She looked abashed for a split second before remembering she was mad at me and turning away with a scowl. I closed the door and leaned against it. Logan plopped down on her bed.

I put my hand on my stomach in a futile effort to calm my nerves. "I got pregnant with you in June; we got married in August before Charlie went to school."

Logan straightened, her face lighting up with skeptical interest as if she couldn't believe I was telling her the truth, and she expected me to clam up without giving the full story.

"You were two weeks late, which made our lie about you being a month premature believable enough."

"Does everyone in town know I'm a bastard?"

"You aren't a bastard."

"Don't avoid the question."

"Yes, everyone in town knows. It's not like you're the first kid conceived outside of marriage in Lynchfield, Texas."

"How long were you and dad sneaking around behind Nora's back?"

"It wasn't like that. It happened after Nora left for boot camp. She'd broken up with Charlie and…" I swallowed. Logan watched me as if she could read my thoughts, as if she could see the truth playing through my mind like a jumpy black-and-white home movie. I wanted to vomit. "She and I had a falling out before she left."

"Over Dad?"

"No. It wasn't an episode of *Gossip Girl*, Logan. Nora left us, and your dad and I… One thing led to another."

"And you fucked your best friend's boyfriend."

I gasped. She hated that word with a fierce passion. "Logan!"

"Well, that's what you did, isn't it?"

"I wasn't the only one in the back of the goddamn truck."

"You did it in the back of a truck?" Logan flopped onto the

bed and covered her face with a pillow. I could hear her muffled voice clear enough. "I was conceived in the back of a truck. Kill me now."

I released the doorknob I'd been gripping. Blood rushed back into my cold fingers. I sat on the edge of the bed. "I'd known your dad my whole life. It didn't take much for us to fall in love." I looked away, ashamed at the partial lie.

Logan lifted the corner of the pillow. "It sure sounds like an episode of *Gossip Girl*."

I smiled. "It does, a little."

She scrutinized me from beneath the pillow. "What's the rest of the story?"

"That's the whole story."

"Why did Nora break up with Dad? What was your falling out over?"

I inhaled. *Tread lightly. Stick to the truth as much as possible. Lie by omission.* "Nora wasn't in love with your dad, and he expected her to marry him. He had their future all planned out, and it wasn't the future she wanted."

"Going to Iraq and nearly dying was better than being married to Dad?"

"It was six years before 9/11. No one thought Nora would be in a war zone."

Logan folded her pillow in half and shoved it beneath her head. "What was your falling out about?"

I took Logan's hand in mine. Her nails were filed short, but I could feel the tiny ridges across the flat part of her nails. "You need to buff these," I said.

"Mom."

I cleared my throat and tried to find the words—*God, why are you forsaking me?*—tried to ignore the explosions of fear going off in my stomach, hoped Logan didn't notice how the palm of my hand had gone clammy, my fingers cold. What would my daughter think if I told her the truth: I was in love with my best friend, but was too scared of the world finding out? Would she allow for how different attitudes were barely twenty years before, or would she think of me as a coward? Something must have shown on my face because Logan sat up. "My God, Mom, what did you do? Did y'all kill someone and bury them in the desert?"

My laugh sounded hollow. "Nothing like that. I've done a lot to be ashamed of in my life, I'm sorry you've witnessed more than your share, but my biggest regret was my falling out with Nora. I've made amends with everyone but her."

"So, it was your fault, why she left?"

I sighed and wondered if there would ever be a time in my relationship with my daughter when she didn't instinctually think the worst of me. I knew I'd brought a lot of her attitude toward me on myself with my binge drinking and standoffishness, but whenever I'd tried to get our relationship on a better footing, she always seemed to sidle closer to Charlie. I suspected he undermined me and our relationship when I wasn't around. Charlie wasn't happy unless he was the superstar of every situation, and there was an openness to him that drew people in, made them trust him. I, on the other hand, had been hiding the most significant part of myself for so long I didn't know how to open up, even to my daughter. Did she sense me holding back a part of myself? If I was honest would it repair our broken relationship, or ruin it forever?

"There was plenty of blame to go around." I gripped Logan's hand tighter and looked her straight in the eyes. "I will tell you what happened, every sordid detail, but not right now. I have to make it right with Nora first. And it's not just my story to tell. It's Nora's, too. I need to ask her permission."

"And Dad's?"

"Your father had nothing to do with our falling out. I need you to promise me something."

"What?"

"Don't tell him about this conversation."

"Why?"

"He didn't want to tell you."

"Why?"

"He doesn't want you to think less of him."

"He said that?"

"No, but I know your father well enough. He wants you to think he's perfect."

Logan rolled her eyes. "It's just sex."

"Don't let him hear you say that. He's already threatening to make you visit Oral Roberts."

"Mom!"

"Don't worry. I won't let that happen."

Logan plopped back onto her bed with relief.

"Since you brought it up," I said. "How long have you and Joaquin been having sex?"

"Mom! We're not…"

"Logan." She wouldn't look at me. "Hey," I said, playfully shaking her until she did. "I don't care."

"You don't care?"

Her eyebrows almost touched, and I couldn't blame her for her astonishment. I'd darkened the church door three times a week her entire life, had taught every Sunday school class she'd been in, and had been a devout evangelical for years. A year ago, I'd joined AA and found more acceptance, peace and community among a room of strangers than I ever had at Lynchfield Baptist. I'd used meetings as an excuse to miss Sunday and Wednesday nights, and had gotten out of teaching Sunday school by claiming it was time for the teens to hear a fresh perspective. I still sang in the choir but spent most of the time daydreaming about drinking or running away. Then I would see Logan sitting with her friends and know I would never leave. I was rooted in Lynchfield, maybe forever.

"It would be pretty hypocritical of me to tell you not to have sex, wouldn't it?"

"Yeah."

"Are you using protection?"

"Yes, Mom. We're using protection."

A tidal wave of questions flooded my mind: *How long have you been having sex? How often? Where? He is considerate of you or only in it for himself? Do you enjoy it? Do you love him? Does he love you?*

I asked none of them. Those were questions for later, once we'd both gotten used to the idea of sharing Logan's secret. Once I got the courage to tell Logan mine.

"Condoms can break. I'm going to make an appointment for you so we can get you on long-term birth control."

"Don't want me to make the same mistake you did?"

I grasped Logan's face and looked into her eyes. "Of all the mistakes I've made, you're not one of them."

Logan twisted out of my grasp and looked away. I stared at the poster of Serena Williams on Logan's wall and remembered the hours I spent lying on my bed, staring at my poster of New York City, dreaming of leaving Lynchfield. Logan dreamed of leaving, too. It was my job to make sure she did it.

I stood. "I'll find a doctor in Austin since you'll be going to UT."

"You won't tell Dad, will you?"

I started to ask, *About the sex or birth control?* but knew the question was for both. Charlie would cause a big scene, act like the world was ending. He would conveniently forget about our summer of daily hookups, about how I had been someone's daughter, too. But, I remembered what it was like to be young and in love, the urge to be with someone every waking minute, the torture when you were apart, the ecstasy of finally coming together, the longing to absorb the person into your very being, the disappointment when you couldn't. I wanted Logan to have that without the underlying fear of being found out, so when the time came for her to decide her future, she decided for herself, not to please those she'd disappointed. Not out of a sense of shame.

"I won't tell Dad." I said it as much for me as for Logan. I didn't want to fight with Charlie about Logan's sex life, and it would be a doozy of an argument, but part of me knew it was inevitable.

I was closing her door behind me when Logan said, "Mom?"

I came partway into the room.

"Thanks for telling me."

"You're welcome."

I closed the door and leaned against it again, relief coursing through me, though my stomach was still roiling. As far as a first step on the road to honesty went, it had been a rousing success. I straightened. Who was I kidding? Telling Logan something she had already figured out for herself was nothing compared to the bombshell of having a closeted mother in love with her former best friend. I pressed firmly against my stomach, but the pressure didn't calm my nerves.

I wanted a drink.

Charlie stood at the kitchen counter, drinking a glass of iced tea. "It's brutal out there."

"No one's making you do it."

"I'm not wasting the money on something I can do myself."

"Right." I opened the refrigerator door and stared at the contents without seeing them.

"Where have you been?"

I closed the fridge and got a glass from the cabinet. "Talking to Logan."

"About what?" His expression was one of supreme unconcern as if our earlier argument never happened. Or with the self-assurance of a man who, after nearly eighteen years of marriage, had no reason to think his wife would go against his wishes.

I filled my glass with ice and poured myself a tea. "Going to a gynecologist in Austin." As much as I loved sweet tea, it was a damn poor substitute for Maker's Mark.

"Everything okay?"

"She's at the age." My phone buzzed with a text message. An unfamiliar area code.

See, I didn't throw your card away.

My stomach somersaulted. I turned away from Charlie and leaned against the counter.

Took you long enough to text.

I drove out to Comanche Springs.

I swallowed, remembering the times we spent out there, sunbathing on the rocks in the shallow river, skinny dipping in the deep pools when we were alone, pushing the limits, the possibility of getting caught heightening the thrill of every touch.

"When are you going?"

I haven't been out there in years.

It's not as full as it used to be. What can I bring Friday night?

An appetite.

Dessert?

My thumbs hovered over the keyboard while I debated how to respond. Safe or bold? What the hell.

Nothing. I'm trying to seduce you with my cooking, remember?

Three dots flashed on the screen for ten seconds, twenty, thirty, while my insides twisted into a Gordian knot.

"Sophie!" Charlie's voice was loud in my ear. I jumped and pressed my phone against my chest.

"What?"

"What's so riveting you've ignored my question three times?" His eyes wandered to the phone.

"Nora. About Friday night. She wants to know if she can bring something."

"Ask her to bring the pound cake she used to make. You re-member?"

"Yes."

Charlie waited for me to send the message. I looked at my phone. The three dots had disappeared, with no new message.

Charlie is requesting the pound cake you used to make.

"Done."

Charlie patted his stomach. "I should probably go for a run in preparation."

"Good idea," I said.

"Hey, watch it." He kissed me on the cheek. "Oh, I was thinking of inviting Avery and Mark, too. Or is that too much?"

"Um, sure," I said, automatically, staring at my phone. "It's okay."

"Let me know what help you need."

"Help with what?" Logan walked into the kitchen with her dirty paper plate and tossed it in the trash.

"Friday night," Charlie said. "We're having a dinner party."

"We're inviting three people and we're using paper plates."

"So, a hillbilly dinner party," Logan said. "Can I ask Joaquin and Lexa?"

"Sure," Charlie said, walking out of the kitchen. "The more the merrier. I'm going to finish the yard."

I gritted my teeth. The dinner I'd planned on being a small family affair with four people now included two extra teen-agers and two Millennial political operatives who would see our house, our food, our conversation and our opinions through DC-colored glasses. There would be very little chance to have a meaningful conversation with Nora, which was what I wanted.

We'd yet to have a conversation not be interrupted by another person or a misunderstanding. There was so much to say, to feel.

"Mom? Is it okay if I invite my friends?"

I smiled and kissed Logan on the forehead. "Of course it is. Go to the store and buy avocados for me, so they have time to ripen."

"Sure. You making fajitas?"

"I am."

Logan pumped her fist. "Yes." She kissed me on the cheek and walked out the front door. I watched my daughter go, my heart soaring. Was it so simple? Was honesty all that had been missing from our relationship?

When the house was quiet, I opened my phone again. A message was there, but not the one I wanted.

The five-flavor pound cake?

Yes.

I can do that.

Up for a game?

I inserted a tennis ball emoticon at the end of the text.

High school?

Thirty minutes?

See you then.

I made sure Charlie was mowing, then I went to change.

ten
nora

Sophie was on the court, hitting balls against the backboard when I drove up. I sat in my car and watched her. She was a little slower, but still graceful, her long legs covering the court with smooth strides, her long arms just reaching shots that would be out of touch for me.

I opened my phone and looked at the text again. I'm trying to seduce you with my cooking, remember?

Provocative, but it would take more than a thumb caress and a suggestive text to make me trust Sophie Russell with my heart again.

She missed a ball and turned to face me. She stopped, smiled briefly and waved.

I walked onto the court. "I don't have a racquet."

Sophie lifted an extra from her bag and handed it to me handle first, like a gun.

"Damn it."

"Come on, cowgirl up. It's only a hundred and one degrees."

"I wasn't lying when I said I hadn't touched a racquet since I left."

"Good. Maybe I'll finally beat you." She volleyed a ball to me.

I returned it and said, "You were serious when you said a 'game'?'"

"Aw, are you too out of shape to play me?"

I pointed the racquet at her. "You're going down."

"You wish."

We hit easy volleys back and forth for five minutes and practiced serves for five minutes more. We met at the wooden bench on the side of the court. Sophie opened a small cooler and pulled out two cold unopened water bottles. "You brought a cooler?"

"It's the mom in me."

"Are there orange slices in there, too?"

"No, smart ass, there aren't."

We watched each other while we drank, while we twisted the caps back on. A truck with a glass pack muffler rolled by, brutally shattering the relative quiet. I flinched, turned abruptly toward the truck and glared at it. Of course, it had a Confederate flag in the back window. When I turned around, Sophie was grinning. "I'm glad I'm not the only one that hates those mufflers."

"They should be illegal."

"I've got something that will cheer you up." Sophie reached into her tennis bag and pulled out a can of balls.

"Is that…?"

I removed the lid to see the silver seal over the top of the can. I pulled the tab back and it hissed like a can of soda opening. I stuck my nose inside and inhaled the unique scent of rubber and felt. Memories of the hundreds of matches I'd played rushed through my mind, and I grinned. "The best smell in the world."

I handed the can to Sophie, who inhaled and grinned as well. "One set, then we talk."

Sophie won the first three games without surrendering a point. When we switched courts, she looked like she'd gone for a brisk walk. "You lied to me when you said you didn't play much."

"Not exactly. I haven't played much since you left. But, I've played a lot recently."

"I'm playing the rest of this set under protest."

"I'll go easy on you."

"Don't you dare." I crouched down in the ready position, determined to break Sophie's serve or kill myself trying.

As we played, my memories of past matches were overshadowed by the sights and sounds of the current game; the pang of the ball hitting the strings, the scrape and squeak of our shoes on the court as we reached for a shot, the ball hanging, suspended, in the air before my racquet whooshed down to connect on a near perfect serve, Sophie's grunt as she returned it, the white lines of the court wavering in the heat, cold water sliding down my throat during a water break.

My muscle memory kicked in, as did my knowledge of Sophie's game. Sophie had east-west range and could drop a shot right on the service line, but she had never liked charging the net, and her backhand, though much better, was still her weakest link.

I broke her serve by charging the net. I pushed the idea she might have let me win the game from my mind and delivered two aces to go up 30-love in the next. When she dropped into her ready stance, the good humor had left her face. The set lasted thirty minutes and when it finally ended, with Sophie beating me 4-3, I put my hands on my knees and wondered if I was going to die.

I walked to the bench with legs that felt like jelly. I licked my lips, salty with sweat. "I thought I was in shape."

Sophie collapsed on the bench. The chain link fence creaked when she leaned back against it. "You're a competitive son of a bitch."

I plopped down next to her and settled my head against the uneven metal. Sweat glistened on our exposed skin. Sophie stretched her long legs out in front of her and crossed them at the ankles. I watched a bead of sweat arch away from its path down the edge of her toned calf, arc across the muscle, hang precariously for a second before dropping down onto the court. Something stirred deep within me, and I looked away.

We drank our water in silence. I was relieved to hear Sophie breathing almost as hard as I was. I lifted the hem of my T-shirt and wiped away the sweat dripping in my eyes. "I don't remember it being this hot growing up."

I caught Sophie staring at my exposed stomach. She took a sudden, and not too subtle, interest in peeling the label off her water bottle. "I can't believe you haven't played in eighteen years and *still* almost beat me."

"The more things change…"

Sophie pushed her sweaty shoulder against mine. "Shut up." She finished her water and reached into the cooler for two more. She kicked off one shoe, then the other, and toed off her socks. She stretched her red painted toes out and flexed her feet.

"Your toes match your nails?"

"Don't yours?"

My nails were natural, as were my toes. I laughed. "I guess so."

Sophie studied me as if trying to gauge my mood. "I didn't invite you to play so you could almost kick my ass. I wanted you to lose quickly so we could talk. Now I'm not sure I have the energy to talk."

I rested my elbows on my knees, holding the sweating bottle of water loosely between them. "What do you want to talk about?"

"The last letter I sent you."

"Sophie…"

"Did you not read it, or did you say that to hurt me?"

I stared across the court at the windscreen on the opposite fence. It was loose and peppered with gashes and slits from age and wear. Weeds grew up on the edge of the court, in the tension creases of the concrete. The high school courts were always just this side of dilapidated, which is why we'd played at the club. Playing here, though, guaranteed a degree of privacy we wouldn't have at the club. Now I understood why she wanted it.

"I didn't read your letters, but I didn't toss them until I read Mary's." I met Sophie's gaze. "She told me about you and Charlie."

To Sophie's credit, she didn't look away. "My letters explained everything. Some of them I'm glad you didn't read. I was so angry…"

"*You* were angry?"

Sophie sat up. "Tell you what, why don't you let me tell my story, then you can pick it apart, okay?"

"Fine."

"Everyone asked me where you went, what happened, when you were coming back. I didn't know what to say. I couldn't very well tell the truth, could I? My mom and your dad cooked up a lie, I think. Something about you getting an earlier basic training slot last minute, which all the adults believed because they didn't give a shit one way or another. Our friends? That was another story. Jamie Luke would *not* let it go. She gave me the idea. About Charlie. Said she'd always thought I'd had a thing for him."

"She always was a moron."

"She's gossipy enough that by the time Charlie came back from vacation it was pretty well accepted you and I'd had a falling out over him. He showed me your Dear John letter."

She cleared her throat. "I figured one time with Charlie would be enough to sell the story. It wouldn't be a total lie, would it? People would move on. Stop asking me about you every goddamn day." She rolled her eyes and leaned back. "Obviously, it didn't happen just once. I um…" She turned her head away so I could barely see her profile. "I thought, maybe…" She cleared her throat. "I realized pretty quick that Charlie could serve another purpose: making my mother believe you and I had been experimenting. When you told her that I was the one who instigated everything…" She swallowed and looked at me with an expression of betrayal, even after all these years. "Is that how you thought of what happened between us? That I *coerced* you?"

"No. But, you did make the first move, in everything. It wasn't like that in the end, but it was in the beginning, and you know it."

"Well, Brenda was beside herself. It was easy to let her catch Charlie and me in the act. My God, the relief on her face. It was a close second to the relief she felt when I told her I was pregnant."

"Did you do that on purpose, too?"

Sophie's mouth tightened, puckered slightly in anger. "No. Broken condom."

I stood and walked to the net, my back to her. When I'd heard about Sophie and Charlie, I assumed it had been accidental. Something that happened when they were drunk and talking shit about me. *Let's show her.* I'd tormented myself for months with images of them touching, kissing, making love, laughing at me. It had never occurred to me that Sophie had engineered the whole thing to protect our secret and to save her skin. Poor Charlie never had a chance. I knew better than anyone how effortlessly Sophie could make someone fall in love with her.

"Did you ever love him?" I said over my shoulder. I was too afraid of the answer to look at her.

"Yes."

I swallowed the lump in my throat and nodded, relieved Charlie hadn't been wholly cuckolded, but jealous all the same. After losing Sophie it had taken me years to open myself up emotionally to another person, but Sophie had managed it within weeks.

"But, not like I loved you." She said it so softly I almost didn't hear her.

"You're eighteen years too late," I said almost as softly as she had. Not sure If I wanted her to hear it or not.

"The final letter," she said, voice stronger, "explained everything, apologized for everything. Begged your forgiveness. I wanted to be with you, wherever you were, whatever it meant."

I spun around to face her, my heartbeat throbbing in my chest, my ears roaring so that I wasn't sure I'd heard her correctly. I hoped I hadn't, but one look at Sophie told me I had. Sophie's eyes and voice were clear, and she looked happier than she had since I'd been back, as if she could float up from the rickety wooden bench she sat on.

"I took over your job at the Char-Grill and had saved some money. Not much, but enough for gas and hotels to get to you. Wherever you were. All you had to do was ask. I knew you were out of basic training, thanks to Emmadean. So I told you to write to me at my grandmother's. I went to visit her like I did every summer and waited.

"At first I thought my nausea was because I was sick with anticipation waiting to hear from you. Every day that passed, I knew you weren't going to write, and I knew if you did, it wouldn't matter anymore. I stopped at a gas station on the drive home. I'd barely finished peeing before the pink lines showed up in the window."

I sat down next to her. Years of pent-up resentment drained away, leaving me saddled with regret. I'd always taken comfort in the knowledge I'd been blameless, at least mostly, in the whole affair.

I took Sophie's hand and held it between both of mine in my lap. I traced one of her smooth red nails with my thumb. "I should have read them. I dreamed...of you coming to me. I wanted that so much." Sophie shifted her hand to intertwine her fingers with mine. "When I heard about you and Charlie, I burned them." I swallowed. "If I'd asked you to come, after you took the test, would you have?"

Sophie shook her head and wiped tears from her cheeks. Her voice was hoarse. "No." Her eyes met mine. "If you'd read the letter, would you have asked?"

I thought of my last conversation with Brenda Russell, her parting threat. "No."

Sophie squeezed my hand and released it. She stood and started putting her gear together. "Then we are both where we were meant to be."

Sophie was tossing her bag in her car when I popped the trunk of my own and pulled two cold beers from a cooler. "I brought a cooler, too." I twisted the caps and offered a Blue Moon to Sophie. "Those orange slices would come in handy about now."

She leaned forward a little, then stepped back. "I would love one but, I, um…" She cleared her throat and looked away. "I'm an alcoholic."

I lowered the beer slowly from my lips. Mary's comment about Sophie being a mean drunk and Logan's overreaction to Sophie drinking my half-empty beer made sense now. I put the beers back.

"You can drink in front of me. It's no problem."

I closed the cooler and the trunk. "I'm not much of a drinker either." Sophie looked skeptical. "The visitation wasn't the norm. How long have you been sober?"

"A year this Saturday."

"Congrats. Thanks for telling me."

"I should have told you in the barn, but I had to pick and choose my issues, you know. There are so many to choose from."

"Soph—"

She fluttered her hand. "No pity, please."

We stood together, not talking, but not moving to leave either. I was afraid this was the beginning of the end, that the air would be cleared but then what? She had her life, her family, I had mine. I'd take care of Ray's estate and leave. Sophie would become a state senator's wife. We'd occasionally text, maybe talk on the phone a couple of times a year. It sounded awful. But, what was the alternative?

We leaned against the back of my car, staring at the street. "So, here's something weird." I reached out for Sophie's hand, not sure what I was doing or why.

"Hmm?"

"My phone doesn't try to autocorrect *impress* with *seduce*."

Sophie raised her right eyebrow, and the right corner of her mouth lifted with it. "So weird. You might want to have that checked out."

She skimmed her thumb against the palm of my hand again and, despite the heat, goose bumps popped up on my arm. Our eyes shifted to each other's lips. Sophie was biting the inside of her lower lip. I wanted to reach out and touch her lips, but I was too afraid of where it might lead.

Sophie inhaled deeply. "The woman who called you the other day. Was that really about work?"

Her expression was tentative, as if she didn't really want to know the answer to the question. I'd forgotten how forthright Sophie was. I'd always admired it, but right now, I wish she would just learn to let us be for a moment, enjoy each other's company, get past the shyness and uncertainty between us, before pushing on to the next issue.

If Sophie saw the photo enough to know it was a woman calling me, she saw enough to see me kissing Alima on the cheek and Alima's expression. I didn't want Alima brought into my time with Sophie. Not when Sophie and I were tentatively back on solid footing. Alima and Sophie couldn't share the same space in my mind right now. Alima had been the first friend to fill the Sophie-sized hole in my life. When we started sleeping together, the parallels to my relationship with Sophie had been uncanny. I loved Alima in a way I hadn't cared for anyone since Sophie, but being back in Lynchfield, seeing Sophie, being with her, had muddled my emotions.

Muddled emotions or not, I reminded myself there was no future with Sophie. My life was in DC, hers was here, with her daughter, Charlie and her career.

"We work together. But, we weren't talking about work."

She released my hand. "Is she your girlfriend?"

"She's married."

Sophie raised her eyebrows. "So, she's what? Your fuck buddy?"

Anger burned through me. How dare Sophie question me, judge me, about my life. How dare she insult Alima like that, dismiss what the two of us had. "Living near Brenda all these years has rubbed off on you, I see. Your lips pucker with disapproval just like hers do."

"They do not. And you haven't answered the question."

"Alima is a closeted lesbian in a loveless marriage with a huge extended family of conservative Muslims. We were friends long before we were lovers. It's probably the healthiest relationship I've ever had. But, she can't commit, and I don't want to. She's good for me, and I'd rather have her when I can than not have her at all. It works for us. She has her husband, I have my lovers, as many as I want, and there have been a lot." I regretted the parting shot as soon as I said it.

"Oh. Okay. So, this. Holding my hand, flirting with me is just a game with you? Another notch on your bedpost?"

"You were flirting with me. 'I'm trying to seduce you with my cooking'? I have to admit, that's a good line."

"Yeah, well someone had to make the first move."

"You're good at that."

"And you're good at running away."

"Am I?" I moved closer to her. "I've learned a lot since I left. We can have fun for a week or two, and I'll leave, and you'll get back to your perfect life."

"Perfect life. Right." Sophie stepped away. "You've made your point, Nora."

"What was my point?"

"To make sure I know I have no right to ask you about your personal life. And, to humiliate me. Good job. Mission accomplished."

She opened her car door and got in.

I kept her from closing the door. "Wait, wait, wait. I'm sorry. Let's start over."

"Is this third time's the charm?"

I grimaced. "I'm a bitch. I'm sorry."

She sighed and let her hands fall from the steering wheel. "Nora, I can't do this. Forgive me or don't forgive me. Be my friend or not. Forget everything else. I can't handle a rollercoaster friendship."

"I don't want that either."

"We can't seem to see each other without fighting."

"It's going to take some time, for us to, um…"

"Trust each other?"

"Yeah. Maybe we should just leave well enough alone for now."

She nodded slowly. "You're probably right. Too much too soon." Our eyes met for a long moment. I didn't know how to tell her what I wanted without risking my heart, and why would she take the chance after how cruel I'd just been? Goddamn it, I was a master at self-destruction.

"Still come Friday," Sophie said. "We can fake it for a couple of hours for Charlie's sake."

"Fake what?"

"A friendship. What else?"

She pulled the door closed so I had to step out of her way, as the truck with the glass pack muffler drove by again, shattering the air around me.

eleven
nora

One day when I was two years old, my mother left Mary and me with Emmadean to go to the grocery store. The skies to the west were darkening with the threat of rain, but when a frazzled mother of two toddlers under four years old needs a break and has a reliable sitter, a little rainstorm isn't going to keep her in the house. She'd taken her time at the store, visiting with friends and going down every row, luxuriating in the time alone. The deluge came when she was in the bread aisle talking to Joyce Wyatt. They'd looked up at the store's ceiling, hearing the drumming of the rain on the metallic roof. "Oh, darn," my mom told Charlie's mother, "we're stuck."

Mrs. Wyatt laughed with my mother, herself escaping from three rambunctious boys.

During a break in the deluge, my mother bid goodbye to Mrs. Wyatt at the front of the Brookshire Brothers. "Be careful!" Mrs. Wyatt called, knowing there was a low point in the road out to our house that flooded during gully washers. Almost immediately after Mrs. Wyatt waved my mother away, the skies opened up again.

My mom drove through the flooded road, eager to get back

to her kids after nearly two hours away. At least, that's the yarn Emmadean told us so often it had become as much a part of the story as the facts we knew. There was no way to know why my mom drove through the flooded road, but that she did wasn't in doubt. Her car was swept down the flooded creek and into the fast-moving river. They didn't find it until the water receded three days later.

I can't say I've missed my mother. I don't much remember her. Emmadean slipped into a surrogate mother role, allowing Ray to delegate all of the parenting duties to her. Except for discipline. Ray was a big one for discipline. But, love, affection, answering questions, teaching us about right and wrong, that was all Emmadean. And though taciturn, Dormer had the gentlest disposition of anyone I'd ever known. Ray might have paid the bills, but Emmadean and Dormer raised me.

I'd retreated to Emmadean's when Ray kicked me out, and she spent the better part of my ten days there trying to repair the breach. I was a shell of myself, my emotions vacillating between mourning the loss of Sophie and fury at her betrayal, and Ray's. Terror of Brenda Russell, her threat to have me arrested for rape, kept me in Emmadean's guest room, door locked against the world. I wouldn't eat, which worried Emmadean more than anything, and lost ten pounds in ten days.

I didn't tell Emmadean what happened between Sophie and me until ten years later when I was in a hospital bed at Ramstein Air Force Base, recovering from my wounds. I told her everything, probably more than she ever wanted to know or more than I would have ever told her if I wasn't high on Percocet; how Sophie and I fell in love, and why Ray kicked me out, how I'd learned about the Kinsey scale in college and had been given a name, a label, for my feelings for both men and women in a junior-level human sexuality class. That for the last ten years I'd gone back and forth between dating men and women, enjoying both, but finding no one who made me feel the way Sophie did.

Emmadean held my hand in silence for a long time. Later, I would realize what a torrent of shocking revelations they would have been to a woman who'd been married to the same man since she was seventeen years old and to who the idea of bisexuality was as foreign as people who put beans in their chili. Regardless, she never judged, or scolded, merely released my hand and pulled me into her wonderful, soft embrace and let me cry.

It was only natural to have negative associations with Ray's house after he'd kicked me out, but it pissed me off that walking to my aunt and uncle's house, a place full of unconditional love, brought back the despair of those final ten days before I left Lynchfield.

I stopped on the well-worn path between Ray's and Emmadean's houses and closed my eyes, chanting serenity and peace with each inhale and exhale. After a few minutes, my heart had settled into its normal rhythm. I took a large gulp of air and continued on, rubbing my cold hands together to get the blood flowing back to my extremities. A dually pickup drove by and honked. I jumped and clenched my teeth together. *Serenity. Peace. Serenity. Peace.* I determined to have a full meditation session after talking to Dormer and Emmadean, and yoga tonight. I shook myself together, put a smile on my face and walked through the back door.

I always craved fried chicken when I walked into Emmadean's kitchen, and this morning was no different. The scent of fresh coffee barely broke through the familiar aroma baked into walls from forty years of country cooking.

"I brought eggs!"

The kitchen was empty and quiet, save the ticking of the mustard-yellow clock on the wall. A frying pan with hardened grease sat on the back burner of the green 1970s electric stove. I placed the eggs in a drawer in the refrigerator before pouring myself a cup of coffee into a Texas Cattleman's Association mug. I sipped the strong brew and made my way through the house. I averted my eyes as I passed the open door of the room I'd lived in. I stopped and listened, hoping for some sign of life. The house felt like a vacuum.

"Emmadean? Dormer? You two decent?"

"Be right there!" Dormer called.

I cringed at the thought I might be catching my elderly aunt and uncle in a compromising position and retreated to the kitchen. I was searching through Emmadean's cabinets when Dormer appeared.

"Mornin'." He patted me on the back and kissed my temple. "Whatcha looking for, Bug?"

"I need to make a pound cake, and Ray's cupboards are empty. Got plenty of eggs, though."

Dormer poured himself a cup. "I'm sure Emmadean's got what you need. What're you baking a cake for?"

"Going to Charlie and Sophie's for dinner tomorrow night."

Dormer's eyebrows raised. "Are you now? That's mighty fine."

"You two sleepin' in? Or did I interrupt something?"

"Nora." Dormer blew on his coffee and shook his head. He slurped his coffee. "It's getting harder and harder for your aunt to get up in the morning."

"Is everything okay?"

"Just gettin' old." Dormer wouldn't meet my eyes.

I crossed one arm and held my coffee cup curled against my shoulder. "Dormer, you know I'm trained to spot liars, right?"

"That come in handy with your job translatin' technical manuals?"

"Don't change the subject."

"Oh, Dormer's an expert at evadin' uncomfortable conversations." Emmadean shuffled into the kitchen in one of her more colorful muumuus. There wasn't a pattern to it, more a jumble of red, orange and yellow blots bleeding together. Her artificially dark hair and those colors together washed her out. She held on

to the back of a kitchen chair to steady herself, then slowly lowered into it. Dormer pulled a clean cup from the cabinet, poured
Emmadean a coffee and placed it on the table in front of her.

"Thanks, darlin'."

I'd been around my aunt and uncle long enough to know
when they were keeping something from me. Neither had a
poker face, and their tell was not looking at each other. As a
child, I learned there were subjects kids didn't need to talk about,
and as a teenager, I didn't care about anyone else's secrets but my
own. I knew I'd never draw it out of Emmadean, but Dormer
was another matter. I just needed to get him alone.

"Mind if I use your kitchen to bake a cake?"

"Course not. What're you baking a cake for?" Her hand
trembled as she raised her cup, and I noticed Dormer had only
filled it halfway.

"Dinner at Sophie's."

"Y'all made up."

I spent a sleepless night going over and over the conversation,
and there was only one explanation: I've been a bitch. Sophie
was right. We'd been on a roller coaster all week, and it was
all my fault. Every time she reached out, I pushed her away. I
didn't want to leave well enough alone. First and foremost, I
wanted my friend back. If anything happened... No. I wouldn't
think about that. Get ahead of myself. Friendship. I wanted her
friendship first, and to regain that, I needed to make amends.

"We're getting there."

"That makes me right proud."

"What kinda cake you makin'?"

"Five-flavor pound cake."

Dormer hummed his approval.

"Want me to make an extra, Dormer?"

"I do, but we got stuff in the freezer still. Thanks all the same."

"How's the cleaning going?" Emmadean asked.

"It's not yet. I could barely get out of bed this morning."

"Still having problems sleeping?"

"Always." Insomnia had been a problem since I'd returned from Iraq, and sleeping pills only nominally helped. It was the one PTSD symptom meditation, yoga, and boxing hadn't helped. None of them were gone completely, but I managed them pretty well. The one thing that helped was sleeping next to Alima, but that happened rarely, and so the insomnia persisted.

"I played tennis with Sophie last night." I rotated my right arm and grimaced. "I'm sore in places I haven't been in years."

"Who won?" Dormer looked at me over the rim of his coffee cup.

"She did. Barely."

My aunt and uncle glanced at each other with amused expressions. They knew how competitive I was.

"I'm going to see if she wants to play again tonight."

"Go easy on her, Bug." Dormer winked at me.

"So you haven't started cleaning, yet?"

"No. I stood in the middle of the den for ten minutes this morning, wondering where to start."

"Sorry I haven't been able to help you," Emmadean said.

I waved my hand at the suggestion. "I left a message for Mary this morning. Told her I was renting a Dumpster and everything was going inside. If she wants something, she better come claim it."

"Oh, Nora. You don't mean it." Emmadean looked horrified.

"I don't want any of it."

"What about the photos? The mementos?"

"I haven't found either, so far. Speaking of, have any idea what Ray did with the stuff I left in my bedroom? *My* photos and mementos?"

Dormer and Emmadean pointedly didn't look at each other again.

"That's what I thought," I said. Still, disappointment stabbed me in the gut. "Why would I give a rat's ass about Ray's stuff if he didn't care about mine?"

"I asked him for them a few weeks after you left. He regretted what he did, I could tell."

"Which part? Throwing me out or throwing out all my stuff?" I held up my hand. "You know what, it doesn't matter. Either way, he was a son of a bitch."

"Nora, now look here. He was my brother, and for all his faults, I loved him. I won't have you talking about him like that."

"And I won't have you defending him in front of me."

Dormer's quiet voice broke in. "We've had this argument before. Ain't nothing changed."

"If I find any photos, I'll bring 'em over."

I finished my coffee and realized I might be performing the same tasks with Emmadean and Dormer's things in the next decade. I turned my back to them and poured another cup of coffee, hoping to hide the shudder of dread that went through me at the thought. "Dormer, think I'm going to shred the pasture today. Can you come over and help me get the tractor started this morning?"

"Not this morning, Bug. I've got some things to do in town. How about this evening when it cools off a bit? I'll bring my tractor over, and we'll knock it out, the two of us, in half the time."

I leaned against the counter. "I'll stay here and make my cake, then. Keep Emmadean company."

"Thought you needed it for tomorrow," she said.

"Pound cakes are better the day after."

I'll admit, I enjoyed watching them squirm. I wasn't an obedient child or a self-centered teenager anymore. If they were going to lie to me by omission and defend my damn father, then I was going to make them as uncomfortable as possible.

"Y'all want to tell me what's going on?" I said.

"Dormer's taking me to the doctor. Nothing special, just my annual checkup."

"Want me to go with you? It helps to have an advocate with you, to ask questions you might not think of."

"It's just a physical, Nora," Emmadean snapped.

I glanced at Dormer, who'd fixed his gaze on the floor. He would be easy to crack. Later.

"Okay." I rinsed my cup out and put it in the dishwasher. "I guess I have no choice but to tackle Ray's house. They said they'd deliver the Dumpster today. They gave me a window of eight to five, if you can imagine. Kim is coming by later to walk through the house to list it."

"Already?" Emmadean said.

"Why should I wait?"

Dormer watched Emmadean, apparently as curious about her answer as I was. Oh, yeah. He'd be a cinch to break.

"It's just all moving so fast. It's good to have you here," Emmadean said.

My knees creaked as I knelt in front of Emmadean. I could never stay angry with her for long. She stroked my face. "I've been thinking; I've got loads of time banked up at work. There's no reason for me to stay away now."

"Since you and Sophie made up."

I smiled. I'd been thinking primarily of Ray being dead. "I'm going to visit so often you'll get sick of me."

"That'll never happen, Bug."

I stood and kissed Emmadean on the temple. "I'll come in the morning to make the cake. That okay?"

She smiled up at me. "Anytime you want." She slid her arms around my waist and pulled me into a tight hug.

I stroked her hair and kissed the top of her head. "Love you."

"Love you, too."

Over the top of Emmadean's head, Dormer finally met my eyes, and I knew whatever they were keeping from me was terrible.

twelve
sophie

My intercom beeped, and my secretary's syrupy Southern drawl came through. "Your mom's on line two."

"Thanks, Sheila."

I stared at the blinking button. I'd dreaded this call every day this week. As the days passed and I didn't hear from her, I'd completely forgotten to dread it. In truth, thoughts of Nora had driven everything else from my mind. I went over and over what had passed between us—every word, every argument, every smile, every touch. I could still feel her fingers intertwined with mine. Hear her laugh.

My secretary had found me staring into space at my desk more than once and had teased me about how I blushed when she did. Lord only knew what she thought I was daydreaming about. She would never guess. Would probably have carpet burns on her knees from all the praying she'd do.

I adjusted the photo of me and Nora that lay on my blotter. It was prom night, and we'd been waiting for our dates at my house. We'd posed and vogued for my father's and Emmadean's cameras, pretending to be each other's dates before Charlie and Joe arrived. The adults had laughed along with us at the absurdity of it. A little over a month later, this was the only photo I managed to save from my mother's frenzied purge of all evidence Nora had been in my life. The faded and wrinkled picture had been held, cried on, wadded up and straightened back out a million times before spending the last fifteen years between the pages of Nora's copy of Jane Austen's *Persuasion*, the last book she'd been reading to me. I'd spent the summer struggling through the rest of the novel to prove the lie to my mother that it was mine so she wouldn't throw it away. Now, eighteen years later, I was still trying to prove the lie to my mother that I was who she wanted me to be.

Maybe we should leave well enough alone.

The memory of Nora's even voice, of her emotionless expression, when she said this made my heart ache, not exactly the frame of mind I wanted to be in when I spoke with my mother. The phone beeped twice. I picked up the receiver and punched the button.

"Mother."

"I made lunch for you," she said.

"You're sweet, but I've brought my lunch to eat at my desk."

"Nonsense. You're the boss. You can take an hour away to eat lunch with your mother. Noon."

I sighed. "Can't we just do this over the phone?"

"Eat lunch? No, that would be impossible."

"You know what I'm talking about."

"I'm sure I don't."

I lifted the photo. Nora smiled at the camera, and I looked down at her with an expression of such blatant adoration it stunned me the entire town hadn't known I was desperately in love with my best friend. I remember wishing it wasn't a ruse, and that Nora and I could walk into the gaudily decorated gym hand in hand, and dance together like any other couple. Instead, we went with Charlie and Joe, and in a strange, almost prophetic twist, Charlie and I were crowned king and queen. He'd given me a polite peck on the cheek, and we'd slow danced to the song you couldn't get away from that year if you tried, Bryan Adams's "Have You Ever Really Loved a Woman?"

I know, right? I caught Nora's eye as she watched us from the crowd, trying not to laugh.

Now, it was almost commonplace for same-sex couples to attend prom together. Maybe not in Lynchfield, but then again maybe so. Logan and her friends saw no conflict between being a Christian and being accepting of others, though Lord knows the church tried to convince them otherwise. Rejection of the "other" was the central tenet of my mother's brand of Christianity. I'd taught it in Sunday school myself and felt like a hypocrite the entire time. Jettisoning nearly forty years of indoctrination wasn't easy. I wondered if a part of me would never accept who I was.

I turned the photo over. "You want to talk about Nora."

"Who?"

I tossed my readers on the desk. My mother was determined to get her way and, like the coward I was, she always did. Turns out being outspoken isn't the same as being a leader. Real strength is quiet and steady, not bombastic. Cowards are always the loudest people in the room. "I'll see you at noon."

In my attempt to embrace my life in Lynchfield I'd gone too far in the other direction. My quiet strength—let's be real; it was long-suffering silence—had turned me into a shell of the girl I was. I would be thirty-six in two weeks, and I'd spent half of my life trying to forget the girl I was in the first half. Tried to fit into the mold everyone thought I belonged in, that I told myself I belonged in—conservative, Christian, straight. Nora hadn't changed a bit, and seeing her, talking to her, being with her, I felt that forgotten girl trying to spread her wings, to push her way out of the grave I'd buried her in when I'd stared into the abyss and decided to live instead of diving headfirst into oblivion. Living was the one brave thing I'd done since Nora left.

I breezed through the Convention & Visitors' Bureau recep-

tion area. Photos of Lynchfield and the surrounding area lined
the exposed brick walls. A pressed tin ceiling and original wood
floors made the room sound hollow. Sheila's Tahitian coconut
candle burned on her desk, making the room smell like tanning
lotion and reminding me of summers by the pool with Nora.

Everything made me think of Nora.

"Apparently, I'm having lunch with my mother."

The old woman smiled. She'd known my mother longer than
I'd been alive. "Good thing she's a good cook."

"I've got Cooper's in the fridge if you want it."

"Oh, thanks, but take that home to Charlie, so you don't
have to cook."

"Excellent idea, Sheila. Call me if anything comes up."

I put on my sunglasses and pushed through the front door
and out into the bright, blazing June day. I stood in the shade
of the building's gallery and surveyed my town. As a teenager,
all I'd wanted to do was escape its stifling smallness. So, karma
had made sure I became the Convention & Visitors' Bureau
president, whose job it was to entice people to visit and help the
chamber of commerce lure businesses to relocate.

Like so many things I hadn't planned to embrace, over time I
had fallen in love with my job. Outsiders were moving in, and
while Lynchfield would never be considered diverse, we were
managing to pull in diverse tourist groups. My hope was some of
these tourists would be charmed by our people, our history, our
quintessential Main Street, our proximity to Austin, and our 300
days of sunny skies, and would return as permanent residents.

The question was, would I be here to greet them?

When Ray died, and I knew Nora was coming back, the cou-
rageous part of me hoped it would be as if no time had passed, all
of the bad feelings would be forgotten, and the connection we'd
had would return. I'd been stupidly optimistic and wrestled with
the question, *What if Nora asks me to leave with her?* What a pipe

dream. We couldn't get through a conversation without fighting, and she had someone waiting for her back in DC. *Alima.*

Still, I pushed the beautiful smiling face I'd seen on Nora's phone from my mind and let myself dream. If she asked, would I leave my family, my daughter, my friends, and the career I'd built for life with a woman who was practically a stranger to me? She seemed like the old Nora, but how much was framing, seeing her in all the places we fell in love? What was she like in DC? What kind of life did she live? Who were her friends? Besides Alima, that is. Whatever her life, Nora had moved on from Lynchfield, and me. If I ever were to put my daydream of escaping into action, the destination wouldn't be Nora's front door, which was where it had always ended.

The door to the popcorn shop beside me opened with a jingle. Tiffany stuck her head out and said, "You okay? You've been standing there for five minutes."

"I'm fine."

In the front window, the old-fashioned popcorn machine was making a new batch. The muted pops sounded like tiny gunshots.

"Want a fresh bag?"

"No, thanks. Going to lunch at my mother's. Maybe later."

Tiffany eyed me suspiciously, and I tried to walk off.

"How's Nora? Kyle drove by the courts last night and saw y'all playing."

My stomach twisted and sweat popped out on my upper lip. "Nora nearly won."

"The more things change, huh?"

"Yeah, but I can still beat you."

Tiffany laughed good-naturedly. "Like I said." She'd just lost to me two weeks earlier, and it wasn't even close. "Will I see you at church tonight? They're serving fried chicken for dinner."

"Wish I could, but I have a meeting, and I'm late for one now. See ya." I turned away, the smell of buttery caramel corn following me, and making my stomach growl despite its constant state of turmoil.

I stopped when I saw Ray's old truck parked next to my car, with Nora half in and half out of the cab. The door rattled when she shut it.

"Oh, hey, Nora," Tiffany said. "We were just talking about you."

Nora raised her eyebrows, and I clarified, "I told her you nearly beat me at tennis."

Nora nodded, shoving her hands into a baggy pair of old jeans. "It was all I could do to keep up. I'm sore today in places I haven't been sore in years."

"You should come to the church tonight for dinner. Wednesday night, you know. Fried chicken," Tiffany said.

"I have so much food at Ray's that I won't need to eat out for a month."

"Are you staying that long?"

"I don't know."

"You two should catch up," I said. "I have to go."

I got into my car as quickly as possible, but Nora knocked on the window. I rolled it down.

"I wanted to talk to you."

"I have a meeting."

"Two minutes."

I sighed and unlocked the doors. She settled into the passenger seat and said, "I need to apologize…"

"You did that last night."

"…for the last eighteen years."

I finally looked at her. Her hair was pulled back in a ponytail of convenience instead of style. She wore no makeup and what had to be an old shirt of Ray's with the sleeves cut off. The only thing that kept her from looking like a Dust Bowl farmer was her brightly colored running shoes. It was a ridiculous outfit.

She was still the beautiful, fresh-faced All-American girl I fell in love with. My heart raced, and the breath went out of me.

Why did she have to come back? Why did I have to see her? I could have stayed away. People would have gossiped about my absence, but hell, I'd been through it already. I'd had Jack Daniel's to console me then.

I loved Nora, still. After all the years away, all I wanted was to be with her. Sit in my hot car for hours staring at her. Talking to her. But, it was impossible.

I glanced out the windshield and saw Tiffany, phone to her ear, watching us. I backed out and pulled around the corner, to an alley behind an abandoned feed store. Nora didn't ask what I was doing, but I said, "Tiffany," by way of explanation. She nodded. I put my car in Park, half turned in my seat to face her and waited.

"Not reading your letters was such a shitty, selfish thing to do," she said.

"We said last night it wouldn't have mattered."

"Maybe not in that way. But, our friendship could have survived."

"No, it couldn't. I couldn't have been just your friend, not after that year. And you couldn't have either. At least I hope seeing me and Charlie and Logan would have..." I rubbed my forehead. "I don't know."

"When you asked me if we could be friends the other day, I said yes, but I'm not sure I meant it. Not then. Now, though. I want that more than anything in the world."

I leaned back against the car door. "Tell me about your life in DC."

"My life in DC?"

"Yeah. We haven't talked about our lives at all. You probably think you've got mine all figured out, small-town mom and all. But, I have no idea about yours. I can't fathom living in a city."

"It's what you always wanted."

"That was a long time ago."

"You like it here?"

"Tell me about your life first."

Nora shrugged. "I work a lot, but I love my job, so I don't mind."

"What do you do?"

"I'm a translator."

"Emmadean told me you know five languages. Is that true?"

"Including English, yes. Spanish, French, Farsi, Arabic."

"I would have never imagined that."

"You don't remember the armed services test? I scored high on languages."

"Right. I'd forgotten." In truth, I hadn't paid much attention to it. Nora wasn't going into the military. She was going to be with me. "You can't work all the time."

"I spar three times a week at a little boxing gym in my neighborhood. I learned in the military. I take advantage of the Smithsonian museums. There's a great bookstore in DC I go to at least once a week. At one point or another, I've seen just about every politician shill a book at Politics and Prose."

"Were you telling the truth last night, about your social life? Or trying to hurt me?"

"I don't have any trouble finding companionship when I want it. But, I'm not out cruising bars every night."

"Hmm." The idea she ever had sent a jolt of jealousy straight through my gut. I glanced at the clock and cursed. Brenda would be calling Sheila any minute now to find out if I'd left. "I have to go. I'm late for a meeting. I'll take you back..."

"You didn't answer."

"My life is busy and boring, just like you think."

"Not about that. Can we be friends even though I probably don't deserve your forgiveness?"

No, we can't. I'm still in love with you and being near you knowing we will never have what we once did is killing me. Please leave town and never come back.

I needed to get Nora out of my car before all those thoughts became words.

"Sure." I held out my hand. "Bygones."

Nora's hand was dry and strong, a little bony. But, her touch sent a thrill through my body that I hadn't felt in years. I stared at our hands, remembering all the times they'd been joined, gripping each other, the panting breaths, the sweat-slicked bodies, the whispers of love. When I lifted my gaze, she was watching me, mouth parted, and I knew she remembered the same things. My body ignited as if a switch had been flipped, in anticipation of what she would say.

I pulled her hand toward me, and she followed. We leaned together and paused, our lips almost touching, as if both considering how stupid this was, knowing what surely lived on the other side, all of the conflict, problems, emotions our lips touching would set in motion. Or in my case, fervently hoping the connection we'd had, the love and desire, was still there. Our eyes met, and I saw Nora's doubts. I was too close to turn back. I could feel her breath on my cheek, see every goddamn adorable freckle on her face. I gently touched my lips to hers, lingered for a long second, and pulled back. Waiting.

She grasped my face and pulled me to her in a tender kiss. Soon we were clawing at each other's clothes, blindly trying to find bare skin to touch. I pulled at Nora's shirt, the pearl button snaps easily breaking apart, and my hand moved automatically to the front bra closure which had always been there before. The next moment her bra opened, and my breath caught at the feel of her in my hand at last, foreign and familiar, her hardened nipple searing a path along my palm. I broke the kiss, and let my lips travel down her cheek, her neck, saying "NoNo, NoNo," desperate for my lips to touch the breast I cupped in my hand. Her hand on the back of my head, she guided me to her, saying my name—has anything sounded sweeter?—her fingers sliding beneath my dress and up my bare thigh to...

The car phone trilled, and we jerked apart. I caught a glimpse of Nora, hair out of her ponytail, lips and chin marked with my red lipstick, her eyes hooded and perplexed. We looked at the dashboard screen and saw the caller's name at the same time.

"You've got to be fucking kidding me," Nora said.

"I'm supposed to have lunch with her. And I'm late."

"Don't go."

"I have to."

Nora raised her eyebrows and pushed the Accept button. She opened her mouth to say something to my mother, but I clamped my hand over it. "Hi, Mother. I'm on my way."

"You're late."

"Yes, I know. I had to stop by the house." Instead of trying to move my hand, Nora kissed the palm, before moving her lips up my wrist and arm to my shoulder. I shivered.

"Sheila said you left twenty minutes ago."

I closed my eyes and tilted my head away to give Nora's traveling lips plenty of access to my neck. She placed my hand that she'd kissed over her breast. Sweet Jesus. "Did I? I must have gotten distracted."

"Is that what you call this?" Nora whispered in my ear, her hand moving deftly along my inner thigh.

I inhaled sharply. "Five minutes, Mom. Maybe ten." I leaned forward, ended the call and was returning to Nora when she removed her hand and mine, sat back, and started setting her clothes to rights. "What are you doing?"

"You have a meeting in five minutes."

"Ten."

Nora buttoned her shirt and looked at me with a pitying expression. She shook her head and got out of the car.

I reached out. "NoNo, wait."

"Tell Brenda I said hi," she said and closed the door in my face.

★ ★ ★

I pulled up to my mother's house thirty minutes late. What was a few more?

I put my forehead on my steering wheel and breathed deeply.

Good Lord, that kiss. Had we ever kissed like that before? I didn't think so. There had been plenty of passion, or what, in our inexperience, we thought of as passion. Today it was hunger and fear and a sense of urgency. I could still feel Nora's steady and sure hands on my thigh, her soft lips. I could smell the scent of coffee that lingered on her clothes, hear the sound of the pearl snaps breaking free. The thrill and joy that came with the discovery that Nora wanted me as much as I needed her.

We had gone from leaving well enough alone to bygones to moaning each other's names to fighting again. What a fucking roller coaster. If I made it through the next few days without drinking a bottle of Maker's Mark in one sitting it would be a miracle akin to the virgin birth.

I would go to a meeting tonight, not only because I promised Logan, but because the urge to drink wasn't diminishing the more I saw Nora but increasing. I'd always thought news about Nora triggered my drinking because she wasn't here, with me, where she was supposed to be. But, Nora was here, in Lynchfield, and when I wasn't fantasizing about her, I was plotting how to sneak a drink.

Obviously, Nora wasn't my trigger.

The last thing I wanted to do was talk to my mother. But, considering there was never a good time to talk to my mother, I might as well get it over with.

"You look flushed," my mom said when she opened the door.

"It's a fucking oven out there."

"Sophie, I won't have that language in my house."

I stepped outside onto the small square of concrete that was generously called the front porch and repeated, "It's a fucking oven out here," and walked inside.

My little rebellion caved at the sign of my mother's disapproval. "I'm sorry, Mother. It's been...a week."

The aroma of a delicious meal didn't greet me as I expected, but the smell of lemon furniture polish almost knocked me out. I walked into the kitchen and saw a bowl of chicken salad next to a small plate of croissants. I peered closely at the chicken salad and turned to my mother. "Is that from Costco?"

"Of course not."

I opened the trash can and pulled out the plastic container. "Are you kidding me?"

"It's as good as what I would have made, and my sciatica has been acting up. Something you would know if you ever called."

"You lied to me."

"Since when did you become a food snob, Sophia?"

"It's not about the chicken salad. It's about you manipulating me to come over here for a conversation we could have had over the phone."

"I don't know what you're talking about." She waved her hand towards the paper plates next to our feast. "Make yourself a sandwich."

"Could you please just say what you want to say?"

"Really, Sophia. Why are you so combative?"

I put my hand on my forehead. The Brenda Headache was coming on strong. I couldn't wait until the meeting. I needed to call Todd, my sponsor, as soon as I walked out the door. I sighed in resignation. "I've seen Nora four times since she's been back. Charlie's invited her to dinner Friday night, along with his campaign staff, so there's no need to worry about us being alone." I turned away to hide the smile that bloomed on my face at the thought of my mother's reaction to what I was doing in my car five minutes ago.

"A dinner party?"

"No, fajitas on paper plates."

"Sophia Elizabeth, I taught you better than that."

"I can't believe the woman who is serving me Costco chicken salad is giving me shit about using paper plates." I picked up her paper plates and waved them at her.

"Your language is vile and insulting." She sniffed and continued with her original harangue. "Charlie's campaign staff are from Washington, aren't they? You can't serve dinner on paper plates."

"Yes, I can. It will reinforce Charlie's down-home bona fides. He's even going to grill the meat. Sleeves rolled up to the elbow like the common man politician he'll be."

"You should take off work that day so you can give the right impression."

"Which right impression are you talking about? That I'm a subservient wife?"

"You say it as if it's a dirty word."

I lifted my eyes to the sky. I couldn't believe I left work for this conversation.

"I'll come over and help."

"Absolutely not. I'll serve the fajitas on real plates. Are you happy now?"

My mother pursed her lips and shook her head side to side very slightly. Brenda Russell had aged well, with few wrinkles on her sixty-year-old face. The glaring exception being the fine lines around her mouth, born of years of puckering disapproval at any idea or action at odds with her ideas of propriety or morality. My urge to needle her was at war with the exhaustion of always being wrong.

"I need to go to the bathroom."

I dry swallowed two Excedrin from the bottle I'd stashed in the medicine cabinet in preparation of the Brenda Headache I always got when I visited. I put the toilet lid down and sat in my childhood bathroom, which I realized now had always looked like the bathroom of a sixty-year-old woman with its gold-and-beige-striped wallpaper, oak cabinet topped with ecru-colored granite. Even the picture on the wall was shades of cream, gold and brown, blending into the wall rather than standing apart from it.

I hated this bathroom.

I thought of Logan's bathroom and how I'd let her make every decision when it came time to decorate it. Watching her bite her lip and tap into her creativity as she deliberated over shower curtains, paint colors and tiles was one of my favorite memories. I expected the result to be a monstrosity of pink and orange and white and was pleasantly surprised when it turned out so well. I would have loved it regardless because of the pride and joy on my fourteen-year-old daughter's face when she saw it completed.

Our relationship went south not too long after. I'd been one of the lucky moms; Logan hadn't turned into a typical teenage girl when she hit thirteen. Unfortunately, she did at fifteen, and we were at the lowest point of our relationship when I'd been arrested for a DUI and turned into the ultimate hypocrite, preaching about drunk driving to my child then acting like the rules didn't apply to me.

My mother and I never had a good relationship to begin with. Being an only child, and a daughter to boot, my father petted and pampered me. Mother never forgave me for distracting my father from her. So, of course she wouldn't have dreamed of letting me decorate my bathroom or have even considered changing it to fit my personality. Her tastes should be my tastes. Her opinions my own. Her beliefs my own. It took me years to realize how manipulative and controlling she was, and that the root of it all was her jealousy towards me for taking a little bit of my father's love and attention from her. I hated to admit it, and I would only do it grudgingly to myself, but there were times when Logan and Charlie's close relationship made me seethe with jealousy. I usually recognized it quickly and pushed the emotion away. I was not going to become my mother. Over the years it had become a delicate balance to distance myself, and my daughter, from my mother's influence without her, or anyone else, cottoning on to it.

I sighed. "Just get it over with, you coward."

When I returned, my mother had made me a sandwich (served on a china plate now, naturally) with plain Lay's potato chips (my favorite) and a glass of ice tea with a sprig of mint in it. I knew the tea would be cloyingly sweet, just the way I liked it. Brenda was pulling out all of the stops.

"I should get back to work."

"I hear Ray left everything to Nora." My mom put her napkin in her lap.

Finally. The tension of dread released slowly, like air through a pinprick in a balloon. I sat down on the edge of the chair, telling myself I wasn't committing to anything and ate a chip, the salt making my mouth water for more. "Apparently."

"What does she plan to do?"

"She mentioned lighting a match to it, but I think she was joking."

"She isn't staying then?"

"In Lynchfield?" My voice rose at the end of the question, but my mother took a dainty bite of her sandwich, seemingly oblivious. "Why would she do that?"

"Emmadean."

I sipped my tea. It was delicious, dammit. "I don't think Nora knows."

My mother raised her penciled-on eyebrows. "I suppose Emmadean doesn't want to guilt her into staying."

I traced the letter N into the condensation on the side of my glass. I'd argued with Emmadean about her decision not to tell Nora about her diagnosis, but that sweet, accommodating, loving woman wouldn't budge. The stubborn streak in the Noakes ran deep. Dormer couldn't even convince Emmadean, and if he couldn't do it, God himself wouldn't change her mind. I expected Mary would be the one to blab so she wouldn't feel obligated to be in Lynchfield as often. Though I suppose it would be as likely that Mary wouldn't tell her sister so Nora would feel guilty for the rest of her life for not being here for Emmadean.

"You two seem to be spending a lot of time together." My mother's lips puckered but her eyes were downcast as if it took a lot for her to admit it.

"Emmadean's a good friend."

"I wasn't speaking of Emmadean. I saw you drive by with Nora the other day, and you've had lunch together and played tennis last night."

"Wow, I didn't realize your network of spies was so extensive, Mother."

"You really should be careful with that woman, Sophia. You know what she does to you."

"No, Mother. What does she do to me?"

My mother twisted her napkin. "Manipulates you into doing things you know are an abomination against God."

"How does she do that?"

"Oh, Sophie, don't say such things. I can't bear to think of it."

"On the contrary, I think you've put a lot of thought into it. What exactly do you think she does?"

My mother glared at me. "I never trusted that girl."

"Oh, please. You loved her. Sometimes I think you liked her more than me."

"She wasn't as disrespectful as you, that's for certain."

I sat back in my chair. "You know, Nora and I probably wouldn't have become best friends if not for your Christian charity." My mother scoffed, but I could tell the idea had crossed her mind before. "This all happened because you gave a motherless girl a scholarship for tennis lessons at the club."

"Coach Cress asked us to."

"And, it was a very Christian thing to do, which led to very un-Christian behavior."

"She coerced you."

I laughed. "No, she didn't."

"You said she did."

"I lied so you wouldn't send me away."

My mom made a small noise of disgust. "She's lucky we didn't press charges."

"Um, I'm pretty sure lesbian sex wasn't illegal, even in 1995."

"Oh, Sophia. Don't use that word. You're not one of those people. I didn't raise you that way." My mom stood, pain clear on her face, and turned away. "You said she forced you."

"Seduced, Mother, not forced. I lied so you wouldn't send me to conversion camp. The attraction was mutual, trust me. We were in love."

"No, you were not." Brenda had ripped her napkin to shreds. "You're just saying that to be cruel."

"I should have told you all those years ago. Nora's the love of my life."

"Charlie is the love of your life."

"I wanted him to be, and I've tried, Mother. I have. But, it's Nora. It's always been Nora."

"Sophie, stop talking nonsense."

I stood and pulled at my hair in frustration. Tears threatened my eyes. My voice shook. "Mother, would you listen to me, just once. Please. I'm—"

Brenda lifted her hand to stop me. "Do not raise your voice to me, Sophia Elizabeth. If you continue to talk this way, I'm going to have to ask you to leave."

I turned away, instinctively obeying my mother's command. I stopped before I'd gotten two steps away. A tear trickled down my cheek. Of course this is how my mother would react. She was an expert at ignoring unpleasant truths, of twisting things to fit her worldview, her beliefs. And I'd let her. I'd let her bend me, mold me into who she wanted.

I sniffed, wiped the tears from my cheeks, and turned around. My mother looked up at me with an expression of supreme confidence, sure that she'd won again. That I would do what she wanted. I wanted to rip that smug expression off her face.

"I'm a lesbian, Mother. Is that what you don't want to hear? Huh?"

My mother turned her head away. I leaned down and got into her face. "Is that the worst possible thing I could tell you?"

"Yes."

"No, it's not." I moved my lips to her ear. "I *hate* you. I've hated you ever since you took Nora away from me."

My mother turned her steely gaze to me. "I didn't *take* her from you. You let her go. I know you, Sophia, and you've never let anyone tell you what to do. If you loved her as you claim, you wouldn't have lied to me, and you wouldn't have let anything stand in your way of being with her. But, you did, didn't you? You let her leave. You let yourself get pregnant by her boyfriend. If it makes you feel better to hate me, to blame me, go right ahead. But, you created your problems. And you're going to do it again if you continue to see that woman."

My chest was heaving with barely suppressed rage. Somehow, I managed to control myself. I straightened, said, "Fuck you, Mother," and left.

thirteen
sophie

The good people of Lynchfield, Texas, would have been surprised to see me stand up a year ago, eyes wide with fear, hands clenched together so tight they were white, and say in a trembling voice, "My name is Sophie, and I'm an alcoholic." Drinking was something I did alone and infrequently, but when I did, the binge would last for days. Charlie became a master at covering for me. After a little trial and error, we'd discovered *migraines* was the best explanation, especially when the binges came too close together to use *cramps* as an excuse.

Lynchfield was dry, so drinking required a one-hour round trip to the next county over, and the willpower to resist opening the bottle on the drive back to town. The stretch between Lynchfield and Kendel County was the highway patrol's favorite honey hole. Somehow, I'd avoided being stopped for ten years until driving back from a convention in Austin three hundred and sixty-three days ago.

The euphoria of my night with a beautiful stranger lasted until I exited the hotel parking garage. I turned my blinker toward Lynchfield, and the reality of what waited for me on the other side of the drive hit me. The lie. I considered turning my car away from my life and driving away. Seeing where the road took me. I knew where I would go, and on whose doorstep I would end up. I might have accepted who I was in the arms of a stranger, but there was only one woman I wanted. Even after all these years.

I sat at the exit until a car behind me honked. I turned automatically and wandered around Austin until I found a dive bar. A real dive, not the ones that no amount of dressing down could keep from looking gentrified. In Austin these days, it's not an easy feat.

With a nine-dollar pack of Marlboro Lights from the cigarette machine by the bathrooms and three shots of Jack with a beer chaser, I watched dog racing on the small television above the bar, said *I'm gay* in a voice so low only I could hear and burst into tears. The bartender, dingy and seedy as his bar, silently poured me another shot and walked to the other end. My hand shook as I lifted the cigarette to my mouth. I closed my eyes and let the smoke mask the aroma of sour beer and vomit, felt the nicotine calm me, but drank the shot anyway.

I considered my three options: drive to the airport and get on a plane to DC. Beg Nora's forgiveness, tell her she was the love of my life and hope we hadn't changed so much that what we had was gone.

Return to my life. A loveless marriage held together by an incredible daughter. A challenging and fulfilling career. Friends? Not really. I'd kept myself apart from girlfriends, knowing I would never find another friendship like what I had with Nora, and afraid I might fall in love with someone else if I did.

Come out. Divorce Charlie but stay in Lynchfield for Logan. I took a drag of my Marlboro Light and thought about what life would be like as Lynchfield's homegrown, token lesbian. Smoke leaked out of my nostrils. I shook my head. "No way in hell," I murmured, downed my shot and signaled the bartender for another one. It came at the same time as a text from Logan.

What time will you be home?

I downed the shot, ordered a burger and coffee and texted a lie to my daughter. Late meeting. Be home by four.

I could see the back of the Kendel County line sign in my rearview mirror when I saw the cruiser make a U-turn and flip on his lights. I failed the field sobriety test and blew a one-point-five. I was still drunk when Charlie bailed me out at 10:00 p.m.

"You have to get help."

"I know."

"Is this the mother you want Logan to remember?"

"Fuck you."

Charlie had never understood his pleas to stop always made me want to drink more. I hated being told what to do, even when it was in my best interest. I would have kept on drinking if I hadn't seen the expression of disgust on Logan's face when we got home.

That was when our typical mother/teen daughter relationship changed from embarrassment to hatred.

Charlie was still at home the next morning when I dragged myself out of bed. I stopped when I saw him, knowing I looked like shit, wishing I'd hopped in the shower. I pretended confidence, poured myself a cup of coffee and leaned against the counter, waiting for the lecture that never came. He turned his computer around to face me.

I leaned forward and read the address on the screen. "I'm not going to an AA meeting at our church."

"You have to get help, Sophie."

"I know, and I will. But, not in Lynchfield."

Charlie furrowed his brows while I tapped out a search and hit Enter. I clicked on a meeting I'd considered going to for a couple of years. I knew if I were to work the program in its entirety, I would have to tell some truths I didn't necessarily want

anyone in Lynchfield to know. And, frankly, I didn't wholly
trust the anonymity the group promised.

Charlie took the day off, and we drove to Dripping Springs
for my first meeting. Todd was the first person who greeted us,
and I felt an immediate connection with him even though he
was a burly bald man with a long beard and covered in tattoos.
His intimidating looks were deceiving; he was a gentle, soft-
spoken hippy who smelled of freshly hewn lumber.

Todd's path to shaking my hand started in a deep East Texas,
white supremacist gang—the family business being hate, in-
timidation, crime and violence—through two stints in the pen,
finding Jesus and joining AA during his last stint, and a move
to the Hill Country and away from his family when he was released. Todd was a barber during the day, a regular at AA meetings at night, and a chainsaw artist who created statues out of
logs on the weekends. Bears mostly. He soon became my sponsor, and after a while, my confidante. To a point. Todd knew
I was holding something back, and I suspected he knew what
I was holding back, but he'd been in the program long enough
to know not to push me.

I might have admitted the truth to myself at that dive bar, but
I'd never said it out loud to another person. Not until today. To
my mother. My last choice for the first person to tell.

I was still shaking from rage when I sat down with Todd at
the rear table of the diner next door to his barbershop. "What
happened with Brenda?"

Todd had never met my mother because I'd never invited her
to my chip meetings. But, he'd heard all about her.

I crossed my arms and put my head down on the table. "I
told her I hated her. Then I told her to fuck off." I sat up. "Or
maybe I said fuck you. I don't remember."

"How do you feel now?"

I sipped my coffee. "Disappointed I don't feel better. I've

wanted to say that to my mother for twenty years and when I finally do? There is *no* catharsis."

"What brought this on?"

I laughed. "How much time do you have?"

"As long as you need."

"You might regret not putting a time limit on this, Todd."

I rubbed my sweaty palms on my skirt and shifted in my seat. Todd sipped his coffee in silence. He had mastered the art of stillness, of letting quietness fill the rare gaps in our conversations. I tended towards chatter, to fill our time with inconsequentialities out of fear something would slip. Now the same urge to chatter and avoid the topic was almost overwhelming. But, I couldn't. If I didn't trust Todd with my full self, I would never be able to trust anyone. It sure as hell couldn't be as disastrous as coming out to my mother.

I closed my eyes and lowered my head, hitting my forehead with my fist. Goddamn her. She stole my coming out. It should have been with someone who would accept me, who I could trust, not her. Never her.

I opened my eyes when I felt Todd gently squeezed my forearm. "Sophie, just tell me the story."

I gripped his hand and sighed. "Okay." I nodded my head quickly. "I have to go back to the beginning, to explain today."

Todd twirled his hand in the air, the universal signal for *get the fuck on with it already.*

"Okay. When I was seventeen, I fell in love. With my best friend." Todd stared at me, waited.

"You want a drink, don't you?"

"How'd you know?"

"You're licking your lips." Todd squeezed my hand. "You got this, Sophie."

I inhaled deeply and said, "Her name was Nora." I waited for Todd's horrified reaction, an expression of disgust, for him to release my hand and sit back in the booth—put as much distance between us as possible—to try to escape as soon as possible. Instead, he held my hand with both of his and nodded his encouragement. Tears of relief welled in my eyes.

"We were best friends since fourth grade. You know how everyone says opposite personalities attract? That was me and Nora. I loved being the center of attention, Nora just stayed back and smiled at my antics. She never told me to tone it down but being around her... She was a good influence on me. I think I was on her, too. I learned pretty quickly she loved reading, so I cajoled her into reading our book assignments to me. I mean, in fourth grade it wasn't a problem, but we got older and the books got longer. I always expected her to say, 'Read your own damn book, Soph'—that was my influence on her, the ability to call people out and not take advantage of her—but she never did. I think she liked it as much as I did. She wouldn't do voices, exactly, but she could make each character distinct. It's probably why, to this day, the only way I can read a book is to listen to an audiobook.

"One day, she laid her head in my lap to read to me. I ran my fingers through her hair for an hour while she read *Persuasion*. We'd long since moved on from required reading to other things. Nora loved the classics, which I would have never touched with a ten-foot pole. When I think of falling in love with Nora, it isn't our first kiss, or the first time we, you know, but it's those moments when she read to me. There was an intimacy to it that is hard to explain. Watching her for all of those hours, I felt like I could see into her soul." I paused. "That probably sounds really stupid."

"Not at all. I fell in love with Ivey watching her care for a patient."

"Ivey is a saint, of course you fell in love with her."

"She is, and she'll be tickled when I tell her you said it."

I cleared my throat. "Our senior year we were a couple, in secret, of course. But, we'd always been so close that no one suspected much. Our friends had joked about us being lesbians for years, and we'd always hammed it up and laughed with them. Charlie was there to attest that Nora wasn't gay in the least."

"Hang on. Charlie, as in Charlie Wyatt, your husband?"

"Yep."

"So, Charlie and Nora were boyfriend and girlfriend?" At my nod, Todd said, "Wow. This is some *All My Children*–level shit."

"Yeah, it kind of is. So, nothing really changed when we got together except the lesbian label wasn't a lie anymore. We managed to fool everyone for our entire senior year."

"That's impressive."

"They guys never believed it, and if some girl was adamant it was true, that our relationship 'just wasn't normal,' I could always wave it off as jealousy. Nora and I were kind of the it girls, and I'm ashamed to admit that we used that to our advantage the entire year. Oh my gosh, what a great year it was. Best of my life. I'd found the other half of my soul. When we'd made it through football season, the prom, graduation, we could see the light of freedom at the end of the tunnel. Then, my mother caught us. Twice." My voice was thick with emotion, at the reliving of the moment as much as the telling. "The first time we were asleep. Naked and intertwined, but Brenda believed us when we said it was a one-time thing. She decided the best thing to do, to keep it from happening again, was to separate us. Mother threatened to tell Nora's father unless Nora joined the army. Brenda knew they were after her to join, and she knew I hated the idea.

"My punishment was attending Oral Roberts instead of Tech." When Todd looked confused, I clarified, "The Jesus university with the praying hands?"

"I still don't know, but I get the drift. Go on."

"Neither one of us liked the options, but we decided the only way to be together was to do what Brenda wanted. Or let her think we were. Nora would join the army and go to boot camp.

When she found out where she would be stationed, I would come to her. Get a job, go to whatever college was nearby. Then, my mother caught us a second time."

I closed my eyes and grimaced at the memory of Brenda grabbing Nora by the ankle and dragging her off me and onto the floor. Grabbing my tennis racquet and hitting Nora with it. Me, throwing myself over Nora to protect her. My father coming into the room at the noise and finding his daughter and her best friend, naked and cowering beneath his wife's wrath.

"There was no denying what we were doing this time. My father calmed my mother down, told Nora to get out and never come back. They locked me in my bathroom. Tiny window, you see. I begged and pleaded through the door, asking them not to tell Nora's dad. I told them I would do anything they wanted, just to leave her alone. I could hear them talking low in my room, then nothing. An hour, maybe two later, my father came back with an empty suitcase and told me they were taking me to a conversion camp." I straightened and moved slightly away from Todd. I couldn't look at him. "I threw Nora under the bus to avoid that. 'I'm not gay. I didn't even really like what we did together. She seduced me. I only went along with Nora because she was my best friend blah blah blah.'" I shook my head. "I saved myself, but I ruined Nora's relationship with her father."

"Your mother told."

"Yes. And told Nora what I'd said. I managed to sneak out the night before Nora left for boot camp. I apologized over and over, but she just looked at me like I was a monster. Which I guess I was. I mean, what kind of friend does that?"

"You were young and scared. With shitty parents."

"She's back."

Todd sat forward. "Nora? Since when?"

"Friday. Her father died. She hadn't spoken to him since she left, eighteen years ago."

"And?"

"We've made up."

"That's great."

I rested my face in my hands.

"I'm still in love with her."

"That's your big revelation? I don't think so."

"It's the truth. I want Nora so much I feel physically ill."

"You just said want, not love."

"I do love her."

"What do you think about more, the everyday life you would have with her, or fucking her?"

"Todd!"

"You need to say it, Sophie."

"Say what?"

He sat back and crossed his arms and let the quietness settle between us.

I sighed. "You know what led me to AA?"

"The DUI?"

"The night before, I had a one-night stand with a woman named Erica. I don't even know if it was her real name. I didn't give her mine." I twisted a thin paper napkin into a long strand. "She's the only other woman I've been with. Telling myself it was just Nora got me through a lot of dark times. Of course, they would always come back because it was a fucking lie."

I untwisted the napkin, laid it out flat. "I was stone-cold sober when the woman picked me up. I was on my first glass of wine at the hotel bar. I'd seen her at the convention. Across the room. There was something about her that drew me. I couldn't keep my eyes off of her. I didn't dare go up to her.

"She came and sat next to me, ordered a drink. When the bartender left, she turned to me and lifted her wineglass. *To beautiful strangers.*"

"Damn, that's a good line."

"Yeah. She had a gorgeous, soft Southern accent, like Melanie from *Gone with the Wind*, but authentic. She wore a wedding ring that was borderline gaudy, and her clothes, the style, the quality, reeked of old money. We talked for a bit, flirted, really. Every question, every answer, was loaded with innuendo. By this time, my entire body was humming with energy. I was worried I was reading something into this that wasn't there when I turned to her and saw this naked expression of... No one has ever looked at me like that. Not even Nora. I don't know how much cash I gave that bartender. Probably sixty or eighty dollars for two glasses of wine. At the door to my room, I turned to ask her if she was punking me, but there was that look again. She told me to hurry up."

I was tearing the napkin now, remembering what happened in that hotel room, how it changed my life for the better and worse. We weren't gentle; we practically devoured each other and shed our clothes as quickly as possible. When I felt her body against mine, her soft skin, her breasts... Even now the thought of her made me burn.

I cleared my throat and continued. "She stayed all night. We parted as strangers. Hard to believe, considering...but we were both uncomfortable. When I opened the door for her to leave, she closed it and kissed me again."

It had been a long and slow kiss, full of regret. Sadness. She stroked my face, said, *Thank you, my beautiful stranger,* and left.

"Reality didn't hit me until I pulled up to the gate at the parking garage and thought about the life that I was driving back to. The idea of sharing the same bed with Charlie revolted me. I couldn't bear the idea of going home, so I went to the nearest bar. That's how I ended up with the DUI. I couldn't deny to myself who I was any longer, but I couldn't leave my life either. Leave Logan."

"What else?"

"What do you mean, what else?"

"The same reason you have to admit you're an alcoholic out loud. You deny it, you backslide."

"Backslide into heterosexuality? I don't think so."

"Look, Sophie, sure, I get the subtext. If you want to move forward, you have to say it aloud. You know that. It's why you called me."

"But, once I admit it, it's real."

"The hard part is over."

I laughed. "No, it's not." I rubbed my hands on the table, inhaled deeply and blurted it out. "I'm gay, I'm still in love with Nora, and I don't know what to do."

"How do you feel?" Todd said, smiling like a proud papa.

The relief at not being rejected was all-consuming. I grinned. "Better than how I felt when I told my mother."

"You told Brenda? Today?"

"Yes. A few hours ago. I don't know if she believed me or not."

"Why?"

"Everything I've done over since Nora left has been running away from it. I can see how she would think Nora was a phase. But, it's not. This is who I am, and I've known deep down since I was little. Then, I didn't have the words to explain how I felt different. With Nora, I could delude myself that it was specifically her I loved, and I did. For years. Until Erica."

"What are you going to do?"

"I don't know. The idea of telling anyone else is terrifying. I don't think I could handle being rejected by my daughter. So, this will most likely be the end of it. My mother will never tell because she will never believe it. You won't tell because you're my sponsor, which means I can go on being a coward for God knows how long."

"A coward wouldn't have told me that story. A coward wouldn't be getting her year chip this Saturday."

I shifted in my seat.

"You *are* still getting your chip on Saturday?"

I shook my head, and Todd's proud papa expression changed to concern.

"It was half a beer." I swallowed. I think I'd dreaded this part of the conversation the most. Admitting my weakness. My eyes burned with tears and knew I wouldn't be able to hold back the building sob. When I spoke, my voice was half pleading, half crying. "I didn't mean to. I didn't want to. I never thought, *I'm going to drink that beer.*" I sniffed back the rivers of snot that were starting to flow. "It was Nora's beer. Her lips—" I pointed to my mouth "—her lips had touched that bottle. That was all I could think about. And, I…" I closed my eyes and touched my lips, remembering the glass, the beads of beer clinging to the edge of the mouth, the yeasty smell, the warmth I imagined was still there from her lips, gone only moments before. "All I wanted was to put my lips where hers had been. That's all I thought about. Her lips. How that cold bottle might be the closest I would ever get to ever touching them again." I opened my eyes. Todd watched me, an expression of wonder on his face, and it broke me.

I covered my hands with my face and cried freely. Todd moved into the booth next to me, his strong arm around me, and the next thing I knew I'd buried my face in his neck and sobbed freely. Still, I tried to talk. "I didn't realize I'd drank it until Nora found it empty. I know it was a stupid thing to do. An entire year of work down the drain and for what?"

"Have you had a drink since?"

"No."

"That's what matters, Soph. Your work's not down the drain."

"But, I still have to start over? Counting?"

"Yeah."

"Fuck."

Todd leaned over and pulled paper napkins out of the holder. I wiped my eyes and blew my nose.

Todd kept his arm around me, supporting me. "You know what?" he asked.

"What?"

"I think this date will mean more for you in the long run. Because it's connected not to a failure or a mistake, but the journey back to someone you love."

"You really are a glass half-full kinda guy."

He smiled and shrugged. "You okay now?"

"Yeah. Thanks for meeting me on such short notice."

"Of course."

He slid back into his side of the booth.

I sniffed again. "All this time, I've thought my drinking was because of the guilt about how everything ended. Lying about Nora. Me and Charlie. And jealousy that Nora escaped, and I didn't. Every time I got news of Nora, I would go on a binge. I never expected the urge to drink would return when she was here, when we'd patched everything up."

"Why do you think that is?"

"I don't deserve to be happy."

"Hell, Sophie, if none of us deserved to be happy based on what we did when we were eighteen, the world would be full of miserable people."

"What would Logan say? Charlie? Having a lesbian ex-wife won't help his campaign. That's assuming he'll divorce me. He hasn't so far, and I've given him lots of reasons to."

"Why does he have to divorce you? If you want to leave him, go."

"It's not that easy."

"The hardest part is admitting it's over. Take it from a man who's done it three times."

"People will ask why."

"You don't have to tell people shit. Ain't none of their business."

"The gossip."

"Fuck that."

"You know, that's easy for a man to say. *Fuck that! It ain't no-body's business. You don't have to tell people shit.* Men leave all the time. No one cares. Women who leave their families? Christ, they're never forgiven. Ever. That's a fucking fact of life, and you know it. And, for me to leave my family because I'm a *lesbian?*" I rested my forehead in my hands. "Jesus, I can't believe I'm even thinking about it."

Todd was quiet so long I finally looked up. "You're right. I'm sorry," he said.

I sat back and pulled my coffee toward me, cradling it in my hands, but not drinking it. "Charlie has been a good husband. A better one than I deserved. He's innocent in all of this. Completely clueless about me and Nora, why she left. I've been lying to him for all this time and…I feel guilty. I used him at first, but I did fall in love with him. Briefly. I love him still, but since last year, it's like I'm sleeping with my brother. I have zero desire, and when it's over, I feel dirty."

"Whatever you do, don't ever tell Charlie that."

"I wouldn't." I motioned for the waitress to refill my coffee cup. After she left, I said, "Taking that sip of beer set me and Logan back. If I came out or left Charlie now, I would lose her forever. On the other hand, I can't bear the thought of Nora leaving town without me."

"Will she stay for you?"

I drank the coffee, felt its bitter bite on the back of my tongue, tried to fool myself into thinking it was Maker's. "We kissed today. In my car. Behind an abandoned building. God, it sounds so sordid."

"The way you're blushing, it probably was."

"It felt…right." I put my fist to my heart. "Like I was finally whole again."

Todd raised his eyebrows.

"To answer your question, I don't know if she would stay for me. But, I know that the spark is still there."

I grasped the back of my neck and closed my eyes, massaging the tension knot that had formed.

"If this was anyone else I would say sleep with her, get her out of your system," Todd said. "But, you can't do that."

"Because I'm married? Charlie's been cheating on me for years."

"No, because you're an alcoholic in your first year of recovery. The rule may be unwritten, but it's there for a reason."

"I'm not going to worry about it right now. I need to make amends. Tell her my story."

Todd reached for my hand. "It's the right first step in truly repairing your relationship. Maybe, in time, you two can be together."

"You know if Nora breaks my heart, you're the only shoulder I have to cry on."

"How'd you like it? Broad enough? Strong enough?"

"Yes. And, please, never stop smelling like fresh-hewn lumber."

"I'll do my best."

fourteen
nora

The Dumpsters arrived at two, one for recyclables and one for the junk, and forced me to confront the daunting task. I hadn't heard from Mary, so I was going forward with the idea she wasn't interested in Ray's things. I knew she wouldn't be. Her house in Austin was decorated in the trendy Texas thrift store style. Mary wasn't sentimental enough to try to shoehorn Ray's worst of the seventies and eighties aesthetic into her own.

Still, I figured someone, somewhere, might want this shit. Before I could talk myself out of it, I put an ad on Craigslist for an estate sale for Sunday, one to four. All prices negotiable! Everything must go! Little did the junkers know I intended to give everything away. I didn't want to cause a stampede, after all.

I left myself only four days to get it ready, plenty of time for a military mind like mine to whip this place into shape. But, I knew I couldn't do it alone. I called Sophie.

"I was about to call you," she said. I could hear the smile in her voice, and my stomach did a little flip at the promise our kiss held, the possibilities I dared not think about.

Kissing Sophie had probably been a mistake, but I couldn't help myself, not when she looked at me with those eyes. The naked vulnerability, the flushed cheeks, her gaze on my lips, her cool hand in mine. I'm only human, after all.

I didn't return to Lynchfield with the intention of making up with Sophie, let alone falling back in love with her. Now I knew it had been inevitable. There was no closure with our relationship, at least not for me. It was why it took me more than a decade to imagine a life with another person, even though Alima was as unattainable as Sophie. I knew, deep down, that Sophie would never leave Charlie, or Logan, or come out in this town. The chance to do that was in the summer of '95 when we could have escaped cleanly. No, she was tied to Lynchfield now and had been denying who she was for too long. If she wanted a physical relationship with no strings, I would give it to her. Especially after the frantic fondling in her car. But, she had to make the move. She had the most to lose.

Regardless of what happened or didn't happen with Sophie, I needed to deal with Ray's house, so I could get back to DC. I missed work, missed the stress, the teamwork, the feeling of contributing something essential to our country, though no one would ever know about what I did. I missed going to yoga and sparring at the gym. I missed the stupid pillow I sat on when I meditated. Four days of intense focus on ridding my life of every last vestige of Raymond Noakes, then I could address the Sophie issue. And leave.

"I have good news and bad news," I said, cutting to the chase.

"Oh. Okay," Sophie said.

"Good news, the Dumpsters arrived. Bad news, I've set up an estate sale for Sunday afternoon."

"This Sunday? What the hell, Nora?"

"I can't stay here forever," I said. "Work understands to a point."

Sophie was silent. I could hear Nirvana playing in the background, and the hum of the car AC on full blast. I lifted my eyes to the sky and silently cursed myself. That came out wrong.

"Sophie, I…"

"So we're going to pretend like the kiss never happened? Okay. Got it. I'll text you Joe's number, though I don't know if he will be able to help on such short notice."

I waited for a beat, barely resisting the temptation to tell her how I felt; that I thought about her incessantly, that each of our conversations were seared in my brain, that there were a million more things I wanted to tell her, to ask her, that I didn't even care that she beat me at tennis because it was so much like our life when we were happy, and our future together was laid out in front of us like a long West Texas road that disappeared into infinity, that I didn't realize how I missed her South Texas twang until I heard it again, that my need for her hummed through my body at all hours of the day, that I was still in love with her, that all of the men and women I'd been with had been a pale attempt to forget her, that I regretted them all.

That's what I wanted to tell her. But, I couldn't do it. I didn't trust that when all was said and done, that she would choose me over her safe life in Lynchfield.

"Nora? Are you still there?"

"Ye-yeah," I stuttered. I cleared my throat. "I wondered if Logan and her friends might want to make some extra money?" I said.

"I'm sure they will. I'll call her. How much will you pay them?"

"Oh. A hundred bucks each."

"A hundred dollars? Jesus. You'll probably get the whole high school out there."

"Then let's limit it to five people."

"Wise choice. Will tomorrow be soon enough?"

"Sure." I heard Sophie's blinker clicking off and on.

"Great. They'll be there at nine. I'm driving so I better…" Sophie said.

"Wait. I have a question for you and I need an honest answer."

"Okay."

"You're close with Emmadean. Is she sick?"

The pause was almost imperceptible. "Why do you ask?"

"Sophie," I said.

"Emmadean's getting old, and she's never been exactly healthy."

Indignation rose in my chest. "What are you saying?"

"Nora," Sophie said. "You need to talk to Emmadean, not me."

"You know what's wrong."

"Not what I said."

"I can tell you're lying even over the phone."

"Oh, you can? Funny, I haven't told one lie yet."

"Yet! So, you're going to."

"Good Lord, stop it. Talk to your aunt."

"Already tried. Emmadean's evasive. Stubborn."

"Sounds familiar."

"Watch it, Sophie. I'm going to get it out of Dormer."

Sophie laughed, and it felt like someone was skipping double Dutch in my chest. "Good luck with that. Dormer is terrified of Emmadean, as am I."

"I have my ways."

"I'm sure you do, J. Edgar."

I barely had time to revel in how quickly our rapport had clicked in when I saw a black car with dark windows drive slowly down the Ranch to Market road in front of my house. "I don't suppose Kim drives a Town Car, does she?"

"No. Why?"

"She's coming by to walk through the house," I said. The car stopped just past my driveway, backed up and turned in. I knew the plates wouldn't be government issue, but I knew the occupant was.

The car stopped in front of my house. The door opened, and a narrow foot in a four-inch wedge stepped onto the ground.

An avalanche of conflicting emotions roared through me and turned my fingers to ice.

"Nora? Did you hear me?"

"No."

"We need to talk; we can't leave what hap—"

"I'm going to have to call you back," I said and hung up on Sophie as my married girlfriend, Alima Koshkam, stepped out of the car.

Alima closed the car door and looked around, a disbelieving smirk on her face. I'd described my childhood home to her, but I'd apparently missed the mark by a mile. The driver retrieved her suitcase, which was alarmingly large, and set it on the porch next to me. Alima gave him a large tip, told him to expect a call for return pickup in the next few days, and turned her attention to me. I knew she was giving me the opportunity to take her in head to foot. She'd struck the same pose many times, leg cocked out to the side, hand on her hip, wearing nothing but her heels. No doubt, she hoped for a similar response from me now.

The car backed out, and Alima strutted up to me, the dust of the driveway swirling around her. "Good Lord, you've gone native."

I looked down at the ridiculous outfit I'd cobbled together from Ray's clothes. "Work clothes."

"Luckily, I broke into your condo and brought clothes that fit you."

"Oh my God, thank you."

"And your meditation pillow."

"You're a lifesaver."

Alima stopped on the bottom step, but with her heels and her height, we were almost eye to eye.

"Are you going to kiss me or stand there gaping at me?"

I looked around, and Alima laughed. "We're in the middle of nowhere, Nora. Who will possibly see us?"

I pinched her chin and pulled her toward me, kissing her lightly on the lips. Her eyes, dark pools of chocolate, met mine. "You're going to have to do better than that."

"Alima…"

"Come on. Show me inside." She preceded me into the house, and I picked up her suitcase and followed.

It wasn't a lie when I told Sophie that Alima was a coworker. She was. Originally. We worked in the same department, managing two different translation groups; Farsi for her, Arabic for me. A friendly competition between us was soon a solid friendship. She was regal and outgoing, the perfect counterpoint to my salt-of-the-earth girl-next-door reserve. I opened up to her in a way I hadn't with anyone, man or woman, since Sophie. The night I told her about Sophie, over two bottles of wine, we ended up in bed together, the wedding ring on her finger a nice safety valve against commitment. I'd half expected her to claim drunkenness the next day, but she hadn't; she'd pretended it never happened. As the weeks wore on, I began to question my memory and my sanity. Then I would remember the round bruise on my inner thigh, and her grin after she gave it to me.

"My husband is going on a business trip to Asia for two weeks," she said casually one day over lunch.

"Do you get lonely when he's gone for so long?"

"Usually."

"Not this time?"

"That depends on you."

Those two weeks I got a glimpse of what a relationship with another person would be like, and I longed for it. The intimacy, the companionship, the comfort of knowing you were the most important person in the world to another. The latter I deluded myself about; Alima was married, with college-aged children and an extended Persian family. A committed, long-term, out-in-the-open relationship with her was impossible. Up until those two weeks, Alima or someone like her had been my ideal lover, and we'd settled into the precise relationship I'd always wanted: passionate, fun and completely free of expectations. I'd told myself I was happy with the arrangement and I was. I am. I'm happy enough I have no desire to cruise the DC area to find someone who could give me a truly monogamous, committed relationship. Maybe I was lazy. Maybe I was content using the obstacle of Alima's marriage to protect my heart. Maybe I loved Alima enough that what we have is enough. Maybe I was happy I'd finally found someone who can stack up to Sophie and was content to have her however she'll have me, and for as long as she'll have me. Maybe it's all of it.

I did lie to Sophie about the number of lovers I've had since I started seeing Alima. I'd had two—one man and one woman—and I'd felt guilty after each one. Alima knew she couldn't very well refuse me lovers; she went home to her husband every night. As far as she knew, I still had occasional one-night stands, but I didn't. I enjoyed monogamy and I especially enjoyed not going to overcrowded bars with overpriced drinks and political operatives who thought the president was either the second coming or the anti-Christ. There was no in-between these days.

Alima and I had stolen lunches and long stretches of coupledom when her husband was away. I loved Alima, and she loved me. I'd given some thought to what our life might be like if she did leave her husband, and I liked what I imagined. But, Alima had never suggested it or even hinted that it was something she wanted. And neither had I. After seeing Sophie again, I was glad I hadn't.

"So, this is where you grew up?" Alima said, twirling her sunglasses and taking in the cheap wood-paneled walls, the flattened shag carpet and the mounds of magazines I'd pulled out of all the cabinets and closets. She picked up a *Field and Stream* magazine, raising her sculpted eyebrows in disbelieving good humor. "You didn't do it justice."

"If this is too beneath you, I bet you can get your driver back here in ten minutes or less."

Her eyes widened, and she dropped the magazine back on the pile. "Touchy."

"I'm not in the mood."

"Because I surprised you?"

"No," I lied. I thought of how out of the way Lynchfield was, and the effort it had taken her to get here. "I'm glad you're here," I said, and I was. She was the closest thing to a best friend I'd had in years, and besides Sophie, she'd been my lover for the longest. *Sophie.*

"Did you miss me?" Alima looked at me from beneath her brows and, though I fought it, felt guilty about it, I felt the familiar stirring.

"I always miss you."

She moved to me, taking the initiative, as usual. I'd never made the first move, with any lover. I needed to be wanted before I could want in return and, God help me, I wanted her. Someone. Desperately.

I pulled her to me roughly, my hand wrapped into her long hair. Her eyes widened in surprise, and I took the lead for the first time in my life.

We fucked in Ray's bed, and I have to be honest, it was some of the best sex we'd ever had. No doubt a psychoanalyst would have a field day with that.

Alima lay next to me, her dark hair splayed across the pillow, a thin sheen of sweat covering her body. "That was…"

"Intense." I propped myself on my elbow. "Amazing."

Her eyes searched my face. "Hmm. Not the words I was looking for." She rose, and sat on the edge of the bed, her back to me.

I moved behind her and kissed her bare shoulder. "What's wrong?"

Alima's eyes were a deep brown, with little golden flecks

around the iris. When they met mine, they were troubled, wary. "You've never made love to me like that."

"Unless I'm mistaken, you enjoyed it as much as I did."

"Yes, but..."

"But, what, Alima? You only like me when you're in charge?"

She rose and went to her suitcase, and I saw a faint bruise on the back of her arm. The shape of a hand. My hand. The passion, confidence from earlier drained out of me, refilled with guilt and shame. "Alima, I..."

"Nora, I've wanted that from you for a long time. To feel like you truly want me."

"I always want you. You know that."

Alima turned and smiled thinly. "Not like today, you haven't."

"Why are you complaining then?"

"I don't like the reason, Nora."

"Because you're beautiful and sexy as hell and you came one thousand miles to help me?"

"Have you seen Sophie today?"

"She has nothing to do with this."

"God, you're a terrible liar."

We were silent.

"Well, then," Alima said. She turned back to her suitcase. "I had today all planned out. In Montreal. Taking you to brunch at L'Express. We would gorge ourselves; their French toast is amazing. We would walk it off through Mount Royal Park and up to Belvédère Camillien-Houde. It's beautiful up there. Very romantic."

She turned and tossed something to me. I caught it awkwardly and looked down at a small square box. Tiffany blue. My stomach lurched. I wasn't sure if I was going to be sick, or sob with joy.

"Open it."

It was a platinum band of a dozen emerald-cut diamonds. Beautiful, simple and elegant. Precisely what I would want.

"I've left my husband, Nora. For you."

"You... But, we haven't talked about this. I thought..."

"You thought I was safe. Unattainable. I was, for a long time. But, somewhere along the way, I fell in love with you."

"I don't know what to say."

"That you love me too would be nice."

"You know I do."

"Who were you making love to just now, hmm? Me, or Sophie?"

"Alima..."

"You don't even know, do you?"

"Of course I do."

Alima sighed and rolled her eyes. She turned around and pulled on a tank top. "I'm not going to play this game with you. You know where I stand. You're holding proof of it." She put on her panties and faced me. "Does your high school lover want you back?"

I looked down at the ring, thinking of earlier, kissing Sophie, her hand on my breast, my hand running up her smooth thigh, feeling the lace of her panties, the warmth, the way Sophie opened her legs, inviting more. The fucking phone call that stopped it all. Life, Sophie's life, would always get in the way.

"Sophie's not a former lover anymore, is she?" Alima said.

"Yes, no. She is. Still former."

"Something happened, though."

I nodded. "It was just a kiss."

Alima laughed. "Oh, I doubt that very much. She's been living in the closet for her entire life. That's a lot of pent-up frustration. She has an itch that needs to be scratched, and you were right there to help."

"It was more than that."

"You're contradicting yourself. Was it just a kiss or was it more?"

I sighed and put the box on the bed next to me. "I don't know. You're making this very difficult, Alima."

"Good." She sat next to me. "It shouldn't be easy, Nora. I love you. I want to spend the rest of my life with you. You know what I'm giving up for you, don't you?"

Her entire family. They would disown Alima, banish her for leaving her husband for a woman. Her children might come around; they held more modern ideas than the older generation, but it wasn't a guarantee. Alima had taken an enormous leap of faith on my love, loyalty and dedication to her.

"Yes."

"A week ago you would have said yes, wouldn't you?"

"I thought we were happy the way things were."

"It's not enough for me anymore. It hasn't been for a while. I want to wake up next to you every morning. Drink tea and read the paper together. Travel. Spend the weekend in bed."

I shook my head in disbelief. "When I imagined a life with you it's just like that."

"But, Sophie."

I shrugged. If I hadn't come home, seen Sophie, kissed her, if Alima and I had gone to Montreal and she had proposed to me on top of Belvédère Camillien-Houde, I would have said yes. Without hesitation. "Yeah, but Sophie," I whispered.

She spoke softly. "You know you two aren't the same people you were twenty years ago, don't you? You're risking what we have for an ideal."

"This isn't exactly fair, Alima."

She leaned back a little. "How so?"

"There's been zero hint that you were considering this. We have an open relationship, so of course if an old lover wants... I'm going to be open to it."

"She isn't just an old lover, though is she?" She smiled and caressed my face. "You're absolutely right. We have an open re-lationship. This ring doesn't give me the right to tell you what to do. I'd never do that regardless. But, listen to me, and listen well: I want you. All of you. All the time. For us to have any chance of a future, you have to settle things with Sophie. I don't want you always to wonder what if with Sophie, and I don't want her ghost in our bed like today. So, go. Have one of your one-night stands—"

"Alima..."

"—get Sophie out of your system. But, when I put that ring on your finger, that's it. For both of us. Full commitment to only each other."

"You're confident."

"Because there's one crucial difference between Sophie and me: I won't break your heart. She has, and she will again. Something to keep in mind before you sleep with her."

Alima put the box in my hand and closed it. "Keep this for now." She rose and walked to the bathroom. "I'm taking a shower. Then I suppose you need to put me to work. No need to waste free labor."

I was in the kitchen making lunch, wondering how my life had suddenly become a train wreck, and plotting how I was going to get Alima out of town without meeting Sophie, when Kim knocked on my front door.

"Kim. I completely forgot you were coming."

"I texted I was on my way."

"Oh, right." I hadn't looked at my phone since Alima drove up.

"Gosh," she said, walking in and looking around much as Alima did, but with less judgment, "I haven't been here since high school."

I smiled, trying to remember when I'd ever invited Kim to my house. Ray hadn't been a fan of slumber parties. Our walls were too thin for him to deal with five or six giggling girls who stayed up until all hours of the night. And most everyone was afraid of Ray. Except for Sophie. He liked her because she talked to him about cows and his job, his two favorite subjects. Sophie had a little bit of Eddie Haskell in her, but my father didn't realize she was manipulating him. If Ray had a soft spot for anyone, he had one for Sophie. Brenda Russell's revelation had been a betrayal to him on two fronts.

"It hasn't changed much," I said.

"No. Mind if I look around?"

"Sure. Hold off on my, um…dad's room. A friend is visiting from DC to help with everything."

"Wow. What a friend."

I suppressed a grin. I wondered if Kim was astute enough to see what kind of friend Alima was. Did I care if she did? Not really. I hadn't come out to anyone in Lynchfield, and I didn't intend to. But, I wasn't going to go to great lengths to keep my sexuality a secret either.

"Have you had lunch? I'll heat us up some King Ranch Chicken."

"A couple of hours ago. Thanks anyway."

"Did I hear someone say lunch?" Alima walked into the den, rubbing her dark, wet hair with a towel, wearing impossibly short shorts and a tank without a bra. For a woman pushing fifty, she was striking. Why would I risk this for the uncertainty Sophie would bring into my life? Talk about a potential train wreck.

Kim's mouth dropped open, and she emitted a little "oh" as someone knocked on the front door.

"Kim, Alima, Alima, Kim," I said, as I went automatically to the door. They were exchanging pleasantries when I opened it.

Sophie stood on my porch, looking unsure of herself, and a little flushed. "Hey."

My breath rushed out of me at the sight of her, and I was right back in Sophie's car. It wasn't the kiss I thought of, but the joy of sitting with her and…talking.

"Oh, hey. I didn't know you were coming by."

"I, um…well…was hoping we could…um…." She pushed her sunglasses onto her head and her gaze drifted to my lips. Her neck turned splotchy. I remembered that reaction. "Talk. About earlier, and other stuff."

She looked past me and saw Kim and Alima. Her confused gaze lingered on Alima. "Hi, Kim."

Oh, Christ. So much for getting Alima out of town.

"Sophie. Have you met Nora's friend from DC?"

Sophie's shoulders lifted along with her chin in a show of arrogance, or dominance. "I haven't had the pleasure."

Alima stepped forward, hand outstretched. She smelled like vanilla shampoo. "Alima Koshkam."

"Sophie Wyatt." They shook hands, and recognition passed between them.

"I've heard a lot about you," Alima said.

"I hope you won't hold any of it against me."

"Not at all. Nora says you two have buried the hatchet."

"You have?" Kim said. "That's fantastic!"

"It's good to have my best friend back," Sophie said.

"For a little while anyway," Alima said.

"How long are you in town for?" Kim asked.

"For as long as Nora wants."

Sophie's eyebrows rose. Neither she or Alima had taken their eyes from the other.

Kim looked between them. "It's a little uncanny how much you two look alike." The women turned to Kim. "Dark hair and eyes, similar complexion." I saw a germ of an idea forming in Kim's mind.

"Why don't you start the walk-through, Kim," I said, pushing between Sophie and Alima and directing Kim toward the hall. "Actually, you can start in Ray's room. At the end of the hall."

"How do you do it?" Kim asked as we walked down the hall.

"Do what?"

"Encourage such loyalty in your friends."

"It's a gift."

She stopped when she saw Alima's suitcase on the floor next to mine.

"It's not what you think." Maybe I *would* go to great lengths to keep my secret in Lynchfield.

"Too bad." Her gaze flickered down the hall toward Alima and Sophie. "It would explain a lot."

"Kim…"

"Don't worry. I've suspected it for years and never said a word. I wouldn't now either. Someone close to me is gay, I…understand the fear." She looked down and away. "Too well." She put a bright smile on and patted my arm. "No need to babysit me. Maybe we can talk later, though."

"Sure," I said.

"There's a little Spanish blood in my family," Sophie was saying when I returned.

"Makes sense. I wouldn't expect to meet a Persian out here in the middle of Texas."

The two women looked at me as I stood there, dumbly, at the end of the hall.

"I, uh, better be going," Sophie said.

"I'll walk you out," I said.

"No need." Sophie stopped at the door. "I don't know if Nora mentioned it, but we're having a dinner for her Friday night. If you're still in town, we would love for you to join us."

"I wouldn't miss it. Thank you."

Kim was at the end of the hall. "Oh, that sounds fun!"

Give Sophie credit; she kept her composure when I knew she wanted to scream at Kim to fuck off. "We'd love for you and Joe to come, too."

"Thank you! What can I bring?"

"I'll text you. See y'all later."

I caught her at her car door. "Wait up."

Sophie tossed her purse into the passenger seat and turned to face me, her sunglasses firmly covering her eyes. "Was she here this morning? Before we…?"

"*No*. Christ, Sophie. Is that what you think of me?"

"What am I supposed to think? It's pretty clear all I'm going to be is a notch on your bedpost."

"No, you're not. I lied, okay, and I'm sorry. Your fuck buddies comment pissed me off. We're in an open relationship, but I'm monogamous. If I knew she was coming I wouldn't have kissed you and I damn sure would have told you."

Sophie reached out and pulled the neck of my T-shirt. "I see you had a nice reunion."

I shrugged away and pulled the collar to cover the hickey.

"Is she why you're so eager to get back to DC?"

"Give me a reason to stay."

Sophie's mouth tightened, and I followed where I thought her gaze had settled. Alima leaned against the front door jamb, watching us with a sly smile. When I turned around, Sophie was getting in her car. She rolled down her window, started her car and said, "That's why I came by."

As her window rolled up, she said, "See you and Alima Friday."

fifteen
sophie

"You invited *who*?"

"Jamie and Trent. Kim just happened to mention you invited her and Joe over. I couldn't very well not invite them, Sophie," Charlie said.

"Yes, you very well could have."

"What's four more people?"

"Four? Who else?" Sophie said.

"Tiffany and Richard."

"Jesus Christ."

"You know the grief we would get if we invited Kim and Jamie and not Tiffany?" Charlie said.

"When are we going to fucking move past high school pettiness?"

"Not today. Calm down. It's four more people, and Trent is bringing two cases of beer."

"Well, the one thing I'm *not* in charge of, nor can I drink, is taken care of. Thank you so much."

"Sophie…"

"And, don't fucking tell me to *calm down*. This was supposed to be dinner for four—you, me, Logan, and Nora. Now it's turned into, what? Sixteen people?"

"We'll use paper plates. And, I'm helping, don't forget."

I inhaled and counted to ten. Charlie's version of helping was grilling the meat and making sure everyone had a beer in their hand. Everything else fell to me. I'd only marinated enough fajita meat for twelve people, assuming Logan and her friends might swing through at some point. Our refrigerator had been decimated too many times by hungry teenagers for me to be unprepared. Now I needed another pound or two of unfrozen, marinated meat, which I didn't have. I would have to send Logan to the store for the prepackaged stuff. I threw up a little in my mouth at the thought. I pulled a scratch pad and pen from the junk drawer and started a list.

The doorbell rang. "Who's thirty minutes early?" I said.

Charlie went to the door. "I asked Avery and Mark to get here early."

"Thanks for the heads up," I said, keeping my focus on the list.

"Brenda," Charlie said.

"Hello, Charlie."

I put my elbows on the counter and rested my head in my hands. *You've got to be kidding me.* I hadn't spoken to my mother since Wednesday, and it had been a pleasant two days.

"Um, nice to see you," Charlie said. "What do you have there?"

"Spanish rice. I know Sophie doesn't ever make it and thought it would be a nice addition to the menu."

"Oh. Sophie, look who's here."

I stood and plastered a smile on my face. "Hello, Mother." Charlie was behind Brenda, shrugging and mouthing, *I did not invite her.* I shook my head at him. "How unexpected."

"I've come to help."

I laughed. She came to keep an eye on Nora and me. "Charlie, would you go get the avocados from the back fridge?"

"Sure."

When he was out of earshot, I said, "I know why you're here."

"I've been waiting for your call, Sophia."

"My call."

"To apologize."

I laughed again.

"That's why I'm here."

"No, it's not. And, you're going to be waiting a long time for an apology. Like until hell freezes over." I turned away from her to stir the beans in the Crock-Pot, but the anger and frustration and shame inside me swirled together until I thought I was going to explode. I turned abruptly toward my mother and pulled her close. In her ear, I said, "I told you something I'd never told anyone, and your reaction…it wasn't one of a loving mother. It was selfish and vindictive and…"

Her blue eyes met mine. "…and every word was true."

"I will never apologize to you, never answer the phone when you call, answer your texts. You're ashamed to have me as a daughter? I'm horrified that you're my mother. Stay tonight if you want, it'll probably be a good show. But, after this? We're done."

"The town will talk."

"I don't give a good goddamn what the town says. I've been run through the gossip mill before, and I can survive it again."

Charlie came back with the avocados. "Here. Start the guac." I shoved the bag in her hand and walked toward the stairs.

Charlie followed me. "Did you invite her?"

"God, no. She's here to make sure I don't use paper plates."

"Are you serious? Of course you are. It's Brenda."

I started up the stairs. "I'm sending Logan to the store."

"I'll go," Charlie called from the bottom.

"Like hell, you will. You need to be here to greet all of the fucking people you invited. And, try to keep my mother away from me."

I knocked on Logan's door and entered without waiting for her reply. Big mistake.

Joaquin's naked brown body blocked my daughter from view except for her splayed legs and tanned face visible above his shoulder with an expression I never wanted or expected to see.

Anger and shock and disgust roiled inside me. What was he doing to my daughter, who just yesterday had been on her bed, lying on her stomach, coloring in an American Girl coloring book, legs bent and scissoring back and forth, brow furrowed as she made sure to stay inside the lines? Or at least it seemed like yesterday. I grabbed Joaquin's ankle to pull him off my daughter. Joaquin flinched, and Logan saw me.

"Mom, get out!"

I stopped, dizzy from déjà vu. I saw myself on the bed, watching my mother drag Nora from me and throw her to the ground, the screaming and tears that followed, the welts on Nora's shoulders from the tennis racket my mother beat Nora with.

I released Joaquin's ankle and closed the door behind me. I kept my back turned, staring at the door, and told Joaquin to take his clothes and get in the bathroom.

"Mrs. Wyatt." I could hear him picking up his clothes. "This isn't…"

"We all know exactly what this is." I grabbed my stomach, afraid I was going to throw up. "Please tell me you're wearing a condom."

"*Mom.*"

"Yes, ma'am."

"Thank God."

The door to the bathroom clicked shut. I turned to face my daughter. She'd pulled a blanket up to cover herself.

"Are you insane, Mom?"

"Logan, shut up. Your grandmother and father are downstairs."

"Grandmother?"

"Yes. She invited herself to our dinner party, the one that's starting in twenty-five minutes. Did you forget?"

"No."

"Right, so you just decided to…" I rubbed my forehead.

Nora and I had sex in my house when my parents were down the hall, so berating Logan for it was the height of hypocrisy. But, seeing your daughter… *Jesus. Don't tell me I'm about to fucking relate to my mother.*

"Forget it. I need you to go to the store. Here's the list."

"Didn't you buy enough?"

I walked to the bed and leaned down into my daughter's face. "You are in no position right now to give me attitude, do you hear me? One day, I'll tell you the story about when Grandmother caught me like this, and you'll know how much worse this could be. Now, here's what you're going to do: get dressed, go to the store, come back and do everything I ask you to do to make this dinner party go off without a hitch. You, too, Joaquin."

Joaquin was trying to tiptoe out of the room. "Me?"

"Yes. That's your punishment for trying to get a quick fuck in before coming down and sitting at my dinner table. Understand?"

"Yes, ma'am."

"Why are you so mad?" Logan seethed. "We just had a conversation about this. I guess you lie about everything now."

I inhaled sharply. "Bathroom. Now."

I put the toilet seat down and sat. Christ, I needed a drink. Or a valium. Both would be preferable. The last two days had challenged my sobriety more than any other time in the previous year. The pull was constant, the desire mingled with anxiety and fear and hurt and anger, a toxic cocktail of emotions for a recovering addict. I'd texted with Todd regularly and he'd managed to talk me down every time. This, though, on top of what waited for me in thirty minutes, might be too much.

Logan came into the bathroom, and I saw my teenage self in her expression.

"Our conversation the other day? Wasn't giving you permission to have sex in our house," I said.

"Oh, so you'd rather us do it in a car at Comanche Springs?"

"Honestly? I'd rather you not do it at all. I'm trying really hard here not to be a hypocrite, to treat you like a responsible... teenager. I meant what I said the other day, but it's a different thing entirely when you see it. It was abstract before, you know."

She crossed her arms over her chest. "I guess."

"Would you want to see Dad and me having sex?"

"No."

I stood and took Logan in my arms. "I'm sorry if I'm confusing you. I'm confused on a lot of fronts these days."

"I'm sorry, too." After a brief pause, she said, "Are you bipolar?"

I held Logan at arm's length and heard the doorbell chime in the distance. "Bipolar?"

"You just go back and forth so much lately. Like, right now."

And here I thought I'd done an excellent job of masking my turmoil. Charlie hadn't seemed to notice, or he didn't want the drama that would undoubtedly result from asking. My daughter, though, she saw everything, and she was right.

I was jealous and angry at Nora for fucking someone only hours after sliding her hand up my dress. It told me I was nothing but someone for her to sleep with and abandon. I might have been okay with that until I met Alima. It was the wake-up call I needed. Nora's life had been a hypothetical before. Coming face-to-face with Alima, her confidence, the air of sophistication that surrounded her, it struck me Alima was the woman I'd intended to be before everything fell apart.

Nora had done it. She was living the life we'd planned, dreamed of, during all our nights together. I wasn't Alima, could never be her, or give Nora the life she had.

Accepting that life with Nora was out of reach had freed me to focus on my work, my family, my life. It wasn't the one I intended, but it was the one I had, and I could either be miserable in it or accept it. I'd looked forward to the dinner party to prove to myself, and Nora, of my acceptance of her friend, and her life. I would ask Nora to meet for coffee, make amends, and move on with my life.

The idea made me sick to my stomach, which I grasped.

"Mom, are you sick?"

"No, honey. I don't think I'm bipolar, just um… I've had some news that threw me for a loop."

"What news?"

I stoked Logan's hair. "Honey, I love you. You're the most important person in the world to me. But, there are some things that I want to keep to myself. You have secrets, things you keep from everyone else, yeah?"

She shrugged one shoulder. "Yeah."

"And that's fine. Really. I'm working through some stuff. I'll be better soon."

"Sure. Okay."

"I do still need your help."

"Yeah. Whatever you need."

I checked myself in the mirror. My hair was up in what Logan called my artfully messy bun that had ironically taken an inordinate amount of time to make look effortless. Natural makeup and lipstick, a sky blue maxidress with a sweetheart neckline and spaghetti straps. I leaned forward, dabbing at my lips, and noticed faint freckles on my chest and down into my cleavage.

"I'm showing too much skin, aren't I? Not very appropriate for a future state senator's wife."

"You look beautiful. Dad's gonna love it."

I smiled at her. I wasn't dressing to impress her dad or his political operatives. I wanted to show Nora what she was missing.

"You aren't going to tell Dad, are you? About catching us."

"No. Can you get to the store and back in twenty minutes?"

"Sure."

I kissed her forehead and told her I loved her. She grasped my hand before I could turn. "What did you mean about Grandmother earlier? Did she catch you and Dad?"

I cleared my throat. "That's a story for another time, okay?"

"Promise?"

I nodded because I couldn't lie outright to my daughter.

I walked down the stairs on shaky legs and saw Charlie talking to his two political operatives.

"Sophie, Avery and Mark are here," Charlie said, stating the obvious.

"Hi, Sophie," Avery said. "Good to see you again."

"You, too."

Avery wore a simple sundress that hit midthigh, and nude wedges. Her long blond hair was pulled back with her sunglasses, and she wore less makeup than when I'd met her previously. Her casual, country look, no doubt. She was dressed a lot like me.

The bespectacled young man stepped forward. "Mark Pryor."

I shook his hand. "Nice to meet you. Have you met my mother, Brenda?"

"Yes, just now."

Brenda's lips were puckered, no doubt puzzling over what to think of Mark. Was he gay, or a hipster? Could either of those two things be a Republican? *What did it all mean?*

"Charlie, can I talk to you for a sec?"

As soon as we were out of sight of everyone, his expression changed to one of frustration. "Are you going to berate me—"

"No. I want to apologize for snapping at you. It was unfair."

"Oh."

"I don't want there to be an undercurrent of anger between us tonight. I know this is important to you. So. No trouble or attitude from me."

He rubbed my arms and smiled. "Thank you." He kissed me gently on the lips. "I love you."

I smiled, and murmured the words back, then went into the laundry room and called Todd. "What are you doing?"

"We're watching…what are we watching again?" A female voice in the background replied. "*Downton Abbey*. Why?"

"Pause it. You're driving over here and having dinner at my house."

"Hang on." I heard a shuffling as Todd got up off the couch. He said, "Pause it for me, will ya?" and the background noise went quiet. "What's wrong?"

"Besides the fact I just caught my daughter and her boyfriend fucking in her bedroom, my dinner of four people has ballooned into sixteen, only two of which I like."

"Calm down, Sophie."

"Why do men always go straight to *calm down*?"

"In this case, because you sound unhinged."

"Yeah, I am a little unhinged. I feel like I'm about to jump out of my skin. I have to keep it together and all that, *pretending*, is just about…"

"Okay, okay. You're right. Tell me."

"My mother just walked in the door, uninvited. My daughter and her boyfriend were naked upstairs. Nora is on her way with her lesbian lover, and six of our high school friends are coming, all of whom want to know why Nora left town eighteen years ago. Oh, and Charlie's Millennials are here."

"His Millennials?"

"Two DC political hacks who think electing Charlie to the Texas State Senate is a great stepping stone to bigger and better things." I barely held back a sob. "Please come. Knowing you're going to walk through my door in an hour is the only thing that's going to keep me from drinking."

"I'm on my way. Ivey will understand."

"Bring her. What's one more?" I exhaled. "And I'd love to see her."

"We'll be there as soon as we can."

· I exhaled and stared at Nora's name at the bottom of my very short Favorite Contacts screen. I touched it and waited for her to pick up.

"Hey," she said. "I'm glad you called. I don't like how we left things the other day."

"Neither do I, but we're going to need to put a pin in our drama for the night."

"Okay, but before we do, I need to tell you something important."

I sighed, wondering what kind of fight this admission would lead to. "Okay."

"I miss you."

My heart skipped a beat. "Oh."

"Now, what did you want to tell me?"

"Um, I need to warn you: Charlie invited Jamie and Tiffany, too."

"Okay."

"You know what that means, right?"

"Oh, yeah. Jamie had a great time fishing when I went to Charlie's office."

"I understand if you want to skip tonight."

"Is that what you want?"

"I suppose that depends on how you introduce Alima."

"Sophie, I would never come out to Lynchfield while you're still closeted."

I sighed with relief. "Thank you."

Nora's voice dropped into an almost whisper. "Look, I'm not sure where this is going with us, but you need to know that no matter what happens, I would never jeopardize your place here, your life."

I swallowed the lump in my throat. I *hadn't* known that. My response was barely audible. "Thank you." I cleared my throat. "There's one more thing."

"Should I be sitting down?"

"Maybe. Brenda's here, too."

"Good Lord. Are you *trying* to get me to beg off?"

"No." I waited for a second, and decided why not? She'd opened the door a crack. "What I want is for us to sneak off. Together. Alone."

The tenor of her voice changed. "I don't think that's going to work tonight."

"Alima is right there, isn't she?"

"Yes. She's looking forward to eating fajitas. She's never had them. Emmadean told her your fajitas are famous."

"Alima's met Emmadean?"

"Yeah. We went over to their house yesterday. To make the cake."

"Oh, right. Yeah. Of course." I felt a jolt of jealousy, afraid Emmadean would like Alima more than me. I immediately felt ridiculous and petty. "Well, y'all hurry on over. People are arriving." Charlie called out to me. "I have to go. See you soon."

I ended the call and took a deep breath.

Nothing terrible is going to happen. This is just like any other weekend, small-town cookout. Joe will drink too much and be loud. Trent won't shut up about his business and how to make beer. Jamie and Tiffany will be side-eyeing everything I do all night. Kim will be the peacemaker. Nora will keep Alima in line, and Brenda? Well, she'll sit on the couch, puckered face, drinking a glass of too-sweet chardonnay and making sure Nora and I don't give ourselves away. This isn't a disaster waiting to happen; it's a challenge.

I'm Sophie Fucking Wyatt. Bring it on.

sixteen
sophie

All of my good intentions, the resolutions I'd made after leaving Nora's house, vanished when Nora and Alima walked through the door. The vision of the two of them, bodies intertwined, the idea I'd been struggling to repress for two days with little success, flickered through my mind. Alima's expression said she saw it all—the hurt, the conflict—on my face.

I knew what I had to do. *Wanted* to do. Risk be damned.

"You have a lovely home," Alima said.

I followed her gaze around the great room that anchored our ranch-style house and tried to see it as an East Coaster would. Exposed dark wood beams on the two-story ceiling, Hill Country sandstone fireplace, scraped hickory hardwood floors, a gourmet kitchen with an AGA stove, comfortable furniture to encourage lingering, minimal tchotchkes on the tables, a gallery wall of framed family photos, windows looking out over the backyard pool with a creek running past beyond. I was embarrassed by how stereotypical it was, how *Architectural Digest* visits the Hill Country it looked, but I loved it all the same.

"Thank you."

Nora stared at everything with an unreadable expression on her face. Was she thinking, *This could have been my life*? Or was she shocked it was mine? It bore no resemblance to my teenage hopes and dreams.

"Let me take that." I reached out for the cake Nora held in her hands.

"Did you decorate?" Alima said, with a motion to the room.

"I did." I lifted the cake, inhaled the buttery scent and smiled.

Alima appraised me and said with a sly smile, "Exquisite taste."

I smiled thinly. "Thank you. Let me introduce you to my mother," I said.

Charlie broke off from talking to the men and came up to us with an outstretched hand. "Charlie Wyatt."

"Alima Koshkam."

"Glad you could make it. Hi, Nora." He leaned forward and kissed her on the cheek. I felt every eye in the room on us, gauging our reactions. I knew that my expression of distaste would be mistaken for jealousy of Charlie and Nora. Instead, I watched Alima. When she caught my eye, my eyebrows rose, and I returned her sly smile.

Nora blushed a little. "Hi, Charlie. Alima and I work together. She came to help me with Ray's house." The explanation was rushed, almost apologetic, but Charlie didn't seem to notice.

"Sophie told me. What a friend. Come on, Alima. Let me introduce you around, get you something to drink. Nora, you want something?"

"I'm good," Nora said. "Thanks."

Alima and Charlie went out to the patio where a group had formed.

"That was smooth," I said with raised eyebrows.

"Did you hear how my voice went up at the end? I sounded like a teenager trying to lie to her parents."

"Charlie's too distracted to notice."

Nora studied me. "You okay?"

"Great."

"You're a shitty liar."

"Don't say that when I'm about to spend the next four hours lying my ass off to everyone in this room." Alima had her back to us, and everyone was crowded around her, listening to her with fascinated expressions. "Come on. Let's put your cake up." I walked off down the hall toward the laundry room.

I was closing the refrigerator when Nora walked in.

"My God, this laundry room is bigger than my first apartment," Nora said, looking around the massive room in awe.

I turned the dryer on. "I know. It's pretentious. I love it."

I pushed the laundry room door closed and backed Nora against it. "This is as close to sneaking off as we're going to get tonight."

Nora's hands went to my hips and she pulled me to her. "This is how I want all of our conversations to start, and end, from now on."

"Stop talking." I cupped her face and kissed her, slowly, remembering the languid makeout sessions we would have in her room. Her dad never at home, we didn't have to worry about being caught by my helicopter mother. Nora's lips were still soft and kissing her was the most natural thing in the world.

She whispered my name.

"I know." I placed her hand over my racing heart. "It remembers."

Nora kissed the back of my hand holding hers, then moved her lips to my collarbone, my neck. I leaned my head back, and her lips traveled to my jaw, behind my ear.

My voice was husky when I spoke. "Seeing you walk in the door with Alima…it shattered my resolve to keep my distance. That was my plan, you know. To let you go once and for all. I can't. I'm jealous of every person you've known, you've been with since you left. I know I have no right to be."

"I'm glad you're jealous."

Nora slipped a spaghetti strap off my shoulder and cupped

my breast. "You look beautiful," she whispered. "I always loved you in blue."

"I know."

She held my gaze as she ran a finger beneath the other spaghetti strap, pulling it slowly off my shoulder. It was all I could do not to let the rest of my dress fall to the floor, to remind myself of the guests not thirty feet away.

"We can't," I said, pushing the strap up.

"We used to," she said, gently pulling it down again. "We were very good at being quiet, remember?"

I inhaled a shaky breath, as Nora kissed my shoulder and moved her lips slowly down my chest. Yes, I remembered the thrill of possibly being caught, how good it was when we were doing what we shouldn't only a few feet away from my parents, or the school hallway, or in the locker room at the club, Comanche Springs. I really hadn't thought through bringing Nora back here. I should have known where it would lead. That not only my heart but my body would remember. But, I couldn't, we couldn't. The time wasn't right. And when this happened, if it happened, I wanted plenty of time.

"When does Alima leave?"

Nora stopped. Alima's name threw cold water on her, like I knew it would. "I'm not sure."

"When she does, we need to talk."

"Talk?" She rubbed her thumb across my bare nipple. I let out a frustrated moan, pulled back and straightened my dress.

Guests. Amends. No relationship rule.

"Before anything happens, I have to make amends."

"Sophie, you don't need to…"

"Yes, I do."

She sighed. "Okay. But, after you talk, we are finishing this." Nora rubbed the edges of my mouth. "Your lipstick is smudged."

I did the same for her. "And you have some on now." We stopped and stared at each other for a long moment. I knew, in that instant, that what I felt for her wasn't just physical, it wouldn't go away after she left. It had never gone away. All these years when I'd consoled myself with the idea it was only Nora who'd made me feel this way, I'd been partly right: Nora was the love of my life. "Oh my God." I turned away and grasped my stomach, fluttering with desire, love and fear.

"You feel it too, don't you?"

I opened the refrigerator door and shoved my head inside to cool myself off. "Yeah."

I turned around and leaned against the refrigerator. We stared at each other, both aware that our relationship was inching closer to the point of no return. The questions were: Could I make love to her and let her go again? Could I stay sober if she didn't choose me?

Magic 8 Ball says, Outlook Not Good.

Still, I never considered turning back.

I moved forward, pulled her to me and kissed her softly. "Get rid of Alima soon." She nodded.

We left the laundry room, Nora loaded with Ziploc bags of prepped peppers and onions while I carried two half pans of marinated fajita meat. My mother stood at the end of the hall, a puckered expression on her face that switched into a scowl when she saw Nora. We passed her without a word.

Tiffany, Jamie, and Kim were waiting in the kitchen when we returned, drinking beer and eating my mother's guacamole. The men and Millennials surrounded Alima, who was nodding and smiling.

"The rumor's true, then," Jamie said, eyes on Nora, whose expression remained inscrutable.

My stomach dropped to my feet. I wouldn't put it past Jamie to follow us and eavesdrop outside the laundry room door. *God, I'm an idiot.* "Which one? There're so many," I said.

"That you two made up."

"We have. Best friends again."

"It's so admirable, Nora, for you to forgive Sophie for what she did," Tiffany said.

"Are you seriously slut-shaming Sophie for something that she didn't do alone?" Nora said. "Charlie's dick was involved, too."

Kim choked on her beer.

"You guys scram. I need to make dinner," I said.

"I'll help," Kim said between coughs.

Tiffany and Jamie offered, too, but I told them I had it under control, too many cooks in the kitchen and so forth. Honestly, anything to get rid of them. I needed time alone to let my heart stop racing, for the flush on my chest to lighten, for me to push down the desire that still thrummed through me.

The guys called out to Nora through the sliding glass door. "NoNo! Come out here and tell us your war stories!"

Nora laughed and shook her head but walked out onto the patio where the men each hugged her in turn. Joe picked her up off the ground and twirled her around like he used to do when he and I were dating. "Kim, you too. Go spend time with Nora," I said. "I've got this."

"I want to talk to you later. Alone." Kim smiled and squeezed my arm. I gave her a weak smile. Nothing good could come of that.

My mother greeted me with disapproval. "Thanks for making the guac, Mother." I lit the gas burner and placed a skillet on it.

"What were you doing back there?"

"Making out."

My mother put her hand over her heart and, for a split second, I thought she was about to drop dead.

"You did that to spite me."

"No, I did that because I wanted to kiss Nora."

"You're making a spectacle of yourself," Brenda hissed.

"No, I'm not. There are only three people in this room who know what happened, and none of us are going to say a word. You invited yourself, so stop puckering your mouth like you're sucking on a lemon, and act like you're having fun. Or leave. Your choice."

"Can I help?" Alima sauntered into the kitchen.

"No," my mother said. She lifted her nose in the air. "You're our guest."

"Alima Koshkam, this is my mother, Brenda Russell."

"Charlie introduced us," Alima said.

"Alima? What kind of name is that?"

A smile played on Alima's lips. "Iranian. What kind of name is Brenda?"

My mother's head wobbled on her neck, and I had to turn away to keep from laughing. I poured olive oil into the hot skillet along with a couple of tablespoons of butter. The peppers and onions sizzled when I dumped them in. Logan and Joaquin walked into the kitchen loaded with bags.

Though I was running behind, too many people in the kitchen would slow me down. I worked best alone and under pressure. "Mother, why don't you go have a seat. I'll have Charlie pour you a glass of wine."

"Just a small one."

I motioned for Logan to tell her dad and helped Joaquin unload the bags.

"Hello, Mrs. Koshkam."

"Joaquin."

The young man blushed to the roots of his dark hair. I caught Alima's eye, and she winked at me, apparently aware of Joaquin's embarrassment. I wondered what had been going on out at Nora's for the last couple of days.

I glanced at the kitchen clock. Todd would be here in thirty minutes. I took a breath. Despite the hum of the conversations from beyond the kitchen, the ticking of the clock overpowered everything.

Alima watched me with an expectant expression. "Are you okay, Sophie?"

I looked up at her. Her mouth curved into a knowing smile.

Leave it to Nora's girlfriend to sense the need swirling inside me, searching desperately for release.

God, she was beautiful. Smooth skin, a few gray hairs around her face, but she was one of those women who managed to make going gray look glamorous. Alima had this way of looking at you as if you were the only person in the world. No wonder Nora was attracted to her. Loved her? I didn't know. I didn't want to know.

I saw the bottle of beer she held and grasped onto it as a conversation gambit. "What do you think of Trent's beer?"

She leaned forward and whispered. "Not a fan, to be honest. I was hoping to be able to pour it down the drain discreetly."

"Want me to make you a margarita?"

"If it's not too much trouble."

I took her beer and placed in the sink. "Not at all. Let me stir my onions."

Alima dipped a chip into a black bean dip. "Did you make all of this?"

Dips and chips lined the island bar. A Crock-Pot of borracho beans sat on the back counter by the stove, and two half pans of marinated beef and chicken sat next to it, ready for Charlie to throw them on the grill. "I did."

"She's a great cook," Joaquin offered.

"Thanks," I said.

"Full-time job, family, and hosting a dinner party and not breaking a sweat. You're a veritable Wonder Woman," Alima said.

"Well, I'm about to ruin your perception of my greatness. I'm serving everything on paper plates."

Alima laughed. "The politicos over there will love it."

"Exactly what I thought. Come on. Let's get you a margarita. Joaquin, will you watch the onions?"

"Yes, ma'am."

"Sweet kid," Alima said when we were out of his earshot. "He was a big help at Nora's."

"Glad to hear it. Is on the rocks okay?"

"Sure. I thought you might come out."

"Come out?" My stomach dropped, and my face flamed with embarrassment.

"Yes. Come out to Nora's. To help."

"Right. I had to work."

I rubbed a cut lime around the rim of a rocks glass, dipped it in a plate of flaky salt, and filled it with ice. I put ice into a metal shaker and poured tequila, sweet and sour, triple sec and Grand Marnier in before clapping on the lid. Our high school friends still surrounded Nora, but she was watching Alima and me. I shook the drink. "Nora mentioned you were coworkers?"

"Yes. We manage two different translation groups. Mostly computer manuals, or how-to instructions. You know, those little pieces of paper you get in your electronics you never read?"

"Yes."

"That. I've enjoyed getting to know Logan the last couple of days. She's very comfortable around adults, talking to them. It's increasingly uncommon."

"I suppose being an only child has something to do with it." I strained the margarita in the glass and garnished it with the lime. I handed it to Alima. Her wedding ring clinked against the glass. I didn't let go of it. "Does your husband know?"

"That I'm here? No. He's on a business trip."

"No, that you're fucking Nora."

She pulled the glass away and sipped it. "Does your husband know you're a lesbian?"

I glanced around, but no one was within earshot.

"Don't worry, Sophie. I'm not that person. Your secret is safe with me."

"Hmm. You and Nora have a nice reunion?"

"Yes, very energetic. Then, we spent the next hour talking about you. A bit of a downer, to be honest. This margarita is excellent. Not making yourself one?"

"I'm an alcoholic."

"Nora mentioned it."

I dumped the used ice into the bar sink and rinsed the shaker. "Then why did you ask? Oh, right. So you could let drop how close you and Nora are. I saw the hickey on her shoulder. I know exactly how close you are. What else did Nora tell you?"

"Everything."

"Nora does love pillow talk."

"I suppose you don't know much about me."

"I expect to, and very soon."

Alima's eyes brightened, and she laughed. "I'm starting to like you, Sophie."

"The feeling isn't mutual."

"I wouldn't expect so. I'm a threat to you. You aren't to me."

"Are you making margaritas?" Tiffany called.

"Sure. Who wants one?"

Four hands went up.

"I'll do the rims," Alima said.

I glanced up from making the drinks and saw Nora watching us. She smiled at Charlie and laughed with the group, and her gaze found mine again.

"Sophie?"

Alima shifted in front of me, breaking my connection with Nora.

"I'm not going to out you, but if you keep looking at Nora like that, I won't need to."

I placed the lid on the shaker and drove it home with more force than necessary, my stomach tying itself up in knots.

I poured the margaritas into the prepared glasses, resisting the urge to throw the strainer aside and gulp the drink from the cold metal shaker until streams of liquid ran out the sides, leaving a sticky trail down my chin and neck before meeting at the center of my chest, dampening the top of my dress. I didn't like tequila, but it had never stopped me from drinking it.

"I'm leaving tomorrow morning," Alima said.

My stomach flip-flopped. Tomorrow I would tell Nora my story. Tomorrow we would...

"My goodness, you're striking when you smile," Alima said.

I focused on squeezing limes into the shaker to take my mind off tomorrow. "Not going to be much help with the estate sale, are you?"

"I'm doing you a favor."

"How so?"

"I've given Nora permission to fuck you."

I fumbled a lime and dropped it on the floor.

"Hey, y'all," Tiffany said, and picked up the lime. "It doesn't take that long to make a margarita. You two seem to be hitting it off."

I handed Tiffany two drinks. "Do we?"

"Sure. Probably having fun comparing the two Noras." She sipped a drink, smacked her lips and said, "Delicious. Sorry you can't have one, Sophie."

I cleaned out the shaker. "So am I," I said under my breath.

"Two Noras," Alima said. "What do you mean?"

"Well, she's different, isn't she? Who would have thought Nora would have gone all city girl on us? I mean, you were always the uppity one, Sophie."

"Would you deliver these, Tiffany? Enjoy your drink, Alima."

I went to the kitchen. Joaquin and Logan stood close together over the onions. Joaquin saw me, jumped away and blushed. Right, I'd almost forgotten about catching my daughter having sex. "Oh, stop it, Joaquin," I hissed. "I knew you were having sex weeks ago."

"*Mom.*"

"You know what, grab twenty dollars out of my purse and go get dinner. I can't deal with you two and everyone else here."

"I'll buy dinner," Joaquin said. "Come on, Logan."

"I'm staying to help my mom," Logan said.

Joaquin and I talked over each other to convince her, but I could read Logan's determination in the set of her mouth. The desire to leave warred with Joaquin's fear that Logan was not happy with him. He rubbed his hands on his shorts and said, "Talk to you tomorrow."

"Whatever," Logan said under her breath.

I welcomed the chance to focus on Logan's life instead of my own, though I wished it was a different subject. "Was that about me walking in on you two?" I whispered.

"No." She moved the peppers and onions around in the skillet, picked up the seasoned pepper and shook a good portion on. "Not entirely."

"Want to talk about it?"

"How are my two girls?" Charlie said, startling us both. He put his arms around me from behind and rested his chin on my shoulder. "You two telling secrets?"

"Yes. Go away," I said.

He chuckled and kissed my neck, sending chills down my arm at the memory of Nora's lips doing the same not fifteen minutes ago. "Is the meat ready?"

"Over there."

He kissed the top of my bare shoulder and said, "You're the most beautiful woman here. Love your dress."

When he left, Logan said, "What's gotten into him?"

"No idea," I said.

Alima returned to the kitchen. "My offer to help still stands."

"No," Logan and I said together.

She nodded slowly and said, "We can finish our conversation later."

"Can't wait," I said.

She wandered over to the two politicos, who looked a little lost and out of place. I should have tried with them, especially since they were going to be a large part of our life for the next year, but I didn't want to.

"What was that about?" I said.

"I can ask you the same thing," Logan said.

"I don't like her."

"Me either," Logan said.

"Why?"

"She looks down her nose at us. Why don't you like her?" Logan said.

"I'm jealous." I shrugged. "She's Nora's friend."

"I think they're more than friends."

My body went cold. "Why do you say that?"

"There's a vibe. Lexa agrees. Joaquin thinks we're crazy. Probably because he's a little in love with her."

Ah. "With Nora or Alima?"

"Alima. You know he said she looks like you. Right after saying she's hot. Like that wasn't a completely creepy thing to say."

"Well, thanks for not saying it's an insult to Alima."

"Soph, we're sucking down your margaritas," Joe called.

"Would you rather drink or eat, Joe?" I called back, smiling.

"Looks like Logan and Charlie're doing all the cookin'."

"I'm supervising," I said. "I'll make a pitcher of margaritas in a sec."

They lifted their glasses to me.

"Are you okay to do that?" Logan asked.

"I'm fine," I lied. "So." I cleared my throat and hoped my voice would sound merely curious. "Would you care if Nora was gay?" I whispered the final word.

Logan scrunched up her face. "Why would I care?"

I relaxed and was about to say something when Logan said, "I mean, it's gross, but to each their own, right?"

"Right."

seventeen
nora

It was plain as day that Sophie needed a drink. Or wanted one, I should say.

She'd been talking to Logan by the stove, and her face fell. She looked toward the bar, and the bottle of tequila she'd just been using to make everyone margaritas, and licked her lips. She turned away just as quickly and busied herself with getting dinner together. I started to leave the group I was in and help her, give her moral support, and damn it I just wanted to be close to her, when Jamie grabbed me by the arm to stop me.

"Sophie's got it under control. She hates it when we try to help."

"Very Type A," Tiffany said. "She never lets us bring anything except beer."

"Sounds like a good hostess to me," Alima said.

"She is. She wants her guests to enjoy themselves," Kim said. "I'd offered to help, and she sent me away."

"Controlling," Jamie singsonged. She drank her margarita and twisted around to glance at the group huddled around the grill, her eyes lingering possessively on Charlie and Avery.

"She's a better cook than you," Kim said.

Jamie glared at Kim.

"Or any of us," Kim quickly amended.

I caught Alima's eye. She tried to hide her smile behind drinking her margarita.

"Tell us exactly what you do," Tiffany said to Alima.

She did, and the three women's eyes glazed over after one sentence of the explanation. Alima was an expert at making what we did sound deadly dull when it was anything but.

"Why in the world did you choose Arabic, Nora?" Jamie sneered.

"I didn't. The government chose it for me. And Spanish, French, and Farsi."

"Say something," Kim said.

"No," I said.

"These good Christians are too blind to see you and Sophie want to rip each other's clothes off," Alima said.

"What did she say?" Tiffany asked.

"What language is that?" Kim asked.

"Farsi. She said dinner smells good," I said.

"What happened in the back?" Alima said.

"Nothing."

"Liar. Maybe Sophie would want to come home with us. We've never had a third. Might be fun. Should we ask?"

"No."

"You're blushing. I think you like the idea."

"I'm not, and I don't."

Alima grinned, satisfied with getting a rise out of me. *"I'm kidding; you're all mine tonight."*

"What did she say then?" Tiffany asked.

"It's rude to carry on conversations in another language," Jamie said.

"You're right. I'm sorry. We're talking about how nice you all are."

"She could say that in English," Tiffany said.

"I like Sophie, by the way. More than I want to."

"Stop it, Alima. You're being rude," I said.

"You sound like a terrorist."

"Jamie!" Tiffany said.

"Well, she does."

I stepped close to Jamie. "Too far." I leaned forward and Jamie flinched. I caught her eyes and saw fear there. "Apologize."

"Or what? You'll kill me with your bare hands?"

I was impressed with her bravado. "You don't think I can, do you?"

"Okay," Kim singsonged, trying to pull me away. "Let's you and me make that pitcher of margaritas for Sophie."

I shrugged her off easily. "Not until Jamie apologizes to our visitor."

Jamie looked around the group, expecting someone to stand up for her, but no one did. "Fine, I apologize."

"Accepted," Alima said. *"Though you're right, bitch; I am a terrorist."*

I laughed. Alima leaned in and whispered, *"That was incredibly hot, by the way."*

I winked at her as Kim threaded her arm through mine and pulled me toward the bar. "When did you become such a badass?"

"I've always been a badass, Kim."

"Can you really kill someone with your bare hands?"

When I didn't answer, she said, "Remind me never, ever, to get on your wrong side. Look," she looked over her shoulder. No one was with hearing distance. She continued, "I know you don't like Jamie, but she'll take it out on Sophie, you know."

"How?"

"She's been sleeping with Charlie for a year."

I dropped some ice into a rocks glass, unscrewed the nearest whiskey bottle and splashed some in, while Kim started the margaritas. I watched Sophie work in the kitchen and threw back the whiskey. The feel of Sophie's lips lingered on mine, her hands cupping my face, the scent in the hollow behind her ear that ignited me as nothing else did. My thumb teasing her nipple, wiping the smudged lipstick from her mouth. She didn't love Charlie, didn't want him, that was obvious. "Sophie couldn't care less."

"Yeah, you're probably right, though it's disappointing." Kim upended the tequila and Grand Marnier for about three seconds longer than I would have.

"Why?" She pressed down on a lime with each hand and rolled them back and forth. "What are you doing?" I asked.

"Loosening the juice and pulp. You don't make margaritas, do you?"

"I use store-bought mix."

"That's disgusting, Nora. Only real limes."

I rolled and Kim cut and squeezed the limes into the pitcher. "Why are you disappointed?" I asked.

"Oh. I've always wanted them to succeed, you know? I mean, she lost her best friend because of it, she might as well have a happy marriage."

"You don't think they've ever been happy?"

"Who's to say? I do know the last few years have been difficult, with Sophie's alcoholism. But, Charlie stood by her. It's pretty obvious who loves who more in the relationship."

I poured another drink and asked Kim if she wanted one. She refused.

"I…um…need to talk to you about something," Kim said.

Brenda Russell sat on a couch between the bar and the kitchen. She stared at me unblinkingly. I winked at her and turned my attention to Kim.

"About what?"

Kim fidgeted, apparently unable to say the words. "You're… gay." She whispered the last word, but it wasn't a question.

"Are you fishing for gossip to share with those two?" I jerked my head in Jamie and Tiffany's direction.

"God, no."

"Y'all seem pretty tight, still."

"Our relationship is like always. Three's a crowd, you know."

"I'm not gay," I said. Now it was my turn to look around to see if we were being eavesdropped on. "I'm bisexual."

"Oh." Her shoulders dropped, and she sighed.

"Why did you ask me that, anyway?"

Kim wouldn't meet my eyes. "I saw you and Sophie once, hugging."

"Friends hug all the time."

"Not like this." She looked at me. "I've known all these years and I've never told a soul. You owe me."

I narrowed my eyes. "Are you threatening me?"

"After what I just saw? Fuck, no. Anyway, I'm not like them," she waved and smiled big at Jamie and Tiffany across the room. "Or you, for that matter. I would never threaten someone. I'm a squishy little Peep."

"Peep?"

"You know, like the little Easter Peeps."

"They're marshmallows."

"Fine, I'm a marshmallow. The point is, I'm not threatening you. I need a favor."

"You want me to kill Jamie with my bare hands?"

"No, though sometimes I've thought of wringing her neck myself. This is a favor for my daughter."

"I'm listening."

Kim looked around to make sure we were alone, caught sight of Brenda staring daggers at me, and turned to block me from Brenda's view. "My daughter, Erin, she came out to me a couple of months ago."

"How did that go over?"

"Oh, well, I mean it was a shock, you know? And, then it wasn't. I've always known, you just don't ever want to admit it. I mean, you know what it's like around here. If you're not hearing it from the pulpit, you're hearing it down at the bakery about gay people this or that."

"Does Joe know?"

"Not yet, and he's said some things he's probably going to regret when he finds out. At least I hope he does." She inhaled deeply and put on a smile. "But, Joe isn't who I want you to talk to. Erin is."

"I don't know, Kim."

"You grew up here and I thought you might be able to tell her it gets better."

"I'm sure there are plenty of LGBT websites that she can go to—"

Kim sighed. "Look, Nora. No one knows about Erin, okay? I'm it. I think you can rest assured I'm not going to let anything slip to Jamie and Tiffany about you two after all these years. It would open up a world of questions I don't want to answer. I couldn't care less who you sleep with. I want to help my little girl. That's it. She is struggling, so much, and I know all about the suicide statistics for LGBT teens. I don't want my daughter to be one of them."

"I don't either. How old is Erin?"

"Fifteen. Going to be a sophomore."

God, poor girl. Three more years of Lynchfield.

I was ready to deflect, to tell Kim I couldn't help her. What did I know about talking to a teenager about being queer in a small town? I hadn't put that label on what Sophie and I had until later when I realized my passion for Sophie hadn't been unique, that I could also find it with other women, the physical desire, anyway. The emotional connection, that was unique. Sharing my experience in Lynchfield meant outing Sophie. But, when I saw the hope and trust and uncertainty in Kim's expression, I couldn't say no. I would have to find a way to thread the needle with Erin.

"I'll talk to her."

Kim threw her arms around me. "Thank you, Nora. You don't know what this means to me."

I hugged Kim back and saw Brenda Russell stand, and come toward us. "Oh, Lord." I pulled away from Kim.

"Oh, hello, Mrs. Russell," Kim said. "You look very pretty tonight. How's your back these days?"

"It's been better, and it's been worse."

"Need another drink, Brenda?"

Brenda's lips puckered, but she held out her wineglass. I turned my back on the two women, filled the glass with ice and whiskey. When I turned around, Kim's eyes were wide, and Brenda did not look amused. "Thought you might want something a little stronger. Being around me must be a tax on your nerves."

"I couldn't," Brenda said.

"Oh, you're right. My bad." I dumped the whiskey and ice into a rocks glass and held it out to her. "Wrong glass."

Brenda smiled at Kim. "Could you excuse us for a moment?"

"Sure." Kim mouthed, *What the hell?* at me.

I shook the glass at Brenda. "Don't worry. I'll drive you home. Or would you rather have a margarita?"

"You have some nerve."

"It's just a drink, Brenda. I promise you won't go to hell."

"Why can't you leave my daughter alone?"

I laughed and shook my head. "Me? I'm always the bad guy in this, aren't I?"

"Sophie would have never..."

I raised my hand. "We had this conversation eighteen years ago. Not interested in having it again, Brenda."

"Stop calling me that."

"You expect me to show you respect? *Deference?* You're out of your fucking mind."

Brenda inhaled sharply and lifted her nose in the air. "You're disgusting."

I leaned forward. "And your daughter loves every minute of it."

Brenda narrowed her eyes. "You need to leave before I…"

"What? Threaten to have me arrested for rape? I'm sorry but what we did in the laundry room earlier was completely consensual, I assure you."

"You are the vilest… I can't even call you a human being. Definitely not a woman."

"Be careful, Brenda, or you're going to talk me into moving back to Lynchfield."

"You wouldn't dare."

"Why not? It would make you miserable, and that's reason enough." I downed the drink I made for her. I licked my lips and looked in Sophie's direction. She had her back turned to us, but Logan was watching. "Now, excuse me. I'm going to help Sophie with dinner."

Brenda grabbed my arm. "Stay away from my daughter."

I pulled Brenda into a hug. She struggled, but I tightened my grip. "You need to leave, right now." And, with a voice shaking with anger, I told her what would happen if she didn't.

eighteen
sophie

When the shit hits the fan, it happens fast, with no warning.

Three things happened at once; Brenda cried out, Logan gasped and said, "Grandmother just slapped Nora," and the doorbell rang.

Charlie was walking in from the patio with a cutting board full of meat when I turned around in the aftermath of whatever the hell had just happened. My mother had her purse and was running to the door as fast as her sciatica would take her. Nora rubbed her cheek with an expression of satisfaction. The rest of the crowd followed Charlie and the cutting board and the scent of fresh fajitas. The doorbell rang again. I stood in the kitchen, holding the wooden spoon I'd been stirring the peppers and onions with, a dread coursing through me, my eyes drawn not to Nora, or my husband, or my mother pushing past Logan, or Todd and Ivey at the front door, but to the bottle of whisky on the bar behind Nora.

Charlie put the cutting board on the island. "What was that all about?"

"I have no idea."

"Todd?" He turned to me. "When did you invite Todd?"

"When my mother showed up."

Charlie moved close to me. "Why the fuck are you making everyone margaritas, then?"

I wiped my hands on a dish towel. "Because no one likes Trent's shitty beer." I threw the towel down and saw Trent and Jamie easily within hearing distance. I went to greet Todd and Ivey.

I hugged Todd. "Oh my God, please put me out of my misery."

He patted my back. "You got this."

"I really don't."

"Sure you do," Ivey Johnson said and gave me a strong hug. She pulled away and caught sight of Logan. "Well, this has to be your daughter. The spitting image of you if there ever was one."

"Yes, this is Logan. Logan, this is Ivey, and you remember Todd."

"Yeah. Hey. Nice to meet you."

"Should someone go after the crying senior citizen who just ran past us?" Ivey asked.

"That was Brenda. She deserves every tear she sheds, trust me."

"Mom, my God," Logan said.

"Give it a rest, Logan."

"You're the one being a bitch, not me." She turned and stomped up the stairs.

"Hey, Todd." Charlie walked up with an extended hand. He looked at Ivey with the expression of a man who'd just won the lottery. Ivey was a short Black woman with gray eyes and dreadlocks tipped with multicolored beads, not exactly Charlie's constituency, I'm ashamed to say. But, that wouldn't stop him pandering to her. "Charlie Wyatt. Pleased to meet you." Charlie, not stupid, had the wherewithal to offer Todd and Ivey non-alcoholic drinks. I directed him to the back refrigerator for the two gallons of tea I'd picked up from HEB on the way home.

Jamie and Trent were still glaring at me, Nora was waiting for me in the kitchen. Logan was going upstairs, apparently done with me for now. My mother was driving home through her tears. Alima watched it all with a cool detachment. Todd and Ivey followed me to the kitchen and asked if they could help.

"No, I just need to cut up these fajitas."

I took up a fork and butcher knife and started in on the fajitas. They never stood a chance. I heard Nora and Alima introduce themselves to Ivey and Todd and have a banal conversation about what they all did for a living. That's why I jumped when I heard Nora's voice so close behind me.

"Need help?" Nora asked.

"I need to know what you said to make my mother run crying out of the house?"

Nora picked up a piece of meat and ate it. "Very good." She leaned close and whispered in my ear. "I told her about our little moment in the laundry room and threatened to tell everyone here."

The knife slipped and clattered to the floor. "Christ, Nora."

"I wasn't going to do it."

Tiffany, Jamie and Kim came to the kitchen bar. "What's wrong with your mom, Soph?" Tiffany asked.

I turned my back and rinsed the knife in the sink. Todd was next to me. "Let me have the knife. I'll cut the fajitas."

"Thank you."

"Take deep breaths. We got you."

Ivey was valiantly trying to make conversation with a group of people who, if they were any whiter, would have burned everyone's eyes from the glare. Charlie's Millennials had edged into the group and Joe and Trent and had started talking to Ivey. When she told them she was an ER nurse, Joe was off with one gruesome question after another. The Millennials caught each other's gaze and rolled their eyes.

Jamie wasn't going to be distracted by idle chitchat. She

moved to the other side of Tiffany, as if to get as far away from Nora as possible. Weird.

"What did you say to Brenda, Nora?" Jamie asked.

"Is your cheek okay?" Kim asked.

"Yes, thank you," Nora said.

My hands shook. I tried to shove them in my pockets, but my maxidress didn't have any. I crossed my arms instead. Everyone was watching me with various expressions of concern, curiosity and conniving. I was pissed at Nora for putting us in this position. What explanation could she possibly give for that slap? The truth wasn't an option.

Charlie walked back into the kitchen, brandishing two gallons of tea. "I've got sweet and un…" Charlie looked around. "What's up?"

"Nora is an atheist," I said.

A hush descended over the room, save a laugh from Alima.

"You insulted Mother's faith, didn't you, Nora?" I asked, staring at her pointedly.

"Yes, that is precisely what I did," Nora said, struggling not to smile.

"You're an atheist?" Tiffany said in disbelief.

Logan bounded down the stairs with her purse over her shoulder, heading for the front door. I followed. Let Nora have the glare of the spotlight for a bit. I caught up to Logan on the front porch and closed the door behind us. "Where are you going?"

"Why do you care?"

"Logan, please. I have enough shit going on in there. I don't need more from you."

"I'm going to check on Grandmother. We'll be lucky if she made it home. I've never seen her so upset, not even when Granddad died."

"I have. Dinner is ready. Will you go back in and help your dad? Play hostess for a bit? I should be the one to check on Mother." I didn't want my daughter anywhere near Brenda. Though I knew

she would never tell Logan anything, I didn't want her to poi-
son my daughter against me and that? She was fully capable of.

"Okay. Sure. I guess."

We walked back inside arm in arm. The locals had surrounded
Nora and were quizzing her. Good. She deserved it. Let her lie
through her teeth like I've had to do for twenty years. She'd be
fine; she was an excellent liar our senior year in high school.

I went over to Charlie and whispered that I was going to
check on Brenda. "In the middle of the party?" he said.

"Yes, Charlie. Everything's ready to eat, and Logan is here
to help. I'll be back in fifteen minutes."

"We aren't making a very good impression here, Sophie."

"I haven't done anything wrong. If you want to chastise someone for ruining your party, go talk to Nora."

I didn't wait for his approval because I knew it wouldn't come.
Todd caught me on the way to the garage. Ivey was right behind him.

"What are you doing?" Todd said.

"Going to check on my mother."

"Bullshit. We're coming with you."

"Todd, I…"

"I know what falling off the wagon looks like, Sophie. That's
why you called me."

Alima walked up behind Ivey and made no bones about having eavesdropped. "Can I come? I don't think I can take your
friends for much longer."

"Sure. Why not."

I pulled up to Comanche Springs and put the car in Park.
Late June in Texas is no time to be turning the AC off to save
gas. During a blissful moment of silence, we watched teenagers
jump off the twenty-foot limestone wall across the pond and
into the water below.

"Um, this isn't your mom's," Todd said.

"No. We drove by Brenda's house. Her car was in the garage. I'll check on her in a minute."

"Ivey, Alima, can you give us a second?" Todd said.

"Sure." The women left the car. Todd stayed in the back seat, and I looked at him in the rearview mirror.

"So that's Alima?"

"Yep."

"How's your resolve?"

"It was good. Until I saw Nora and Alima walk in the door."

"Has anything happened between you and Nora?"

I shook my head, feeling only slightly guilty for lying to him. Todd scooted forward in the back seat. I turned so we were face-to-face. "I'm proud of you, Sophie. Damn proud."

Now I felt guilty. "Todd, I don't know if I can do it."

"You can. Don't let your jealousy and competitiveness derail your recovery."

"What does that mean?"

"It means that woman out there shouldn't factor into your actions at all. She is insignificant. What's important is you make amends with Nora so you can move past this."

"Move past it. Move past the fact that I'm a closeted lesbian in a miserable marriage?"

"No, Sophie. Move past Nora."

I grimaced and looked away.

Todd was silent, and we watched Ivey and Alima talking a few yards away.

"If you and Nora were a one-time thing, I'd look the other way," Todd said. "But, I don't think it is, and you risk your sobriety if you go through with it and it ends badly. Which, it probably will."

"I'm not under any illusions, Todd. I know this ends with her leaving. Do I want her to stay? Yes. Will I try to get her to stay? Hell, yes. I know it's a dream. But, I'll be damned if I'm not going to take the opportunity to feel alive again, to feel whole, even if it is for a week or two. I want—I need—to live in this new skin, to live with my sexuality as much as possible while I have the chance. I'm not going to be closeted forever. Late in life lesbianism. It's a thing, you know."

I got out of the car and called out to Ivey, who met me halfway. "She wants to talk to you."

"Should I be worried?" I murmured.

"Nah. She puts on her pants just like we do. You'll be good. If you need me to kick her ass, just give me a wave." Ivey winked at me and went to the car.

Alima waited for me near the river bank. "We need to get back, so make it short," I said.

"I've known Nora for about five years. We've been lovers for three."

I swallowed down the jealousy blocking my throat. I crossed my arms over my chest. "Sounds like you're gearing up for a story."

"We'd still be merely coworkers if I hadn't seduced her. When we saw each other at work the next day, you'd have never thought we'd been sweaty and naked the night before."

I lifted a hand. "Okay, I don't need the details."

"So, I waited. To see what Nora would do. It wasn't until later that I discovered Nora didn't commit. Ever. She was easy enough to get in bed, but after that, nothing. Which is perfect for me, because I didn't want to be a couple, I wanted to be lovers. She was all right with it, too. She has her men and women on the side; I have my husband."

"Men and women?"

"She's bisexual. You didn't know?"

"No." Did she mention it during one of our fights? It was possible, but she never said *bisexual*. That I knew.

I couldn't fathom wanting a man. Though I'd been sleeping with Charlie for years, I'd never felt desire when I watched him get out of the shower, his muscular body slicked with water. I knew he was gorgeous, and I was lucky, but looking at him was like looking at a beautiful sunset. I appreciated its beauty, but I didn't want to fuck it. I'd long since stopped fooling myself that I enjoyed sleeping with him, or that he or anything he did made me come. The only way I'd ever been able to come was to think about women, mostly Nora, but also the occasional stranger. And Cate Blanchett.

"Nora isn't an amateur. She's been with lots of—"

I raised my hand. "Please stop. I really don't want to know about Nora's love life."

"You want to think you're the only woman she's fucked?"

"Meeting you ruined that fantasy for me."

"The only woman she's ever loved?"

Our eyes met, and I nodded slowly.

"Sorry to tell you, but she loves me."

I looked away. I closed my eyes, lifted my face to the setting sun and inhaled. Why wouldn't Nora love Alima? She was the type of woman I would have been, if only... "Are you ever going to leave your husband for her?"

"I have. Last week. Sophie, I understand what you're going through. Being my authentic self—well, when I was young that wasn't even a phrase, let alone an option. I was married as a young woman to a man my father chose. I was lucky; Davoud was a good and kind husband. We had a nice life. I raised the children and he even let me have a career. He was much more liberal than my father thought, much to his consternation. But, liberality only goes so far, and we are devout, in our own way. I was perfectly content with my life until I fell in love with Nora. Still, it's taken me years to get up the courage to leave. It's not a decision that can be made so quickly, is it?"

"No."

"Go ahead. Seduce Nora. Trust me; you'll enjoy it. But, in the end, you won't leave your family, and Nora hates Lynchfield, and you, too much to give up her life, career, and me."

"Nora hates me? She didn't seem to in the laundry room."

Alima studied me for a moment with the same knowing smile I'd seen at the house. "Under different circumstances I think you and I would be friends. I like you much more than I thought I would, especially after everything Nora told me about you."

A sharp pain pierced my heart. According to everyone, including my daughter, and now Nora, everything had been my fault.

"Nora wants to sleep with you, and I can't blame her for that. She'll never trust you, and can you blame her for that?"

I shook my head and looked away.

"I'm sorry to be cruel. I only want what is best for Nora."

"And you are what's best for her."

"Yes, I am. We have a great relationship, and we love each other. I'm giving up a lot to be with her, just like you would, so I understand what's going on in that beautiful head of yours. It took me three years to get the courage and you'll have what? Two weeks? Maybe three. So, yes. I feel confident."

"Great. You've made your point. What time do you leave tomorrow?"

Alima smiled. "I've scheduled a car to pick me up at 8:00 a.m."

"I'll be there at 8:01."

"I'll make sure not to wear her out too much tonight." She winked at me and walked to the car.

Fucking bitch.

nineteen
sophie

When we returned from Comanche Springs, everyone was on the back patio, eating. I made sure Alima, Ivey and Todd were fed, and was puttering around in the kitchen, taking my time serving myself, hoping Nora would take the hint and come inside alone. She did. She stood next to me and made herself a fajita. We didn't speak for a bit.

"How's your mom?"

"Her car was in the garage. I'm sure she's fine."

"Where did y'all go?"

"Comanche Springs."

"What did Alima say to you?"

"She wants what's best for you." I scooped guacamole on my plate and Nora's and added the rest of the corn chips. I grabbed a fresh bag of chips from the back counter and replenished the bowl. "We disagree on who that is."

Nora placed her hand over mine, and I finally looked at her. "She says she's leaving tomorrow morning," I said.

"Is she?"

"Are you disappointed?"

She ran her thumb over the back of my hand. "No."

"Can I come by tomorrow morning?"

"Yes." Her voice was quiet but full of emotion.

"Promise me you won't sleep with her tonight."

Her hazel eyes met mine. "I didn't intend to."

The men came inside with empty plates. Nora released my hand and went outside to join the others.

The rest of the party was uneventful. We somehow managed to not talk about politics, though there were more than a few pointed questions for Alima about Islam (she's not devout) and where she was from (Virginia). She handled it all with seemingly good humor, but I caught her exchanging disbelieving expressions with Nora. When she and Nora were leaving, I pulled her a little aside and apologized for the other guests.

"Thank you for inviting me. It was everything I expected, and more."

She didn't mean it as a compliment, but I let it pass. I didn't want to do or say anything that would keep her in town.

For all my talk of taking happiness while I could have it, I wasn't sure if I could sleep with Nora, and then wave at her as she drove out of town. But, I didn't like the alternative either: coming out to Lynchfield meant throwing my life into turmoil. It meant an ugly scene with Charlie and Logan. It meant stares in the produce section at Brookshire Brothers. It meant arrested conversations when I entered a room. It meant being churched or, even worse, included on every prayer list in town. Did I love Nora enough to endure that? I had no idea.

So, I lay awake all night, listening to Charlie's drunken snores, my mind spiraling with a million scenarios, counting down the minutes until I could go to Nora, hoping Nora kept her promise, trying not to think of how Alima and Nora were saying goodbye if she didn't.

I rose as soon as the clock ticked over to 6:00 a.m. I showered and dressed as if I were going to stand up in the AA meeting and tell my story, the smell of stale coffee in the air, a cardboard box of cheap donuts on the table, the runny glaze where the donuts met their neighbors no deterrent from being eaten.

Charlie didn't move when I left the bedroom. I thought of peeking in on Logan, of watching her sleep, making sure she was still breathing, a habit I'd gotten into when she was a baby and did to this day. I hadn't talked to her since my blowup the night before, and I knew the sight of my daughter might erode my resolve or sidetrack me into a conversation I wasn't ready to have. Yet.

I stopped at Giesmann's Bakery downtown for a cup of coffee and a box of kolaches and settled down at one of the patio tables with Saturday edition of the *Austin American-Statesman*. I should have driven to Dripping Springs for my meeting. Get a little strength from the group before stepping off the emotional ledge I was inching toward. But, I didn't want to go and have to say, "I'm Sophie and I'm an alcoholic. It's been seven days since my last drink." The need for Nora hadn't abated in the night. Waiting would be torture. And, I really wanted to get this over with. To tell her everything. To know one way or another if my thirst for her would be quenched. Finally.

I was reading the editorials when a dark-windowed Town Car drove down the street from the direction of Austin. I swallowed the knot in my throat and returned to my paper, but the words swam on the page. I was still staring at the page when the Town Car drove by the other way. The windows were too opaque to see inside, but I knew Alima watched me from its darkened interior. I drank my coffee and was surprised to find it lukewarm. I folded the paper neatly and left it on the table for the next person.

Nora's rental was in the driveway next to Ray's truck, but there was no answer when I knocked. I heard chickens squawking from the barn. I walked around the house, the sounds of unhappy chickens getting louder and louder.

"Oh, give it a rest MacArthur, you prima donna. Take a page from Patton here. See how she calmly moves out of the way so I can get the eggs? Ow! You did not just peck me! I'm gonna have Emmadean fry you up and serve you with cream gravy if you're not careful, you spiteful little chicken."

I burst out laughing as much from nervousness as from watching Nora fight with a chicken. Her surprised expression changed to one of embarrassed good humor in a flash.

"That chicken's on thin ice," Nora said. "She was probably Ray's favorite. Bet he coddled her."

"Ray didn't seem like the type to coddle chickens."

"People do strange shit in their old age."

She put the bucket down and came toward me. "I like your dress."

This one was white with small periwinkle-blue flowers all over it. "Thanks. It's one of my favorites."

She nodded to the box in my hand. "What do you have there?"

"Coconut cream kolaches."

"My favorite."

"Used to be."

"Still is. I had one the other day." She took the box from me and balanced it on top of the bucket.

Her head tilted up as her hand caressed my cheek.

"Are we really, finally alone?" she whispered.

"Just us and the chickens."

"You seem nervous."

"I am."

"Don't be." She gently pinched my chin and brought my lips down to hers. Her mouth was soft and gentle, and I had to force myself to let her kiss me, to not pull her to me roughly, to release the pent-up passion and frustration that had been building for nearly twenty years. I was glad I didn't. My mind emptied of all the worries, the what-ifs, the second guessing, of all the regrets and lies and sadness. I was seventeen again, kissing my girlfriend, exploring the new world that had opened up between us. Allowing myself to feel good without guilt or judgment or fear.

When Nora finally pulled back, I kept my eyes closed, not

wanting to leave the moment, vaguely knowing there was some other emotion besides joy that would greet me when I opened my eyes. I wanted to linger, but Nora broke the spell when her thumb rubbed along the bottom of my lip.

"Smudged lipstick."

"Hmm."

She picked up the box of kolaches. "Let's get this talk over with so we can do that again." She held out her hand, and I took it. "And, more."

My stomach twirled around like a ballerina in a spin. I inhaled. "Last night, did you and Alima...?" I hated myself a little for asking.

"No."

I sighed with relief. "I know I had no right to ask you not to, we aren't—"

Nora put her fingers on my lips to stop me from talking. "You had every right to ask and if I were in your shoes, I would have asked the same thing."

I nodded and inhaled. It was time. "I hope you have coffee on."

"I do."

The coffee was hot, and the kolaches were pillowy and sweet. The air was thick with anticipation, and a fair amount of dread on my part. My palms started sweating. I sipped my coffee and placed the mug on the table with a thunk. I inhaled and exhaled slowly.

Nora reached out for my right hand. She outlined my hand with her index finger, her featherlight touch sending chill bumps up my arm. She gently twisted our friendship band between her thumb and forefinger. "What do you want to tell me?"

"I'm scared."

"No need to be scared of me. Ever." She squeezed my hand in encouragement.

I nodded and stood. I paced in the small kitchen, gathering my courage, pressing my hand to my tumbling stomach. *Pretend it's a meeting and Nora is a stranger.* Finally, I stopped and faced Nora. "Hi, my name is Sophie, and I'm an alcoholic."

"Hi, Sophie."

I laughed, mostly from nerves. I inhaled and dove headfirst into my greatest fear. "It's been one week since my last drink. Some of you are probably surprised by that. Today, I was supposed to get my one-year chip. Instead, I'm back at seven days, thanks to two swallows of beer." Nora opened her mouth as if to interject, but I held up my hand. "I've almost completed my twelve steps, thanks to my sponsor, Todd. But, there has been one glaring hole in my program: full amends to the person I hurt the most. Telling my story is the start."

I swallowed and met Nora's eyes. "The summer after eighth grade, my best friend got her first serious boyfriend. She'd had a crush on him for years and was beyond excited. I was excited for her. We'd all grown up together, and for the last couple of years we'd traced with fascination the progress of the happy trail of curly hair growing up out of Charlie's swim trunks." Nora laughed. "Charlie was partial to tight jeans, too, and we'd spend lots of time pretending not to see his bulging crotch. He knew we were looking."

"Yeah, he did," Nora said.

"You can imagine the excitement when he finally asked Nora out. But, she was nervous, too. She'd never kissed a guy and didn't want to do it wrong. Lose Charlie before she had a chance to keep him for a while. Since I'd kissed a boy before, I told her I'd show her how.

"I have to confess here: I talked a big game. I'd only ever kissed one boy, and it had been a wet, sloppy disaster. He enjoyed it, I suppose, because he kept at it. The story I told my friend was a little more impressive. There was this way she would look at me sometimes, wide-eyed, almost worshipful." I closed my eyes, remembering. "I would do anything, say anything, to get her to look at me like that." When I opened my eyes, Nora was watching me intently. "I'm sorry."

"I did worship you, Queen Esther."

I swallowed. "Naturally, I would be able to show her how to kiss, based on all of the false experience I said I had. We knelt on my bed and giggled each time we leaned toward each other. Finally, we kissed."

Nora's eyes hadn't left mine, and her mouth parted slightly.

"It wasn't a peck on the lips either. After—and we kissed for a good, long while—I assured her Charlie would have no complaint. We didn't speak of it for four years, but I remembered. I obsessed about it for weeks, about her, about how she made me feel. Eventually, it faded. She had her boyfriend, and I tried to date, kissed as many boys as I could, lost my virginity to one, but no one could make me feel... After sophomore year, I stopped trying.

"My life changed in September my senior year. It was a Friday night at a football game, and I saw my best friend kiss her boyfriend—same guy—like I'd seen her do a hundred times before and I thought, *That should be me. I* want *that to be me.* I shocked myself but knew deep down it was the truest thought I'd had about myself in years. Later, when we were alone, I brought up our kiss. I can't believe I did it. I was young and fearless. As it turned out, she hadn't forgotten it, either."

I looked down, the memory of that night sending a pleasant warmth rushing through my body. I didn't dare look at Nora but felt her unwavering gaze on me. I cleared my throat and continued. "We kept our new relationship secret from everyone. I got a boyfriend, immediately started sleeping with him. Better to have the reputation as a slut than a lesbian." I grasped my hands, twisting the band, wishing Nora would look away or stop me from continuing, say *I understand, no need to go on.* She didn't.

"Those months with Nora were the happiest of my life. We planned our future. College together, moving to a city and living together. There would be no need to 'come out.' We weren't gay, after all. We loved each other. Everyone knew we were best friends, living together would be the most natural thing in the world. We would ignore the pointed questions about when we were going to find husbands, and eventually, they'd stop asking. It was mostly my idea, my plan, with Nora going along with it. That's why, when I betrayed her, she cut me out of her life completely. And I deserved it."

I peeked up at Nora, who was staring at the kitchen table now. She sat rigidly, her hands folded neatly in her lap.

"If I hadn't made the first move that night our senior year, we would have continued to be best friends; she would have come back to Lynchfield and married Charlie, had a passel of kids. She would be the one helping plan Charlie's first political fund raiser. With her all-American girl-next-door looks and her adorable freckles, she would have been the perfect political wife.

"I'd always thought I was the strong one. I put up that front for years. But, when my parents threatened me with conversion camp, I cratered."

Nora's head jerked up. "What?"

I nodded.

"That bitch."

I held up my hand again. "I betrayed Nora completely. I lied about everything, told them I'd only gone along with Nora's advances because I didn't want to lose her friendship. I didn't think about what my lies would mean for Nora. I never expected my mother to tell Nora's father, that my lies would destroy her relationship with her family. All I could think about was saving myself. It was selfish and cruel and unforgivable. And the biggest mistake of my life.

"I started drinking the summer after she left. I quit three months later when I got pregnant and stayed clean for two years. With a breastfeeding infant, and a husband I was putting through college, I was too exhausted at the end of the day to drink. Whenever I would hear news of Nora, drinking would numb me, help me forget. I went on this way for years, drinking in secret. Outside, I had a perfect life. But, inside I was miserable. Something was missing."

I inhaled deeply. "A part of me knew what was missing, but I'd managed to shove that tiny bit of knowledge so far down and away from my life I'd convinced myself the desire I'd felt was unique to Nora. I would never find it with another woman. In sixteen years, I'd never looked at or desired another woman. It must have been the person, right? I decided to test the idea." I swallowed. "It wasn't."

Nora stood and poured herself another cup of coffee. With her back to me, she drank her coffee and stared at the cabinet. Finally, she turned around and leaned back against the counter.

"My final binge happened in a dirty little bar in Austin. I told myself I was drinking because being with the stranger had brought back all the memories of my friend, my betrayal. But, it wasn't. I didn't realize until this week that all those years I've been trying to drink away the gay. It didn't work that day either, but it did land me in a jail cell for DUI. Charlie, God love him, stood by me. Part of me had always hoped he would one day have enough and divorce me. But, even when his wife was in the drunk tank with a blood alcohol level that might torpedo his political career before it started, he didn't. I'm sure you're thinking, why didn't you leave? Cowardice. Loyalty. How could I betray a man who'd stood by me through so much?

"I knew something had to change when I saw the expression on my daughter's face when I came home after my arrest. She's seventeen now. I don't have her for much longer. I decided I wanted to see her through sober eyes every morning, and I have. For three hundred sixty-five days.

"So, why am I not getting my one-year chip? My best friend returned. I went to apologize to her, to make amends. She shut me down. I don't blame her. I deserve every ounce of hatred she had for me. She left half a beer on a table and... I picked it up. Tilting the bottle up and drinking was instinctual. When I pulled the bottle away, I wasn't thinking of the beer flowing down my throat, that I'd just torpedoed one year's worth of work. I thought of my lips touching the same glass hers had touched moments before, and I knew I couldn't let Nora leave without making amends, without apologizing to her, without telling her this story. Most importantly, I couldn't let her leave Lynchfield without telling her I love her. Still."

Nora didn't move; it didn't look like she was breathing. I took one step forward, knowing there was more, that I had to lay myself completely bare. "NoNo." My voice broke, and I swallowed. "I've been an ass, and I don't deserve you or your forgiveness. But, I've never stopped loving you, and I never will."

Nora placed a hand on her stomach, her chest rising and falling, finally. She came to me, setting her coffee cup on the kitchen table. Being this close to her the years fell away, and I looked into the face of the girl I fell in love with. I reveled in the tiny flecks of brown in her hazel eyes, the freckles dusting her nose, the way her eyelashes lightened at the tips. I knew one of her front teeth jutted slightly in front of the other, that if you pressed your thumb to the center of her chin, you could feel the cleft, though you couldn't see it.

She reached up and ran her thumb beneath one of my eyes, then the other, wiping away tears I didn't realize were there, but her eyes wouldn't meet mine. *"Say something,"* I whispered, feeling fresh tears. "Anything."

Her expression, so inscrutable, softened as her eyes met mine. The corners of her mouth lifted into a gentle smile, and she cradled my face in her hands. "I've never stopped loving you, and I never will."

twenty
nora

I would have never thought the torture training I learned in the military would be put to its hardest test while listening to the woman I loved lay herself bare in front of me.

After wiping her tears away, we embraced for a long time, Sophie crying quietly on my shoulder while I rubbed circles on her back.

I wished more than anything that I could take back everything I told Brenda about me and Sophie. If I hadn't pushed Brenda she wouldn't have threatened Sophie with conversion camp and we might have been able to have gone through with our plan for Sophie to meet me after boot camp. But, listening to Brenda berate me, call me the vilest names she could think of, made me snap. I didn't only tell her Sophie instigated the relationship, I gave her details. Graphic details. It felt good, seeing Brenda's face transform from haughty condescension to horror. If I ever considered how Brenda would take it out on Sophie, I don't remember. But, at the time I didn't think it could get much worse than going to a school with a statue of praying hands. Knowing what I know now about conversion camps, I know it gets a lot worse.

"I'm sorry."

She sniffed. "For what?"

"Everything. It's all my fault."

Sophie pulled back. "No, it's not. That's not why I told you the story."

"Conversion camp? That's because I told Brenda about us. In detail."

"No wonder she looks horrified when your name is mentioned."

"The beer?" I said. "If I hadn't been such a bitch in the barn, if I'd shown you just a little bit of grace…"

"I didn't deserve it."

"Yes, you do. You deserve all of my forgiveness, and more." I held on to her tightly. "You are so strong, Sophie Russell."

"If I were strong, I'd walk out that door, let you go back to your life. But, I can't."

Sophie's hand was at the small of my back, pulling me to her, her other buried in my hair, easing my head to one side so her lips could travel up my neck to my ear. "Do you really forgive me?" she whispered.

"Yes. Do you forgive me?"

"Yes," she breathed in my ear.

My body was barraged with tiny explosions of desire and, deep down, I grieved for all the years this had been missing from my life, that Sophie had been missing. I wanted her as I'd never wanted before, and when our lips met, I fell into her. My God, Sophie knew how to enchant me.

"Wait, wait," I said, against her mouth.

Sophie continued to kiss me, walking me backward toward the hall to the bedrooms. "Please stop talking," she said between kisses. Her hands were under my shirt, caressing my sides, my back, moving up my stomach to…

I pulled away. "This isn't fair to you."

She exhaled sharply, frustration evident in her expression. "I know what this is, Nora. Okay? No strings. A fling. Whatever you want to call it."

"Is that what you want?"

"I want to say *fuck everyone* and do what I want, which is to be with you, if only for a couple of weeks. I don't care. I need you, Nora. I can't eat or sleep. I haven't gotten shit done at work because I spend all day staring at the only photo I have of you. I mean, isn't the bedroom where this was always going? I know I'm not as experienced as you, but those were the signals you were sending. You just told me you've always loved me. What am I missing?"

"I've dreamed of this, you know. Even when I hated you, I wanted this. I've compared every woman I've been with to you, and no one has stacked up. So, no. You didn't read the signals wrong. Of course I want you."

She moved toward me. "Shut up and show me."

We were in each other's arms again, kissing frantically, our hands moving across each other's bodies. Tilting my head up to allow her full, sensual lips to travel up and down my neck, to my ear, and to my lips. My mind started wondering what I would do to her first, what I would teach her...

I held her face in my hands. "I know how the program works, Soph. Us being together is against the rules. I've already caused you to backslide, I don't want to be the cause again."

She inhaled slowly. "If this ends badly, you mean."

"Yes."

She nodded. "I appreciate that, more than you know. But, the chances are the same if I can't have you now, or if I lose you later. Besides, my drinking is my problem, my choice. Let me worry about it."

Sophie tried to kiss me again. I moved my head away. "I couldn't sleep last night, fantasizing about today. Anticipating. Dreaming. Remembering. Then, I thought of the after. It took me years to get over you, Sophie. But, in all the daydreams about it, the one thing I always imagined it as was a beginning, not the beginning of the end. You say you're fine with a one-night stand, but you could never be that for me. You're the love of my fucking life."

She stepped back. "What are you saying? You love me so much you don't want to make love to me?"

"I am not going to open myself up to being hurt again. I'm not going back to that shell of a woman."

The desire in her eyes was dimming, being replaced with indignation, and a little bit of anger. "Oh, but it's okay for me to?"

"You've got a lot of fucking baggage, Sophie. You've been living a lie for eighteen years. I haven't, and I'm completely comfortable with myself, and my life."

"And you have Alima to skitter back to when this is over."

"Skitter?"

Sophie huffed. "And you wonder why I said 'you won' that first day. Fine. Do you want to fight? Let's fight. There is nothing safe about me being here. If any of this came out it would torpedo my life, ruin my relationship with my daughter. I *still came* because I love you more than my miserable, small fucking life, I guess. We talk a good game, say we love each other, but what if when we get into it, we realize we aren't who we once were together? Or you decide you'd rather have Charlie than me? Or Alima. Then what do *I* have? A bunch of broken relationships and life alone in a small town."

"Charlie? Why would I want Charlie?" I said.

"Because you're bisexual."

"Alima told you."

"Yeah. Why didn't you?"

"I wasn't sure you would understand."

"You're right. I don't. Charlie might as well be a fence post for all the desire I feel for him. I want you, and only you."

"And I want only you. The fact that I'm attracted to men, too, has nothing to do with it."

"How can I be sure?"

"The same way anyone is sure of their partner's loyalty: trust."

"Why should I trust you? You don't trust me. Yeah, Alima told me that, too. And she told me you hate Lynchfield and me."

"Sophie…"

"*I'm* the trustworthy one, Nora. Christ, I've stayed with a man I don't love for nearly two decades because of his loyalty to me, and because of my love of my daughter. I stayed, faced the town, faced my mistakes. You're the one who ran and didn't come back. I came here this morning knowing you're going to leave again, to break my heart again. And why? Because I want to be with the woman I love, the only person I've ever loved. I want to feel your skin against mine, to be reminded how beautiful making love can be when you're with someone who you want to absorb into your very being because the thought of ever being without them fills you with sense of despair so complete, so bottomless, that you're sure you'll never smile, or laugh, or feel whole again. I'm willing to risk my family, my sanity, my sobriety because I fucking love you. You say you're risking your heart, but you aren't. Not when you have someone waiting for you. Someone who gets you. I don't have that. I've *never* had that, and if I lose you, *when* I lose you, I never will. So don't talk to me about fucking *risk*." Sophie took her purse off the back of her chair and draped it across her body. "You don't want to fuck me? I'll find someone who does. Enjoy your kolaches."

It took a moment for my mind to catch up with my emotions. Sophie was out of the kitchen and heading for the front door.

"Sophie, wait." I lunged after her and was stopped at the door of the kitchen when Sophie pulled me into her arms, her mouth finding its way home to mine.

twenty-one
sophie

"When do you have to be back?" Nora's voice was lazy, her words almost slurred, and I felt a little arrogant in the knowledge it was because of me.

"Noonish. What time is it?"

She reached over me, her bare skin sliding across mine, and woke her phone. "Eleven hundred."

I kissed her and got out of bed.

"Where are you going?"

"To buy us more time."

I walked down the hall naked as the day I was born, picked up my purse from the couch where I'd flung it on our way to the bedroom. I texted Charlie and Logan.

Going to brunch with Todd & Ivey. I'll text when I'm on my way home.

I hesitated before I hit Send. Lying to Charlie didn't bother me. He'd been cheating on me and lying to me for years. Lying to Logan was another story, especially after the promise I made to her only days before. I removed her name from the text and hoped she wouldn't question me too deeply about my morning.

I followed our clothes back to Nora's bedroom, discarded on the floor like a trail of breadcrumbs left to find your way home. I stopped before I got to her door. I was home. Nora was my home. I took a shaky breath, terrified and thrilled at the same time. I couldn't go back to the life I had before, but I didn't know how to go forward either. I pushed the fear of the future to the back of my mind, determined to take full advantage of the time we had now.

I pulled a book out and dropped my purse on the floor. "We have another hour."

"Gosh, whatever will we find to do?"

"I have something for you." I held the book out to Nora.

She grinned. "*Persuasion*. You kept this all this time?"

I sat down on the bed next to her. "It was the only thing I had of you."

She opened the book to the photo of the two of us.

"And that photo," I said.

"It looks like it's been through the wringer."

"You have no idea. Here." I took the book from her and flipped to the end. "This is my favorite part."

"You've read *Persuasion*? On your own."

"Yes, multiple times. Now, I've read a couple of Austen's novels. *Pride and Prejudice*."

"Everyone's read that."

"*Emma*. I love her."

"She reminds me of you. 'Sophie Russell, handsome, clever and rich…'"

"You think I'm clever?"

"Definitely handsome and rich."

"Ha ha. Well, *Persuasion* is my favorite, and this is why. 'You pierce my soul. I am half agony, half hope. Tell me not that I am too late, that precious feelings are gone forever. I offer myself to you again, with a heart even more your own than when you almost broke it eight and a half years ago.'" I closed the book. "Every time I read that, it gave me hope."

Nora took my hand and kissed it.

"I would drink when I heard of you, but when I sobered up, I would read this book, and fool myself into thinking we could have this happy ending."

"We may yet," Nora said. She pulled me down into a soft and languid kiss, as if we had all the time in the world. "I dream about your lips."

"Shut up."

"It's true. Remember how we would kiss for hours, and never get bored?"

"Yes."

"I've missed that, and everything about you."

"When did you become such a sweet talker?"

"I'm not," she whispered. "I guess you bring out the sap in me."

We took our time familiarizing ourselves again with the curves and planes we once knew so well. My hand stopped on Nora's abdomen, and I broke our kiss. I traced the most prominent scar with my finger. "Tell me what happened."

"Our convoy hit an IED."

"And?"

Nora kissed me then whispered against my lips, "I survived. Let's talk about it another time."

It was tough to stay focused, but I somehow managed. "You used to tell me everything."

With a small sigh, Nora pulled back and looked at me. "I'm out of practice. I don't usually open up to lovers."

I resisted the urge to mention Alima and pushed her out of my mind. "Can I ask you a question?"

"Anything."

"When we were together, did you enjoy sex with Charlie, too?"

"Goodness, that's a complicated question."

"I just, um, assumed you hated it like I hated having sex with Joe. But, if you're bisexual..."

"Being gay or straight or bi isn't just about who you're sexually attracted to. It's as much about emotional connections, maybe more so. I had both with you. With Charlie—" she shrugged "—the emotional connection faded, so the sexual attraction faded, too. He noticed, and you know Charlie. He's a fixer. The night before he left town, he pulled out all the stops. That was the only time that I felt guilty about sleeping with Charlie, because I knew my reaction to him was a betrayal of what we had."

It's amazing how a slight from years past can still pierce a person's soul. I tried not to show my hurt, but of course Nora saw it. She pulled me down next to her. I laid my head on her chest and listened to her heartbeat while she finished.

"I went to Tech and honestly just assumed I would date guys, and I did. But, I lived in a dorm full of girls, beautiful girls, girls who reminded me of you. It was a very confusing time for me.

"There was a class, human sexuality, that was tough to get into. You had to be an upperclassman to have any chance. People took it for all kinds of reasons and there was a lot of elbowing and snickering when the professor talked about sex, and condoms, and orgasms. That ramped up to a hundred when we got to the section about sexuality. That was back when calling guys *fags* and girls *lesbos* as a joke was okay. Looking back on it now, I suspect there were a lot of people in that class like me, questioning themselves, who they were, what it meant. I was hoping to find an easy answer for myself. What I learned was if you're looking for a clear definition of bisexuality, you won't ever find it, especially in a human sexuality class that's determined to give you all the options, to encourage you to have an open mind. I can tell you what it means to me, why I use the term. I enjoy connections—emotional and physical—with both genders. I've only had two relationship where the emotional and the physical have existed side by side. You and Alima."

"What about friends? Please tell me you had friends."

"Of course. The army's training is focused on building camaraderie, on a soldier's willingness to do everything they're
ordered to do to protect the life of the soldier next to them.
Friendships, that's one reason I loved the army so much. Then
I lost good friends in the IED attack. Best friends. The pain reminded me of losing you. It was easy to avoid connections after
that. They just weren't worth the pain. Then I met Alima and
she wasn't having any of that."

"Are you in love with Alima?" I whispered.

"You're the love of my life, Sophie."

As nonanswers went, it was a pretty good one. "You asked me
the other day to give you a reason to stay. Would you?"

"And sneak around? No. Can we get back to kissing?"

Her hands and lips shut me up for a few minutes until I pulled
away. "We need to multitask here."

"It's hard to make out and talk at the same time, Soph. And
we only have thirty minutes left."

"I'll talk fast."

She sighed. "You're killing me, Smalls. Go on. Hurry up."

"If I came out, left Charlie. Would you stay here in Lynchfield, make a life with me?"

"What would I do?"

"Raise chickens? You seem to have an affinity for them."

"I hate the little fuckers."

"You do not."

"I'm not raising chickens, Sophie."

"It was a joke."

"Come live with me in DC. You would love it," Nora said.

"I'm not leaving Logan. It's going to be bad enough I'm a
lesbian. If I skipped town to be with my girlfriend? My God,
could you imagine the gossip?"

Nora propped herself up on her elbow. "What do you mean,
bad enough you're a lesbian?"

"I mean people are going to freak out is all, and I'm not looking forward to it."

"You're not looking forward to finally being honest about who you are?"

"Don't twist my words around."

"This is why I didn't want to talk." Nora started to get up, but I grabbed her arm.

"Hang on. Come back."

Nora settled back down beside me. We lay on our sides, faces close like we used to. "First things first," I said. "I think your bed has shrunk."

"It's always been a twin. Are you complaining?"

"Right now? No. Second, I love you, I love you, I love you."

"Ditto."

Ditto was the code word we used to say *I love you* when around other people. We'd used it sparingly because there was nothing teenagers loved more than trying to figure out inside jokes.

I pushed her shoulder. "Say the words."

"I love you, I love you, I love you."

"So, let's remember that first, okay?"

"Okay."

"This 'what happens next' conversation? We need to have it because I'm not sure I'm going to be able to let you go."

"Me either."

"But, let's not have it right now, okay? Let's just enjoy today. Each other. We only have a little bit of time left, and I don't want to spend it fighting. We have two more weeks to do that."

"You started the conversation, Soph. I wanted to make out."

"Shit, you're right. I'm sorry. Tell me more about how much you love my lips. When did this start? You never told me before."

"When I didn't have them." Nora traced my lips with her finger. "Have you ever noticed Cate Blanchett's lips?"

I started laughing. If she only knew. "Yes."

"Yours are like hers, except yours are here, begging to be

kissed." Nora pushed me on my back and straddled me, holding my arms up over my head. "Now, whatever will we find to do for the next thirty minutes?"

"I don't know, but this looks promising."

Nora leaned down and brushed her lips against mine. "You have no idea…"

The was a thump in the distance.

"Was that a car door?"

"Shouldn't be. I told the high school kids not to come."

A child's squeal of laughter cut through the air.

"Shit," Nora said, rolling off the bed. "It's Mary. I forgot she was coming."

"Our clothes are in the other room."

"Nora," Mary called. "Is that Sophie's…"

"Look, Mommy, Aunt Nora's clothes are on the floor like mine," Hunter said.

Nora went to the dresser and pulled on panties and a T-shirt. Mary's voice dropped, and I could hear her talking to her husband. "Kids," Mary said in a too-loud voice, "I forgot, we're supposed to meet Aunt NoNo at Emmadean's." The door closed loudly, and we were alone.

"Shit," I said.

"I'll get the clothes."

Nora opened the door and Mary stood there, arm raised to knock. Her eyes went wide at the sight of me sitting on Nora's bed, naked and disheveled. I pulled a sheet up over me.

After the initial shock, Mary started laughing. "Holy shit."

"Out," Nora said, pushing her sister through the door and closing it behind her.

My body went numb, my mind blank. This wasn't on the level of my mother walking in on us, but it was close.

Nora was back quickly. She closed the door behind her and handed me my clothes. "I'm sorry I forgot," Nora said.

I shook my head and got dressed. It seemed my decision as to if and when I would share my secret was made.

"I'll talk to Mary. She won't tell."

I laughed. "Mary has never liked me."

"That's not..."

I silenced Nora with a look. We both knew it was true. I ducked down to look at myself in the dresser mirror, running my fingers through my mussed hair. I applied lipstick carefully, as if it was a typical day and I was getting ready to run errands. I stared at myself in the mirror, impressed that I didn't look like I wanted to vomit, which I did. Turned out telling Nora my story had been the easy part. I shouldered my purse and faced Nora, who'd put on a pair of jeans.

"Not how I wanted to spend our extra hour," I said.

"Me neither." She pulled me close and tucked a strand of hair behind my ear. "When can I see you again?"

Despite the fear swirling through my stomach, I smiled. Something to look forward to, to keep my mind off... "I don't know when I can get away. I'll have to text you," I said.

"Okay."

I took a deep breath and walked out of the room, with Nora behind me. Mary sat cross-legged in Ray's chair, waiting for us like a sentinel on duty. I wasn't about to give her the satisfaction of being ashamed. "Hello, Mary."

"Well, this explains a lot."

Nora took my hand.

"Dad found out, didn't he? That's why he kicked you out."

"My mother told him," I said.

"Holy shit. Brenda knows? I bet that was a scene."

"Could you not act so thrilled?" Nora said.

Mary's head jerked back, and her smile slipped. "I'm not thrilled. I'm glad to finally, after all these years, understand what the hell happened. I can't believe you managed to keep it secret."

"I know you don't like me," I said, "but I'm begging you not to tell anyone. To give me a chance to do it."

"Tell anyone? Tell them what?"

"That I'm gay."

"Wait, you're gay? This isn't just revisiting a teenage experiment?"

"I'm bisexual, and gay people pretend to be straight all the time," Nora said.

"You're gay, and you're bisexual?" Mary stood. "Wow. I can't even wrap my head around this."

"You promise to keep it to yourself," Nora said.

"Yeah, sure. What would I have to gain by telling anyone?"

I almost laughed at Mary's complete self-involvement but knew better. "Thank you." I turned to Nora. "I'll text you."

"Okay."

She squeezed my hand and gave me a brief smile. I leaned down and gave her a lingering, soft kiss. "Love you," I whispered. When we pulled apart, we saw Kim and her daughter, Erin, framed in the screen door.

I jerked back in surprise. "Shit."

Kim's mouth gaped in slack-jawed astonishment, and Erin looked at us with an expression of wonder—and relief?

"Kim, what are you doing here?" Nora asked.

"I brought Erin. Like we talked about."

"Like you talked about?" I asked.

"Well, yeah, but we didn't say when, or where," Nora said.

"I'm sorry, I just figured you would be up and about with the sale tomorrow and all." Her astonished gaze shifted to me.

Mary had the good grace to get up and excuse herself. "I'm going next door to Emmadean's." She left through the kitchen.

"Come on in, I guess," Nora said.

As they walked in, I turned to Nora and whispered, "What's going on? Why is she bringing Erin here?"

Kim inhaled. "I suppose this is a safe space."

Nora sighed and put her hand to her forehead. Kim continued. "Sophie, Erin is…"

"Mom."

"What? Nora knows, and I'm pretty sure Mrs. Wyatt isn't going to tell considering we just saw them kissing."

I looked away and pushed my hair behind my ear. "Oh my God," I said softly.

"I'm as shocked as you are," Kim said. "After meeting Alima and realizing about Nora, I just assumed the big fallout was because it was one-sided. It explained so much. I had no idea it wasn't. I mean, knock me over with a feather."

I looked at Erin Stopper. She was a sweet girl, quiet and respectful, with big blue eyes framed with a pair of black cat eyeglasses. She was awkward in the way fifteen-year-old girls used to be before the beauty industry and society and the Kardashians came along and convinced children they should look and dress like adults. She wore clothes a size too big and frequently changed her hair and her look. Most of Lynchfield chalked her oddness up to her being a geek girl, in love with science and gaming and being the smartest girl in her grade. I guess she had been testing out identities and trying to hide from scrutiny at the same time. It made sense now.

I'd known Erin her entire life. I'd rocked her to sleep when I volunteered in the church nursery, taught her in vacation bible school and Sunday school, and babysat her periodically on Saturdays when Kim and Joe both had to work. Though she and Logan were a couple of years apart and they'd always gotten along well, they weren't exactly what you would call close friends. I wondered if Logan knew she was gay.

"Come here, Erin," I said.

She stopped in front of me. There were four thin braids on one side of her head, one dark purple, but it barely stood out against her dark hair. "Can I hug you?"

She nodded, and I pulled her into my arms. She was considerably shorter than me, so I kissed the top of her head. I leaned my cheek against her head and whispered, "You're not alone."

She cried, softly at first, before it turned into full-fledged sobs.

twenty-two
nora

"I have a few minutes if you want to talk, Erin," Sophie said when the girl stopped crying.

Erin nodded and wiped her cheeks roughly. "Yeah."

"Does anyone want a Blizzard? I suddenly have a hankering for a Blizzard," Kim said.

"I wouldn't turn a Reese's blizzard down," I said.

"Double chocolate-covered cherry," Sophie said. I smiled. Same order from our high school days.

"Just a chocolate malt," Erin said.

"I'll, uh, go pick those up. Give y'all time to chat."

Kim held her purse across her body in a white-knuckle grip. I went to her and edged her toward the door. When we were outside on the porch, I cleared my throat. "So, about what you saw."

"Nora, you don't…"

"Listen. You know what Erin's going through? How concerned you are about her? That's what Sophie's going through, too. Sophie has a lot to lose if this gets out."

Kim nodded. "I know that."

"I don't know what Sophie will tell Erin, but we need to

know you won't quiz your daughter about it, and you won't tell Joe about us. It's our story to tell, understand?"

"Yes. Absolutely. I'll be back in a jiffy."

I watched her leave, not entirely confident she would be able to keep what she saw to herself. When I saw Sophie's expression as she sat across the kitchen table from Erin, I knew the same worry was on her mind.

Sophie and Erin were silent, their familiarity getting in the way of honesty. I sat down between them, took Sophie's hand, and squeezed it. Erin's eyes went straight to our enjoined hands and stayed there.

"Erin, I'm Nora. It's nice to meet you."

"Nice to meet you, too. I've heard a lot about you."

I cleared my throat. "Your mom wanted me to talk to you, but uh, I've never done this, so I don't know what I'm doing. Or what to say. I'm bisexual, so my experience might not be like yours."

"You like guys, too?"

"Yes, I'm attracted to men, too."

"Are you, too?" She looked at Sophie, who stared at the table for a long time. Finally, with a squeeze of my hand, Sophie shook her head almost imperceptibly.

Sophie inhaled and met Erin's shocked gaze with a smile that I knew took a lot of courage. "I've known since eighth grade. What about you?"

"Fourth." Erin picked at the edge of the table. "I didn't really understand until a year ago. There was a girl, at space camp, last summer."

"Have y'all kept in touch?" I asked.

"Yeah. She lives in East Texas, and is in pretty much the same boat I am."

Sophie nodded. "You haven't told any of your friends?"

"God, no. Just my mom."

"You're lucky you have a mom who was understanding. I didn't," Sophie said. "Still don't."

"What about Mr. Wyatt? And Logan?" Erin asked.

"No one knows, Erin. I'm not ready to tell, and I'm trusting you and your mother to keep my secret, even from your father. Like I'll keep yours."

"Yeah. Okay. But, you two are a couple, right?"

"No, Erin. We're not," I said. "Sophie is married, and I live a thousand miles away." Sophie pulled her hand from mine and placed it in her lap. "We've just reconnected, and we're trying to figure out what's next."

"So, you're just hooking up."

"No," Sophie said, a little too forcefully. "We fell in… I fell in love with Nora in high school. Senior year."

"*We* fell in love is right. We kept it a secret, of course."

"You dated my dad," Erin said.

Sophie grimaced. "I did."

"He was your beard."

"Yes, I suppose he was."

"Like Mr. Wyatt is now."

"Erin…" Sophie stood, and started pacing the room. She put her head in her hand and murmured, "Christ." She dropped her hand an inhaled deeply again. "No matter how bad you think Lynchfield is now about gay people, it was much, much worse twenty years ago. My choices were all awful, and they were limited. Things are different now. At least for you." Sophie said the last bit in a soft voice and turned away.

"I'm tired of not being me, you know?" Erin said. "Going along when everyone talks about how hot guys are. If I never have a conversation again about Chris Bird's ass, it will be too soon."

"I'll just assume he's the big man on campus," I said.

"Yeah," Sophie and Erin said in unison.

I waited for Sophie to say something, but she kept her back turned.

"I'm definitely not the person to tell you to come out or not," I said. "But, I can tell you this: it's easier when you get outside this bubble. I'm not going to say it's easy. It's not. There are fucking homophobes everywhere. But, you will find a community, people to support you. People like you. College was a real eye-opener."

Sophie leaned against the kitchen counter with apparent nonchalance, but her white-knuckled grip on the edge of the Formica gave her away. "I would hope that kids would be more accepting," Sophie said. "It seems your generation is more tolerant, about everything. I imagine Logan wouldn't..." She bit her lip and looked away. So, Logan wouldn't be good with it.

Erin leaned back in her chair and crossed her arms over her vintage NASA T-shirt. "Have you forgotten the Sunday school classes that *you* taught to me?" Erin said.

Sophie didn't answer for a long moment. When she spoke, her voice was strained. "No, and I'm sorry for that. I'm a coward and a hypocrite, Erin."

Kim called out from the other room. "Blizzards are here!" She came into the kitchen with a drink carrier and passed out the ice cream. It wasn't until she finished that she noticed the tension in the room. "Is everything okay?"

"Yes, everything's fine." Sophie squatted down in front of Erin. "I'm sorry. Truly, I am. I knew what I taught was wrong, but I didn't dare say no. It helped my cover, you see, to hate what I was. What I am." Sophie's voice broke, and though I couldn't see her face, I knew she was crying. "I'm probably not the best example for you, I know that, and any advice I give you I should probably take for myself first. But, I'm here if you need me." She squeezed Erin's leg and stood. "I need to...to get home. Thanks for the Blizzard, Kim."

Sophie darted toward the door, and I had to run to catch up with her. "Hey, hey, hey. Hold up." I grasped her arms, moved closer and lowered my voice. "Stay here. We need to talk."

She pulled her arms free. "No. I've been here too long. Logan's texting me."

Kim and Erin bustled through the den on the way to the front door. "We're going to head out."

"Thanks, Mrs. Wyatt. Nora." Erin threw herself into Sophie's arms. Sophie held her arms around her awkwardly, one hand still holding the Blizzard. Erin looked up into Sophie's tear-stained face. "I'm here if you need me, too."

Sophie finally lost it. She clung to Erin and buried her head in her shoulder. They were whispering low so that Kim and I couldn't hear. They pulled apart and gave each other encouraging smiles.

"Come on, Mom," Erin said.

I locked the front door behind them. "Stay here," I said, and left to lock the kitchen door. "No one is interrupting…"

Sophie had her hands in her hair, and she was crying. "Oh my God, oh my God, oh my God."

"Sophie, just calm down."

"Calm down? Why does everyone go straight to fucking calm down? Kim Stopper just saw us kissing. I came out to her fucking daughter. Your sister caught us in bed. And you're telling me to calm down? Christ. The number of people in town who know I'm gay just doubled in five minutes. You know Kim's going to tell Joe. There's no way Kim will keep that to herself."

"I don't think she will."

"Yes, well, it's only a matter of time, isn't it? So, I get to live with the constant fear that she's going to out me, or that Erin accidentally will. That's going to be fun. What do you care? You'll be a thousand miles away."

"That's not fair."

"Isn't that what you said? We aren't a couple, and you're a thousand miles away? So, I know not to expect any help from you."

I gritted my teeth to keep from lashing out and took a deep breath. "You're jumping down my throat because you're scared."

"Scared? You think I'm scared?" She moved close and said,

"No, Nora. I'm *terrified*. Do you want to know what all I'm terrified of? It's a long list. Oh, wait. It's a lot of *baggage*."

"I forgot what a bitch you can be."

"And I forgot how selfish you can be. How cold and unfeeling."

"You want to know what I'm afraid of, Sophie? Why I didn't want to sleep with you? Didn't want to forgive you? Because I knew you would pull me back in. And you did. And I knew, too, that this would happen. That you would betray me to save your reputation."

"Betray you? How can I betray someone who isn't interested in commitment? Who tells me at every possible opportunity that I'm not enough for them. That me, a life with me, could never compare to what you have in DC. With Alima."

"Not fucking Alima again. I'm turning her down, okay? She's no threat. When I imagine my future, it's with you. Not Alima. I love you, Sophie. Only you. How many different ways do I have to tell you?"

Sophie stilled and leaned back a little. "Turning what down?"

Fuck. I pinched the bridge of my nose. I didn't mean to let that slip.

"Turning what down, Nora?"

"Her marriage proposal."

"Marriage. Alima… She *proposed* to you? When?"

"The day she arrived. Did you not hear the second part of that? That I love only you? That I imagine a life with you?"

"Turning down. Pretty sure that's future tense."

"I was going to call her tomorrow."

"Why not last night? Or this morning? Or when she fucking asked you? I'm pretty sure that was after our kiss in the car."

"And I didn't say yes, did I?"

"So, if we hadn't kissed, or if you hadn't come back, you would have?"

"You and I were nothing to each other a week ago, Sophie.

It is completely unfair for you to be angry about the life I had without you, the people I've loved and been with."

"Sounds like you're hedging your bets. With both of us."

"Honestly, Sophie? I was waiting to make sure you didn't fucking betray me again, but it looks like you're going to. Logan won't accept us, will she?"

Sophie sighed. "I don't know. She said something last night... It doesn't matter."

"Bullshit. You won't come out if it would hurt your relationship with Logan." I heard myself finally, how angry and hateful I sounded. I was lashing out at Sophie when all she was doing was asking fair questions of me, holding me accountable for my actions. My voice gentled. "I don't *want* you to risk your relationship with Logan."

"So, where does that leave us?"

I took Sophie's hand and held it to my chest, chanting *peace, calm, peace, calm* inside my head. *I love this woman, and I'll fight to win her.*

"I want to spend as much time with you as I can before I leave. We'll figure everything out. I believe we're meant to be together, one way or another. I didn't realize until I saw you at Mel's that you've held my heart in the palm of your hand all these years. Right now, I'm offering you my heart, Sophie. My soul. Can you promise me a future?"

Sophie closed her eyes and exhaled. "I want to, I really do. But, I don't know, Nora. I really don't."

I dropped her hand and stepped back. Sophie's phone vibrated in her purse.

"That's probably Logan."

"Mmm-hmm."

"We can't leave it like this."

"Sophie, you know where I stand. Where we go from here is your decision, and I'm not going to beg you to make it."

I unlocked the front door and opened it for her. She left without a glance or a word.

twenty-three
sophie

"How was your meeting?"

I poked at my chicken fajita salad and mentally went through my schedule for the week. Conference calls, meetings, taking Logan to Austin for her doctor's appointment, making personal calls to potential donors for the fund raiser next Saturday, grocery shopping, dinner, laundry. Hardly a minute to myself. But, I had to find a way to see Nora.

It's your decision, and I'm not going to beg you to make it.

There was no way to see Nora at night without Charlie. Sure, I could say we wanted to visit as much as possible before she returned to DC, but Charlie would inevitably want to come. He had a history with Nora, too. No, there was no possible way I could spend time with Charlie and Nora together. Not after this morning.

Which meant I was going to have to sneak out, and Charlie is a light sleeper.

"Mom."

"Hmm?"

We sat at the kitchen table eating leftovers. Charlie scrolled through his email, or Facebook or Twitter on his phone, and didn't seem to be paying attention, but Logan was watching me with one of her suspicious expressions as if she knew I was about to disappoint her in some way.

"How was your meeting?" Logan said.

"Oh." I shrugged one shoulder. "Fine."

"Are there a lot of people there on Saturday mornings?"

"Usually."

"How many were there today?"

"I didn't count."

"A ballpark."

Charlie looked up from his phone. "What's with the third degree?"

"Just trying to make conversation. Isn't that what families are supposed to do? Talk at dinner?" Logan said.

Charlie turned his phone over. "I played an awful round of golf today. Lost a hundred bucks."

"Whatever will your constituents think about your gambling?" I said.

Charlie ignored me. He picked up a fajita. "You were gone when I woke up this morning."

"Couldn't sleep. Went to the bakery for a coffee and read the paper before going to the meeting."

"What did you do, Logan?"

"We were supposed to go out and help Nora get ready for the sale tomorrow."

My stomach dropped to my feet. I looked at my daughter, who was staring at me. "But, she told me to take the day off. Probably wanted to spend time with her girlfriend."

Charlie laughed. "Girlfriend?"

Logan looked at her dad. "Alima. They're gay, you know."

Charlie laughed even harder. "No, they're not. Alima is married."

"Nora's not."

"That doesn't mean she's gay, Logan," Charlie said.

"Look at the way she dresses. It's almost masculine."

Charlie furrowed his brows. "She didn't look masculine last night. But, Nora never dressed very... She was always a T-shirt and jeans kind of girl. Not everyone loves clothes like your mom. Or looks as good in them."

"Thank you," I said automatically, though I couldn't take my eyes off my daughter. She was pointedly looking at me now.

"What do you think, Mom? She's your best friend. Is she gay?"

"We haven't..." I started a denial, a deflection, and stopped. "What would it matter if she was?"

"Is she?" Charlie said.

Technically, she's bisexual, and I'm in love with her.

The confession was there, ready to be voiced, eager to spread its wings and soar into the world before anyone else could out me. Mary, my mother, Kim, Erin and possibly Joe. I had the sudden image of Luke, Han, Chewie and Princess Leia in the trash chute, frantically trying to keep the walls from closing in and crushing them. My chest grew heavy as if being squeezed between a vise. I should get out in front of it, confess. But, did I want to destroy everything I had? Try as I might, I couldn't imagine a different life. I imagined Nora with me, in this life. The fact was, to free my inner life, I had to give up the safety and security of my outer life.

Everything had come down to this moment, sitting at my kitchen table, eating leftovers. A piece of chicken fell out of the end of the fajita Charlie held in his hand. There were deep furrows in Logan's hair where she ran her fingers through it to pull it back into a hasty ponytail. The spicy, smoky aroma of the fajitas made my stomach tighten with nausea. Charlie's expression was shifting before my eyes, from questioning disbelief to a real consideration, as if connecting the dots to a picture he realized had been hiding in plain sight for years. How long had I been sitting in silence?

"Not as far as I know."

Logan sat back in her chair, and Charlie laughed a little nervously. "Of course, she's not." He rebuilt his fajita. "When is she leaving?" he said.

"I don't know," I answered. I drank my sweet tea, trying to rid myself of the shame lodged in my throat.

"She doesn't need to stay on after the estate sale tomorrow," Charlie said. "She can leave as early as Monday. Everything else can be done electronically, closing on the house, finalizing the will."

"I thought you wanted Nora to stay on for the fund raiser next weekend," I said.

"I got the impression from Alima that Nora needs to get back to work," he said. "Doubt she'll contribute anything anyway."

"Is that the only reason you want her there?" I asked.

Charlie shoved his chair back from the table and picked up his plate. "I'd rather financial supporters eat my barbecue and drink my beer." He rinsed his plate and put it in the dishwasher. Was he clanging the dishes around with more force than necessary, or did I imagine it? His expression was neutral. "We have a meeting tomorrow afternoon with Avery and Mark at the dance hall. Two o'clock."

"We? I thought my job was to make phone calls and show up and look pretty."

"Avery thinks you should be more involved in the planning."

"I was going to help Nora tomorrow."

"She has a family to help."

"I'll help her," Logan said.

"There you go. You can help your husband get elected. I've got to run up to the office for a bit." Charlie twirled his keys around his forefinger and left without looking at me.

The garage door went up and back down before Logan spoke.

"Why did you lie? I know Nora's gay."

"How could you possibly know? Did she tell you?"

"No."

"Then it's none of your business." I took my plate to the kitchen and dumped my uneaten salad in the trash. I squirted dish soap on the plate and washed it.

"I know you were at her house today."

The plate slipped from my hand. I glanced up at Logan, who was watching me like a hawk. I picked the plate back up and continued cleaning it. "What makes you think that?"

"Find My iPhone. What were you doing over there?"

"I stopped by after my meeting to visit. Nora's leaving soon, and I want to spend as much time with her as possible." I hated the shaking in my voice and hoped the sound of running water covered it.

"Why did you tell Dad you were going to breakfast?"

I put the plate in the dishwasher. "I was afraid your dad might decide to come by."

"Why would that be bad?"

"I know it's been a long time, but it's weird for me to be in the same room with them, you know?"

"Because you stole Dad from Nora?"

I sighed, the relief of being almost honest with my daughter dissipating with my breath. It seemed in the past, present and future, I was always going to be viewed as the villain. Everything came down to me, to my decisions or indecision, my courage or cowardice.

"Yep, Logan. You've figured me out." I threw the sponge in the sink and went to bed to crawl under the covers, and never come out.

twenty-four
nora

"Come here, Nora. Look at this one."

Mary and Emmadean sat on Ray's sofa, a cardboard box of photos at their feet, rifling through what my unsentimental father had shoved in the back of his closet after my mother died. Since I'd avoided touching Ray's room out of disgust or fear, I wasn't sure which, I'd never seen the box before Mary had dragged it from its hiding place. Even in childhood. A quick glance at the visible contents—a dozen or so school photo envelopes—and I knew how much the box, and the memories it contained, meant to my father. It was easy to envision him tossing my and Mary's latest leftover school photos in the back of the closet and forgetting about them. Thinking back, I realized it had always been Mary and I who had asked for money for the photos, and Emmadean had always been the one with the camera at our significant life events. The photos on the wall had been put there by me and Mary and Emmadean.

All those years I'd been alienated from Ray, I'd never given much thought to how unique our relationship had been or realized that after my mother had died my father had always been more bystander than a participant in our lives. He met our basic needs and left the parenting up to his sister. Instead, I'd focused on the unfairness of Ray's reaction, his refusal to talk to me, to let me explain. I'd picked at that scab off and on for years, letting it heal over before worrying it again, but never moving on to a different wound. That one had been enough. Life defining. But, there had been so much more that might have helped explain everything, help me move on emotionally. Allow me to open myself to people in a way I've never been able to. Or wanted to. I'd never considered how easy it must have been for Ray to cut ties with me. He'd effectively done it when my mother died.

I was jittery with the urge to leave Lynchfield, to run far away from Ray's memory, Mary's judgment (I'd caught her staring at me with amazement a few times), Emmadean's secret and Sophie's emotional baggage, and to set fire to the world before I escaped. I didn't need the drama.

I was afraid I'd already opened myself up too much to Sophie. *I love you. You've always had my heart.* What was I thinking? You don't tell anyone that until you are sure of their commitment, their trust. I'd never told anyone that, not even Alima. Maybe that was what had held me back from accepting Alima, the knowledge deep down that I couldn't tell her those two things, that as much as I loved her and desired her, it wasn't the same sort of love I felt for Sophie. As I sat here, looking blankly at the photo Emmadean held, that surge of emotion I felt when I told Sophie was fading, being replaced with the soul-crushing grief of abandonment I'd felt in those last days in Lynchfield all those years ago.

Emmadean's hopeful expression as she held out a photo stopped me from jumping out of my skin, but my mind was working on the quickest and easiest way to make my getaway.

I took the photo from Emmadean's shaking hand. Her eyes met mine, and she pulled her hand to her chest in a futile hope I didn't notice. I pretended to ignore it and looked at the picture. It was the last family photo the four of us had taken for the church directory, a perfect storm of '80s fashion. We looked happy. Were we? I couldn't remember.

My mother stared at me from the past, and it was like looking in a mirror, even down to the freckles sprinkled across the bridges of our noses. Sure, people had always told me how much I looked like her, but I'd always shrugged off the idea as polite small talk, something people felt they had to stay to make sure I didn't forget her, or would somehow continue to feel connected to her as the years slipped by. I realized now I was older than my mother was when she died. How different would my life have been if my mother hadn't driven home in the storm? Sophie and I wouldn't have become best friends, and we wouldn't have fallen in love. Ray wouldn't have kicked me out, and I wouldn't have joined the military. Hidden among the disasters were genuine moments of happiness: my senior year in high school when I knew pure, unconditional love; the discovery of a real talent for languages; a fulfilling career; making a difference in the world, though not one I could share or discuss; a full, happy life with friends and lovers who accepted me, loved me, for who I was, not who I was expected to be. Would I trade the good things to have a mother growing up, and here with me? I wasn't sure.

Emmadean and Mary watched me. I handed the photo back. "I'm leaving on Monday."

"Monday?" they said in unison.

As soon as I said it, I knew it was the right thing to do. The only thing to do. I was glad I'd come home, filled in the blanks of the past with Sophie, made love to her one last time. I could move on now. Maybe with Alima, maybe not. Maybe I wasn't meant to have a life partner. On a deep level, I knew it would not be Sophie. I knew she loved me, but I wasn't sure she loved me enough for the sacrifices she would have to make. The end of our most recent conversation didn't give me much hope.

"That's the day after tomorrow," Mary said.

"There's still so much to do," Emmadean said. "You've only been home…"

"A week," I said, and that's a week too long. "And Lynchfield hasn't been home in eighteen years."

Emmadean inhaled and dropped her head.

"What the hell, Nora? Do you hear yourself sometimes?" Mary said. She placed her arm around Emmadean's shoulder and whispered in her ear. Emmadean wiped at her eyes and shook her head. Mary glared at me. "Just because you fought with your girlfriend…"

"We didn't fight…"

"Your girlfriend?" Emmadean said. Her watery eyes widened. "Alima?" she whispered.

"Sophie," I said, and the corners of Emmadean's mouth turned up into a tentative smile.

"You knew Nora was gay?" Mary said.

"Bisexual," I corrected her.

Emmadean kept her eyes on me. "Nora told me about her and Sophie when she was in the hospital after her accident. I was trying to convince her to come home to recuperate. So I could take care of her."

"I wasn't about to give Ray the satisfaction of ignoring me."

"You didn't want to see Sophie," Emmadean said.

"That, too."

Mary's arm fell from Emmadean's shoulder. She leaned away from our aunt. "I can't believe y'all kept this from me all these years. Though I don't know why I'm surprised. You've always liked Nora more than me." Mary rose from the couch.

"That's not true," Emmadean said.

"There she goes," I said, "making everything about her."

"Oh, shut up, Nora. You're the most selfish person in this family. You don't even care about what's been going on with Emmadean. And don't tell me the super spy hasn't noticed."

"Mary," Emmadean snapped.

"Hello?" A man's voice called from outside.

The three of us looked at the front door. "Who's that?" I asked.

"I don't know. My x-ray vision is on the fritz," Mary snapped.

I rolled my eyes and opened the door. Charlie Wyatt stood on the other side of the screen holding a six-pack of Mockingbird Toasted Pecan porter. "Hey," he said. "I knocked, but don't think you heard me."

"Charlie," Mary said. "I'm so glad to see you."

Charlie smiled like a good politician, but there was doubt there. What had he heard? I grabbed his arm and practically pushed him off the porch as I left the house. "Help me check the chickens." I glared at Mary and slammed the door behind me.

"Family spat?" Charlie handed me a beer as we walked around to the barn.

I twisted the cap and threw it against the house. "Something like that." I gulped the beer. "God, that's truly awful beer."

"Yeah, sorry. It's all we had left over from last night."

"No idea why," I said.

"Poor Trent can't seem to settle in on anything. It's a real tax on Jamie."

The chickens were squawking and scratching the dirt for feed when we walked into the barn. I grabbed a handful of seeds and tossed them into the coop while Charlie opened a beer. He watched me with narrowed eyes and a sly knowing smile. Could he somehow tell I'd been making love to his wife only a few hours earlier? Impossible. Charlie didn't like to lose, and his wife cheating on him, especially with another woman, would never cross his mind. I upturned an empty bucket for him to sit on as flashes of my time with Sophie flittered through my mind: the subtle scent of perfume in the hollow behind her ear, tracing her full lips with my finger, Sophie counting the freckles on my nose, her hand lightly stroking my arm while we talked.

My heart raced with longing. Christ, the mere memory of being with her was softening my resolve to leave.

I leaned against the stall door to keep my legs from buckling beneath me and tried for nonchalance. "What brings you out here?" I said.

He sat down and placed the six-pack at his feet. He shrugged and drank. "I haven't gotten to spend any time with you alone since you've been back. Thought it might be nice to."

I nodded and drank the skunky beer. No conversation ideas came to mind, and Charlie seemed more interested in analyzing me through narrowed eyes than talking. I remembered that Charlie's favorite subject had always been himself. Young, in love (or so I thought), and raised to believe in a female's subservient, secondary role to men, I'd never given it a second thought when we'd dated. I'd long since grown out of that and silently thanked Ray for freeing me from Lynchfield, Charlie, and the old-school outlook I was raised to have.

"It looks like you're right on track for the governor's mansion."

Charlie grinned, showing the Deadly Dimple. "It's early days yet, and our current governor is pretty well entrenched. But, there are other offices besides governor."

I nodded. "So, the GOP is grooming you for greatness?"

He shrugged one shoulder. "They seem optimistic. I have the background, the family, the right outlook on the issues."

I clenched my jaw, knowing full well that *right outlook on the issues* meant restricting my rights. It wasn't worth arguing with Charlie. Texas had nothing to do with me. I would leave here in two days and return where I was accepted. Or at least I wasn't overtly hated. "To the future of the party," I toasted.

He lifted his beer. "As long as there's no scandal to derail me." He drank his beer but kept his eyes on me.

I nodded. "You might want to stop sleeping with Jamie Luke, then."

"What makes you think I'm sleeping with Jamie?"

"Do you want me to list the ways I know?"

Amused, Charlie said, "Sure."

"Jamie was protective and territorial when I visited your office, she couldn't take her eyes off you last night, but you did your level best to avoid her altogether. I don't think you ever even looked at her. Probably didn't want Avery to catch on."

"I'm sleeping with Avery, too?"

"Yes. She's probably safe. She knows how Washington works, and as long as you don't betray her professionally, she'll keep the secret. You aren't the first politician she's slept with, and you won't be the last."

Charlie's smug smile slipped. Poor thing, he'd been the golden boy in little Lynchfield for so long he didn't realize how insignificant he was to the broader world.

"Jamie, though. She won't take rejection well. She's a concern. Unless you intend to leave Sophie for her."

"Good thing I'm not sleeping with her, then."

"Charlie, cut the shit. Sophie told me all about you."

Charlie laughed. "Oh, did she? What did she say?"

"Besides that you liked your affairs? That you would try to seduce me."

"I haven't, though, have I?"

"Isn't that why you're here?"

"Will you be disappointed if I say no?"

"Not really."

Charlie rocked the bucket back off the ground. "Wow. Don't spare my feelings, NoNo."

"Don't call me NoNo."

"Why? I used to call you that all the time. So did Sophie. In fact, I heard her call you NoNo last night, and you didn't blink."

I drank my beer so I wouldn't have to answer. NoNo had been my nickname since childhood, but I couldn't hear it, or think of it, without hearing Sophie's voice whispering it in my ear, or calling it out when we made love. Like she did this morning. I looked away. "I've outgrown it."

"I suppose Sophie can get away with things we mere mortals can't."

I glared at Charlie. "Why are you here?"

He finished his beer, put the empty in the six-pack, and took out another. The bottle opened with a *pfft*, and he stood. "I need you to leave town."

"You what?"

"For Sophie's sake."

I pushed away from the stall door. "What's wrong with Sophie?"

Charlie's eyes sparked as if I'd confirmed his suspicion. "She's an alcoholic, for one. A terrible mother most of the time because of it. A habitual liar. A master manipulator."

"That's not the Sophie I know. That's the disease," I said.

Charlie scoffed. "Alcoholism isn't a disease. It's a weakness, one that Sophie had finally overcome. She'd been sober for nearly a year. She was getting her life back together, her relationship with Logan. Our marriage. Then you came back in town, and the drinking starts. The lying. And, I started thinking back over the years, and you know what every binge she went on had in common?"

I remained silent.

"News of you. Your deployment, your injury, every other little piece of news Emmadean spread around town as if you were the second coming of Christ." Charlie stood a mere foot away from me. I looked up at him and met his gaze with a fierce determination I didn't feel. His voice lowered and softened, became intimate. "There have been many times over the years when I've wondered how different my life would be if we'd gotten married like we'd planned. Usually during the difficult times, and there have been many, many difficult times with Sophie. You know how volatile she can be. But, something funny happened that summer after you left. I learned what it was like to be in love. I'm not telling you this to insult you. I loved you, Nora, and we would have had a good life, I think. But, with Sophie, I've had *passion*. That volatility has its benefits, especially in the bedroom."

I clenched my jaw but didn't blink. I knew it was a lie. Sophie loved me. Wanted me. Told me how she felt nothing when they had sex. But, the image of them making love that I'd tortured myself with all those years ago, and my own experience with Sophie's passion, wasn't so easy to forget.

"The bad times make me appreciate the good times more. We're a great team, me and Sophie, and we're just getting started." He moved forward a half an inch, and his voice hardened. "And, you're not going to take that away from me."

"Take what away?"

"My wife. My future."

My heart soared. Sophie'd told Charlie and Logan, about us, about herself. She'd leaped, and I was going to be there to catch her. "Sophie told you."

"Yes."

"And, you're here to try to intimidate me to leave?" I laughed in his face. "I won't go into what they did to prepare females for capture by extremist forces, but you might be able to imagine it. A two-bit small-town lawyer like you isn't going to intimidate me by getting in my face. Especially when it comes to being with the woman I've loved my entire life." I shoved him back and walked away. "Go home, Charlie. You're embarrassing yourself."

"So, it's true? You're gay."

I turned to face him. "What?"

"Sophie didn't tell me anything. She lied for you to the end. So much for your training. This two-bit small-town lawyer got you to confess pretty easy."

It took great discipline to keep my face impassive. Inside, I was begging Sophie to forgive me.

"So, are you?"

"Gay? No. I'm bisexual. Did Kim tell you?"

"Kim? She knows?"

"Who told you?"

"Logan. She asked Sophie if you were gay. Not an hour ago. Sophie said she didn't know. I knew she was lying."

Charlie didn't know anything for sure. The entire conversation was a fishing expedition, and I might as well have been tossing the fish into the boat for him. I could salvage this. Keep Sophie's secret until she was ready to tell it herself. But, why? She'd had the chance to tell Charlie and Logan and had chosen to lie. The small amount of hope I'd held about Sophie selecting a life with me evaporated. If I told Charlie everything, Sophie would be forced to choose, and I would finally, definitively, be free of this limbo.

Patton squawked and fluttered into the air. A bead of sweat trickled down the small of my back. Mary's children laughed in the distance.

"I've been in love with Sophie since high school. When you went on vacation, I told her. Confessed everything. She rejected me, said it was you she always wanted, so I enlisted. Left town. Stayed away all those years because I couldn't bear to see her with you. She came by today, after her meeting, and I told her I still loved her. She rejected me again."

Charlie searched my face, searching for the truth. When his face relaxed in relief, I knew he believed me. His life, his plans, his future, were secure. "Good." He picked up his six-pack of beer. "Did you ever love me?"

"Yes."

"And, our last night together? That was all fake?"

"No, Charlie. I'm bisexual."

"Explain that to me, how you can want to fuck men and women."

"Google it."

He scoffed. "When are you leaving?"

"Monday."

"All of the paperwork for the will and the house can be handled electronically. Have a safe trip."

The smug expression on Charlie's face, his supreme assurance he would never lose, grated on me.

When Charlie was at the barn door, I called out to him. He turned. Sunlight backlit him, so he was more shadow than a man. "Do you even love her, or do you just need her to sell your brand to the voters?"

Charlie stepped forward, his expression almost hurt. "Do you know how easy it would have been to leave? To give up on our marriage? I didn't because I love her. I love the life we have, who she is when she's not crawling around in a bottle. Hell, yeah, she will help sell me to voters. She's beautiful and she can talk to anyone about anything. My God, can she charm people." He chuckled and shook his head. "Men and women alike. So, yeah. I want her by my side, not only because she makes me better, but because I love her, despite everything she's put Logan and me through."

"You'll never love her like I do."

"Maybe not, but it hardly matters, does it? Have an nice life, Nora."

twenty-five
sophie

Nora, I hate how we left everything today. I want to be with you. Only you. We can figure this out. Together.

I'm coming over tonight after Charlie goes to sleep. We have to talk this through.

Hello?

Your silence speaks volumes.

If you don't want to be with me, you've got to tell me to my fucking face. Ignoring my texts won't save you.

When Charlie's breathing settled into its steady rhythm, I slid quietly out of bed and into the bathroom. I had to see Nora, finish our conversation from earlier. I dressed in the closet, barely paying attention to what I put on, brushed my teeth and pulled my hair back into a messy bun. I turned the light off and was waking my phone to check if she'd messaged when the door opened to a brightly lit room. Charlie stood in front of me.

"Where are you going, Soph?"

"For a run. I can't sleep."

"In flip-flops?"

I looked down and cursed myself.

"Going to see Nora?"

"Why would you say that?"

"I went to see her today."

"Oh. That's uh, good," I said. "You two haven't gotten to spend much time together."

"Won't get to spend much more. Nora's leaving on Monday."

"Is she?" My voice was unnaturally high.

Charlie nodded. "Seemed anxious to leave. She was relieved when I told her we would handle the paperwork electronically."

That was it, then. Why Nora wasn't replying to my texts or picking up the calls I had made before Charlie returned. She was leaving me. She'd decided I wasn't worth the trouble.

"Oh. Well. I'm sure Nora's anxious to get back to her life," I said, my throat almost closed with emotion.

"Logan was right, by the way. She's gay."

"She told you that?"

"Yes. Didn't hesitate. Nora said you knew."

I cleared my throat, hoping my voice would sound normal. "It wasn't my secret to tell."

"You're a good friend, to keep her secret all these years. She told me all about it."

The room swam in front of me, and I leaned against the doorframe for support. "Told you what?" I whispered.

"That she was in love with you. That you rejected her all those years ago. And again today."

Charlie pulled me into his arms. "No wonder it ended your friendship. How could you be around her knowing she fantasized about you? It's disgusting. Degrading." He kissed my neck and slid his hands under my shirt and across my back. When he found no bra strap to unhook, his hand moved to cup my naked breast. His growing erection poked into my thigh, and the thickness in my throat turned to bile. His free hand guided mine beneath the waistband of his underwear. I tried to twist my hand away, so I didn't have to touch it, but he was stronger than I was. He held my hand around his semihard cock. "Remember our first time," he asked. "When you slid your hand beneath my shorts?"

"Charlie." I tried to push him back, but he wouldn't budge. His hand squeezed my breast harder. "Ow. Charlie." Two could play that game. I squeezed and twisted his dick before pushing him away and stepping back at the same time.

He cupped his cock. "Fuck, Sophie. That hurt."

"Oh, but you squeezing my boob didn't hurt me?"

"But, you like it rough. Angry."

"Not tonight."

"Not tonight, what? Do you want to make love gently? Or you don't want to at all?"

"I'm not in the mood tonight."

"Are you ever really in the mood, Sophie?"

I sighed. "Can we not?"

"Yes, let's not. Let's start with not fucking lying to me anymore. How does that sound?"

"Charlie..."

He moved forward threateningly. "Cut the shit, Sophie." His eyes blazed with a rage I'd never seen before. For the first time in our marriage, I was afraid Charlie was going to hit me. "Tell me exactly what went on between you and Nora, and don't lie to me. If you do, I'll make sure your daughter never believes another word you say. You and I both know it won't be difficult to do."

My throat constricted and my mind immediately went to alcohol. I licked my lips.

He scoffed. He knew me too well. "You're pathetic."

"Charlie, you don't understand."

"No, I think I do. Nora's been your trigger for all these years, and now I think I know why. But, I want to hear it from you."

I took a deep breath and exhaled. I walked around Charlie and sat on the edge of the bed.

"Nora isn't the trigger."

"Oh, really."

I shook my head and kept my gaze on my hands. I rubbed my red thumbnail. "Every time I heard about Nora it reminded me of when we were together. How happy I was. How complete she made me feel."

"What do you mean *when you were together?*"

I looked up at him. "You know what I'm saying."

He crossed his arms over his bare chest and looked away. The muscle in his jaw working. "How long?"

"All of our senior year."

"Jesus Christ." He rubbed his hands over his bald head and started pacing. "You dated Joe senior year."

"We dated y'all so no one would suspect."

"So, your jealousy about Nora and me was because of Nora, not me?"

I nodded.

His fist balled and his jaw clenched. I leaned away from him, and he caught himself. He turned away. "Nora lied to me today."

"Yes." I took a deep breath and told him the full truth.

I should give Charlie credit, he listened to the story from beginning to end without interrupting, but his thoughts and emotions were written plainly on his face. I tried to mask the relief I felt at finally being honest, at the possibilities of a future with Nora.

"And, today? Were you with her today?"

"Yes."

"And, did you...?"

"Yes."

Charlie turned, screamed and slammed his fist into the wall. He immediately swore and shook his hand.

"Charlie!" I went to him, reaching for him. He flinched away from me.

"Don't touch me."

"Charlie…"

"Just shut up, Sophie."

I dropped my hands. "I'm sorry."

"You're *sorry*? *Sorry*? You fucking lied to me all these years, and that's the best you can manage? Sorry?"

"Shh. You'll wake Logan."

"You don't want her to hear about how you trapped me into marrying you by getting pregnant?"

"That's not what happened," I said.

"Sure what it looks like."

"If the condom hadn't broken, I would have gone to Nora. Begged her forgiveness."

Charlie shook his head and looked at me in disgusted amazement. "You never loved me. You used me. All this time."

"I did love you."

Charlie waited as if hoping for more. When nothing came, he walked out of the room.

I exhaled. It was over. Done. I reached out for the dresser to steady myself. Now I needed to find the words to tell Logan before Charlie did.

I practically ran out of the room and down the hall. Charlie stood in the kitchen, filling a Ziploc bag with ice. He closed the freezer door, balanced the ice on the back of his injured hand and pulled a beer out of the fridge. He realized he couldn't open it and motioned toward me. "Do you mind? Or are you desperate for a drink?" I opened the beer for him. The kitchen lights were dim, softening Charlie's sharp features. He drank the beer, keeping his eyes on me. "We meet Avery and Mark tomorrow at one. The fund raiser is next Friday night. There's lots to do."

"Charlie... I... I just told you I'm gay."

He laughed. "You told me you messed around with your best friend in high school and got caught. Lots of people experiment."

I stared at my husband in wonder. If there hadn't been a bag of ice on his hand, I would doubt the angry conversation we had five minutes earlier had happened. "It wasn't an experiment. I love her. I've always loved her."

He set his beer down on the counter and took my hand. His was cold and slightly damp from the bottle. "Look, Sophie. I know you struggle with mental illness—"

"No, I don't."

"—lying, manipulation, addiction. I suppose I shouldn't be surprised there's a sexual aspect to your sickness as well."

"Being gay isn't a sickness, Charlie. It's who I am."

"Obviously, AA isn't enough for all of your problems. I've never wanted to mention this, but I think it's time you went to see a shrink."

"A *shrink*? What are we, in 1950? Yeah, I probably should have gone to therapy, and maybe I will. But, here, *now*, you aren't *listening to me*. I can't live this lie anymore. I want a divorce." I finally said it. If I'd have known about the feeling of lightness, of relief that would follow, I would have done it years ago.

"That's not how this works, Sophie. You don't get to manipulate me, trap me into a marriage, lie to me for years, and then ruin my reputation and future by waltzing away with your dyke lover. Being married to you has been a nightmare, but I've stood by you. Through it all. You. Fucking. Owe. Me. You want to eat pussy? Fine. Do it on the side. Out of town. I don't care."

I flinched at how he turned my time with Nora, something beautiful and full of love, into something crude and dirty.

"But, you aren't leaving, and we aren't getting a divorce."

With sudden clarity, I realized there was a ruthless, vindictive side to Charlie I'd never seen because he'd never lost in his life.

"I've betrayed you, and you want to get back at me by making me miserable."

"Miserable? How is your life so miserable?" He swept his arm around the house. "You live in a beautiful house, you wear designer clothes, you have a wonderful daughter, and a good career. I've supported you in absolutely everything. I've been an equal partner in parenting, and you know that is not the fucking norm around here. I've done everything I can to help you overcome your addiction. Have I ever, once in our marriage, said no to you? Or discouraged you from doing something you wanted to do?"

I looked away and shook my head.

"Sorry, I can't hear you."

"No."

"Now, you think I'm being unreasonable for being angry at being betrayed for twenty fucking years? Just listen to yourself, Sophie. Jesus Christ. I'm not the bad guy in this situation."

"You've never been faithful."

"Because you hate having sex. Now I get why. Do you realize we went nine months without having sex once? *Nine months.* I mean, come on. But, I never even considered leaving you."

"Because you love me so much, or a divorce wouldn't look good for your political future?"

He exhaled sharply. "Believe what you want, I don't care. But, after all I've done for you, you owe me some goddamn public loyalty, and you can start by helping me plan this fund raiser and winning the election."

A year and a half. That's what Charlie was asking of me.

"You're right, Charlie."

I love you. It's always been you.

A year and a half of penance for my betrayal.

"I owe you."

You've got a lot of fucking baggage.

A year and a half of lies, of not being myself. A year and a half of worry that someone would out me.

"I'll do whatever it takes to make sure you get the future you've worked so hard for."

I'm offering my heart. My soul. Can you offer me a future?

No, I can't. Not right now. I have debts to pay, only after will I be free of guilt and clear of conscience to be my true self. The woman Nora would get now would be riddled with guilt. Nora deserves better. She deserves my honesty, and then the decision of what our relationship would or wouldn't be will be up to her.

"Good," Charlie said.

"On one condition."

Charlie laughed. "I hardly think..."

"Promise me you won't tell Logan."

He took a drink from his bottle, then showed a great deal of interest in the label. When he said, "I promise," without looking at me, I knew he was lying.

twenty-six
nora

I spent all day Sunday watching Emmadean and knew within an hour that she was sick and trying her darnedest not to show it. She was her usual, cheerful self, laying out defrosted funeral food on every available space in the kitchen.

"Emmadean, this is an estate sale, not a potluck." I snagged a sausage ball from a Tupperware container.

"You're selling the freezer, or have you forgotten?"

I swallowed the dry sausage ball and followed it with a swig of coffee. "Oh."

"And, we're not letting this food go to waste, what with you leaving tomorrow."

She wouldn't look at me, hadn't looked at me full-on since she arrived. I put my arm around her shoulders. "We need to..."

She moved out from under my arm, unsteadily. She caught herself on the back of a chair. "Is Sophie coming?"

"I doubt it."

"Are y'all on the outs again?" She sounded irritated.

"Honestly, I don't know what we are."

By lying to Charlie, I'd given Sophie the ability to stay closeted if she wanted, or to come out.

I hadn't answered Sophie's texts because it was her life that would be upended, and I didn't want her ever to doubt her decision, to ever be able to point to my influence during an argument and say, *if you hadn't...* I expected her texts to change when Charlie told her about my lie. When they didn't, I assumed it had worked. Charlie had believed me. When she hadn't shown up by 2:00 a.m., I knew it was over.

"You need to stop being so damn stubborn, Nora."

"What? *Me?*"

"Yes, you. If people don't do what you want them to do, you write them off. I love you, Nora, I do. But, you're one of the most selfish people I know."

I choked on another dry sausage ball. Why was I eating them? I drank more coffee. "That's unfair."

"Is it?"

"I could have told Charlie everything last night, forced Sophie's hand, but I didn't. After all she put me through, I think that was pretty goddamn magnanimous."

"All she put you through. Have you ever considered what she's lived through?"

"Of course I have."

"Humph."

"Sophie knows I love her."

"No, you don't. Love means making sacrifices, putting others before yourself most of the time." She looked me in the eye. "When was the last time you did that?"

"Yesterday, when I lied to Charlie to protect Sophie's secret."

"You lied to Charlie so you wouldn't have to decide to stay or not. It's all up to Sophie now, isn't it?"

Jesus, it was easy to forget what a gift of discernment Emmadean had. She sure knew how to puncture my high opinion of myself. Of course, this wasn't just Sophie's decision. Mary and Emmadean were right; I am incredibly selfish.

Madison and Hunter ran into the kitchen and launched themselves at Emmadean. She laughed and hugged the troublemakers with one arm, the other tightly holding on to the back of the chair for balance. Mary and Jeremy walked into the kitchen. "Kids," Jeremy said, "Y'all are too big to barrel into Emmadean like that."

Mary surveyed the table. "Ooh, sausage balls."

"Sorry, Emmadean," Hunter and Madison said.

"You'll never be too big to hug me, just a little gentler."

"Are you feeling okay this morning?" Madison petted Emmadean's arm and looked up at her with her brown, soulful eyes.

"Yes, angel. I'm feeling fine. What can I get for you two to eat?"

"Special breakfast!" Hunter said.

"I don't think Aunt Nora has Eggo waffles."

"Awwww."

I motioned to the spread of funeral food. "There's lots of options, kids. Please, help me eat up this food."

"They're kids, Nora. They eat four things," Mary said. "Jeremy, take them to town to get donuts."

My brother-in-law, who had been watching me, turned to his wife. "You take them. I need to talk to Nora about the chickens."

"Why?"

"Because I'm building a coop in our backyard for them."

"Yes!" Madison said.

"No, you are not," Mary said.

"Yes, I am."

"And, who's going to be left taking care of them? Me. Just like I have to take care of everything."

"I've been reading up on them, Mom. I'll help. Nora, Patton is a Golden Comet, MacArthur is a Rhode Island Red. They lay the most eggs," Madison said.

"No joke," I said. "Sold. When can y'all take them?"

"Never," Mary said.

"I'll take an apple fritter," Jeremy said and held the back door open for me.

"Chocolate cake with chocolate icing for me," I said to Madison. "I can't hardly find those in DC. Old-fashioned if they don't have it. You're a peach, Mary."

Grasshoppers flew around us and chattered with displeasure as we disturbed them walking to the barn. Patches of dry and brittle grass testified to the coming of July. By August, the grass would be worn down to stubble and dust. "Having a bad morning?" he asked.

"More like a bad week."

Beads of sweat ran down my back when we walked into the shaded barn.

"A week, huh?"

I suspected I knew where this was going.

Jeremy went to the chicken coop, gave it a cursory glance before turning to face me. "Emmadean has Parkinson's."

Not where I thought it was going.

"She was diagnosed about six months ago."

"Why didn't anyone tell me?" I sounded petulant and annoyed, even to my own ears. It only took a glance from Jeremy to make me feel shame. It was my own fault I didn't know. This was the unintended result of separating myself from my family.

"She didn't want us to. It's killing Mary not to tell you. I'm telling you because I'm sick of listening to her bitch about you, and how she's so put upon all the time. She's already complaining about how the brunt of taking care of Emmadean is going to fall on her."

"Typical Mary."

"Is she wrong?"

I shifted from one leg to another.

"Don't misunderstand, she isn't complaining about taking care of Emmadean. We all love Emmadean and would do anything for her. Mary is complaining about *you*, Nora. It chaps her hide that you can be so selfish, can shirk your responsibilities to Emmadean and you're still her favorite."

"I didn't know Emmadean was sick. Now..."

"Come on, Nora. You worked in Army Intelligence, for Christsakes. You knew something was wrong. You didn't want to know the details because you didn't want to be bothered."

"That's not true. I was going to talk to Emmadean today."

"She wouldn't have told you anything. She's made us all swear not to tell you. She wants you to stay because you want to, because this is your home, not because she's sick."

"This isn't my home. And don't act like living in Lynchfield is some dream. It's small, petty, spiteful. You don't live here, and you could. You fucking *work* from home."

We were silent, looking around the barn. Finally, I spoke. "I've got tons of vacation, and sick leave saved up. I can come down for a four-day weekend once a month to help out. Go to doctor's appointments. Whatever they need. How bad is it? Her Parkinson's?"

"They have her on Sinemet, which has been helping. But, still. There's no cure. It's a matter of how fast you go downhill."

"Shit." I turned and looked at my chickens. MacArthur, the preening little shit, was strutting around like a rooster while Patton watched stoically from her roost. Ike was asleep. I opened the coop and went in to gather the eggs, making a basket with the bottom of my shirt. I stroked Patton's feathers before gently nudging her off her nest. "Come on, girl. Give it up." I stared down at the egg I held and thought of Sophie. *You could raise chickens.*

I shook my head. I didn't want to raise chickens, and I didn't want to live in Lynchfield. What Sophie didn't realize when she asked me to stay, and what I had ignored with my impulsive request to ask her to convince me to stay, was that there were very few spaces for people like us to be ourselves, and Lynchfield wasn't one of them.

Jeremy watched me through the chicken wire. "I got quite an earful about you and Sophie last night."

"Did you tell her you knew?"

"Hell, no. And you better take that to your grave."

I'd confided in Jeremy over a ridiculously expensive bottle of red wine during one of his business trips to DC years earlier. He had been the first person I'd told the entire story, from beginning to end, leaving nothing out. Emmadean knew most, but the version I told her was a PG-13 tragic love story. I hadn't intended to bare my soul, but the wine was good, and he was a damn fine listener. Jeremy never flinched or blushed. Merely watched me with steady eyes and offered his hand to hold at the absolute perfect time. It was cathartic, a turning point in my life. I met Alima not long after.

"I can't stay, Jeremy. Everyone will see me as the one who 'turned' a loving wife and mother into a lesbian."

"Move to Austin."

We could go to Austin and come close to feeling comfortable in our skin, but the threat of violence against us was everywhere. Red state, blue state. It didn't matter. Sometimes, the most well-meaning people, the "advocates," would say things and remind you that small-minded people were all around us. Luckily, Logan was almost of age so custody might not be an issue. It was almost a certainty that a homophobic small-town Texas judge would rule against Sophie and require supervised visitation. Too few people would see past the one thing that made us different to see all the ways we were the same. "I have a job."

"Think Sophie would…"

"It doesn't matter." I stepped out of the coop. "Sophie won't come out, and if she did, I would never ask her to leave her daughter."

"I hope you're wrong."

"So, are you going to take my chickens?"

Jeremy raised his eyebrows. "Your chickens?"

"Ray's."

"Yeah, probably. The kids want them, and I love eggs."

"Mary is right in that she'll be the one taking care of them."

"Oh, she talks a good game, but she's only truly happy when she's complaining about something."

"How can you stand it?"

"She's a great mother and wife." Jeremy leaned close. "And, that fire? Translates in private."

"Oh, hush. I do not want to hear that." We walked back into the blazing heat.

"One more thing." Jeremy stopped in the middle of the yard. I squinted up at him against the bright sun. "I confronted Ray. After you told me."

"You what?"

"I was so pissed for you. I had a big idea I could heal the rift."

"You're the best of us, Jeremy."

"He got angry. Told me to mind my own business."

"No surprise there."

"But, after that, he asked me about you all the time. He'd get me alone out here with the chickens and quiz me without actually ever asking about you. It was the damnedest thing, how he did it. He was proud of you."

"Humph." I looked out toward the pasture that still needed shredding, though the heat would take care of the weeds soon enough, and swallowed the lump forming in my throat.

"I asked him once if he wanted your number. He said he'd had the same home phone number for forty years. You knew how to get in touch with him."

"Stubborn to the end."

Jeremy put a hand on my shoulder. "Take a lesson, sis. Don't let your stubbornness get in the way of your happiness."

"I can't believe we didn't sell more."

Emmadean looked around the half-empty den with a sad expression. I followed her gaze and caught Mary's eye. Neither of us was surprised. Ray had kept the bones of the house up—the plumbing, electricity, the roof, etc.—so chances are we wouldn't have much trouble selling it. But, the inside, the decor? Hadn't changed since the Reagan Administration. The first one. Every piece of furniture had thirty years of wear on it. Everything was shabby, and not in a chic sort of way. The junkers found nothing inside to entice them and focused on things in the barn. That was Dormer's domain, and he held on tightly to things I would have given away. The hipster estate buyers from Austin practically turned their noses up at Ray's stuff, eliciting from me an unexpected, and alarming, defensiveness. Even the locals found little to like, though the women cleaned out the kitchen quick enough. Privately, I hadn't expected the shabbiness to matter to country folk, had expected all Ray's crap to be scooped up within a couple of hours. It turned out they were more discerning than I thought. Now I was left with a house that was still full of shit I didn't want to deal with. In my rush to be done with Lynchfield, to blow out of town, I'd extended the time I would have to be here.

"I should have used Joe."

"Yep," Dormer said. "That horse is out of the barn, though."

"He probably couldn't have sold much more than we did," Mary said.

"But, he would have someone haul off what's left, right?"

"I guess."

"I bet he'll hook you up with someone who'll take it off your hands," Jeremy said.

"Doubt it. 'Hey Joe, I didn't use you to sell my stuff, know anyone I could call to take it now?'"

"Call Sophie," Mary said, with a small smirk. "I bet she'd love to help."

"I need a beer." I walked out of the den. "Who wants one?"

"We're heading out," Jeremy said. "I leave for Boston tomorrow."

"And the kids have swim practice," Mary said. "Where are they?"

"With the chickens," Jeremy said. "I'll get them."

He kissed me on the temple. "Remember what I said," he whispered and squeezed my arm.

I peeked into the kitchen at the destroyed remnants of the funeral food. Instead of being on the downhill side of the mountain I needed to climb to escape Lynchfield, it seemed I was back at the bottom of the ascent.

"I better get working on the kitchen," Emmadean said.

"No. I'll do it. You're wiped out, and you've done more than your share today."

Her face slackened with relief. "If you're sure."

"Positive."

"I'll take you home, Em," Dormer said.

The kids came in with Jeremy and took the few cookies that were left, thinking they were chocolate chip. I didn't have the heart to tell them they were oatmeal raisin. Plus, less for me to clean up.

After a flurry of goodbyes, I was alone in Ray's house.

Right back where I was a week earlier.

twenty-seven
sophie

The parking lot in front of the run-down building was full of potholes, trash and weeds. A couple of Harleys were parked in front, and a nondescript pickup was parked on the side of the building.

"Um, this isn't the Magnolia Café."

Through the front window of my car, I looked up at the square midcentury sign hanging from a steel pole above the door and laughed. "Nope."

I opened my car door and stepped out.

"We aren't going in there, are we?" Logan asked.

"Yep." I waited at the bar door for her.

"What the hell are we doing here, Mom?"

I pointed up at the sign. "Hitting Rock Bottom."

It took a moment for my eyes to adjust to the dark room, but the smell was shockingly familiar. Logan moved close to me and put her hand in mine. "Mom, this place is creepy."

I squeezed her hand. "We're okay," I said, though I was starting to doubt my decision to bring my young daughter here. I led her to a table near the back by the old-fashioned jukebox and cigarette machine.

The bartender threw his towel over his shoulder and ambled over to us. "Minors aren't allowed."

"Okay," Logan said, standing. I held her hand to keep her seated.

"She's not drinking. We won't be here long."

The man narrowed his eyes at me and seemed to come to a decision. "Jack and beer back, right?"

"Not today. Two Cokes, please."

"You've been here before," Logan hissed when the bartender left.

"Unfortunately."

"And you brought me here, why?"

"I need to tell you a story. I thought I'd start at the end, but I'm not so sure now."

"This place smells like vomit."

"Most bars like this do."

The bartender put two Cokes in front of us and returned to the bar. A biker went to the jukebox next to us and leaned over it, deciding on what to play. He chose his music and ambled back to his friend. Johnny Cash's smooth voice filled the dark bar.

"I can't imagine what kind of story ends here." Logan eyed the patches on the back of the biker's vests. These weren't white-collar weekend bikers. They looked like extras from *Sons of Anarchy*. "I mean, I can't believe you got out alive."

I sipped my Coke and gathered my courage. I ran this conversation over and over in my mind the day before, during every tedious minute of the meeting with Avery and Mark about the fund raiser, trying to grasp enough of what they were saying to be engaged, but not caring a bit about anything they decided. I'd managed to focus during Logan's first gynecological visit, but immediately after my mind went to this conversation, how I would start it, how it would go, how it would end. Now, here we were and all I wanted to do was leave and keep my secret for one more day.

"This was the bar I was at before my DUI."

"Oh."

"I didn't realize until today it was called Rock Bottom. Pretty appropriate." I placed my hands flat on the sticky table and leaned back, inhaling deeply.

"Mom, what is it? Are you dying or something?"

I laughed. "No, though it might be easier than telling you I'm gay."

I went completely still, shocked that I'd said it so nonchalantly. My plans for easing into our heart-to-heart ran out the front door, screaming.

Logan's eyes were wide and fixed on me. "You're *what*?"

"I..." I started to apologize for how it came out, to explain how I'd had a big conversation planned to help her understand, but what was the point? I didn't want to apologize for who I was. But, I knew this was going to upend her world, her perspective of me and our relationship, and I felt guilty I was doing it to her, even though it needed to happen.

"I'm gay, Logan. That's what I wanted to tell you."

Her eyes narrowed. "Nora did this, didn't she?"

"No."

"You were fine until she came back to town."

"No, I wasn't."

"That fucking bitch. I knew it."

"Logan," I snapped. "Don't you dare call her that. And don't rush to judgment when you only know a sliver of the story."

Logan flounced back in her chair and crossed her arms over her chest, but her eyes flicked toward the front door. Toward escape.

"I've known I was gay since eighth grade. Oh, I've denied it, ignored it, tried to change it, most of my life." I closed my eyes and shook my head, thinking of all the lost years. I opened my eyes to my daughter watching me. "I can't anymore. I'm so tired of pretending."

Arms still crossed over her chest, she pursed her lips and studied me. "Is that why you're an alcoholic?"

I nodded.

Logan leaned forward, put her head in her hands and stared at the table. "I can't believe this."

"You can't believe I'm gay, or that I'm being honest with you?"

"Both." She waved her hand at me. "Look at you. You don't look gay. I mean, Nora is one thing. But, you?"

"Logan. I'd hoped I taught you better than that, but it looks like your father's and my mother's influence is peeking through."

Her eyes widened. "Does Dad know?"

"Yes. I told him, but Charlie doesn't want to believe it."

"Are y'all getting a divorce?"

"He doesn't want one."

"He doesn't? But, why would he…"

"Want to be with someone who doesn't love him?"

"You don't *love* him?"

I cringed. This wasn't going the way I hoped. "I did. In the beginning, and for years after. Up to a few days ago, I would have said I loved him, still."

"What happened?"

My palms dampened. I didn't want to turn Logan against her father, but I'd also promised myself I would be completely honest with her, that total honesty would be how I saved our relationship. But, it could also destroy it. "He threatened to use you to keep me in our marriage. To lie to you about me, and my past."

"Dad's not the liar. You are."

"Yes, I lied to hide my drinking. I tried to keep it a secret, and to keep how bad it had gotten from you. Yeah, it was selfish and wrong but I was trying to protect you. To protect our relationship. Lying wasn't the way to do it, I know that now, and I'm sorry. I wish I could take it all back, but I can't. I'm opening myself up to you, sharing a big secret, because I don't want to lie to you about my sexuality. I've just come to terms with it. For the most part, anyway. Your dad refuses to."

Logan's eyes burned with what? Hatred? Skepticism? "Why would Dad want to lie to me?"

"I think he's afraid having his wife divorce him for another woman won't play well with his conservative base."

She shook her head vigorously. "No way. How can you be so mean…" Logan's brows furrowed. She held up her hand. "Hang on. What other woman?"

I looked away, but not before I saw her face turn to stone.

"Nora."

"Yes."

"I knew it. You just lied about that." Logan stood suddenly, taking me by surprise. I grabbed her hand before she could walk off.

"You need to sit down and listen to me."

"Why? You're doing what you said Dad would do. Trying to turn me against him. What's next? You leaving us for that dyke?"

"I'm not leaving you, Logan. I will never leave you."

"No, you'll pretend we're a happy family for all these years. So much for only lying about your drinking. You lied about why you were at Nora's, didn't you?"

I nodded. "I'm telling you everything now, so I don't have to lie anymore."

"Dad's right. You're manipulative."

I held myself upright and immovable, afraid if I moved I would shatter into a thousand pieces. "When did your dad say that?"

Logan squirmed, realizing she'd told me something she wasn't supposed to.

"Logan?"

"He says it all the time."

I gritted my teeth to keep from screaming. I'd long suspected

Charlie undermined me with Logan, now I knew it for sure. That fucker. Any qualms about what I was doing vanished.

"Why should I listen to anything you say?"

"Because I'm risking the most important relationship in my life by coming out to you. Because if you're going to hate me, you need to hate me for all of it, not just for the end."

Logan looked toward the door, then over her shoulder at the bartender, who'd stopped talking to the two bikers and was watching us with mild interest. Willie and Waylon sang about Pancho and Lefty. Reluctantly, Logan sat down.

The story poured out of me like whiskey from a new bottle, in fits and starts at first, before finding its rhythm and sliding into an ice-filled glass.

When I stopped, Logan stared into the distance with an unreadable expression. The bartender brought two fresh Cokes and a basket of boiled peanuts. He nodded to me in understanding, glanced at my stunned daughter and walked off. I was reasonably sure the music had drowned out my story from the men at the bar, but I suppose he'd seen enough in his time to know a confession when he saw one.

Logan wouldn't look at me.

"Say something." My stomach was in turmoil. "Do you hate me?" I said my voice barely above a whisper.

Logan sighed. "Yeah. Maybe a little."

A sob burst from me. Every one of my deepest fears was coming true.

"Did you think I would say, 'Yay! My mom is gay! My whole family is a lie! Let's get some pancakes'?"

"Your family is not a lie. My sexuality doesn't change the fact that your father and I love you. Loving you, not wanting to fail you, is the only thing keeping me from taking that bartender up on his Jack and beer back offer. All I want to do is to get drunk and forget this conversation ever happened."

"Fine. Let's go eat pancakes. Anything to get out of this shit-hole, and you away from the booze."

Only a few tables were occupied when a waitress led us to a booth in the main room of the Magnolia Cafe.

"Coffee," I said, as we sat.

The waitress looked at me full-on. Her brows furrowed slightly, no doubt at my red eyes, but being the professional she was, she ignored it.

"Same," Logan said. "Black."

"Coffee?"

"I feel like I've crossed over from childhood in the last hour. Might as well start obtaining the vices of an adult."

"Keep it to coffee, and you'll be good."

"I will."

My alcoholism, my lies, my many failures, my secrets hung in the air between us.

The waitress brought us the coffee. "Ready to order?"

"Gingerbread pancakes and crisp bacon," Logan said.

"Same."

"Short stack?"

"Nope," Logan said. "We're living it up."

"You got it."

Logan drank her coffee and grimaced. I chuckled. "Want some cream?"

"No. I'm good." Her voice was strangled. "That's terrible."

"By the time we leave here, you'll be used to it." I drank my coffee, set the thick ceramic mug down and twisted it around on the table. "So. Ask."

"Ask what?"

"Don't you have a million questions?"

"I probably will later, but right now, I have two."

"Okay."

"Did you only tell me because you were afraid Dad would?"

"No. I decided Saturday that I couldn't live a lie anymore, but I, um, couldn't work up the courage to tell you, or your Dad, that night. I should have." I reached across the table and grasped her hand. "I know you have no reason to trust me, but I swear I'll never lie to you again."

She raised her eyebrows, and I knew she was going to ask a question to test the theory. "Would you have married Dad if I hadn't come along?"

"Probably not. I don't think Charlie had any idea of marrying me either. We found comfort in each other, and when you came along, we named it love."

Logan drank her coffee again, and only grimaced slightly. "And Nora?"

I studied my mug for a moment, then forced myself to meet Logan's eyes. "I knew I was still in love with her when I saw her at the funeral. I wasn't crying for Ray, that's for damn sure."

The waitress returned with our pancakes. We were silent while we slathered the butter and syrup over the delicious-smelling gingerbread. The waitress freshened our coffee and left us alone again. We ate for a few minutes.

"Does Nora know you're talking to me?"

I shrugged one shoulder and crunched into my bacon. "If she's been reading my texts, she does. I haven't heard from her since I left her house Saturday."

"Why?"

"I have no idea." I cleared my throat. "Well, I have a suspicion." Logan waited. "Your dad went to see her Saturday night. I have no idea what he said to her, and he hasn't let me out of his sight since."

Loyalty to her father warred with her tentative trust in me. I was torn between not wanting to seem like I was trying to turn Logan against Charlie and giving him too much leeway.

"She made a comment on Saturday about me having, and I quote, *a lot of fucking baggage.* She's been living her life openly for years. I suppose I can't blame her if she's not interested in taking me on."

"Mom, look. I'm glad you told me, but there are just some things I don't want to think about, like you being in a relationship with another woman. I'm sure one day I'll be fine, but right now I just can't deal with the visual."

"Right. It's 'gross.' I get it."

Logan's eyes widened. "No, I didn't mean... It would be weird if it was with another man, too. Just you with anyone. I mean, even Dad. I think that's gross."

"Stop, okay. I know exactly what you meant Friday night."

"Mom, please. I didn't know."

"I've dropped a bombshell on you, so I'll extend a little grace to you that you haven't necessarily given me. You know, there comes a time in everyone's life when they have to realize they can't just say whatever comes to their mind whenever it comes to their mind. Today is that day for you, I think." I gestured to the waitress for more coffee.

"I'm sorry, Mom," Logan whispered.

"Apology accepted." The waitress poured my coffee. "Thank you." I smiled and she left. "Don't worry; I'm not leaving your father."

"You're not?"

"If I left, came out to the town, how do you think it would go over?"

"Well, Grandmother would go ape shit."

"I don't give a shit about my mother. I'm thinking about you."

"Me?"

"I don't want you to have to endure a year of people teasing you about your lesbian mother."

"Oh."

"You need a little more time to get used to the idea, I think. And, I want you to enjoy your last year before going off to college, not be dealing with the fallout of my coming out. Plus,

I want to help your father get elected to the State Senate. He's worked hard, and it's what he's always wanted. It's the least I can do."

"Are you going to be miserable?"

I sighed. "The only thing that would make me miserable is if I lost you. So, I'm going to make a promise to you, okay?"

"Okay."

"Complete honesty. Within what you're comfortable with, that is."

"What does that mean, exactly?"

"Don't ask a question you don't want to know the answer to."

"Oh."

"Hey, I don't want you ever to think I've hated my life. I don't. I love my job; I love you. Your dad is a good husband and a great father. What's been miserable is denying who I am to myself, and not being honest with the people I love. Telling you, even though it's going to take you time to fully accept it, I feel light as a feather. You are the only person whose opinion I care about."

"And after I go to college?"

I met Logan's eyes but didn't answer.

"That's not fair to Dad, is it?"

"After the election is over, I'm doing what's best for me."

Logan drank her coffee and didn't wince. "Going to Nora?"

I crossed my fork and knife over my half-eaten pancakes and pushed the plate away, suddenly nauseated. "Nora is leaving today. I assume she didn't change her plans. Which tells me whatever my future holds, she's not interested in being part of it."

twenty-eight
sophie

I couldn't help myself; I drove out to Nora's Tuesday after work. Rumors were swirling that the estate sale had been a bust. I'd been asked by at least a half dozen people how long Nora was staying and was there any chance she might stay permanently?

I told myself during the five-minute drive out of town that the rumors had been wrong, that Nora had left the day before as planned, that I wouldn't see her and be confronted with the decision I made about staying with Charlie for the time being. So, it was with mixed feelings when I saw a small figure on a tractor in the far corner of the pasture. I parked in the front yard between an overflowing Dumpster and Ray's truck. I walked around behind the house, leaned my arms against the top rail of the pasture fence and waited for the ancient John Deere to make its painfully slow progress to me.

Nora stopped the tractor next to the fence, pushed and pulled various levers until the tractor died, leaving a stony silence behind. After a few seconds, the grasshoppers and crickets started up their summertime chorus.

"That's an interesting look." Nora wore tan coveralls at least two sizes too big for her, running shoes, Oakley sunglasses and a sweat-stained and dirty straw cowboy hat.

Nora jumped down from the tractor. "I didn't bring any work clothes. I borrowed this from Dormer and found the hat in the barn. The glasses and shoes are mine. Goddamn, it's hot."

She pulled her arms out of the coveralls, letting the top part hang down from her waist. The white tank top she wore was soaked through with sweat and left nothing to the imagination. Little bits of grass and dust stuck to her sweaty face, and the smell of motor oil was overpowering.

"Why did you stay?"

"The estate sale was a flop."

"I heard."

Neither of us seemed to know what to say, where to start, so Nora went with good manners.

"Want some iced tea?"

Inside the house, the AC was cranked down low, chilling the sweat that had popped out on my body in the ten minutes I'd been outside. "Are you sure it's a good idea for you to be out in this heat?"

Nora handed me a glass of tea in a red Solo cup. Tiny goose bumps covered her arm. "Yes, Mom. I'm fine."

I grimaced at the unsweetened tea.

"Don't like it?" Nora said.

"I drink sweet."

"It's not good for you."

"I'm not giving up every vice."

"I would offer you some sugar, but I'm pretty sure someone bought the sugar bowl and the hardened sugar inside. The kitchen was the one room the junkers cleaned out."

I glanced in the empty den. "It looks pretty cleaned out to me."

"I went scorched earth on the house yesterday. If I could carry it, it ended up in the Dumpster. They're bringing me an empty one tomorrow."

"Eager to get out of town?" *Back to Alima.*

"Did you know Emmadean has Parkinson's?"

"We're going to avoid it? Okay. Yes, I've known for months."

"Why didn't you tell me?"

I opened my mouth to respond, but Nora continued. "Let me guess: Emmadean said not to."

I nodded. "I tried to talk Emmadean into telling you, but she's pretty stubborn. How did you find out?"

"Jeremy told me."

"Was Emmadean mad?"

Nora drank her tea and shifted on her feet. "I haven't talked to her about it yet."

"You're avoiding that conversation, too."

"I'm not." She stared into her cup. "I don't know."

"If you talk to Emmadean, you're afraid you'll need to stay, and you don't want to."

She didn't disagree or look at me. We stood as far apart in the kitchen as was possible. Nora leaned against the sink, and I stood near the door to the den, the kitchen table a substantial barrier between us.

"I told Logan."

Nora's head jerked up. Her mouth parted slightly, but still, she didn't speak.

"I told her everything."

Nora's eyes widened, lifting her eyebrows almost to the brim of her ridiculous hat.

"You didn't think I'd do it, did you?"

"No. How'd she take it?"

"Not as good as I hoped, but much better than Charlie. He caught me trying to sneak out to come see you Saturday night."

"You told Charlie?"

"Yep. Thanks for warning me that he came to see you."

"From your texts, I assumed he believed me and didn't say anything."

"Oh, he said something all right."

"What happened?"

"He assumed it was an experiment. Or at least, that's what he wanted to believe. I wouldn't let him."

"It would have been easier to."

"I'm tired of lying. I'm tired of not being myself. More than that, I'm tired of fighting with you every time we see each other. I don't want to think about tomorrow, or next week or next year. I just want to be with you while I can. As much as I can."

Nora nodded slowly, her gaze never leaving mine. "I need to clean up."

I grabbed her arm as she went past. "Wait." The scent of hay and motor oil hovered around her. "I'm not leaving Charlie."

Nora narrowed her eyes. "I thought he would leave you."

"I have to stay. For Logan."

She swallowed nodded. "I understand."

I smiled. "No need to look like I just kicked your puppy. We will be together by next Thanksgiving. Logan will be in college, I'll have helped Charlie get elected to the State Senate, and then we'll can be together."

Nora shook her head. "You want to be around for Logan's last year, fine. But, you don't have to be married to Charlie to do it."

I stroked her cheek and smiled. "You sound jealous. I like it."

She leaned her cheek into my hand. "I don't. I can't stand the idea of you being with him."

"Me either. I'm never sleeping with another man again. That's why I moved into the guest room last night."

"Oh."

"You can pretend to be jealous for a little longer. It's good for my ego."

Nora rolled her eyes. "How did Charlie take it?"

"When he realized Logan knew, and it hadn't ruined our relationship, he pretended to be okay with it. I think he's going to try to get back at me, somehow."

"Through Logan?"

"That would be my guess, but I don't think it'll work. At least I hope it won't. One year, and I'll come to you, wherever you are."

"You aren't asking me to stay?"

"Would you?" I could see the answer in her eyes. "Forget it. It would be too hard to sneak around, anyway. Will you wait for me?"

"I've been waiting for eighteen years. What's one more?"

I kissed her again, hard and quick. "Clean up fast. I don't have much time."

"So, this was a booty call?" Nora ambled through the den and down the hall to the bathroom.

"Yep. Get it in gear. I have fifty calls I need to make tonight for Charlie's campaign."

"I don't get why you're helping him." She started the water in the bathtub. I leaned against the doorjamb and watched her undress.

"He says I owe him, and I agree."

"Owe him? For what?"

"Using him?"

She was slim and fit, and it took all of my willpower to stay in the doorway. She pulled the lever to switch it to the shower nozzle, stepped in and closed the shower curtain. "He's controlling you, Sophie."

"He's trying. We aren't going to be interrupted by anyone this time, are we? No late afternoon appointments?"

"No. Did you hear about Erin? It was all the locals could talk about at the estate sale."

"Yeah. I'm a little ashamed that a fifteen-year-old has more courage than I do."

"You've got more to lose, Soph."

"I suppose. Logan suspected, about Erin. She was very supportive of her. Kim told me."

"Think it will help her come to terms with us?"

When we'd gotten home from church, Charlie went off to play golf at the club. Logan had come to me and hugged me tightly. "I love you," she said.

"Aw, sweetie. I love you, too."

"I'm sorry I didn't tell you that the other day. At the Magnolia."

I pulled back from her. "Didn't you?"

"I couldn't remember. I know it took a lot for you to tell me, and I probably didn't handle it well."

"Better than I expected."

"Well, I love you, and I support you. Always. Just like you've always loved and supported me."

At that point, I burst into tears. We both had. I would tell Nora about it, eventually, but I wanted to hold that private moment between me and Logan within myself for a little while longer.

"I think she already is," I said to Nora.

Steam billowed up to the ceiling, and rolled out into the bathroom, bringing the scent of peppermint shampoo with it. "I would have liked to have been in that Sunday school class, though," Nora said. "Think Erin was sending you a message?"

"Maybe. And here we were supposed to be the ones helping her."

I leaned down and checked myself in the mirror. I pulled my sunglasses off my head and ran my fingers through my hair.

"I think we did. She came out the next day."

"To a room full of Baptists. Guaranteed to spread it over town like wildfire."

The water cut off, and the shower curtain rolled back. "As long as she keeps your secret," Nora said.

"Quick shower."

"I'm motivated."

"Are you going to be in town on Saturday?"

Nora toweled herself off, grabbed me by the hand and pulled me into her bedroom. "Are you inviting me to Charlie's fund raiser?"

"Yes." I pulled my maxidress over my head. Nora had unhooked my bra before the dress was off, and had started pushing my panties down.

"If you want me there, I'll come."

"Oh, I do." We knelt on the bed in front of each other, our hands already exploring. "I want you here, there and everywhere."

"Ditto." She kissed the promise ring she gave me when we were seventeen years old.

twenty-nine
sophie

We couldn't get enough of each other.

It wasn't easy, but we saw each other every day. I'd skipped my AA meeting on Wednesday and met her in a hotel in Dripping Springs instead. I'd avoided Todd's calls, texting instead that I was okay, no drinking, and that I'd told Logan. He told me to get my ass to a meeting and I promised to Saturday morning before the fund raiser. Thursday, I begged out of tennis, citing a recurring tennis elbow problem I hadn't had in months, and went to her house, parking my car in her barn on the off-chance Charlie drove by. Friday, she'd driven out to Cooper's to pick up dinner for my family, so we could spend the two hours I would have been on the road out near Comanche Springs. We parked on a secluded road and made love in the bed of Ray's old truck, which Nora had taken to driving. Or tried to make love, at least.

"You're a million miles away, here. What's wrong?" Nora said.

I pressed my hand to my sweaty forehead and shook my head. "Nothing."

Nora lay down next to me. Sunlight rippled back and forth across our bodies as the leaves above us danced in the wind. She lightly held my hand, the summertime heat too intense for extended skin-to-skin contact. "Come on, Soph. Spill it."

"How do people sneak around like this all the time?" I said. "It's stressful."

"It's easier in a city."

"Right. You're used to affairs with married women. Do you prefer married men, too? Or just women?"

"I don't make a habit of sleeping with married men and women. Yeah, it happens sometimes. I don't want to shock you, but people lie when they are out to get laid, and sneaking around to do it is easier in big cities."

"Defensive much?"

"Tell me, are you accusing me of being a slut, or of being immoral? Or maybe it's both."

"No, I'm not."

"Or maybe you're just jealous that I've had multiple partners and you haven't."

I grimaced and looked away. That was exactly it, and of course Nora had seen through me. She'd always been able to.

Nora held my hand. "That was cruel of me. I'm sorry I snapped at you. But, we don't have much time together and we don't need to be fighting over petty stuff like this. We can't change the past, we can only cherish the time we have now, and look forward."

"I know you're right, but I dread you leaving so much, and it makes me lash out." I put my head on her shoulder.

"Come with me."

"You know I can't."

"I know, but I keep asking, hoping the answer will change."

I swallowed. "If I left Charlie now, would you stay?"

She stared at me for a long moment, the conflict clear in her eyes.

"You don't have to come out when you leave him."

"If you stay I will."

"I'm not giving up my career."

"I'm not asking you to. I'm sure translators work from home."

"I'm not that kind of translator."

"Technical manuals require your presence in a particular office."

"I work for the fucking government, okay?"

My mouth dropped open. "The government?"

Nora looked at the woods surrounding us, in frustration? Or was she searching for eavesdroppers?

"I can't tell you what I do, but it's not technical manuals."

"Oh." So much for that dream. Nora had always been a rule follower (well, for the most part), and was responsible to a fault. She'd always been as good as her word, and I imagined being in the military had only sharpened that part of her personality. I couldn't compete with Nora's sense of duty.

Nora straddled my lap. "Sophie, listen. I've been thinking about your problem, a lot."

"My problem? Isn't being together *our* problem?"

Nora sighed. "Will you please listen? I've been trying to figure out how we can both get what we want."

"What exactly do you want, Nora? Your life, uninterrupted?"

"You separate from Charlie for the standard, boring reasons people get divorced, irreconcilable differences or whatever. People will ask questions, but will they wonder? Charlie's been cheating on you for years, and chances are everyone in town knows it. They think you've finally had enough. It's the oldest story in the book."

"Um, that sounds to me like you're getting what you want, which is me away from Charlie. All I'll get is a bunch of gossip and questions, which is what I don't want. But, okay. Let's say I do it. What will you be doing during this year? Running around with your married men and women in DC? Alima?"

"Jesus Christ with the Alima stuff."

"Have you broken it off with her yet?"

Nora shook her head.

"Even after I told you we'd be together next year? I even gave you a fucking date!" I pushed her away and stood up, retrieving my dress. "How dare you accuse me of not being able to commit and mocking my jealousy. I'm outta here." I jumped out of the truck bed and started walking to my car.

Nora jumped over the side of the truck and got in front of me. "Wait, wait. You're right. About all of it. I'm being a shit, I'm being selfish and I'm not being fair to you."

"Is this what our relationship is going to be like? Fighting all the time? Because I don't like it one bit."

"No, it's not. I swear to God. I…" Nora cleared her throat and looked down. "I can be self-destructive when I don't feel… in control. That's why I… It's a pattern I thought I had grip on it, but I guess I haven't really."

She looked so broken, so lost, I did what came naturally. I pulled her into a hug and asked, "What can I do to help you?"

Nora broke down and sobbed into my shoulder. She clung to me as if I was her life raft and that was enough to banish my shock at her uncharacteristic emotional breakdown, pull her closer and wait.

When she'd cried herself out, she pushed away. She wiped her cheeks roughly and laughed uneasily. She wouldn't look me in the eye. "I…um…don't usually do that in public."

"Hey." I cradled her head and made her look at me. Her eyes were red and watery, and tearstains were streaked across her cheeks. I kissed her eyes, her cheeks, her forehead, her temples. She rested her hands gently on my hips and she released a long sigh while I peppered her face with kisses. "I'm not just anybody, Nora," I whispered. "There was a time when I knew you better than anyone in the world. We told each other everything. I want that again, desperately. I know it seems like all I want to do is fuck you—" Nora barked out a laugh, and I chuckled "—obviously, I do. But, I miss *everything* we had." I put her hand on my heart.

"The connection. The laughter. Being able to look at you in a group of people and know exactly what you're thinking, and you being able to do it with me, too. Remember?"

Nora nodded.

"You were always the first person I thought of when I had a problem because I knew you would listen and not try to solve it for me but solve it *with* me. Let me be that for you. Now."

She pressed her forehead against mine, sighed and closed her eyes. "Thousands of vets have this same story. I'm not unique."

"That doesn't make your problems any less important."

She moved away and sat on the truck's tailgate.

"I told you in the IED attack I was in, I lost friends. Good friends. I didn't tell you I lost a lover, too. No one knows about Will, actually. Not even Alima. It hadn't really gotten past hookups, but he was a great guy. Fun, loyal, very good-looking. I knew by then no one would ever stack up to you, but I was tired of being alone. I deserved to be happy, too. Like you and Charlie."

"Oh, Nora."

"If I only knew, right? Will'd started to drop hints about meeting parents and stuff. I knew I'd have to tell him about us. About being estranged from Ray. I was not looking forward to it, but I decided to take the leap. And he died. Just like that." She snapped her fingers. "Along with my two closest friends. That just proved to me that opening myself up emotionally to people only led to disasters. So, when I recovered and was discharged, my life became about one-night stands and keeping friends at a distance."

I leaned against the side of the pickup. "Sounds lonely."

"It was. I know that now. At the time I thought I was handling everything pretty well. My job saved me. It was tense and high-stress and— I've already told you more than I should.

"Then one day, I got a call from a man I didn't know. I'd given my number to his wife for the next time she was in town.

No, I didn't know she was married. I expected angry, but it was the hurt in his voice that I couldn't get over. I didn't like being the other woman, even if it wasn't my fault."

"Would you have slept with her if you'd known?"

Nora scoffed and shook her head. "Yeah, probably. I was more careful after that. Then I met Alima.

"We were friends first. She wouldn't let me keep her at a distance. She told me later that she knew within minutes of meeting me that I was broken, and she was determined to break through my shell to help me. She introduced me to yoga, to meditation, which helped with my symptoms tremendously."

"Symptoms?"

"PTSD. Insomnia. Nightmares. Headaches. Anger. Control issues. Impatience." Nora stood and moved toward me. "I know I've been angry and impatient, and cruel to you, and I'm so, so sorry. I don't want to be, and I'm working on myself every day to not be. I didn't realize how much my structured life helped me manage my symptoms. Cutting ties with Alima is about more than ending a sexual relationship. She's been my anchor for a while now, and I'm scared shitless of the person I'll become when I lose that."

The expression in her eyes was raw vulnerability. Fear. She'd stripped away her cynicism, given up control, to tell me this, and it had cost her. We were both broken, in our own ways. Could I ask her to give up the stability she'd found with Alima for a year and a half of uncertainty she would have with me? I wanted to be her rock, but could I be with all of my issues? Was it really fair of me to ask Nora to risk her mental health to make me happy? No, no, and no. I loved her too much. I embraced her. "Thank you for telling me." I stopped and swallowed the sob that threated to escape my throat. I inhaled and pulled away to look at her. I smiled, though I knew it wasn't genuine. "We'll spend as much time together as we can while you're here. I won't ask you about it again. I love you, and I want what's best for you. If that's Alima…" I cleared my throat. "I hope Alima will understand if we remain friends. I want that, NoNo. I can't lose you completely again."

I really, really wanted to vomit right then. I meant every word I said, I knew it was the right thing to do, but I hated myself for ruining my chance at happiness. I couldn't imagine finding happiness with anyone but Nora, and the thought of searching for it, of being alone? I really needed to leave before I broke down. I would call Todd and tell him to expect me tonight. I'd ask Logan to go with me. I was going to need someone in my corner, a shoulder or two to cry on.

I looked off into the woods thinking, something is missing. Then I realized: my mouth wasn't watering. I wasn't thinking of Jack Daniels, or Maker's Mark or Old Crow. Today, I didn't want those old, reliable friends. I wanted the community I'd found a year ago when a bunch of imperfect strangers had opened their arms to a lost, shattered woman. Tonight, I wouldn't be going as a broken woman. Heartbroken, maybe. But, I knew as long as I believed in myself, and let others believe in me, I would never be that shell of a woman again. It was time to stop thinking only of myself and my problems, and start helping others, and that included Nora most of all.

Nora hadn't said anything but watched me with an unreadable expression. "Well." I cleared my throat. "I need to get back to work." I kissed her on the cheek and headed to my car. The sobs started, but I managed to keep them quiet. I refused to make a scene.

I put my seat belt on and didn't look at Nora. I couldn't bear to see her standing there, just letting me go. I understood a little better the betrayal she felt all those years ago. I started the car and jumped when Nora knocked on my window. She had her phone to her ear. I heard her side of the conversation through the window.

"Hey, Alima. Yeah. I'm good…the estate sale was a bust…

Yeah, it was a bunch of junk…How are you? How's work?"
Nora laughed. "He's always been a dick…Sophie?"

I met Nora's gaze. "She's good. A few times, yeah…that's what
I'm calling about…I wanted to do this in person…Yes, it's a Dear
John call…I know…you might be right…I'm willing to take that
risk…" I turned the car off. "She's my soul mate, Alima. I can't
change that. I don't want to." Nora turned away and dropped her
voice. "I know, and I love you, too. I always will. You've given
me so much, three wonderful years. You'll find someone else…
What?…You're kidding…" Nora turned toward me again, brows
furrowed now. "You never told him why you were leaving. Wow,
well, hedging bets seems to be going around…I'm not sure when
I'll be back. Probably next week sometime. I'll bring the ring…
Right. Okay. Take care."

Nora opened my car door and stepped into the gap. "You
were really going to let me go."

"Here I thought you were letting me go."

"Not on your fucking life. You're who's best for me, Sophia
Elizabeth."

"I have a lot of baggage."

"You're never going to let me live that down, are you?"

"Probably not."

"Well, surprise. I have a lot of baggage, too."

"Yeah, I noticed."

"Call the office and tell them you have a migraine."

"Sheila will think I've started drinking again." Nora leaned
across me and unbuckled my seat belt.

"Tell her you're about to have mind-blowing makeup sex with
your girlfriend." She took my hand and helped me out of the car.

"That wasn't a fight."

"I know. See all of the progress we're making? Get in." She
nodded toward the bed of the truck.

"So we can have fake makeup sex?"

"No, so I can make you forget everything and everyone but me and you for the next hour."

"An hour? That sounds promising. I suppose I do need to text Sheila." I did and tossed my phone in the cab of the truck.

She was very bossy, telling me where to lie down before she straddled my lap and took my face in her hands. Her thumbs traced my bottom lip. Her voice was intimate. "Sophie, I meant what I said. You're my soul mate. You have no reason to be worried about me going back to DC, or to be jealous of any woman or man. I plan on coming back at least once a month, for long weekends. To be with you, and to help out with Emmadean."

"Once a month?"

"If not more. And you can visit me in DC, too. I have lots of time accrued, and I've never asked off. It won't be a problem."

"Unless there's a terrorist attack."

"That's what I work to stop. That's why I can't quit."

"Christ, I guess I can't compete with the safety of our nation."

"Sophie…"

"No, I get it now. I can't expect you to give that up. It would have been nice for you to tell me sooner, so I don't sound like such a belligerent, selfish bitch."

"You're not belligerent." She tried to hide her smile.

I pinched her side. "Hey. Watch it."

We kissed again, long and slow.

"All that's important right now is figuring out how we can spend every waking moment together," I said. "The thought of going back to work, of being away from you, fills me with dread." I kissed her left breast. "The thought of having to sit across from Charlie and eat the dinner you bought for us makes me want to vomit." I kissed her right breast. "When I'm not with you, I'm miserable. Almost as miserable as I was for eighteen years without you."

She grasped my face gently and raised it, so our eyes met. "I hate the thought of being so far away from you, too," Nora said.

"You're doing what's right for Logan, and I respect that. Me going back and forth isn't the best solution, and if you've got a better one that solves our problems, I'm all ears."

The thing was, I didn't. Having Nora home once a month was probably the best I would get for the next year.

"Hey. A year isn't so long, and think of the reward at the end. Us. Together. Forever. That's what this is about, right? Because that's what I'm planning. If you're not, you better say so right now."

The intensity in her eyes made me smile. "Are you asking me to marry you?"

She chuckled. "Boy, you *are* a lesbian."

"What does that mean?"

Nora looked up to the heavens. "She doesn't even know the lesbian stereotypes. You have so much to learn."

"You're avoiding the question."

"Well, I was going to wait until you'd left your husband, and actually come out." She looked around the woods we were hidden in. "I wanted to do it somewhere more romantic, but sure."

"*But, sure?* Be still, my beating heart."

"Leave your husband, and you'll get a romantic proposal."

"I'm leaving him eventually, you know."

"And, you will eventually be proposed to." Nora pulled my dress up.

She was right, my mind didn't wander even once.

thirty
nora

I gave a perfunctory knock on Emmadean and Dormer's back door and walked inside. They sat at the kitchen table, with Emmadean holding a cigarette up to her mouth. A smoke filter hummed on the table. Emmadean started coughing when she saw me.

I grinned. "I didn't know you were a closet..." That when the smell hit me. I looked closer at the cigarette. "You're smoking weed?"

"She is," Dormer said. "It helps her shakes."

"Dormer." Emmadean's voice was sharp, not softened at all by the weed.

"It's okay. I know." I pulled up a chair and sat down looking back and forth between my elderly aunt and uncle. Emmadean held the joint between her thumb and forefingers as if she'd been toking for years, but her expression was one of acute discomfort. "Go on. Don't mind me."

She held the joint out.

"No, thanks," I said. "Drug testing at work."

Emmadean took a hit, held the smoke in, and exhaled. "How'd you find out?" She turned her stink eye on Dormer.

"Jeremy."

"That little traitor."

"Don't be too hard on him. He was sick of listening to Mary complain about me." I reached out and took Emmadean's hand. "I'm here to apologize."

"For?"

"Not talking to you about it earlier. I… I didn't want to know because if I knew the extent of it, I'd stay. I'd *want* to stay. For you. But, I couldn't stay in the same town with Sophie and Charlie. I…" I shook my head and released Emmadean's hand. I traced a scratch on the table. "There was too much pain there."

"I know, honey. But, you've made up now, right?"

I nodded quickly. "More than made up."

Dormer shifted in his seat. He lightly grasped his hands and held them in his lap, head down, listening.

"She told Logan about us, about her."

"What did Logan say?"

"She took it pretty well, I think. But, Sophie's staying with Charlie until Logan graduates." My throat tightened. "She doesn't want Logan to have to deal with it all. You know how small towns can be. So she's staying with Charlie for a year. I'll come down here at least once a month. And not just to see Sophie. To help you. Go to doctor's appointments with you. Be your advocate. Do whatever you need. Financially, too. I've plenty of money to help. Whatever you need."

Emmadean patted my hand. "We're okay right now, but we may have to take you up on your offer one day."

"No, we won't," Dormer said.

I lifted my hand. "Let's argue about it later."

"Well, that sounds like a right good plan," Emmadean said. Her words were slightly slurred, and I had to smile. "Course, I want you down here all the time, but I understand you have a high-powered career up there in DC. We're just gonna be happy to see you more often."

"I'm going to be glad to see you more often, too. But, that means more goodbyes. I hate goodbyes."

I thought of all the goodbyes I would have to say to Sophie over the next year. Today's parting had been horrible. Neither of us had wanted to leave and had held on to each other's hands, silently wishing there was something we could do to fix everything, to stop having to say goodbye. I'd held it together for her, because I saw the quiver in her chin, the waver in her voice. When she was gone, I sat in my truck and cried.

I wouldn't see her until Saturday when we would be surrounded by a hundred of Charlie's donors, and there would be no chance to be alone. It would be a real test of our acting skills, to pretend to be only friends. We'd done it for nearly a year in high school, but for the life of me, I didn't remember how. On Monday, I would leave, say my first goodbye to Sophie, return to my life in DC. I'd been antsy to go almost since I drove into town. Now that it was here, I didn't want to go.

Today, Sophie had taught me a lesson about true unselfishness. She'd been willing to let me go, to do what she thought was right for me and sacrificing her happiness in the bargain. It was time I did the same.

"Sophie accused me today of being selfish." Emmadean and Dormer glanced at each other but didn't comment. "Seems to be a theme with everyone. Y'all are all right. I didn't want my life interrupted. I wanted her to leave Charlie so I wouldn't have to think of her down here, in his bed."

Dormer shifted in his chair again.

"Oh, settle down, Dormer," Emmadean said.

"I guess I'm more like Ray than I thought."

"The good news is, it's not terminal," Emmadean said.

"Emma," Dormer gently chided.

"No, I deserve that," I said. "You've always given me everything, and I've never given you anything."

"That's not true."

"It is, but that changes now." I nodded, my mind working. "I need to call my boss."

"Are you quitting?" Emmadean said. "But, it's such a good job, and the *benefits*!"

"Make up your mind, woman," Dormer said. "You've been jawing about her moving down here for weeks, and now she's on the verge and you're mourning her loss of the government teat."

"I wouldn't call it a teat," I said.

"Nora. Don't you quit your job because you don't think I can handle taking care of my wife, 'cause I can, and I will." He got the set to his mouth that always told he would not be moved.

I laughed. "Selfishness isn't terminal, but it ain't instantly cured, either. I'm going to try to keep my job, work remotely. I might not be down here full-time, but I'll be down here enough you'll start to get sick of me."

"Never happen."

"Welp," Dormer stood. "There's things need doing." He kissed me on the head. "Glad you're staying, Bug, but I knew you'd stay all along."

"Oh, you did?"

He held open the screen door. "Yep. And, I know it ain't because of Emmadean or Sophie, either. You love them chickens too much to leave them." The screen door slapped shut behind him.

"No, I don't!" I called. "I hate the little fuckers!"

Emmadean held out her joint, and I shook my head. "He's right, isn't he?"

"Yes, damn it. I love those little bastards."

thirty-one
nora

The Comanche Springs Dance Hall was tucked in the woods off a curvy oil top road about ten miles outside of Lynchfield. Horace Clark turned his barn into a hill country speakeasy well before the area became the Hill Country with capital letters, selling moonshine from his still to farmers and doughboys back from the war. It was men-only for years until the fighting got out of hand and Horace decided having females present would keep everyone on their best behavior. Or, at least they'd stop fighting over dominoes and cards and fight over women, which happened often enough, but his customers seemed to be more passionate about dominoes. As an afterthought, he laid down some planks in the back of the barn, got his half-deaf grandfather to pull out his banjo, and the dance hall was born. Nameless for years, until some drunk came up with Comanche Springs, even though the springs were a good fifteen miles away, on the other side of town.

The barn hadn't changed much over the years. Boards got replaced as they rotted, the new lumber resembling Band-Aids until time and rain and wind weathered them to a uniform gray. Large openings had been cut on the sides to catch the breeze, screens covered the openings to catch the flies, and shutters to close it all up when the rain came. Ceiling fans hung down from the rafters to keep the un–air-conditioned air from being stagnant, and a large, ten-foot industrial fan sat whirling and humming in the corner near the bar, keeping the dancers cool while they waited for their cold beer.

I parked Ray's '85 GMC in a line of pickup trucks and stared at the dance hall. It was twenty thirty, thirty minutes after the party started, and the sun was still high enough that the Christmas lights strung up inside the hall contributed little to the atmosphere. Country music drifted through the open windows, along with laughter and the hum of conversation.

Avery, Mark, and Jamie Luke manned the registration table set up at the door.

"Nora." Jamie looked behind me. "Where's your terrorist girlfriend?"

"My what?"

"Alima. She's your girlfriend, right? That's what the kids who helped y'all last week seem to think."

"Glad you could make it," Avery said, cutting Jamie off and giving her a cold stare. "I'm sorry to hear your estate sale didn't go very well."

"Yeah, well, whaddya gonna do? It was a bunch of junk anyway."

Mark was tapping away on his iPad. "We don't seem to have you in our database."

"Probably because I'm a Democrat." I started to walk off but turned around and leaned in close to Jamie. "FYI, you aren't the only woman Charlie is fucking behind Sophie's back." I cut my eyes to Avery, and I walked away. I felt a little sorry for Avery; I liked her well enough. But, I had no doubt she would come out on top of any showdown with Jamie.

I wandered away from the table pleased with the look of astonishment on Avery's and Mark's faces, and the look of horror on Jamie's. I scanned the crowd for Sophie. It didn't take long to find

Joe Stopper twirling her around the floor. She wore a floral thigh-length dress with a pair of red cowboy boots. Turquoise earrings dangled from her earlobes, the blue-green stark against her dark hair, and a dozen thin silver and beaded bracelets encircled her right wrist. She and Joe were laughing as they circled the floor.

I made my way to the bar.

Charlie put his arm around my waist and pulled me into a one-armed hug. "So glad you could make it, NoNo." The people in the line around me smiled and greeted Charlie. His dimple was in full force.

"Two Lone Stars," Charlie said to the bartender.

"I don't like—"

The beers were uncapped, and Charlie was ushering me away before I could protest. He steered me to an open space on the far edge of the dance floor, nodding to people as we passed, but with a determined enough air, no one stopped us. "Cheers." He clinked his bottle against mine and drank.

"God, this is terrible. It's like drinking water."

"It sets a mood, and that's what I wanted to do."

"Shiner or Real Ale sets a better mood."

He drank, staring out at the dance floor. I knew he was watching Sophie. "She's always been a great dancer. Better than you were, sorry to say."

"Yes, well, I've realized since I'm better at leading."

Charlie looked down at me, his jaw working. "So, you're the man in the relationship."

"No, Charlie. I'm a woman. That's why we're lesbians." I drank my beer. "I'm staying."

"Staying where?"

"Here. In Lynchfield. Emmadean's sick, as I'm sure you know. I'm taking a personal leave from my job to help out."

"For how long?"

"I'm not sure."

"Is that the only reason you're staying?"

"No." I resolutely held his gaze.

He sighed. "Why are you doing this?"

"She's the love of my life, Charlie. And, she's worth fighting for. Don't you agree?"

Charlie didn't answer.

I nodded. "Sophie deserves better than a marriage of convenience. For you."

The song ended. Sophie said something to Joe, but her eyes were on Charlie and me. They parted, and she walked over to us.

"Nora. You made it," Sophie smiled and sighed. Maybe other people saw her glowing face and thought she was flushed from dancing. But, I knew better. I'd seen that face a thousand times, every time Sophie told me she loved me. For eighteen years I'd been searching for that expression from men or women. I should have known it was right here in Lynchfield all along, waiting for me to return.

Charlie moved next to Sophie and put his arm around her protectively. Sophie leaned away from him, slightly, but he kept his arm firmly around her. "Let's dance."

"I want to take a break."

"How does it look for my wife to be dancing with everyone but me?"

"You wanted me to schmooze with the men, so I have. Now I'm taking a break to talk to Nora."

"No, you're not."

"It's okay, Soph." My eyes met Charlie's. "I'm not going anywhere."

Charlie took Sophie's hand and twirled her away. She looked at me over her shoulder with a puzzled expression. I mouthed, *I love you*, and she grinned.

thirty-two
sophie

Charlie wasn't as good a swing dancer as Joe, but he was better than most of the men I'd danced with so far. Between the fast-paced song and the twirling moves he was putting me through, there was very little time to talk. But, I felt the anger in his leading, and I saw it in the set of his jaw. Charlie pulled me into two-step between swing moves.

"Can we slow down for a minute? I'm out of breath."

He led me around the floor smoothly, but the tension in his shoulders didn't lessen.

"What's the matter? Are you angry? I think the party's a success so far."

His jaw snapped open. "Have you seen Nora behind my back?"

I almost deflected, answered him with a question. It was second nature to me to lie about who I was. But, no longer. "Yes."

Charlie led me off the dance floor and out the back door by the stage. He pulled me along until we were a good ways off from the barn. He swung me around and released me. "Are you trying to destroy our family?"

"Calm down, Charlie."

"Calm down?" His voice dropped to a growl. "You've been

sneaking around with your lesbian lover in our hometown. Where anyone could see you."

"We've been careful."

"Oh, well, that makes the fact my wife is cheating on me all better."

"Fuck you. You've been cheating on me for years."

"Not with a man."

"Is that why you're so angry? Because it's a woman? Does that somehow emasculate you more than if it was a man? Or is it because it's Nora?"

Charlie moved toward me and stuck his finger in my face. "Stop seeing her."

"No."

"Sophie, so help me God."

"You know what? Fuck this. I'm done."

Charlie grabbed my arm as I tried to push past. "What do you mean, you're done?"

"I'm leaving you. I won't come out, so Logan won't get ridiculed, and for you to save face. But, once Logan goes to college, I'm leaving town to be with Nora."

"You owe me more than that."

"If you weren't such a shit about everything, then I would gladly pretend a while longer, help you with the election. But, you've been nothing but hateful and threatening since you found out. I'm not going to live like that."

"You're the most selfish person I know."

"Me? Do you think living a lie for eighteen years has been selfish? I did it for Logan because I thought it would be best for her. I did it because I felt guilty that I didn't love you more. I wanted to feel something, but it wasn't in me."

"I'm going to turn her against you."

"And how is that different from what you've been doing for years?"

He smirked. "Logan worships the ground I walk on. It won't take much for her to see you for the selfish bitch you are."

"Dad?"

Charlie and I turned toward Logan's voice. We'd been so busy arguing we hadn't heard or seen Logan follow. Her eyes were wide with an expression of horror.

"Logan," Charlie said. "Honey. What are you doing out here?"

"Avery sent me to find you. It's time for the cake."

"What cake?" I asked.

"For your birthday." Logan kept her eyes on her father as she answered. "It was supposed to be a surprise."

"Oh, how sweet." I moved forward and put my arm around Logan's shoulders to direct her back into the dance hall. "I'll act surprised." But, Logan wouldn't move.

"Dad, what were you saying?"

"Nothing." He turned on his charming smile. "Your mom and I were talking about election stuff. Come on. Let's cut some cake."

Logan pushed away from us and stepped back. "Would every-one please stop lying to me? I want to know what's going on."

"Logan, now isn't the time," Charlie started.

"I'm leaving your father," I said.

"Sophie," Charlie warned.

I kept my focus on Logan. "Don't worry. I won't come out until after you leave for college. But, I think staying will make for a miserable home life. I don't want that for you. Or us."

"Why would you try to turn me against Mom?"

"I didn't say that."

"I *heard* you."

"Logan, it's complicated…"

"No, it's not. People get divorced all the time. Big fucking deal. Why would you want to turn me against my mother?"

Charlie clenched his jaw and nodded briskly. "Thanks for this, Sophie."

"Me?"

"If you hadn't been fucking that cunt—" he pointed toward the back door where Nora stood holding a beer "—none of this would have happened."

"Oh my God, Dad," Logan said. "What is *wrong* with you?"

"I'm watching my future go up in flames, that's what's wrong with me." Charlie strode off toward the dance hall. Nora stepped out of his way. He leaned in and said something to her as he passed.

"I'm so sorry you had to hear that, sweetie."

"I can't believe you were right." Logan's voice cracked.

"And I hate it. I do. I wanted to be wrong, for your sake."

"That's fucked up."

"Logan, when all of this is over, we need to have a conversation about your language."

"Seriously?"

Logan looked over towards Nora, who was hanging back by the dance hall, waiting. "You've been seeing her this week, haven't you?"

"How did you know?"

She smiled up at me, a little sadly. "You've been happier than I've ever seen you. You were singing in the car this morning on our way to your meeting. I can't remember the last time you did that."

"Well, I don't listen to Kidz Bop anymore, do I?" I brushed her hair from her face. "Logan, you make me happier than anyone else."

"I'm not jealous, Mom. I'm sad because I'm going to miss you."

"Miss me? I'm not going anywhere."

"Yes, you are. I don't want you to stay here for me. I want you to be you."

I pulled Logan into a hug. "Hearing you say those words is the best gift I've ever been given."

"I meant it when I said I would always support you."

"Yes, you did." I squeezed her, then held her at arm's length, my eyes burning with unshed tears. "But, I'm not just staying for you. I want to be here and experience all your lasts with you. I can't do that from a thousand miles away. I don't want you to have to live with your father. I don't think he's going to take this well."

"Obviously." Logan glanced at Nora, who was still lurking. "Is she ever going to come over here?"

"Probably not until we ask her." I leaned forward and whispered, "She never makes the first move."

"Too far, Mom."

"Sorry."

"I like who you've been this week."

"Guess what? I've liked me, too. Thanks for going with me this morning."

"Yeah, of course. Whatever you need to not want to drink, Mom."

"I always want to drink, but I've got other, more pleasant things to think about. Like you, and how proud I am of you."

"And Nora."

"Yes. And Nora."

"You should tell people."

"Tell people what?"

"The truth. I'd much rather have a happy lesbian mother than an unhappy straight one."

"Are you sure? People will talk."

Logan motioned for Nora.

"Sneaking around might play well in a romance novel, Mom, but in real life, it's tacky. You need to control the narrative."

"Control the narrative? Where'd you come up with that?"

"I overheard Dad and his millennials talking strategy."

I hugged Logan. "I love you so much."

"I love you, too."

thirty-three
nora

I walked over to the mother and daughter a little hesitantly. They talked in low voices, and Logan gave a brief nod before I got within earshot.

"What happened? Is everything okay?"

Sophie was glowing. She grasped my cheeks and kissed me. Right in front of her daughter. When we pulled apart, I looked at Logan, who was trying very hard to be nonchalant about seeing her mother kiss another woman. "Come inside. There's a surprise."

"What kind of surprise?"

"A birthday cake for me, and a present for you."

"Me?"

Holding both our hands, she led Logan and me inside and left us near the front of the stage.

"Do you know what's going on?"

Logan was studying me with a hostile expression. "Do you love my mother as much as she thinks you do?"

"Your mother is the love of my life."

"She better be."

"What is she about to do?"

One corner of Logan's mouth turned up into a smirk. "Nervous?"

"A little, yeah."

Across the room, Sophie was talking to Avery, Charlie and Mark. Their body language was tense, with Avery playing peacekeeper. Mark went off to the bar, and Avery led Charlie to the stage, whispering in his ear the whole time.

"Did you start a rumor about Alima and me?" I asked.

Logan's face turned beet red. "Yeah. I blamed you for my mom's drinking and being in such a shitty mood. And Joaquin was making such an idiot of himself about Alima."

"How is Joaquin?"

"I don't know. We broke up."

"Sorry to hear that."

Logan shrugged. "I'll get over it. I'm sorry I started the rumor. It was stupid and immature. That was before Mom told me about...you know, being gay."

"It's different when it's someone you love, isn't it?"

"Yeah."

Charlie took the mike, and the crowd started clapping. "Thank you!" Charlie said. "Thank you all for coming and being so generous with your donations. For those of you who didn't donate—" he glanced at me "—there's still time to redeem yourself." The crowd laughed at the lame joke, and Charlie went on with a shortened stump speech about conservative values, yada, yada, yada. Watching Sophie cross the room to join us, it was easy to tune him out. She was clutching her stomach and gave us a nervous smile. I suddenly knew what she was going to do.

"No, Sophie. Don't."

"But, I couldn't have done any of this without my family. My wife, Sophie, and my daughter, Logan. You're why I get up every morning, why I want to fight the good fight." A smattering of applause as everyone's attention turned to us.

With a big smile, Sophie waved. Logan's was embarrassed, a

small wave from the hip. When the focus returned to Charlie, Sophie looked at me, her smile wavering. "Don't what?"

"As you may know, Sophie's birthday is next week, and I couldn't have a party without celebrating the woman who has supported me and propped me up all these years."

"Do what I think you're about to do."

"Are you having second thoughts about us?"

"No. Never."

The band struck up "Happy Birthday," and a waitress walked onto the stage carrying a cake with two lit candles shaped like a three and a six.

"That's my cue." Sophie leaned down and kissed me on the lips. Some in the crowd gasped, while others soldiered on with the song, unsure what to do until finally the singing faded off like ellipses at the end of a sentence. She grinned at me and said, "There's no turning back now."

"Holy shit." Logan covered her mouth, and half laughed.

In the ensuing silence, Jamie Luke blurted out loud enough for the entire room to hear, "Well, that explains a lot."

Charlie froze, the mic held down at his side. The band stepped back into the shadows. Sophie whispered something in Charlie's ear and took the mic from his hand. He smiled, turning on the Deadly Dimple, and kissed Sophie on the cheek. Charlie stepped lightly off the stage and stood by Avery and Mark, who were busy bombarding him with whispered questions. He held up a hand and kept his attention on Sophie, his face a mask of impassivity.

"Thank you, Charlie, and thank all of you for the birthday wishes." Sophie fiddled with the top of the mic stand. "Whew. I wasn't planning on doing this today, to be honest. So, I uh, don't have prepared remarks. See, Charlie. I wouldn't make a good politician's wife after all." The crowd's laughter was as forced as Charlie's ensuing smile. "The beginning is too far back, so

I'll start at the beginning of the end. This is the story y'all have been dying to hear since 1995. The full truth. Well, most of it."

Sophie cleared her throat. "I fell in love with my best friend the September of my senior year. Somehow, I was brave enough to tell her the very night I realized. Sometimes, I wonder where that brash girl went. I haven't seen her for years."

"This is pretty damn brash, Soph," Trent called out. Joe and Kim stood next to Trent, watching Sophie with expressions of fascination and respect. Joe put his arm around Kim and looked over at me. He smiled and nodded, and I knew Kim had told him about Sophie and me. Sophie had been right; with the rumor Logan started, and so many people knowing, it was only a matter of time before the whole town found out. Joe winked at me and returned his attention to Sophie.

Maybe coming out in Lynchfield wouldn't be the disaster we feared. A quick glance around the room showed about an equal number of hostile and stunned expressions. Better than I expected.

"Good point. Imagine my surprise, and relief, when she told me the feeling was mutual." Sophie met my eyes. "It was the best year of my life." A ripple went through the crowd. I smiled and nodded. She inhaled and continued. "After graduation we were caught, threatened, shamed and separated. The details don't matter, but the short version is, I was persuaded what Nora and I felt was wrong. Dirty. Sinful. We would go to hell unless we repented, changed our ways. I see a few of you nodding along. I know most of you agree, and I get it. I do. It's difficult for you to understand, but gay people fall in love like you do. We love as deeply, and as long." She met my eyes. "Longer."

Sophie's voice strengthened. "When Nora left I was angry, at myself mostly, for being a coward and not fighting for us. But, I also started to believe what I was being told about myself, and I told myself I wasn't gay, it was just Nora I loved. We'd taken a close friendship and perverted it. When Charlie and I started spending time together and became a couple, it seemed to prove the point." She turned to Charlie. "I'll always love you."

I couldn't tear my eyes from Sophie. My heart pounded in my chest with dread, with anticipation.

"When I discovered I was pregnant, I told Charlie everything."

The entire room gasped, and my eyes shifted along with everyone else's to Charlie. His hands were on his hips, and he was smiling. He nodded encouragement to Sophie as if he'd been in on the plan all along.

"Son of a bitch," I said, and almost laughed out loud.

"What's she doing?" Logan said.

"Saving Charlie's ass. He's going to come out of this smelling like a rose."

"I expected him to desert me, but I didn't give him nearly enough credit. He stood by me, told me we'd work through it all together, the important thing was we loved each other, and we were bringing a child into the world. For eighteen years, he's stuck by me. God knows it hasn't been easy for him. He's a goddamn saint."

The crowd laughed, the tension broken, happy their hero was firmly back up on his pedestal.

"We were happy and might have gone on together forever." She smiled down at the floor. "We all know what happened next."

She lifted her head as she inhaled. "Nora and I hadn't spoken since she left, but I knew the moment I saw her that my feelings hadn't changed. Would never change. Charlie and I have been talking and praying about what to do since, and today we finally realized the best thing for both of us. For our family. Me, standing up here in front of you, confessing, is my public amends for the lies of self-preservation I've told. To those of you I've hurt, I apologize." She found me in the crowd, and everyone and everything else fell away. "Nora, my heart is more yours now than when you broke it, eighteen years ago. You're the love of my life, and I want to spend the rest of it proving it to you."

Every eye in the room turned to me, and I blushed under the scrutiny. Everyone expected a grand gesture from me, but what? I was dumbfounded she'd done it, bared herself in front of the whole damn town, and all for me. I walked toward the stage and looked up into her nervous, expectant, exquisitely beautiful face. The woman I loved. The woman I wanted to spend my life with. I held out my hand. She took it and jumped off the stage. I wrapped my arms around her in a fierce hug.

"Now who's the sweet talker?" I whispered in her ear.

"You bring out the sap in me."

"I love you so much, you know."

"You better."

There was scattered applause. I pulled away. Sophie wiped the tears from my eyes with her thumbs. She looked deep into my eyes and my nervousness about showing affection to another woman in public faded away until all that existed was this woman who'd taken the biggest risk of her life on me. On my love. I pulled her to me and kissed her, pouring into her every bit of admiration I had for her generous heart, gratitude for her courage, and hope for our future. When we pulled apart she was flushed, and the crowd around us had thinned, but the ones who surrounded us were clapping and cheering. It wasn't universal acceptance, but it was a start. We endured five minutes of congratulations and everyone talking over everyone else. It was nice, but overwhelming, too. I could tell Sophie felt the same.

"Let's go home."

"Oh my God. Please."

thirty-four
nora

"How did I know I'd find you with the chickens?"

I pulled my head out of the chicken coop and saw Sophie walk into the barn. She wore a flowing knee-length sundress with spaghetti straps and an enticingly low V-neck. Her Jackie O. sunglasses were perched on her head, pulling her hair away from her beautiful face.

"How did I know you'd look like you walked off the pages of an Anthropologie catalog?"

She grinned but didn't stop until her lips were on mine.

"Hi," I said.

"Hi. Am I to assume from that kiss that you've forgiven me for making a spectacle last night?"

"Almost. You're going to have to pay a little more penance."

"Oh, I can't wait. Are you done with the chickens?"

"Yes, the little bastards. How did it go with Charlie?"

After leaving the fund raiser, I took Logan and Sophie back to their house. After a lengthy discussion, disagreement more like, Sophie convinced me to let her stay there alone to wait for Charlie. "We have a lot to work out, and there's no reason to rub his nose in it with us."

"Isn't he going to have to get used to it? With me staying in Lynchfield?"

"You're staying?"

"Yeah, didn't Charlie tell you? Isn't that why you went all Hester Prynne on Lynchfield?"

"Nice *Scarlet Letter* reference." Logan filled three glasses with ice.

"No. I did it because Charlie pissed me off, and I knew he was going to make the next year miserable."

"He was," Logan interjected. She poured tea into the glasses. "But, the way you spun it. Fucking baller, Mom."

"Logan, your language really is vile."

"You're focusing on the wrong thing." Logan pushed a glass across the counter to each of us. "Nora's staying in Lynchfield. Why?"

"For Emmadean, and because I didn't want to be away from your mother."

Sophie leaned over and kissed me. "I love you."

"I know I have to get used to this, but it's weird seeing you kiss someone besides Dad," Logan said.

"Sorry. So, has word gotten around to your friends?" Sophie asked.

"Yeah, I've gotten a few texts," Logan said.

Logan glanced at me, probably wondering if I would tell Sophie about the rumor. I shook my head slightly. She would have to confess to her mother in her own time.

"And...?"

"Everyone's shocked. I mean, with Erin no one knew it, but it wasn't a surprise, you know? It's was like, oh yeah, that makes sense. And, no one cares. It's like, okay, cool. Erin's a lesbian. You, on the other hand, were a shock. But, no one is being hateful yet. Gross, but not hateful."

"Gross how?" I asked.

"Chris Bird came up with an acronym for you."

"I'm afraid to ask."

"LILF."

"LILF?"

"Lesbian I'd like to fuck," I said. I covered my mouth to keep from laughing.

"I've never heard of that. Is that a thing?" Sophie asked.

"Chris Bird is a douchebag," Logan said.

Sophie reached across the table and took Logan's hand. "I'm sorry, Logan. I shouldn't have done it in such a public way. I was caught up in the moment, of finally being true to myself."

"I can handle it. Fuck the haters."

"I think that'll be my mantra for the next year. *Fuck the haters*," Sophie said.

"We'll make T-shirts," Logan said.

I'd finished my tea and left them to wait for Charlie.

Now, Sophie draped her arm across my shoulders as we walked from the barn to the house. "It went pretty well. Avery was with him. She'd convinced Charlie I'd done him a huge favor, spinning it like I did."

"Where did that come from, anyway?"

"I have no idea. But, it was pretty brilliant, if I do say so myself."

"And you will."

"Everyone got what they wanted."

"I'm happy. I got what I wanted."

"Me, too," Sophie said. "I do have some bad news."

I opened the kitchen door for Sophie.

"Oh, Lord, what?"

"Logan and Lexa are holding us to the tennis match."

"Shit. I'd hoped they'd forgotten about it," I said.

"Nope. They want to do it tonight. I told them we would."

"Tonight? I'm not in good enough shape."

"Let's let them beat us and get it over with."

"No way am I letting them win," I said. "And have to listen to them tease us about it for the rest of our lives?"

"I do love your competitiveness." Sophie kissed me.

"And I love your lips."

"Always with the lips."

A suitcase sat next to the kitchen table. "Is that yours?"

"Yeah. Is that all right?" Sophie asked.

"Absolutely. It's just, I got rid of everything before I decided to stay."

"Not everything, I hope."

"Did you hear something?"

"Nope." Sophie traced her fingers down my bare arm.

"It sounded like a car door."

Her hand collapsed on my wrist. "Oh. It's probably Logan. She wanted to come with me this morning, but I told her we needed to talk first." She disentangled herself from me and reached for her dress, discarded on the floor.

"Talk?"

She pulled her dress over her head and shrugged. "She knew what I meant, and only grimaced a little."

I pulled on my T-shirt. "Is this going to weird Logan out? Seeing you and your girlfriend walking out of a bedroom is a lot different than seeing us kiss."

Sophie ran her hands through her hair to straighten it. "I suppose we're about to find out."

I heard a perfunctory knock on the front door as I pulled on my panties. "Sophia Elizabeth!" shouted Brenda Russell.

"Shit," Sophie said, eyes wide. "In all this, I forgot about my mom. I haven't talked to her since the barbecue."

"Why wasn't she there last night?"

"She's down in her back. I can't believe she's here. She must be drugged to high heaven. I hope she didn't drive."

She started to leave the bedroom, but I caught her. "No. We go together."

I pulled on my jeans and held my hand out for Sophie. With a nervous smile, she took it.

Brenda Russell clutched her purse in front of her in the middle of the empty living room, glaring distastefully at Sophie's suitcase in the kitchen. When we walked in hand in hand, her face puckered. "I knew it," she said.

"Mother..."

"You." If she was drugged up, she did a good job of hiding it. All I saw was years of pent-up hatred. "I knew you would coerce my daughter into sin again."

"There was no coercion, I assure you."

"Shut up, shut up, shut up!" She lifted her chin. "Come on, Sophia. I'm taking you home to your husband and daughter."

"You're taking me home?"

"Yes."

I stepped in front of Sophie. "Not this time, Brenda. We're too old to be manipulated by you."

Sophie tugged on my hand. "Nora, wait."

My heart dropped to my stomach. Brenda straightened her shoulders, confident in her ability to guilt Sophie into doing whatever Brenda wanted. I couldn't help it; a small part of me expected Sophie to go. To be persuaded once again by her mother that we were deviants. I dropped Sophie's hand. Brows furrowed, Sophie looked from our unjoined hands to my face. Her expression cleared. "I suppose I deserve that." With a smile, she cupped my face and gave me a sweet, lingering kiss.

Brenda gasped in disgust.

Sophie faced her mother and sighed.

"You need to let this go, Mom. I get it now. What you did. I would do anything to protect Logan, and that's what you thought you were doing twenty years ago. You've told yourself that everything you've said and done has been from a place of love, for me, to protect me from making a mistake. But, loving

Nora isn't a mistake, being honest about who I am isn't a mistake. Leaving her, betraying her all those years ago was the mistake."

"Have you even thought about your daughter?"

"Logan understands, or at least she wants to."

"You're corrupting that child."

"Being around two people who love each other isn't corrupting."

"You're ruining Charlie's chance at the Senate."

"Charlie will be fine, trust me. Anyway, this isn't about Charlie. This is about me being who I am, loving who I want in the open, and it feels wonderful. I know it's going to take some time, but I hope that once you see how happy we are, you'll come around. I don't want to cut you out of my life, but if you can't accept us, if you actively try to hurt us, I will."

"It's her. She tempted you."

"Here we go again," I said.

"The biggest mistake of my life was listening to Ray Noakes. I should have called the sheriff on you like I wanted," Brenda said.

"Called the sheriff? What are you talking about?" Sophie said.

"It was rape, what she did to you."

Hearing the words again hit me in the gut, even after all this time when the threat was hollow. Sophie moved closer to me, and I was glad for it.

"Mother! No, it wasn't."

"She would have been sent away for a long time; your father would have made sure of that."

"What do you mean, you shouldn't have listened to Ray?" I said.

"Ray promised me there'd be no need, that he would make sure you two stayed apart."

I found Sophie's hand and clutched it, needing her strength to remain standing. "Is that why he sent me away? To keep you from following through on your threat?"

"Your threat?" Sophie's head jerked from me to her mother. "You threatened Nora with…a rape charge?"

"She forced you!"

"No, she didn't! How could you do that to her? To me? To us!"

"It was for your own good."

"Oh my God," Sophie said, her face a mask of shock.

"Is that why Ray sent me away?"

Brenda's head jerked back, shocked at my raised voice. "Yes."

"Mother, that's horrible. Even for you."

"You bitch." I moved forward with every intention to snap her head off her wobbly little neck. Sophie held me back.

"You are a vile human being," I said.

"Me? You two are the wicked ones. Everyone in town is making fun of you, talking about what you do behind closed doors. If you insist on flouting your sin, you should leave while there's still a chance to save Logan from your deplorable influence."

"Leave?" I said. "We're not leaving."

"What?" Brenda's voice shook, and she reached out to grab something to stabilize her, but there was nothing there. She swayed, but neither Sophie nor I moved to help her. When she saw that, she straightened quick enough to show her weakness for the ruse it was.

"I'm staying in town to take care of Emmadean," I said. "Logan has another year of high school and, I have to confess, I don't want to miss it. We might not be able to legally make a family in Texas yet, but the time is coming when we will. You can't keep us apart anymore, Brenda."

Sophie pulled me away from her mother and cradled my face in her hands. "I love you so, so much."

"I love you, too."

Sophie stepped a little in front of me to face her mother, whose mouth was curled in disgust. "*You* need to leave. Now. Don't bother coming back until you can accept that Nora will be in my life—will *be* my life—from now on."

"Sophia…"

Sophie turned away and led me down the hall to my bedroom.

When the door closed behind us, Sophie hugged me. I buried my face in her neck, the smell of her perfume comforting, calming me. I clung to her, to the sense of love and protection that had been missing from my life for too long.

When we pulled apart, Sophie rubbed my upper arms. "Are you okay?"

I nodded but still felt a little dazed by Brenda's claim. "Do you think Pop did it for me?"

Sophie pushed my hair behind my ear. "It sounds like it."

I sat down slowly on the bed. Brenda Russell had thrown everything I'd thought, felt, believed for the past eighteen years into doubt. Sophie sat next to me and took my hand. "You have to believe, I knew nothing about my mother's threat. I would have been on the road to you as soon as I knew."

"I'm sure that's why she never told you."

"That's why you didn't reply to my letter, isn't it?"

I nodded. I stared into space with Sophie. "So, my pop wasn't as bad as I thought, and your mom was worse."

Sophie breathed a heavy sigh. "She'll never come around."

"Does that bother you?"

"Not as much as it should."

"You were fantastic."

"I should have stood up to her years ago."

I placed my fingers over her mouth. "Shh. No more regretting the past."

"No more regretting the past."

I took both Sophie's hands in mine and kissed the ring I gave her the night we promised to love each other until the day we died. "I love you, I love you, I love you."

"Ditto."

★ ★ ★ ★ ★

acknowledgments

The Secret of You and Me started as a modern-day retelling of Jane Austen's *Persuasion*, but it quickly morphed into its own vibrant story when I realized my heroine was in love with her best friend.

Nora's character came to me first (I envisioned her as my Anne), but I struggled with who the romantic hero would be. No one seemed right. None of them seemed worthy of Nora. The only character who was worthy of Nora, and who Nora was worthy of, was Sophie. As soon as I realized that, everything else fell into place.

I've had more fun writing this novel than any of my others, and I couldn't have done it alone.

There have been many, many people who have helped me with *The Secret of You and Me* along the way.

To Kat Cook for being my first reader and such a dear friend. I miss you every Wednesday at workshop and still have hope that you'll come back some day.

To Steve W. for helping me with the AA portions of the story. You are a true inspiration to me.

To Brooke Fossey, John Bartel, and Jenny Martin for your

wonderful developmental edits and suggestions. Except you, Bartel. I ignored your advice. (Just kidding.)

To my agent, Alice Speilburg, for supporting and encouraging me no matter how far out of my "lane" I get, and for being able to sell multiple genres to multiple houses.

To my editor, Allison Carroll, and the entire team at Graydon House for loving Sophie and Nora as much as I do, for your enthusiasm, and your support.

To my family and my friends who encourage and inspire me.

To my sons, Ryan and Jack, who humor me when I ask questions about teen lingo but also make me swear never to use it in front of them.

Finally, to Jay. Every scene, every sentence, every emotion I wrote about Sophie and Nora falling in love, I was writing about falling in love with you.

Love is universal.

—ML

discussion questions

1. What did you think of the title of the novel? What does it mean to you? To whom and what does the title apply?

2. Which of the two main characters (Nora and Sophie) do you most relate to and why? Do you relate to any other characters in the novel?

3. Sophie is not living the life she expected or wanted when she was eighteen years old. Does your life resemble the dreams you had when you graduated from high school? Are you happy with the results or disappointed you didn't follow your dreams?

4. What are some of the themes the novel touched on?

5. Family is an important theme in the novel. Discuss the family dynamics shown between Nora, Sophie, Brenda, Emmadean, and Charlie, with each other and with their various families.

6. We all make decisions in our lives that seem, in the moment, to be everyday and inconsequential, but as we get older, we

realize were pivotal moments that changed the direction of our lives, for good or for bad. Discuss these decision(s) and whether or not you'd make the same choice(s) now, with years of experience.

7. All the characters change over the course of the novel. Discuss how and why. Who do you think underwent the biggest change?

8. Did the novel surprise you or change you? If so, why?

9. Discuss setting. How did it enhance the plot and/or the themes of the novel?

10. Have you read other books by this author? How did they compare with this one?

11. Share a favorite quote. Why is it your favorite?

12. Who would you recommend *The Secret of You and Me* to? And why?